Run, Run Rudolph

FAIRY GODMOTHERS AND OTHER FIASCOS
BOOK TWO

JEAN ORAM

Run, Run Rudolph
A Christmas Romcom Romantasy

Fairy Godmothers and Other Fiascos, Book 2
By Jean Oram

© 2025 Jean Oram
All rights reserved
First Edition

Oram Productions First Edition: November 2025

This is a work of fiction and all characters, organizations, places, events, and incidents appearing in this novel are products of the author's overly active imagination or are used in a fictitious manner unless otherwise stated. Any resemblance to actual people, unicorns and other mythical creatures, alive, dead or extinct, as well as any resemblance to events or locales is coincidental, except for when it isn't. (See Author's Note and Glossary, or check a map of Canada.)

For nondigital editions, the print location of this book is stated on the last page. Published by Oram Productions in Alberta, Canada.

COMPLETE LIBRARY OF CONGRESS CATALOGING-IN-PUBLICATION DATA AVAILABLE ONLINE

Oram, Jean.

Run, Run Rudolph / Jean Oram.—1st. ed.

Ebook: 9781998476527

Paperback: 978-1-997734-24-6, 978-1-997734-25-3

Large Print: 978-1-997734-26-0, 978-1-997734-27-7

Audio: 978-1-997734-28-4

Front cover design Elizabeth Mackey

To you, my dear reader. May this book tickle your funny bone.

Hugs, love, and endless maple syrup,
XO,
Jean

RUN, RUN, RUDOLPH

Quick note from the author:

To add to the authentic Canadianness of this Canadian story, this (Canadian) author uses Canadian spellings. Enjoy!

P.S. If you need it, there is a glossary of Canadian terms at the back of the book.

CHAPTER 1

~ *Tamara* ~

Was Travis Tritt single? And if so, how old was he? Because that man sure could croon some Christmas carols, and the rightness of his voice singing *All I Want for Christmas Dear is You* sent my mind spinning down romantic avenues as fat snowflakes flew past my windshield.

It was the night before Christmas Eve in the Rocky Mountain foothills, and I loved a white Christmas—which it most definitely was. Although the winter storm was maybe a bit too thick for my liking as I drove home from a family dinner. Tonight, my mom, after giving up on trying to convince me to take another crack at dating my ex-boyfriend Kade, had come dangerously close to badgering me into accepting a date with my former high school English teacher. The man was only four and a half years my senior, but date Mr. Devilson? No way. His real name was Mr. Derekson, but none of us had called him *that*. I might be single, and I might not have someone to curl up with in front of the fireplace in my old farmhouse tonight, but I wasn't desperate.

Dejected about my options? Most definitely.

But I left the desperation for my mother. Ever since I'd moved back home last summer to reunite with my ex-boyfriend, Kade, she'd renewed her mission to get me down the aisle before 'all the good ones were taken.' I think she might have hidden in her room to cry it out when our romantic reunion had only lasted a few weeks.

Or it could have been the very public way it had combusted, and the delight in which the gossips had swarmed her in hopes of getting the straight goods under the guise of returning old casserole dishes or borrowed books. I was pretty sure my mom now had more of both than she'd ever loaned out.

To rights, the final breakup fight between Kade and I had been rather epic. We'd covered everything under the sun, from who had changed the most in the years we'd been apart, to whether or not his recent ex-girlfriend's botanicals (AKA herbs, supplements and vitamins) actually worked and were worth the high prices, to who'd scratched his new F-150.

The answers: me, maybe, and me again.

Yes, my time in the city had changed me. Everyone kept saying that, and yet my life didn't feel that much different. Same small town, a job that was going nowhere, no horses of my own, and still single.

Although, I did have a better sense of myself now, and was more willing to stand up for what I wanted. Hence the epic break-up fight.

As for the scratched truck, Kade didn't have any evidence, and my lips were sealed forever, due to the way he'd defended Jannifer's botanical vitamins with a vigour that had raised my hackles to their fullest, prickliest heights. I'd died on that hill— one so mighty that if I ever even needed so much as a bottle of Vitamin C, I'd have to drive to the next town over and buy them in secret, or hear about it until the end of time.

Back to the truck. There was only one witness to the paint

scratching, and that was Kade's super-smart, handsome, womanizing older brother, Haden. He'd been there when I'd backed the borrowed pickup and horse trailer past a fence post, and had accidentally screeched along some barbed wire.

I was pretty sure Haden wouldn't give me up to his sibling, though. He tended to avoid me and my endless curious questions about animals—he was a veterinarian. However, over the years, I'd caught him smirking with amusement whenever I'd finally make a dig or two back at Kade. It was likely nothing more than some sort of sibling rivalry, and the resulting joy at seeing his gregarious, do-no-wrong younger brother get a bit of pushback.

It certainly didn't stem from a fondness for me, a woman eight years his junior. And anyway, I was a bother to him, someone often in need of rescue. I was so clueless about being a bother that Kade had needed to pull me aside when I was seventeen and give me a heads up. I'd bothered Haden for *years*, assuming his patient kindness and depth of knowledge was an invitation to pummel him with questions.

Really though, was it any surprise that I'd been led on? Haden had a whole fan group in Eagle Ridge, as well as the surrounding county. They ran a constant parade through his veterinarian clinic with what I suspected were fake emergencies. I was also fairly confident that he loved it, as I'd never once, in all our years of sharing the same town, seen him with the same woman more than a time or two.

Yeah, he was *that* guy.

On top of it all, he was a practical small-town vet, sure and reliable. And I was the gal with the ooey-gooey love for my little fur babies. He didn't do ooey-gooey. How was he even brothers with Kade, who'd found my fur-baby tendencies adorable?

I tightened my grip on the steering wheel and grumbled to myself. At least Haden would no longer have to suffer through seeing me at the Powell family dinners, vacations, or other family events. He'd always slip in just in time for Christmas Eve dinner, bordering on being late as he took the spot on my other side at his mom's big table. I suspected he hid out somewhere until supper because of me.

Come to think of it, Haden *might* reveal my truck-scratching secret to his brother. But, if he was the good businessman I believed him to be, it would be in his best interest not to. After all, I was the primary guardian of my landlord Carl's ageing horse, and Haden would want to ensure those hefty vet bills got paid out to his clinic, and not his back-up veterinarian friend one town over, who generally dealt with his overflow emergencies.

I slowed my car as another wash of flakes reduced my visibility, and I squinted out into the night, waiting for the snow burst to wane. When it did—and still feeling the sureness of the hard-packed, snow-covered gravel road beneath me—I sped up again.

My life might not be perfect, and it might be lacking a husband and kids, but at least it was, for the most part, filled with things I was choosing for myself. That included everything from my wonderfully cheesy horse-themed Christmas sweatshirt to my rented farmhouse and barn, to the semi-adopted horse, Dolly, and my new job as a teacher's educational assistant.

Even my bestie Char could see I was happy to be back in the country again after my stint in the city with her...although, she worried I wasn't finding enough adventure. Which I could understand. Some days I was lonely, and wondered what I was doing with my life. Was I wasting my best years? Would I ever find anyone out here?

Days like that had me tempted to drop it all and move closer to the Spruce Meadows horse training facility in the slim hope of getting to work with horses. I was inexperienced, but maybe I could muck out barns or back up trailers. Or just muck out barns. I didn't have a great track record with backing up a trailer.

As for adventure, though? I didn't want or need it in the way Char did. And after her run-in with the magical world last summer, I was fine right where I was, thank you very much. It turned out fairy godmothers were real, and Char, as a result, had landed herself in some hot water. Try owing a fairy godmother over one-hundred grand thanks to a backlog of granted wishes, and then face the ogre accountant while sorting out repayment. I shivered just thinking about it. Thank goodness I was past helping Char through all of that business, and my life was blessedly back to normal. No magic. No magical creatures. Just me living alone in the country.

So alone.

The only male in my bed was my rescued tomcat stealing the blanket in the night.

Sighing, I wondered for the eight millionth time if coming back home had been a mistake. I'd never find a husband out here. That meant never starting a family. And with my current salary, never being able to afford a hobby farm on my own.

A gust of wind obscured the dark road with another flush of falling snow, and I squinted, leaning forward in the driver's seat again. It was only a bit after seven o'clock, but for those of us in the northern hemisphere, especially Canada, we were fully into the depth of shorter days.

I rubbed my left eye and peered out at the endless snow tumbling from the sky, making it impossible to see. Sensing movement to my hood's right, I snatched the bunch of mistletoe I'd rather optimistically hung from my rearview mirror and tossed it onto the passenger seat. Why I'd thought I'd be driving a single man around in my car this holiday season

—or that we'd find ourselves 'under the mistletoe' so-to-speak —I have no idea. I blamed my mother and her constant campaign to get me married off. (Or worse, back together with Kade.)

Maybe instead of moping about being alone, I needed to spend more time with my friends. I should ask the GAL PAL squad—my former roommates—to stay over for longer than our planned, one-night New Year's celebration. They could stay an extra day, and we could bake, watch movies and give each other pedicures.

I tapped the brakes as something reflected back at me from the ditch, my heart thumping. Was that an animal?

No. Just a reflector on a buried line marker. Country roads were the worst at night. I thought anything that flashed in my headlights' glare might be animal eyes.

I couldn't wait to get home, stretch out on my couch in front of the fireplace and Christmas tree, take off my bra and sip hot chocolate.

My phone chirped with a text, and I wished again that I was home so I could read it.

No, not a real wish.

I didn't need to follow my best friend Char into massive fairy godmother debt with some ill-thought-out wishes. Even several months later, I could still barely believe that fairy godmothers were real—and that they charged exorbitant amounts when they granted wishes. It made me very leery of using the W word—*wish*.

As for reading texts while driving, I was simply *envious* of vehicles where a person's phone and car stereo spoke to each other, and thus the driver.

Anyway, it was likely only Samantha texting the group, which meant it could wait. She'd been fighting with her very lovely boyfriend Malachi for weeks, and seeing that they lived together, she needed a friend to calm her down every so often so she didn't break up with him. Which lately, seemed to be a couple of times a day.

But I knew someone else would talk her off the ledge in our group chat. It used to be called GAL PAL—Giggle and Laughter, Pouring our hearts and Listening. Now, it had been renamed to Save S&M. I didn't like the new name—it made me think of sadomasochism, and not saving Samantha and Malachi. I couldn't wait until her relationship was on solid ground again so I could change the name back.

Ignoring my phone's bings and boops, along with the phantom eyes in the ditch, I leaned back, relaxing my grip on the steering wheel. I was almost home.

I stretched to twist the radio dial, cranking up Travis Tritt as he finished singing *All I Want for Christmas Dear is You*. Maybe one little wish to Estelle, the fairy godmother, wouldn't hurt...

How much would it cost to wish for love?

When I glanced back at the road from the radio, it was like someone had emptied a bag of bounding reindeer in front of me.

Wait. Reindeer? We weren't *that* far north, despite what some tourists believed. We only had mule and white-tailed deer in the foothills. And the occasional moose or elk.

My thoughts were quick as I jammed on the brakes. My convertible Sebring slid one way, then the other. I furiously corrected and braked, squealing as the herd jumped around on either side of my car. Antlers created finger-like shadows in my headlight's beams. In front of me. Behind me. Surrounding the car were furry hooves and wide, dark, terrified eyes.

There was a thud as a hoof hit the door on the passenger side. A white-and-brown belly blocked my view as a reindeer leapt over the hood. How many were there? It felt like they'd never stop jumping and landing.

A small red light appeared before me. I made a hard left, spinning as I jammed the brakes, afraid I was about to rear end someone I couldn't see due to the falling snow and flying deer.

I could have sworn the deer were intermittently flying.

But if they were, they wouldn't be on the road, would they?

There was another flicker of red as my car finished its spin. I was still moving forward. A deer jumped in the same direction I was heading, and my bumper made contact with a dull thump.

Then the reindeer were gone. There was nothing but darkness and empty road as my car finally slid to a halt, sideways across the snowy country road, sending tunnels of light into the ditch's grove of bare trees.

It had only been a few seconds of twisting my way through the herd, but it had felt like minutes.

I unclenched my hands from the steering wheel and flicked on my emergency flashers, grateful I hadn't hit the steep, snow-filled ditch. I left the car running, as per my mom's advice about collisions and the ignition kill switch that wouldn't allow you to restart a vehicle post-accident. I hopped out to check the damage, ensuring my thick winter coat was zipped up to my chin.

In the glow of Benjamin's—my car's—headlights, I could see my bumper had lost the quick battle. It hung crookedly, the blue plastic sporting a jagged hole bigger than a hoof, and there were bits of brown fur stuck around it.

Oh, no.

I scanned the dark road behind my car. Something red was flashing on the ground, almost in time with my car's flashers. Had one of the deer kicked out a taillight? I walked toward it, my car highlighting the road with a rosy red glow every half second. My lost taillight was by a deer who was lying on its side. Weird that the light was still working.

I approached slowly, and tears wet my eyes as guilt took over. The poor thing! The deer had its back to me, ribcage heaving. What if it was severely injured, and I had to call someone to put it down?

Stupid Travis Tritt and the stupid radio. Why hadn't I been watching the road?

I pulled out my phone to use its flashlight to help me see better as I approached, talking softly so as not to startle the animal, like Haden had once taught me when I was a teen. The deer was smaller than I'd expected, and as I took it in, I ruled out the possibility that it might be a mule deer. It wasn't a white tail, either. It seriously looked like a woodland caribou—AKA reindeer—like they kept at the Calgary Zoo. Had one gotten out and travelled all this way undetected?

As I circled the beast, I located the blinking red light. It wasn't a lost taillight. Not at all.

The blinking red light was on the end of the reindeer's nose.

THE MAGICAL WORLD WAS BACK. Back in my life, where it didn't belong. Where I didn't want it.

With a shaky voice, I commanded my phone to call Char as I ran back to the warmth of my car. If anybody would know what to do, as well as not to immediately jump to the conclusion that I was crazy, it was my best friend since ninth grade. The day we'd met, she'd saved me from a very scary spider, nonchalantly scooping it into her hands—her *bare* hands—and saving me. We'd been best friends ever since.

And right now, I needed her spider-scooping hands and level head.

We'd dealt with some rather *unreal* things last summer, thanks to her fairy godmother, but nothing quite like this. There'd never been magic in Eagle Ridge. This small town had always been perfectly, *safely* boring.

I bit my bottom lip and dropped into the driver's seat as Char picked up, closing the door behind me to keep the heat inside the cab.

"It's piña colada time!" cooed my friend, obviously enjoying the open bar at the all-inclusive Mexican resort she and her boyfriend James had gone to for Christmas. His family had basically adopted Char, and his parents had overlapped their own trip so the four of them could spend a few days together over the holiday. She lowered her voice, suddenly serious. "I think she's going to break up with him."

Samantha. She must be reading the GAL PAL texts.

"Are you drunk?" I asked, my voice wavering.

"Yes. And giving Samantha the best romantic advice ever, right James?"

My phone binged with another text to the group chat. I skimmed Char's message and sighed. That was not good advice for our commitment-phobic friend. Not even close.

In the background, I heard a deep male voice say through the phone, "Merry Christmas, Tamara!"

"Merry Christmas, James. And family."

"He can't hear you, and his parents are still at supper. You're not on speaker."

"Char, I need you. And I need you completely focused because I hit something with Benjamin!"

Benjamin, my car, had bumped a lot of things in his time, but never any wildlife. Not even gophers, though everybody else in town hit them. Especially in the summer, when they swarmed the roads like little devils.

But *shh*. Don't tell that to my cute gopher buddy, Felipe.

He'd moved into the top floor of the old boarding house the five of us gals had been renting in Calgary, and we'd promptly adopted him. When we'd all gone our separate ways last summer, I'd brought Felipe with me, figuring the country air would do him good. But apparently he was an indoor creature now, with absolutely no desire to go back outdoors. He was an odd little animal. He was even friends with my cat.

Back to my current situation, and the deer sprawled on the road.

There was a short pause on the other end of the line, then a giggle.

"I'm serious, Char."

There must've been something in my tone because her amusement vanished, and she replied very soberly, "Start at the beginning."

"I hit Rudolph. He's on the road."

"How do you know it's him?" Char asked, the music in the background of the call fading. My guess was she was finding somewhere more private, so she could be the bestie I always counted on. Here for me. Always. Even though she was in Mexico toasting her ta-tas in the sun while I was in Canada, freezing mine.

Then again, she could be slipping somewhere private because Estelle had made it clear we weren't to discuss the magical world with non-believers. Which happened to be two of our close friends—Samantha and Gabby.

Likely, James didn't know about Estelle, or the magical world. And hitting Rudolph? That was right up there with discussing fairy godmothers.

I found it funny that our interactions with fairy godmothers and ogres hadn't been the thing to send Char to therapy. It had been her strong fear of love and stability. And her desire not to mess it all up once she'd finally managed to snag it. But look at her now. Happy, and in a healthy relationship. What I wouldn't give for something like that.

Well, I wouldn't give money to Char's fairy godmother Estelle to make it happen.

"How do you know it's *him*?" Char repeated.

"His nose blinks red."

She swore under her breath. "It's almost Christmas, Tam-Tam."

Her accusatory tone magnified my guilt. "I know."

"What was he doing on the road? It's too early to be out! Christmas Eve isn't until tomorrow. Are you *sure* it's him?"

"What other reindeer has a blinking red nose? And I know it's almost Christmas. He should be...I don't know. At the North Pole!" Not on the road. Not injured. "I didn't make a wish! Why is the magical world revealing itself to me? Why—why—was he on the road? I hurt him!"

I rubbed my forehead, trying to pull myself together. Boys and girls around the world were going to be devastated if Santa didn't come tomorrow night. Christmas was a magical time, and I loved the spirit of the holiday. But that didn't mean I wanted a one-on-one with it.

"Tell me everything," Char said calmly. "From the beginning."

"Fairy godmothers are real. So Rudolph has to be real, too, right?" I was blubbering now, talking fast, probably not making much sense, my car still angled across the road. "Except that it's the night before Christmas Eve, and I just hit Rudolph, and he's lying there with his nose blinking, and I don't know what to do."

"You hit Rudolph with your car," Char repeated back slowly. There was a gravity in her voice, and I had a feeling she'd been smacked by the cold, hard hand of sobriety. "Is he still alive?"

"He was breathing and his nose was glowing." My voice sounded small. I was not the independent, strong, capable, take-charge-of-anything-and-come-out-on-top woman I'd sometimes thought I was since moving home again. I'd had a good run of faking it with renting a farm, and taking care of my elderly landlord's horse for him. But now that reality was hitting the fan—or my bumper—it turned out I wasn't so bravely handling my life after all.

"Is Santa there?" Char asked.

The question was so ludicrous, I would've laughed twenty minutes ago, but now I found myself hopefully craning my neck, looking behind my car.

Santa! Of course. He must be around. Right?

Right?

But he wouldn't be doing his Christmas Eve deliveries for another full day, so why would he be here? Then again, why would Rudolph? And where had the rest of the reindeer gone? There'd been at least half a dozen of them, maybe more.

I scanned the dark road, illuminated intermittently by my car's flashers. The snow had let up a tiny bit, but the visibility was still crap.

"I don't see him," I said. "I saw all of his reindeer, and now I don't see any of them. Except Rudolph."

"Is there a sleigh?"

"No, they were all on the loose." The image of them bouncing around me like a dropped bag of marbles had my voice shaking again.

There was a long silence. "Let me get in touch with someone," Char said finally.

"Not the funny farm!" I blurted out before remembering who I was dealing with. She was the one person I knew in this universe—other than our friend, Josie, who was a walking contradiction with her logic-loving mind and her passion for all things romantasy related—who would believe just how real this was.

"Hey," Char said gently, "you didn't call them on me when I told you about Estelle. I'm not calling them on you."

Satisfied, I hung up the phone before realizing I didn't actually have a solution and didn't know who she was calling. It wasn't like she had Santa's phone number.

Probably.

Something—or someone—knocked on my window and I jumped, squealing, tossing my phone in the air. It clattered somewhere behind me as it fell.

The person at the window was short, their rapping knuckles only reaching part way up the door. Was there a child outside? In this weather? What new madness was this? I quickly opened my door, careful not to whack them with it.

The person stepped around the edge of my door and I squeaked, shoving myself against the console between my seat and the passenger side. I wanted to reach for the door and shut it, but the snarly-looking elf was now between the handle and my seat, a stubby finger pointed accusingly at me.

"Who are you?" He had a gruff, masculine voice that didn't fit his tininess.

"Nnnhn. Nhn." I was nearly hyperventilating. Elves were supposed to be cheery. Adorable, cute, and cuddly. This guy was none of the above.

I mean, I was pretty sure he was an elf. He had the ears for it, and was wearing a green-and-red striped pointy hat, a green button-up shirt with a red vest that was embroidered with fat, white snowflakes, and the most unstylish squarish green pants shoved into fuzzy brown boots.

I'd met some scary creatures last summer when Char had gone through the thing with Estelle, and I'd learned enough about the magical world to be terrified of all that I didn't know. And you could fill a library or two with that.

This guy might not even be an elf. He could be something evil. Add to that, I was a female on the road alone. In the dark.

"Well?" he demanded.

My mouth wasn't working properly. I was not holding it together. I hadn't really held it together last summer, either. Even with Char standing beside me, her shoulders pushed out wide, ready to protect me as we met her fairy godmother. She'd practically had to carry me when my legs went all weird and jellylike after meeting what I still believe was a real-life witch.

Right now I was alone, and with no BFF backup. It was just me, and I wasn't made for this.

I wanted to close the car door, lock it, and ignore the elf's existence. But if I tried to move past him, I'd have to get dangerously close, and he looked like a biter. I'd been meaning to get my tetanus booster shot and hadn't. What would happen to you if you got bitten by an elf? It would be so much worse than a kindergartener, I was sure of it.

"Who are you, and what are you doing here?" he demanded. He leaned alarmingly close, trapping me, his finger jabbing the air around me.

"Let me out!" I snapped, lifting my foot like I planned to plant it in the elf's chest. Really, I just needed to keep his snarly face away from anything biteable, such as my entire being.

He stepped back, and I popped out onto the road, scooting away from him. The cold snow crunched underfoot, and I darted a glance over my still idling car and toward the hurt reindeer. Nose still blinking.

"Who are you?" the elf asked.

"Are you with Rudolph? Is he going to be okay?"

The elf made a funny noise. "Rudolph? Who's *that*?"

"The—the—" I pointed toward the deer, then touched my nose with a mittened hand. "His nose. Isn't that Rudolph?"

The elf leaned back, eyes narrowed. Then he was on the attack again, pushing me back with every step, a finger jab aimed at my kneecaps. "How can you see him? Who are you?" Every word out of his mouth was cut off, as if he was out of patience and brimming with anger.

Then again, I suppose this was the elf's busiest time of year, so I should allow him a bit of room to be stressed out. Especially since I'd apparently taken out Santa's lead reindeer the night before Christmas deliveries began.

The heavy feeling in my stomach grew worse and my breath hitched unsteadily.

"How can you see him?" the elf repeated.

"I don't know. I just can." When I'd gone with Char and our three friends to meet Estelle at the offices of Your Fairy Godmother, only Char, Josie and myself had been able to see the magical appearing door. Theoretically, it was because we believed. Samantha and Gabby didn't, so they hadn't seen the door. They'd also stayed outside in an alternate reality when the rest of us had entered the building. Was something like that happening to me right now? I could see something that others might not?

"How can I see you?" I asked.

"My choice. Why did you hit Rudolph? Who sent you here?"

"It was an accident."

"You're trying to ruin Christmas," the elf announced, a quiver of fear in his voice.

"I'm not," I said calmly. "Truly. I'm not. I'm a big fan of the holiday."

"You're ruining it and trying to keep them apart."

"Who?"

"You know who!"

Beneath the elf's toughness, I caught a hint of bluster. He was scared. And rightly so. A human had just mowed down Rudolph out of season. Not that there was likely a season for mowing down Santa's herd.

Now that I was standing and no longer cornered, I realized the elf was about the size of a kindergartener. Maybe even shorter, reducing his threat level, despite the appearance of a creature who'd enjoy biting someone.

Time to get this little magical creature on my side.

"Um, well, I'm going to check on Rudolph. Do you want to help me?" I reached into the cab and popped my trunk as the snowflakes started falling faster again. Poor Rudolph was still on the road, and was probably getting cold as the snow piled on top of him. If he was alive.

No. Positive thoughts only. It was Christmas. Miracles happened. They *had* to happen.

"How? By running him over again? Where did you learn how to drive?" the elf sniped at me. "Did you get your license from a crackerjack box?"

"As a matter of fact, yes." I slammed my car door and whirled on the elf, causing him to take a step back.

That's what I thought. Tough, but most of it was bluster.

"I almost ate it. Good thing I didn't."

Moving around to the trunk, I tried to tune out the elf's constant stream of abuse, focusing instead on the things I could do to help Rudolph. I had a blanket and a First Aid kit which had been pushed onto me by my mom years ago as part of my car's winter safety kit. She'd even found one in the tones she believed my future wedding theme colours would be—teal and black. Yes, she was stuck in the nineties. As well as on the dream that I'd soon marry, even though at the moment I felt terminally single.

With shaking hands, I pulled out the kit, blanket, and a lantern I'd forgotten about, leaving the trunk open. The elf was starting to get under my skin, his unrelenting verbal assault reminding me a bit of Kade.

Kade hadn't been a bad boyfriend, or emotionally abusive by any extent, but he had a stubborn persistence, making it impossible for him to let something go. Such as my introverted side. He was the life of the party, whereas I leaned more toward enjoying a night in. He felt that if I just stepped outside of my comfort zone, I'd soon realize that I loved being social.

Without a doubt, he didn't understand why I wanted to live in the boring country all alone. And yeah. Occasionally, it was lonely. But I knew where to find people when I felt like socializing.

I appreciated the way Kade had always encouraged me to get out more and to try new things back in high school. I'd needed that push, and he'd prompted me to step out of my comfort zone and to follow my heart a bit more. Although, in the end, Kade had exhausted me by wanting me to be more outgoing like he was, and to go out more, make more friends, join more clubs, and have more parties.

I now understood that changing someone to be more like yourself wasn't how a good relationship worked. Same with trying to be someone you weren't.

Despite the insights I'd earned by dating the man, it still didn't mean that being hounded hadn't become a hot button issue for me.

"What is Santa going to do now that you've hit Rudy?" the elf continued. "Huh? Do you know how *important* Rudolph is? Do you? I bet you do!" The elf had stepped right up, practically toe to toe with me. Now that he was wound up again, his lack of a height disadvantage didn't seem to impact his confidence one iota.

I peered into the dark night, down the empty road at the blinking red nose, wondering if the elf would let me near the reindeer.

Sure enough, whenever I tried to sidestep the elf to move toward Rudolph, he blocked me.

"You're going on the naughty list. *Forever*! You just ruined Christmas for every child in the world! We're all trying to save Christmas, and here you are ruining it all!"

"Look. Can you help or not?"

He'd backed me toward the trunk again, and the idea of Christmas being in limbo, and us just standing here while he verbally assaulted me, was really starting to steam my muffins. It felt like the final weeks of my relationship with Kade when he'd go on and on about all the ways we were no longer a perfect couple. Probably because the last thing I wanted to be was his version of 'perfect.'

"I really love Christmas," I said, thinking about how the holiday had pulled me out of a deep funk when I was thirteen, "and want to help Rudolph." The idea of the holiday now being in limbo had me itching to make things right again.

"I really love Christmas," the elf mimicked. "Especially ruining it! Mrs. Claus is going to kick your—"

Without thinking, I shoved the elf. His butt and back hit the bumper, and he tumbled backward, his torso and arms landing over my trunk's threshold as he gave a dramatic flail. I grabbed his legs, lifting them, finishing the job of dropping him inside, then slammed the trunk shut.

I gasped and stepped back.

Santa's elf was yelling, his feet kicking from inside my car.

"You're a tootie-fruitie, no-good, rotten sugar plum!" he shouted, his voice muffled.

I froze halfway to the trunk's release button. On second thought, maybe he could keep himself occupied searching for the trunk's emergency release, a glow-in-the-dark handle, while I checked on Rudolph.

"You're a frozen polar bear turd!" he screamed. "You smell like a reindeer fart! Mrs. Claus is going to freeze you into a giant ice sculpture and all the dogs will pee on it!"

Not only was he short like a kindergartener, his insults were at their level, too.

"You can stay in there until you learn how to be cooperative," I said loudly, leaning over the trunk, hoping he could hear me over his banging. "And you had better not dent my car!"

Turning on the lantern, I made my way back to Rudolph. As I waved the light, I caught the odd flicker like someone—or several *someones*—were watching me from the snowy ditches.

"I mean no harm," I called, feeling spooked. I'd just done two very bad things—hitting Rudolph and locking up an elf, and I tried not to think about what sort of consequences the magical world might lob my way.

I crouched beside Rudolph, who blinked at me. He lifted his head, then slowly rested it on the road again.

"I am *so* sorry. Are you okay?" I watched his black eyes for a long moment, then cautiously unfolded the blanket, shaking it out with gentle, slow moves so as not to scare the reindeer. "I'm going to put a blanket over you, okay?" I draped it over his snowy torso, an eye out for dark pools on the white snow around him. No obvious bleeding. That was good, right?

As I tucked him in, I wondered if I was actually helping him, or just causing him stress. A strange human touching him and covering up his fur coat, which was meant for this weather.

But you kept a person warm after an accident in case they went into shock, so surely it wouldn't hurt a reindeer to do the same?

I crouched in front of him again, not sure what else I could do for him. He wasn't a massive animal, much shorter than I'd expected. Beautiful. And also in the middle of the dark, snowy road.

"Are you going to be okay, Rudolph?" My eyes filled with tears. What had I done to this poor creature? "What can I do to help you?"

Hearing crunching in the snow, I looked up to find myself surrounded by at least a half dozen reindeer, the reflective layer in their eyes making them glow an eerie, evil red. It was then that I realized my knowledge of the magical world was very, very limited.

CHAPTER 2

~ *Tamara* ~

Over the sound of the elf's tantrum in my trunk, I put down my car's soft roof, and helped an injured Rudolph into the back seat. My Sebring was a two-door, making it extra awkward, and I was pretty sure that in the light of day I'd find hoof scrapes down the side panels of the car from where Rudolph tried to climb in over the door.

If Haden could see me now, helping a (technically) wild animal into my car so I could take it home to help heal it, his eyes would roll so far back in his head, he'd sprain an eyeball. But what else was I supposed to do? Leave Rudolph on the road and let Christmas, the most magical time of the year, come to ruin, decimating the hearts of billions of children just because I'd been distracted by a Travis Tritt song?

I didn't think so.

And anyway, all of Rudolph's pals seemed to feel this was a good idea. When I'd asked them if they had any magic to heal him, they'd just stared at me. But when I'd suggested I take him to my barn so he could rest somewhere safe, they'd begun directing me, pushing me around with their noses. It was terrifying, and also the coolest thing ever. Way better than Char's fairy godmother, not to mention the cranky witch who worked as her receptionist.

Although, the non-talking magical creature bit was making communication tricky.

Rudolph's ankle and foot, which had gone through my bumper, were scraped but not bleeding too terribly, and it was difficult to decipher how severe his injuries might be. He was definitely dazed and stumbling. He also smelled oddly of tequila. In fact, all the reindeer seemed to have distinctive boozy, fermented scents, which could be a side effect from bad feed. Yet, I doubted very much that Santa would take shortcuts with his animals and their food.

The elf in my trunk had mentioned a party. But a reindeer party with alcohol? That felt too weird to be true—even for the magical world. Although, maybe the North Pole had Christmas parties just like a regular office did.

But this close to Christmas Eve seemed excessively risky. And shouldn't they be too busy to celebrate?

Either way, with Christmas less than twenty-four hours away, Rudolph's condition was not good.

Earlier, after setting up the back seat for Rudolph and retrieving my phone from where I'd thrown it after being surprised by the elf, I'd counted off the reindeer names in my head. So far, I had only spotted eight of the nine animals from the songs and stories. They were all wearing red collars with a silver medallion with their names engraved on them, and it appeared as though Vixen was absent. I hoped the reindeer hadn't met a fate worse than Rudolph's.

Once Rudolph was settled in the back of my car, the elf still banging and yelling at us from the trunk, I asked the other reindeer, again, for confirmation about what I should do.

"You want me to take Rudolph to my barn so he's safe? And then maybe call a veterinarian?" No nose nudges to help me out. What did I expect? One of them to break out a to-do list for me or start writing in the snow?

The elf had seemed surprised that I could see the reindeer, and I wondered if it was possible because I believed in magical beings. Only three of us in the GAL PAL group could see Estelle, Char's fairy godmother, and her offices. It had all been invisible to Samantha and Gabby, our nonbeliever friends. Would Haden, a serious, grown man, even be able to see Rudolph?

Haden. I really didn't want to call him for help. Yes, he was a skilled veterinarian. He was kind, calm, super knowledgeable, and animals trusted him. But what would I do if he answered my call, came, and then was unable to see Rudolph?

The reindeer looked at each other, then back at me. They seemed to understand me, but so far had been only using their noses to nudge or prod me in the direction they wanted me to go. Maybe the magical veil between our worlds didn't allow them to interact like Estelle or the elf could? Or maybe, because they were deer, they simply couldn't talk.

"So? To the barn? Yes?" I repeated, feeling nervous. I wished someone would take charge, and make me feel less like I was about to kidnap Santa's most-famous reindeer. I hunched further into my parka, stamping my cold feet. The snow was already piling up in my convertible's interior, and the drive home was going to be awful with the roof down. The sooner we got going, the better.

Comet—the reindeer with the most white in his muzzle—stepped closer. I figured he must be second in command, and now in charge, since Rudolph was basically down for the count. I braced myself for another fuzzy nose nudge. At first I'd been delighted to be nuzzled by the beasts, but then one of them—Dasher—had nudged me a bit too hard, and I'd gone flying onto the snowy road, landing on my knees.

"Okay, I'm taking that as a yes," I told Comet, noting that he had some sort of small red sack attached to his collar. None of the others had a sack, and I wondered what was in it.

"The barn will be fine while we decide what to do," he replied in a deep, sage voice, and I jolted.

"Comet!" another scolded, his voice soft. I craned my neck, reading his medallion. Prancer.

I crossed my arms over my bulky winter coat, tucking my mittened hands in my armpits while I hunched down inside my parka and struggled not to react. The reindeer could speak—and in English. I didn't know whether to faint or let out a sigh of relief.

"Talking is more efficient," Comet replied to Prancer.

"No talking to humans," Prancer said. It sounded as though he was quoting a list of rules.

"Hugo did," someone said.

"He's a traitor. A hypocritical, two-faced narc," the one named Donner snapped. He had something green in his antlers, and I realized it was a lot of holly and mistletoe.

"Wait," I interrupted, scanning the name medallions. "Which one of you is Hugo?"

"I am!" came a muffled voice from my trunk.

"Oh. Nice to, uh…" I was going to say 'nice to meet you' to the elf, but I didn't make a habit out of lying. I pulled my toque a bit further down on my head as a blast of icy snow hit me. We really needed to get off the road.

"How does she see us?" one whispered to another, dark eyes watching me. "She saw his nose, but didn't have to touch him first."

"The wall between worlds…?" Prancer said pointedly. There was a warning in his tone, and it sparked a collective inhale, followed by a rise in overlapping chatter I couldn't follow.

"Look," Donner said loudly, and the side-chatter died

immediately. He smelled like beer and corn chips. "She locked Hugo in the trunk."

I shifted nervously, and considered popping the trunk, aware these guys could easily paw and stamp me to death with their big furry hooves.

"So, she can't be all that bad," he continued.

Wait. Had I scored a few points by immobilizing the rude elf, even though I'd basically run down their leader?

The group of dark reindeer eyes with their beautiful long lashes studied me.

"So, to the barn, and then call a vet? Because I know a guy. He's really good." I felt like a stuck record. But the more I thought about our predicament, the more I wanted someone like Haden checking Rudolph over. I might not adore the man any longer, my childhood crush and infatuation long ago squelched, but I still admired his skill set and calming strength in emergencies.

A riot of reindeer arguments for and against calling in a vet swirled around me like a sudden windstorm. My phone rang, and I stepped out of the circle of antlers to answer it.

"Hello?"

Char launched into conversation, sounding a bit breathless. "Estelle says Santa's reindeer are real."

I rolled my eyes. "I figured that out, thanks. They also talk."

"Of course they do. Why wouldn't they?"

"I don't know. They're reindeer?"

"Anyway, she's going to call Santa. I hope it's okay I gave her your number to pass along."

"Yeah, no. Of course." I wiped my forehead with a mittened hand, relieved to know that this mess would soon be in someone else's capable hands. "What do I do until he calls?"

"I don't know."

"You didn't ask?"

"No."

"So what do I do?"

"I don't know. Make sure Rudolph doesn't die, so you don't ruin Christmas?"

"Thanks," I said dryly.

"You could make a wish, and have Estelle fix it."

"Never." I nearly ended the call on that note. There were some things I never wanted to experience. And being in debt to the magical world and having a drooling ogre eye me up like I was his next lunch... I shuddered just thinking about it. Even though Estelle said her ogre buddy was vegan, I wasn't sure I believed it. Real-life vegans were known to make exceptions. What if eating a human was an ogre's version of a cheat day?

"I might still have some credit on my account at Your Fairy Godmother," Char said, her voice rising like this was tantalizing information.

"Nope. Not risking it."

"Why not?"

Why not? Was she kidding me? She'd wished like a crazy person and ended up owing Estelle more than she earned in a year. And to top it all off, she'd only had ninety days to pay it all off. Had she somehow forgotten about that mess, and how we'd all come together to help bail her out?

"Are you forgetting how awful it was? It was freaky and stressful."

"You can use as many of my credits as you want. And, anyway, it all turned out okay."

True. But I feared that if I decided to dabble in wishes, I might accidentally do it wrong and completely ruin Christmas.

Having Estelle contact Santa on my behalf felt safest. What was the point of having a fairy godmother if she couldn't help you out in a pinch?

Char and I finished our call and, with a sigh, I turned back to the car. All eight reindeer were watching me, their giant antlers intimidating weapons in the illumination put off by my car's flashing orange lights.

"Um. All decided?" I asked tentatively.

Comet said definitively, "Take Rudolph to your barn."

"You're coming, too, right?"

"Yes."

"We trust you, but not that much," one said. I think it was Dancer.

One of the more muscular reindeer stepped from the herd. His fur was glossy, and there were faded words painted on his rump that said *Hitch me up*. "Beat you there!"

"You don't know where we're going," I grumbled, climbing into my car. Or maybe he did. Who knew how Santa's visits really worked. Maybe his reindeer had internal GPSs as well as a mapped-out list of every human's home address.

"Yeah, Dasher," one of them chided, clearly delighted by the way I'd inadvertently put Dasher in his place.

"Are you flying behind me? How fast should I drive? Can you see without Rudolph guiding you?" I asked, aiming the car's heater vents at my face, and feeling certain I was going to freeze to death driving between here and home with my convertible's top down.

The reindeer began talking at once, with everyone having an answer, but Dasher's was the loudest. They postured and pushed each other aside with their shoulders or antlers, trying to be heard, and to be the one in charge.

Men. It didn't matter the species. They were all the same.

I put the car in gear and drove off without them.

CHAPTER 3

~ *Estelle* ~

"The girls need me! Char and Tamara!"

I'd withstood four long months of them claiming they didn't need a fairy godmother in their life, and I was giddy to be back in the game.

"Report, Estelle," the head fairy said with a sigh, as though I exhausted her.

"Yes! Right!" I was supposed to be filing my trainee report on what I'd done today here at Your Fairy Godmother. Not share my excitement that Char and her friends had made contact with me after several disappointing months of silence.

I cleared my throat and straightened my shoulders, trying to act more like the trainee who'd won the creativity award last summer. Winning an award in your first year was basically unheard of. Not to brag. Or rub it into the faces of anyone in particular, such as Trish, my primary rival who was also eager— make that overeager—to prove herself.

The head fairy was waiting, watching me with her lavender eyes.

"As you will recall, Char was our best client last year," I stated unnecessarily.

29

And she was mine. All mine.

"I remember." I caught a small, impatient eye roll.

I'd also won an award for most wishes granted, thanks to Char.

Last quarter was rather dire, though, and this one wasn't shaping up well, either. We trainees only received a certain number of clients each year, and two of mine—Char and Tamara—hadn't made a single, chargeable wish. I was falling behind.

"I also recall the mix-ups, broken rules, and errors." The head fairy was clearly tired, ready to go home, but she had a duty to listen to all of us lower ranked trainees at the end of each day. Provide guidance, remind us of the rules, keep us in line, and guide us so we could pass our next levels and basically become like her.

Right down to the barf-a-rific pink dresses I refused to wear.

Still, I think the head fairy liked me. And not just because we were related. She'd been in this job for a few hundred years and seen everything. And again, not to brag, but I continued to surprise her. And that wasn't solely due to my accidental rule-bending and breaking.

My fairy godmother trainee colleagues all knew the rules by heart as their families had put them into fairy godmother-specific private schools from an early age, preparing them for today.

Unlike my family. I was truly a trainee, learning everything for the first time, and our jobs were beyond complex.

But, it turned out, I was good at finding loopholes and bending rules. Probably because my fellow trainees were already so well-trained on how to behave, there wasn't much leeway for them to surprise our head fairy.

I took the wins wherever I could get them.

Especially since sometimes I could see a little spark of pride in Gram-Gram's eyes when I did something unexpected. Oh, how I lived for those sparks.

"I will bring magic and goodness to their lives!" I told Gram-Gram.

"Have either of them made a wish?"

"Well, no." So, technically, I couldn't jump in and fix things for Tamara. But I could grease the wheels over here in the world of magic. Then Tamara would see that I wasn't as scary as she believed, and she'd start making wishes for me to grant.

"Then why the optimism and excitement?" the head fairy asked.

"I was asked for a favour."

"We don't grant favours. We grant wishes."

"Yes, I know." You got paid for wishes. Not favours, or anything else for that matter, and there was a cost to running the offices of Your Fairy Godmother. "I need access to the regional communication system."

"RCS?" The head fairy leaned forward, eyes narrowing. She was pretty in her pale pink dress with the sparkles and matching hair clips. I'd been told by Trish that tomorrow the head fairy would celebrate Christmas Eve by wearing red and green. Red was my favourite colour, and I couldn't wait to see someone else in the agency wearing something other than pink. Baby pink, flamingo pink, bubblegum pink, cherry blossom pink... The list of yack-inducing shades went on and on.

I was surrounded by so much pink I swear my estrogen shot through the roof every time I walked into the bullpen of fairy cubicles. I was the only one who refused to wear pink. I was also the only one wearing stilettos and black leather pants. *And* the only one with dyed red hair.

Was the whole wearing-red thing for Christmas simply

Trish trying to pull my leg again? She knew I didn't understand the fairy world as well as everyone else. I might come from a very long line of fairy godmothers, but some of this stuff just wasn't in my blood. And some of it—like the wardrobe—I didn't want in my blood.

"Why?" the head fairy asked.

"Sorry what?" I was still trying to picture Gram-Gram in something other than pink.

"Why do you need access to the regional communication system?"

"To call the North Pole. To speak with Santa Claus."

"And why is that?" Gram-Gram was instantly suspicious. Obviously she'd heard about the solstice party, and the ensuing, lengthy fight between Santa and Mrs. Claus, thanks to me and my social blunder.

But it was an easy mistake to make. Santa hadn't been in his red suit, and Trish had told me he'd been eyeing me all night, and that he was a high wizard. Feeling brave, I'd gone over, and we'd flirted over appies for almost an hour.

How was I supposed to know he was Santa? Wizards might also let out a 'ho, ho, ho' when they laughed. Trish sure had been pleased with herself once I was in Mrs. Claus's line of sight. I shuddered at the threats Santa's wife had made against me.

"I'm following the client rules," I said, thinking on my feet. "Keep the client safe, happy, making wishes, and improve their lives."

"Cut the unicorn-crap, Estelle."

I sighed. Fine. "Tamara, my client, hit Rudolph with her car."

"How? Where? With what?"

"Um. What do you mean?" I'd been expecting some sort of concerned panic from the head fairy, with it practically being

Christmas Eve and all. But she seemed more befuddled than anything.

"Well, first of all, how did she see him? He'd be at the North Pole. So, are you sure it's Rudolph? And if it is, how would your human get through the shroud?"

"I don't know." It was a special time of year where some types of magic were stronger. But so, too, were the protection spells, such as the ones around Santa's reindeer, so children and others couldn't see or harm them while they made their deliveries on Christmas Eve. Come to think of it, it was a bit odd that Tamara had not only seen Rudolph, but managed to hit him with her car.

I knew that when someone believed, they could see us. If we wanted them to. But why would Rudolph want to be seen by a human?

The head fairy sat back in her chair, her pink painted nails against her lips. "Tamara believes."

"Yes." She'd been in our offices and seen all of us. That was ironclad evidence.

"I think there's something more at play."

I quirked my head to the side. "Like what?"

The head fairy sat forward, her brow creased. "Something doesn't feel right."

"Is something wrong?"

"I think we'd better check on a few things."

"Okay." I nodded, eager to learn something new and special or odd. Something that fairies like Trish might not get to see or learn in their first year.

"When did this happen?" Gram-Gram asked, her expression growing more concerned, as though the news was finally sinking in past the disbelief that an accident of this type was not only possible, but had actually happened so close to Christmas.

"Just now. More or less."

The head fairy stood up, face pale. She wavered slightly, as if she was standing in a gale force wind. It wasn't until then that I realized that my client might have a major magical world problem.

CHAPTER 4
~ *Tamara* ~

I parked in front of my red barn with the white trim, letting the car's heater blast me for a few more seconds before getting out. It was so cold, it felt as if my entire face was going to break off. Even with the heat cranked, and me, driving hunched over my steering wheel with all the vents angled at my fingers and face, I was frozen. My jaw chattered so hard, I feared I might shatter my teeth. Driving with the roof down in a Canadian blizzard was not something I'd ever recommend.

My joints creaking, and the fabric of my winter coat crackling in the cold, I got out of the car. The snow that had swirled into the cab and coated my shoulders and lap dropped to the ground like a sudden avalanche. I held the big wing of a door open for Rudolph and looked to the sky for the other reindeer. I hadn't seen them while driving, and feared I'd lost them. What was I going to do with Rudolph if they weren't here to guide me?

Moments later, I relaxed as they silently landed in the snow, careful not to knock over my lit-up reindeer lawn ornament, which was significantly less beefy than they were. There was something off in the way they moved. Their movements were slightly uncoordinated, and they walked with a fluid grace that made me more and more convinced that they were tipsy, if not flat-out drunk.

The boys surrounded Rudolph and the car, and I stepped back to shoot off a quick text to the GAL PAL text group, cringing as I hit Send.

ME

Benjamin met Rudolph tonight. Advice? Have him at barn. Char called Estelle. Haven't heard back. SOS!

I knew Samantha and Gabby wouldn't be helpful since they didn't believe in the magical world, or at least, they hadn't last summer. Josie was in the chat thread, though, and she was our resident expert, seemingly understanding way more than Char and I did despite her lack of forthcomingness whenever we ran into an issue.

I opened the barn door, the doorway strung with multi-coloured Christmas lights, and turned to find the herd of reindeer coaxing Rudolph along. He was limping, collapsing down into his hips when he walked, which didn't look very promising in regards to a speedy recovery. His nose was blinking slowly, and I swore his eyes spun with pain.

We maneuvered Rudolph through the doorway, and I went to close the door behind us. One of the herd was rubbing noses with the reindeer ornament, which was a white, wire-frame deal with white lights. I left the door open for the straggler and helped Rudolph into an empty stall near the back of my four-stall barn.

Once Rudolph was situated, I returned to close the door, so what little heat trapped in the uninsulated building didn't escape. I checked my phone with half-frozen fingers while hunching further into my parka. I pulled my toque further down over my ears and eyebrows, trying to fight the intense wave of shivers taking over my core.

SAMANTHA

u drunk?

I think Malachi is going to propose. 😏 What do I do? 🫣

GABBY

Yay! Say yes!!!!!!

I smiled. Gabby was the most optimistic and romantic of the five of us, and naturally she saw the bright side of Samantha's mostly likely doomed relationship. She was the one we relied on for hope, and I bit my lip as I scanned her next message, eager to see if she had anything helpful for me despite her lack of belief.

GABBY

Please tell me u don't mean Rudolph as in the reindeer...

I could picture her rolling her eyes. It looked as though she still didn't believe in the magical world.

ME

Yes. That Rudolph.

CHAR

Nothing from Estelle or the jolly fella?

ME

Not yet.

GABBY

Um? So we're doing this again?

> **SAMANTHA**
> They're drunk. Ignore them.

Dots appeared under Josie's name, and I held my breath as I waited for her to chime in.

> **JOSIE**
> This is bad. Very bad. It's almost Christmas Eve! What were you thinking?

I shivered, and not from the cold. Her message should have been the helpful one I'd been counting on. Instead, it only gave me a deep, unwelcome sense of foreboding.

> **ME**
> I didn't ask for this! I didn't make a wish.

Why was this happening to me?

> **CHAR**
> Call Haden.

No. I pocketed my phone.

I couldn't do that. He was my ex's brother. He didn't like me, and would have things to say about me bringing a 'wild' reindeer home. One with a blinking nose. Assuming he could even see any of this. He probably couldn't even help me, and would think I was nutso, or trying to lure him into something like one of his HAGs—Haden Appreciation Group fan club members.

What was I going to do?

Maybe Rudolph could allow Haden to see him, but not his magical blinking nose.

Haden. He was the kind fixer, and I was the girl in need of fixing.

My long-ago crush on him had formed on the first day of

grade one. I'd fallen and torn my knee open on the steps leading up to the elementary classrooms. He'd been going past me to the junior high, and had helped me up, dried my tears, and handed me off to a sweet teacher to get bandaged up. He'd been in grade seven and he could have acted cool, and walked on by like dozens of others. But he hadn't.

Moments like that dotted our existence.

Well, until Kade had put a record-screeching stop to it all by informing me that his older brother was merely tolerating me.

Ugh.

And if he came here tonight and failed to see the magical flying reindeer in my barn... Yeah, no. There was no way I was calling Haden. We needed to wait for Santa or some other solution.

I checked for more deer outside, then closed the barn door. From behind me, I heard someone with a Spanish accent crooning softly. Cupid, I figured, although his accent was much more pronounced than it had been earlier. Turning, I spotted him at the first stall, which was occupied by my landlord's mare, Dolly.

"Who do we have here?" Cupid asked her, his voice warm and smooth like melted butter. He received a delighted horsey snort in reply.

I hurried back to where the rest of the herd was surrounding Rudolph.

"Can someone call off Cupid?" I asked, as a few chickadees swooped down from their spots in the rafters, almost landing on my shoulders before veering away. They thought it was feeding time, even though I fed them, and the other birds that used the barn for protection, in the morning. "The last thing I need is to try and explain some creature that's half-horse and half-reindeer to Dolly's owner, Carl."

Prancer gave a derisive snort. "That can't happen. He's magical. She's not."

"Ever heard of demigods?" I muttered.

"I like her," Donner stated.

"Thank you," I told the beer-scented reindeer with the holly and mistletoe in his antlers. "You're very handsome."

Donner tipped his head up as though basking in the compliment.

Rudolph had slumped into the clean straw lining the empty stall, and I fit the car blanket around him a bit better. Then I snagged a horse blanket and wrapped it around my lower half and shivered, trying to warm up. It was warmer in the barn than outside, but still well below freezing.

"Ignore Cupid," Comet advised me. "He'll have forgotten all about her by tomorrow."

That wasn't particularly reassuring. Dolly was snuffling in a, dare I say, flirty way. Even flirtier than when she wanted another carrot. With reluctance, I let the duo be, and returned my attention to Rudolph. I crouched beside him, my worry returning.

"Do any of you have magic that can help?" I asked.

"We're reindeer," one of them replied. I couldn't see who, but I think it was Prancer.

"Is that a no?"

"Yes."

"No," another one argued. "You mean no."

"Yes, it's a no," Prancer insisted. "Are you still drunk?"

There was the clack of antlers hitting each other.

"Guys!" The antler clacking stopped. "Do you have magic that can help us right now?"

"No!" the two bickering deer chorused.

"Okay. Thank you." Yeesh. These guys were as testy as kindergarteners who'd missed snack *and* nap time. "How about Santa? Is there a way we can call him?"

I was certain Estelle would get the job done of contacting him, but it wasn't a bad idea to use everything at my disposal, seeing as Christmas Eve was looming up on us.

The reindeer became very busy studying my barn's inner architecture instead of considering my suggestion. They looked more like my class of students when they were up to no good and trying to go unnoticed.

There were a couple of pranksters in my class, and over the first few months of the school year, they'd mastered that same look of innocence. Well, if you considered looking way too obviously innocent 'mastered.' They thought I was psychic because of the way I always seemed to know when they were up to something. The teacher and I had shared a few private giggles over that and their cuteness.

In other words, these reindeer didn't seem to be much different from the five-year-olds I worked with. My guess was that getting drunk and injured would possibly get them into trouble, and they were hoping an innocent act would keep me oblivious to the severity of their misdeeds.

"What did you boys do?" I scolded, automatically falling into my teaching role, hands on my hips.

"Nothing," Dasher replied quickly.

"Party on!" Blitzen called out. Had Christmas tree ornaments always been hanging from his antlers? How had I missed those earlier?

"We were bonding," Comet said carefully.

"Male bonding," Donner added.

I turned to him. "Is that why you smell like beer?"

Prancer snickered beside him.

"And you smell like peach schnapps."

Prancer's spine straightened.

"Chiquita knows her drinks," Cupid said, coming closer.

"Party on!" Blitzen repeated, the shiny glass ornaments swinging from his antlers.

Dancer, stockier than the others, and his coat, mostly a pale brown other than a flash of white on his chest, spoke up. "We were celebrating." He had a heavy Swedish accent, and the way he weighted his words, it gave them a certain gravitas.

"Christmas?" I asked.

"Christmas Eve is tomorrow night. I need to be able to fly," Rudolph said. "Do you know someone who could help me feel well enough to do that?"

"I'm so sorry." Guilt instantly overtook me for my distraction, and I crouched beside him. "How are you feeling?" I tentatively stroked the spot between his ears. "Is it okay if I pet you? Who should I call? Santa? How do I do that?"

I looked up to find the other deer watching Rudolph, eyes wide. Then they broke into a chorus of comments ranging from "You're okay. Walk it off, man" to "Are you sure?" to "Mrs. C. can*not* find out."

"Um. So?" I asked tentatively.

"Let the elf out of your trunk," Rudolph said.

The others gasped.

"Not on your life!" Donner grumbled.

"Might be," Rudolph said ominously.

I felt a fizz of panic taking an unpleasant meander through my nervous system. "Sorry, what am I doing? Am I letting him out?"

Releasing the elf was going to make this difficult evening a lot worse, but I supposed I couldn't lock him up forever. The magical world was particular about their rules, and I was sure that holding an elf hostage would make the lengthy list of no-nos.

Donner told Rudolph, "We don't need him."

"He's locked in her trunk," Rudolph said pointedly. "Mrs. C. will be very angry."

"It's unkind," Prancer added primly. "You know the rule about kindness."

"Wet blanket," one of them muttered.

"Killjoy."

One of the reindeer made some poorly disguised mutterings under a fake cough that sounded a lot like "The elf's a narc."

"Mrs. C. won't stand for it, and you know he'll tell her," Rudolph pointed out, putting an immediate halt to the insults and digs.

Donner grumbled, "He's just got to ride in the seat that suits him best."

Dasher snickered. "How's he going to tell her if he's in the trunk?"

"Yeah, he's stuck here. He can't go tattle."

"In my trunk?" I confirmed, getting the feeling that the elf was stuck here in more ways than one. "He's not really stuck. There's a glow-in-the-dark emergency pull cord that will release the trunk's latch. It's dangling beside him. I can't imagine it taking him much longer to find it."

More elf-directed insults started up again, these ones centred around Hugo's intelligence or, rather, lack thereof.

I opened my mouth to ask more questions, but Rudolph piped up with a plaintive, "I hurt." His big deer eyes turned to me. "Especially where you hit me with your car."

"I know. I'm so sorry. We're going to get you fixed up. I promise." I stroked his flank. "Can Santa help you? Should we call him?"

"No." The reindeer surrounding me all shook their heads.

Okay, so that pretty much confirmed that they had been out doing something bad and could get in trouble for it. Got it.

"What do I do?"

"Call a doctor?"

"Oh. Um." Haden. Ugh, no. "Can a veterinarian even see you?"

"Not a good idea, boys," Prancer said under his breath. "Repercussions."

"What kind of repercussions?" I asked, imagining Estelle's ogre in accounting with the big slobbery mouth. I shivered involuntarily.

I reminded myself that this had all been an accident, and that I was doing the best I could to help the herd. Nothing bad would happen to me. I hoped.

But I was starting to get frustrated with the lack of forthcomingness, my imagination, no doubt, acting on a much more grand scale than reality.

"What do you think I should do?" I asked. "Can you come to a consensus?"

Rudolph sighed into the straw. "Resting isn't helping me feel better. A vet is the answer, and we all know it."

Mentally, I ran through all the reasons that was a bad idea. There were a lot. More so, now that I knew the other reindeer felt it was a bad idea, too.

On the flip side, the consequences of not getting Rudolph proper medical treatment as Christmas Eve reared up on us was possibly worse.

The reindeer had fallen silent, and Rudolph's word appeared to be the final say.

I sighed. "Okay. I'll call Haden. He's a vet." The idea left a leaden feeling in my stomach. "You'll make sure he can see you, so I don't look crazy?"

"Call him," Rudolph said wearily.

"Oh, boy," Prancer muttered.

"Other ideas?" Rudolph snapped at him.

He received a lengthy sigh in reply. Then Prancer said, "Told you tonight was a bad idea."

"Shut up," Blitzen sniped. "There's no rule we can't go out and party. We only work one night of the year. We have the best job in the world, but not if we sit at home with our rule books stuck up our furry little—"

"Enough!" Comet barked. "We are a team."

I began backing away from the brewing fight, patting my parka, wondering which pocket I'd dropped my phone into. My bulky coat was far from flattering, but it was warm and had a plethora of giant pockets, making it ideal for Canadian winters. I found a wad of clean tissue, lip balm, cat treats, Benjamin's fob, numerous hair elastics, a gas points card I used as a windshield scraper, and then finally my phone. I waved it in the air. "I'll just go over there and...."

I marched myself to the other end of the barn, scrolling through my contacts until I found the name of the local, large-breed veterinarian. I closed my eyes and sighed in defeat. Haden Powell.

Did I even have enough in my bank account to pay him? I wasn't totally broke, but what did it cost to fix up a magical being, especially as an after-hours emergency? Maybe I could ask Haden to work as fast as humanly possible, and then kick him out. That was probably the best plan—just hurry him along to save both my wallet and our tentative friendship.

Friendship? It wasn't even that anymore. If it ever had been. More like once was (one-sided, of course), never to be again, and relegated to acquaintances who knew each other fairly well. Was there a word for that type of relationship?

Sighing, I skipped over Haden's personal number, opting to try his clinic first. Pretty much every cat, dog, goat, horse, sheep and cow in the county were all getting way more check-ups these days than the average Canadian animal did, and would until the man was married off. But I bet nobody had ever brought him a reindeer emergency before.

While I waited for the clinic's after-hours recording to pick up, where I assumed I could leave a message, I put my phone on speaker and read through the GAL PAL texting string. My friends didn't have anything helpful to offer in regard to my reindeer problem, so I scanned through Samantha's current list of relationship issues. None of them would be big in my world, and I started to grumble over her lack of gratitude. She had no idea how lucky she was to have such a sweet boyfriend who wanted to keep her.

Although, I did understand her annoyance with him not getting her parents a gift even though they were spending Christmas Day with them. Samantha came from money and manners, and while she acted like a regular gal, and not a woman who was independently wealthy, she had a tendency to forget herself and brought hostess gifts to friends' houses, even when said friend still used a cardboard box as their coffee table.

I hoped Malachi was currently running out to pick out a gift.

I was annoyed at how easily Samantha found great men, but never kept any of them. Meanwhile, I was floundering about as a single woman—probably for the rest of my life.

ME

He loves you. Nothing of this matters.

GABBY

I agree. It's hard to find a man who loves you back.

Poor Gabs. She was in love with her bestie, Lamonte, and her feelings weren't returned. She said she'd moved on, but I think she'd just done a good job of burying how she felt. When it came to love, she was in the same boat as I was. So single it hurt.

JOSIE

Listen to really loud, angry music. You'll be
fine.

She attached a link to a playlist, which I was pretty sure was the one she sent me when Kade and I broke up. Music was her solution to everything.

ME

Love's hard to find. Hard to keep. Malachi
doesn't have to be perfect. None of us are.

I could see the line of dots indicating that Samantha was typing up a reply—probably something that would annoy me and my lonely heart even further, so I typed one last thing as fast as I could and jumped out of the thread.

ME

Char—still waiting to hear from Santa.
Reindeer said to call Haden.

I should have sent the text to only Char. Now, next time I opened the group chat, I'd have an annoyed Samantha still complaining about how much her boyfriend loved her, *and* Samantha or Gabby mocking me for believing in magic.

What if Haden actually got my message and came here? My heart thumped at the thought of spending one-on-one time with Haden, and without a distraction, such as his brother, to hide behind. I avoided Haden as much as I could, along with that penetrating gaze of his that went right through me like an x-ray machine, seeing everything. And I meant everything.

So it was wholly unfair, seeing as he looked at everyone with shuttered eyes, allowing nobody to see even one speck of his kind-hearted soul.

Realizing that the clinic's emergency line was waiting for me to record my message, I quickly explained that I'd hit a deer, and that I had it in my barn, and could Haden come look at it.

Mulling over the recording I'd left, I winced. It sounded like I was going to be here, waiting for him in nothing but lingerie, tempting Mr. Hot Bachelor to visit my little love trap.

I was certain he already thought I was loony. Now, saying I'd hit a deer, had brought it home, and was requesting Haden, specifically? Yeah, that was bad.

No, he knew me.

He knew I'd spent too long dating his brother when we clearly weren't a strong enough match. His gaze made that clear. The way he'd look at me when I'd roll over and let Mr. Gregarious Kade take over our social life. Not only was I an ooey-gooey animal lover softie, I was a softie with his brother, too.

I guess tonight would be just one more thing Haden could add to his list.

And anyway, it didn't actually matter what he thought. He already knew I was a bleeding heart when it came to animals, so my message wasn't that weird, was it? He understood that I sometimes treated animals like they were my non-human children.

Not that I would ever take a dog for a walk in a stroller—they had legs, and even I had my limits. But I did believe that animals had rights, and should be treated as though they had feelings. Because they did.

Honestly, I think he agreed with me on that one.

Although, he hadn't thought it was cute—at all—that I'd dressed up my rescued tomcat for Halloween. I mean, a black cat was just begging to wear a Batman costume, right? Everyone had agreed he was adorable. Well, everyone except Haden. He'd been the one bit of rain in the comment section of my kitty's social posts.

Ugh. Why did I even care what he thought? I mean, he was following my cat's account. What did he expect?

And my voicemail had been to the point, which was something he appreciated. Although, maybe I'd given him too much information, or the wrong kind of information, and now he was going to have me put on Fish and Wildlife's Wild Animal Bad People list for hurting and transporting an undomesticated wild animal without a license or whatever you needed.

I wouldn't blame him if he reported me.

I dialled the clinic again, leaving a new message, telling him to contact me before anybody else.

I groaned as I repocketed my phone. That was worse. Now I sounded suspicious. He probably thought I was going to make venison stew or something. Bringing the animal home... Could that be construed as poaching?

No. Only if it was dead.

I glanced toward the back stall, surrounded by arguing reindeer.

Rudolph had better not die.

CHAPTER 5

~ *Haden* ~

My phone buzzed and, out of habit, my eyes shifted from the dark snowy road to the screen on my truck's dashboard. There was a new voicemail on the clinic's after-hours emergency line. I rubbed my twitching left eye, wondering when my day would end. It had started long before winter's dawn, and I was ready to go home, eat supper, and kick up my feet. Then, maybe wrap up the Christmas gifts for my parents and brother.

After tapping a few buttons, the voicemail played over the truck's speakers. I frowned. Tamara Madden.

My brother's ex-girlfriend. The most curious, animal-loving woman I knew. Her curiosity had fuelled my own, leading me to veterinarian medicine.

She sounded stressed. Why hadn't Tamara called me directly?

Right. Despite once being friends, she no longer wanted to be around me. My brother Kade had made it clear she believed I led women on, and that I wasn't nearly as charming as the rest of the world seemed to think I was. She was likely hoping

50

someone else was covering my after-hours emergencies tonight so she could avoid me.

I frowned as the message ended, a spear of alarm awakening my nervous system. Why did she have a deer in her barn? Didn't she understand she wasn't Snow White, and could get seriously hurt trapping an injured wild animal indoors? Yes, she was good with animals, but that would be dangerous for anyone.

The next voicemail played—having come in while I'd listened to the first one. It was another from Tamara, and my senses shifted into high alert as she begged me to call her before anyone else. Me.

She needed me tonight.

What on earth was going on over at Carl's old farmstead?

I slowed the truck, turning it around on the dark, snowy road. Then I pushed the accelerator down as far as I dared.

CHAPTER 6

~ *Tamara* ~

I returned to Rudolph's stall, noting that Blitzen was nudging the cooler where I was making yukaflux. I'd taken a combination of chopped fresh fruit along with the vodka and rum leftovers from my housewarming party a few months back and mixed it all together. The boozy concoction was something I'd be serving at the small New Year's party I was holding for the GAL PALs where we'd live up to our group name. We'd Giggle And Laugh, Pour our drinks And Listen to each other. Just like when we'd all lived together back in Calgary. I missed them and those days, but not the city.

"Get out of there," I told Blitzen as I walked by. He looked up at me with rounded, deep dark eyes, the Christmas tree ornaments swinging from his antlers, clinking as he moved.

His innocent act might work on Santa, but not me. I clicked the lid closed, locking him out of the boozy fruit.

"I left a message with Haden, the vet, since it's after hours," I told Rudolph and his buddies, refraining from letting them know I had the man's personal number. "By the way, where's Vixen? According to the song and stories, there are nine reindeer. Is he lost or hurt or something? Should we be out looking for him?"

"We know where Vixen is," Comet replied.

"And he's okay?"

"*She.*"

"Oh. Sorry."

I swore Comet rolled his eyes at me for my assumption that they were all male.

Wait a second. "All of the reindeer have antlers in the picture books."

"And?" he asked dryly.

"Only male deer have antlers." I hadn't made a sex-based assumption after all!

"Both male and female reindeer have antlers," Rudolph informed me from his prone position.

"Oh." I glanced at the antlered beasts surrounding me. "Why do you still have your antlers? Don't you lose them in the fall?"

"We're a special magical breed," Comet said in a bored tone, like he got asked this a lot.

"Oh. Right." Every time I opened my mouth, I proved how little I knew about them and their world.

"It's just the guys tonight," Dasher told me.

I grumbled under my breath about gender politics in the workplace.

With a sigh, Prancer said, "We were having a stag party."

Dasher chuckled flatly. "*Stag.* Get it?"

"Are stag parties the same in the reindeer world as they are in the human world?"

"I'm getting married," Dasher said.

I aimed a "Congratulations" his way. Suddenly, their booziness made sense. As well as the absence of Vixen. And the painted words *Hitch me up* on Dasher's flank.

"Wait." I held out a hand, working to piece it all together. "Santa let you go out and get drunk the night before you all have to fly around the world—the *planet*?" A whirl of panic did a devilish spin through me. Referring to the world as a planet made their job feel extra-large.

Blitzen sighed. "I already told you. No rule against it."

"There should be," Prancer muttered.

I clapped a hand over my mouth as I realized what they'd done. "You snuck out! And now Santa's going to be mad because Rudolph got hurt," I whispered loudly. Automatically, I'd leaned in as though someone might overhear us and, thus, their secret.

"We can leave the compound at any time," Dasher said stiffly.

"This is *really* good," someone said from behind the group. I craned my neck around Comet's rump and spotted Blitzen, antler deep into my cooler, his antler ornaments swinging wildly.

"Get out of my yukaflux!"

"We don't have fruit like this at the North Pole," Blitzen said, his muzzle pink and dripping from the alcoholic mix.

Dasher, with his hitch-me-up painted flank, and Donner, with his mistletoe and holly, zeroed in on either side of him. They tried to angle Blitzen's head out of the way so they could try some yukaflux, their antlers clacking as they collided. One of Blitzen's ornaments hit the barn floor and broke.

"Aw, guys," he complained. "Look what you did. Now I'm not as festive."

"Dude, you're pigging out. Save some for us," Dasher whined.

"You gulp everything like it's a race. I needed the head start."

"You finished it!"

"That's alcoholic punch." I marched over, pushing their heads out of the way. "You've found enough trouble tonight, thanks to booze."

They were incredibly strong, but also surprisingly obedient. I was grateful that my disastrous mixing with the magical world had at least brought me sweet, bratty reindeer and not drooling ogres. Although, in terms of meeting scary beasts, I was sure there was still time to meet some more.

With the lid closed on the mostly empty cooler, I rubbed my throbbing temples, and walked out of the barn, trying to get my head wrapped around my life. I hoped Haden showed up and managed to pull off a medical miracle.

Gently, I coaxed the frozen cloth roof of my convertible back into place. Then I plugged in the car's block heater so the engine wouldn't freeze up on me—assuming that hitting Rudolph hadn't triggered the engine's accident ignition kill switch thingy, and Benjamin would still start for me later. Although, maybe my car didn't have one of those switches, or it was broken, because I'd bumped into quite a few things, and Benjamin had never refused to start again afterward.

Cheered by the thought that my car was basically invincible, I took the snow brush and cleared off the seats as well as the incredible amount of fur Rudolph had shed in the back.

Maybe I could ask Santa for a new car if I managed to resolve this growing reindeer problem. That was a bit more practical than my usual Christmas request, which was a boyfriend.

That was an embarrassing request. I should stop asking for that. Or at least cease mailing away my letters to Santa like I was still five-years-old.

I debated calling Char again, but knew there wasn't much she could do from Mexico, especially since she'd already reached out to her one contact in the magical world.

Josie, however, knew a lot about the magical world, thanks to her love of romantasy novels. But her text message hadn't offered up anything helpful other than pointing out the obvious around how bad this all was.

Which left me again with Haden as my answer to all things reindeer-related. Was it too soon to call his personal line? I shoved up the sleeve of my parka and checked my new smartwatch. It had only been about five or ten minutes since I'd called him. I should give his voicemail monitoring service a bit longer to reach him. Although, maybe the voicemails went directly into his inbox, and he had gotten over his compunction to fix me and my problems, and was ghosting my craziness. If I called a third time, it would only secure any belief that I was bonkers.

And honestly, I wasn't sure where I stood with the man, now that his brother and I were finally kaput. He kept so much locked up behind his guarded dark blue eyes. I feared if I misstepped, it would become super awkward, like it was with his parents whenever we bumped into each other around town. Mrs. Powell didn't know if she should hug me or simply say hi and keep going. We'd often ended up in an awkward sort of hug, mumbling niceties over each other.

It didn't help that Kade and I had broken up very publicly, which I think had embarrassed both families.

Remind me to never break into tears while throwing bags of chips at someone.

But seriously. Kade had aired a whole laundry list of ways that I'd changed, and how I wasn't the same, and now I was less fun and a total hermit. Where was my sense of adventure? Life was for the living! It had been a lecture and break-up speech, all in one. And this was after I'd moved my entire life back home to be with him.

So much for allowing a sense of nostalgia for the comfort of our old relationship, time spent within the folds of his family, and my familiar hometown to guide my life decisions.

Standing there in the grocery store with my heart breaking, and people I'd known all my life quickly turning their carts to avoid our aisle and my tears, I'd felt so powerless, so unwanted and undesired. So...unworthy and outright plain.

I inhaled sharply at the wash of memories from the past. I shook out my cold hands, wishing I could shed this emotion like the reindeer fur that was stuck to my mitts.

The snarky elf was muttering and clunking in the trunk, and I leaned closer, feeling guilty for leaving him in there.

"Are you warm enough?"

I turned an ear, listening. I was pretty sure he said something about frozen reindeer turds.

"Are you okay? The boys don't want to let you out. They say you'll tattle on them."

More insults.

Right. Nice guy. I could see why he was so well liked.

I checked my watch again. When did the herd need to be back at the North Pole? It was already nearing eight, and Blitzen was going to need some time to sober up.

And what about the weather forecast? Tonight's storm would end sometime early in the morning, but there was only a short reprieve before a second storm rolled in on the heels of this one around noon tomorrow. It was too early to know if the forecasters' predictions were on target. But chances were, there would be no clear skies on Christmas Eve, and Santa would need Rudolph at the helm to help guide his sleigh filled with toys.

His sleigh.

I inhaled the sharp, bitterly cold air, and tilted my head back, peering up at the dark sky and ignoring the shouting elf.

Snowflakes landed and melted on my cheeks as I let the magic of the night sink in.

Elves were real.

Flying reindeer were real.

Santa was real.

I loved the holiday season, and the traditions I had with my family, and in particular, my grandma, who I called Oma. She'd saved Christmas for me when I was thirteen and my parents had separated for a few weeks. We started a lot of traditions that year, Oma and I. In the end, I think some of them, along with the spirit of the season, were what brought my parents back together on Christmas Day.

That, for me, was what Christmas was about. Love. Hope. A second chance to get things right. Caring about each other. Time with family. There were so many things about the season I adored and held dear.

One of the traditions my Oma and I started that year was for us both to wear the same ugly Christmas sweater. We used to rotate years, so she'd pick out something one year, and then I'd do it the next. But after a particularly raunchy sweater the year I turned eighteen, I took over the task of finding us our seasonal sweaters. I'd revealed them tonight at supper, and was still wearing mine. I'd gone horse-themed with "Oh, what fun it is to ride" across the front with a horse and rider jumping a fence below it. Oma wasn't as into horses as I was, but she'd dutifully put on the sweater with a chuckle, like always.

That was my favourite tradition, beating out helping Oma bake for her cookie exchange, and maybe even her special, rich and creamy, Christmas rice dessert that she made just for me. However, tonight, meeting the reindeer had made the season feel even more magical. The myths and stories were all real.

I patted the trunk's lid and said to the elf, "I'll be back out in a bit. Don't go anywhere."

A string of flavourful, Christmas themed insults rose from the car.

"Yeah, well, I hope you burn your Christmas baking, too," I muttered, returning to the semi-warmth of the barn. I pushed Cupid away from Dolly as I passed him. "Leave her be."

I aimed a finger at Dolly. "You're old enough to know better." She tossed her head back with a mighty snort of displeasure.

Standing in the middle of the barn, I commanded to the reindeer, "Gather around."

The reindeer obediently shuffled closer, Blitzen giggling. That guy seriously couldn't hold his liquor. Although, I had poured a couple of twenty-sixers in the cooler, and he'd drunk every last bit of those large bottles of liquor. Plus, there was still whatever else in his system that he'd enjoyed during the stag party.

Maybe Comet's little bag was full of booze. I'd have to find a way to ask about it later and make sure they weren't taking nips here and there and making this boozy problem even worse.

"Why is the elf with you?" I gestured in the direction of the closed barn doors where my car was parked on the other side.

"He's a narc," Donner complained.

"Total buzzkill," Blitzen added.

"Yeah, you mentioned that earlier."

"He's a spy," Dancer added in his Swedish accent.

"Okay, but *why* is he *here*?" I asked.

They all repeated themselves, talking over each other.

"He's spying on you guys? But why? So he can tattle to Santa?"

Their heads moved back and forth. No.

I felt that stirring of uncertainty and its trusty companion —fear. There was too much I didn't know or understand about tonight or their world. I turned to the tawny reindeer to my right. "Prancer?"

"The elf chose his side," Donner said gravely, not allowing Prancer to answer.

"Which side?"

"Not ours," Comet said. "Wrong team."

"Okay. So, there's some sort of fight going on?" Nobody said anything, but I could tell my guess was correct.

"Mrs. Claus is mad at Santa," someone toward the back said.

"And the elf is on Mrs. Claus's side?" I hazarded.

I got a nod.

"I see. And he'll tattle on you, and that'll make the fight worse somehow?"

Another nod.

"But it's not like Santa can ground you for sneaking out— it's almost Christmas Eve. Doesn't Christmas have to go on, no matter what?"

The reindeer shared looks. A few of them pawed the ground.

"Wait. Is something else wrong with Christmas?"

My stomach dropped as I caught their expressions. But before anyone could answer, cold air hit the back of my neck, and I turned to see the barn door had opened. My veterinarian acquaintance-almost-once-a-friend, all tall, dark and handsome with melting snowflakes twinkling in his wavy hair, was watching me curiously.

Crazy animal loving lady. Yup. That was me. Talking to a herd of reindeer in her barn about Christmas.

I turned back to the reindeer, my cheeks heated. Haden had to think I was an absolute loon. I tried to think up some brilliant reason as to why I suddenly had eight talking reindeer in my barn.

But the barn was empty.

~

"Hey," Haden said, taking me in with that patient, assessing way of his as he came deeper into the barn, a hefty medical bag in hand. He had the kind of gaze that made you feel thoroughly seen from the bit of toothpaste you missed at the corner of your mouth, down to the fact that you flushed a tampon into your septic system—which was a huge no-no.

But sometimes, secretly, it also made me feel like I was okay because, even though he probably saw all of my flaws, he didn't cross the street if he saw me coming. Sure, we avoided each other, but nothing that would hit the obvious-about-it scale. Occasionally, he smiled, as if reading my less savoury thoughts about someone and finding them amusing.

And did I mention he was a good listener? Whereas most women wanted men to be better at listening to them—like I had been with Kade—with Haden, I wanted to put stoppers in his ears. It felt like he caught everything. And right now, he'd just caught me talking to a herd of reindeer about Christmas being in trouble.

Not that the reindeer were making themselves visible. Which meant, I'd simply looked as though I was losing my mind.

"I got your message, Trademark," he said, and I refrained from rolling my eyes at the nickname. My initials were T.M.— Tamara Madden—and so, of course, he called me Trademark. As far as I knew, he hadn't given anyone else a nickname, so I wasn't sure if I was special, or just that annoying to him. I was fairly certain it was the latter, as Kade had explained when I was seventeen, that I was a bother to Haden, but he was too polite to tell me so. I'd been mortified and had essentially avoided

Haden ever since. I'd thought he'd enjoyed showing me the things he was learning in veterinarian school, and it had felt like we were having some really nice moments, connecting as future siblings-in-law.

Apparently not. On all accounts.

"I was just down the road," he said, his voice that calm deep pool of comfort that soothed animals and their worried humans. "Thought I'd pop by on my way home." He bent slightly, brushing the snow from his hair with crooked fingers.

"Great. Thanks," I said, my voice too high and cheery. I couldn't see a single reindeer, and wondered if they'd done some sort of spell to make themselves invisible to me, as well as Haden. "He's over here."

"You brought him in here?" the vet confirmed, his tone careful. Even though it was chilly in the barn, he unzipped his thick winter work coat, exposing a softly worn red-and-green check flannel shirt buttoned up over a white tee.

Oh, and those hands. I remember watching them deftly and confidently show me how to reshoe a horse. They were strong and capable. The kind of hands that could hold someone firmly, that could tickle, or stroke or protect.

I cleared my throat, trying to focus on our conversation, wondering why I was swooning over the man's hands. That wasn't like me. I'd chased away my childish semblance of a crush years ago.

"He was in the middle of the road." I began moving toward the stall, eager to get Haden out of here. Because as much as I'd love a friendly face at my side during this crisis, his wasn't it. "I'm sure you want to check him out and get to other emergencies before this blizzard gets worse."

"You should never approach wildlife, especially if they're hurt. It's not safe." His tone was firm, and the usual tension that vibrated between us like a tight cord returned. "And never move an injured animal of this size on your own. They can be unpredictable."

A flash of resentment milked my anger over how I cared about his opinion of me.

"He was in the middle of the road in a snowstorm," I snapped, my hands landing instinctively on my hips as I turned to face Haden. "What was I supposed to do? Leave him there for somebody to run over?"

I heard a soft "yeah" of agreement from behind me, followed by a hiccup. Blitzen. I casually scanned the barn, but saw nobody.

Then a flicking tail. They were hiding in the space just past the last stall, which was Rudolph's. I could see them, but could Haden?

The man in question was silent for a long moment, his jaw flexing as he studied me. He was no doubt holding back the lecture sitting on the tip of his tongue, ready for stupid, well-meaning citizens such as myself. There was a flash of impatience in his dark gaze, and he suddenly looked tired.

"Can I see him, Ms. Florence Nightingale?"

I forced my hands to flatten at my sides when all they wanted to do was curl into fists. His tone was too tight, too falsely gentle, and it bothered me. It made me feel as though he was trying to soothe the unhinged, or that same bothersome young girl who'd asked him to save an injured mouse.

Although, he'd actually been really good about that when my eleven-year-old self had shown up at his house with a tiny mouse in a pink shoebox. He'd nursed it back to health for me. What nineteen-year-old man did that? No wonder I'd crushed on him so hard, and then taken his attention the wrong way. Even though he was clearly too old for me.

He'd done a good job of taking my worries seriously, and making me feel seen and important.

"Maybe you *can* see him," I said flippantly. "I don't know."

"You don't know?"

"Yeah, I don't." My confidence and sassiness faltered. If Rudolph's ability to let Haden see him failed, then what? "Also, please note that your name calling is not funny," I grumbled, leading him to the stall where Rudolph was napping, and hopefully sobering up. "You're not as cute as you think you are."

"So I've been told." He stroked Dolly's long nose on his way past, earning an affectionate huff from the old mare.

"And you haven't bothered to correct that fatal flaw, huh?" I asked. "Figure you'll find someone who loves you just the way you are?"

Behind me, Haden said smoothly, his tone light with amusement. "My self-confidence comes from media indoctrination. I believe I'm *perfect* just the way I am."

"That's the message for women. Not men. Men still need work."

"My mistake." He was right behind me now, and the gentle warmth of his deep voice chased away my earlier chill.

"Thank you for recognizing your room for growth," I told Haden, testing how far he'd let me take the teasing.

"I'm an evolved man. Or at least trying to be."

I gave him a second glance. We hadn't allowed banter or teasing between us in a really long time. Not since before Kade had told me I was annoying his older brother with my endless animal questions.

Maybe Haden didn't mind me as a person, but had simply wished I'd leave him alone.

That didn't feel quite right, though. None of it did. I think that was why when Kade had told me how his brother *really* felt, it hurt so much. I normally did a decent job of reading people. And I hadn't gotten the vibe off of Haden that he wanted me to leave him alone when I was younger. I could still remember reshoeing his dad's Clydesdale, the two of us shoulder-to-shoulder while working on the massive beast's front foot. He'd been patiently showing me everything he'd learned at vet school, and his years with horses. I was new to horses, and infatuated with them, and he taught me how to be confident and calm around them. That had involved me talking to the animal while touching its flank, and running my hand all the way down to its hoof.

Apparently, Haden had only meant I should speak to the beast before touching it, but I'd taken it to the extreme, giving a full diatribe of my day while we worked. Haden's mouth had quirked in amusement when we'd finished, explaining I didn't need to talk the entire time. I'd felt a flash of immaturity and childishness in the shadow of his solid, sophisticated maturity. And yet, I hadn't felt judged by him, just a bit silly for taking his tip to excess.

We'd gone to work on the next horse, with him letting me take the lead. Kade had come into the barn and, when we'd virtually ignored him, he'd later sat me down to tell me the truth. Haden was tired of me following him around the farm asking questions, but felt obligated because I was practically family.

He also told me his older brother frequently led women on, and one of his best tricks was acting interested, and doing that attention-giving thing of his.

I'd fallen for it, clearly. But to make it worse, I was dating Kade, and had been mortified that he'd thought I was flirting with his older brother.

After that, I'd noted the flirty glances that followed the eldest Powell brother around town, and the way he had time and a smile for everyone.

That day was the last time Haden ever offered to show me

anything about horses, reinforcing the idea that I'd been a bother.

Now in my barn, I held my breath, very aware that Haden might not believe in anything magical, such as Rudolph, and may see nothing but an empty stall. If so, I'd have to find myself a new vet for Dolly and my cat, Boots.

I led Haden into the stall, crossing my fingers, hoping Rudolph would be like Hugo the elf, and allow this kind human to see him.

CHAPTER 7

~ *Haden* ~

There was something not quite right about what I saw in the stall, and it wasn't just the way Tamara was behaving. The first tip-off that things were odd, of course, were her voicemails about bringing an injured animal home. The second was the fact that she was talking to an empty barn, as if someone else was there. Third was the teasing. She hadn't teased me in eons, as she only teased the people she liked. I did not make that list.

In other words, something was up.

But even more odd than any of that was the animal she'd called me about.

"This is a woodland caribou," I stated, my voice flat as I took in her car's victim.

"A reindeer," she confirmed.

"Yes."

She nodded, looking relieved.

"The *rangifer tarandus* are a species at risk," I said. "Sorry. Latin. They're threatened. Their natural range is west and north of here." I shook my head and backed from the stall, fishing my phone from my jacket pocket. "I need to make a call."

"What?" Her tone became panicked, and she grabbed my sleeve. "But what if he's bleeding out right now? You have to help him, Haden."

I looked down at her slender hands, now wrapped around my wrist and freezing from the cold. She repeated my words back to me. "He's a species at risk!"

Her big brown eyes were filled with concern for the animal, and my heart softened. She'd once convinced me to nurse a mouse back to health with those sweet eyes of hers. A mouse! They were pests on a farm, and she'd had me feeding one in a shoebox, the whole time worried sick that Kade would discover it and kill the small thing. I accused her of being the softie, but clearly that was a two-way street.

Against my better judgement, I pocketed my phone, noting another text had come in from one of my clients, asking me questions I'd already answered. Flirting via her chihuahua. Who needed to go on the dating apps when you were a single, small-town veterinarian? Well, maybe I did, if I wanted to find the woman of my dreams, because so far, she hadn't walked into my clinic. Knowing my luck, the woman of my dreams would be allergic to animals.

So far, only a few of my more persistent clients had managed to trap me into a date. A date. As in one. Get tricked once, you're a man. Get tricked twice and you're a fool who wasn't sending out the correct, uninterested signals.

With my phone away, I took a moment to study Tamara. Usually her thoughts were a billboard and easy to read, but tonight something was off. She was locked up like a secret.

The more I stood there contemplating this novel disaster, I came up with more questions. Such as, how did she get this several-hundred-pound wild animal into her barn on her own? And why did I keep catching wafts of booze? Was it coming off

Tamara? Had she been drinking and driving? That didn't seem like her.

I cautiously entered the stall and crouched beside the animal, the alcohol scent growing stronger. The reindeer was smaller than I'd expected. Male. It still had its antlers, which was concerning, seeing how late in the season it was for shedding. Was it unwell? Diseased?

I gave it a visual once over while I debated my options. The animal didn't seem spooked by us, or by being enclosed in the barn. He was breathing a bit too fast, a sure sign of stress, but there was no apparent blood in the straw, so that was good.

I'd checked Tamara's car on the way into the barn and spotted the hanging bumper with the hole. Nothing too extensive in terms of damage. So, by the looks of things, she'd been lucky, and so had the deer. Around here, the wildlife and the vehicle were often both goners after a collision.

"I think it's his back end," Tamara said, crouching beside me. I could smell her gentle cocoa butter scent, something that always reminded me of Christmas. Probably because, years ago, my mom had given her a jar of the stuff, and she'd slathered it on, then seated herself beside me at Christmas dinner. It had been all I could smell, permanently linking her and her cocoa butter scent to my favourite holiday.

"You should give him space," I warned as she crouched in close. "He's a wild animal. His antlers could do a lot of damage."

"It's fine."

I refrained from sighing. She was too trusting, and while I admired her love for all creatures, I'd never dress up my cat in a Halloween costume. That was too far. Or get too close to a caribou unless necessary.

"Really, you should back up."

She held my gaze, then reached out and stroked the reindeer's forehead. I froze, ready to get between her and the beast. But nothing happened.

"This is okay, isn't it?" she cooed softly to the caribou. It blinked its big dark eyes at her.

Huh.

Go figure. Tamara had the thing tamed already.

"He's got a scrape," Tamara pointed out. I nodded, having noted the injured back leg. The long gash likely didn't need stitches, but it would need a bandage at some point. "I think he kicked my bumper when he landed in front of me on the road."

"Always the wildlife's fault," I muttered. If people slowed down and watched the road and ditches a bit better, I'd enjoy a greater number of free evenings.

"Well, according to insurance companies, it *is* their fault," she said rather indignantly.

"You already called them?"

"No, I just...know."

I held in a smirk, aware that she was sensitive about the things she'd bumped with her car over the years. Honestly, other than being a bit alarming, it was kind of cute.

"He must have gotten out of a petting zoo," I said, eyeing the sprawled beast. That would explain why it wasn't freaked out by humans, and was okay being snuggled by Tamara.

"Yeah, maybe," she said, her tone suggesting she was humouring me.

I reached out to touch the caribou's scraped back leg, and Tamara froze. I did, too. "What?"

She glanced upward, then quickly down, when I started to follow her gaze. "Is it okay if Haden touches you?" she whispered to the caribou.

Her bleeding heart. Seriously. "*Tamara.*"

"He's a veterinarian," she said to the animal.

I blinked hard. Had the animal just nodded? I turned to Tamara. What was going on here?

She caught my eye, her lips forming a small pout. "Quit looking at me like that."

"Like what?"

"Like you think I'm a cracked softie."

I tried to erase any trace of expression from my face, certain my brain had been playing a trick on me over the head-nod thing.

"Consent is very important," she said, drawing herself up. "Even with animals."

I swallowed my chuckle. "Yes. Yes, it is." To distract myself from how cute she was about this potentially dangerous animal, I began to work on the caribou, checking out his back leg, and watching for other injuries. Out of habit, I talked softly to the animal while I worked. I had been trained to speak while approaching the animal to avoid startling it, but had learned it was often more soothing to my patients if I spoke during the entire check-up, helping it track me.

I kept one hand on the deer while I worked, very aware that he could suddenly turn on me. But I was even more aware that I might look like a softie with all my chit-chat—something Tamara may not let me live down, since I'd once laughed at her for that very same thing.

But, again, I didn't dress up my cat.

Or bring home injured wildlife. Clearly, I took them to my clinic.

"Have you noticed any bleeding?" I asked.

"Hmm?" Tamara struggled to look up from my hands, and I glanced at them in case something was out of the ordinary. Just my regular old hands with slightly chapped knuckles thanks to being out in December's dry cold, helping animals.

"What? No." She peeked up at me. "You're talking to him."

"Yes."

"But I mean...talking. A lot. Not just to let him know you're there, and going to touch him."

She remembered that day when we'd worked on my dad's Clydesdales, too. I wondered if the memory held the same fondness that it did for me.

That had been the last time we'd helped an animal together, other than the awkward moment when she'd brought Boots in for his first appointment after she'd taken in the stray tomcat.

My dad still had that Clydesdale, and whenever I worked on him, or any horse's shoes, I thought of Tamara and that day. While we reshoed, she'd chatted to the horse the whole time, and he'd rewarded her with a quick nuzzle when we were done. I'd never seen him do that before. Or follow anyone like he did whenever Tamara showed up.

"A woman I know taught me it's better to talk to them the entire time."

"She did?" Her voice was slightly breathless, and I dared to dart a glance her way, holding her gaze for a long steady beat.

"Yeah."

"And so now you talk to your patients the whole time?"

"Pretty much." I cleared my throat, feeling the weight of her stare. "They seem to appreciate it." And a calm animal was much easier and safer to work on, and the outcome and experience was better for all involved.

"What do you tell them?"

"Whatever they need to hear."

I waited for the glimmer of amusement in her gaze to translate into teasing me.

"A lot of animals and their owners depend on you," she said, seriously. "Some days, it must feel like it never ends—the things we all need from you. It must take a toll."

I glanced at her, noting she was watching me with an insightful gaze, like she understood me in a way even my family didn't. A lot of people believed working with animals was nothing but romantic charm. It was until the sick cat bit you, or the hurt horse lashed out with a well-timed hoof to the shin. Or until you had to help a family assist their beloved pet over the rainbow bridge.

I loved my job, but I loved even more that Tamara could see the whole picture. And that made me miss our old friendship with astounding severity.

Clearing my throat, I tried to keep talking to the deer while I worked, but found myself suddenly tongue-tied and self-conscious in front of the woman I'd always felt most at home around.

"Their noses are interesting," she said, her tone oddly casual and strangely testing.

"Fur-covered," I stated, not looking up from my work. She used to ask me for all sorts of facts. Was she over her snit with me, and allowing her curiosity to get the better of her at long last? Because I was a walking encyclopedia of animal facts, and I loved how enthusiastic and interested she'd been about my knowledge. It wasn't about ego, but something else. A bonding of sorts, I guess. Kindred spirits and all that.

"Not wet like other deer," I added.

"Why is that?"

A tightness that had been in my chest since her voicemail unspooled and loosened with her follow-up question.

"It helps them with temperature regulation. Did you know that in really cold weather, the blood vessels in their noses can dilate, making them appear reddish or pink?"

"I...didn't." Her tone was delighted, just like when she'd been a kid hanging out on the farm as part of Kade's friend group. It didn't matter what fact I offered her from veterinarian school, she ate it up. "Does his seem red to you?"

I glanced at the animal's nose, curious about the odd squeaky lift in her voice. "No. Was he able to walk?"

"But it's quite cold in here."

"Apparently, not cold enough. How did you get him in here? Could he walk?"

"Yeah, but his back end didn't seem right."

"Did you get a horse trailer?"

"No."

"Then how did you bring him here?" I couldn't exactly imagine this big guy riding shotgun in her convertible. The mental image, however, brought a smile to my face. If anyone could pull off something so impossible, it was Tamara. "Lead him on a leash?"

I'd been there a few months ago when she'd borrowed my brother's truck and trailer to transport Dolly, a retired barrel-racing mare, in from an acreage where she'd been boarded after her landlord, Carl, had moved into a nursing home. When Tamara had started renting this place, she'd offered to bring Dolly back home for Carl, and to take care of her. Honestly, it was a perfect match for all three of them, and I was glad my mom had suggested this place to Tamara.

Maybe she'd borrowed my brother's trailer again? But then, where was Kade? If he'd let her take his unfamiliar rig out in this storm to move an injured animal, and not helped her, he was going to have some major explaining to do.

"He," Tamara coughed, cheeks flaming red, "followed me home?"

I could feel my eyebrows settling low at her poorly crafted lie.

She let out a giant sigh. "Fine. He rode in the back seat of my car."

I said nothing, knowing there was no way this animal had ridden shotgun.

Flustered, Tamara added, "It's a convertible. He and his antlers fit fine."

I sat back on my heels, studying Tamara. She was serious. My earlier mental image of the reindeer riding beside her hadn't been that far off the mark.

I shook my head, dazzled by this woman and the way she continuously caught me off guard. If her story was true, then she was indeed a modern-day Snow White—but without the stepmother trauma—when it came to animals adoring and trusting her. If she wasn't careful, she'd have a full farm within a matter of months. Which would be a stroke of luck for the animals that found their way to her. Sadly, I didn't think she could afford it.

I went back to my check-up before craning my neck to look at her again. "You're serious?"

She nodded, brown eyes wide with apology.

"Cold ride," I said matter-of-factly.

"Very cold," she said. Her eyes twinkled for the first time tonight. "Also, he sheds a lot."

No part of this scenario was amusing, but we grinned at each other like idiots over the image of her giving a caribou a ride in her convertible in a blizzard. The wary tension that had been thickening between us broke as we laughed. But it was just a quick, involuntary burble of mirth, similar to an air bubble in a stream as it split open at the surface.

Honestly, this was such a stupid thing for her to do. Completely reckless and dangerous. So why was I laughing?

Because charming a wild animal was so completely Tamara.

I focused on the reindeer again, still unable to sort out how she'd lured it into her car, and then kept it there while she drove down the road. Knowing sweet Tamara, she'd probably convinced it to put on its seatbelt.

Were there legal implications in regards to transporting an injured wild animal? As a veterinarian, was I liable or obliged to take some sort of action in this scenario? Fish and Wildlife would certainly want to know about this out-of-range caribou and its injury. And its unshed antlers.

"In your car," I muttered.

"What else was I supposed to do?" Tamara asked softly. "I wasn't going to leave him to get hit again."

"No, yeah. Of course not."

"And for your information, I missed more than I hit."

"Caribou? There was a herd of them?" Oh, man. I definitely had to report this to Fish and Wildlife.

I pulled out my stethoscope. "What have you named him?"

"I haven't."

I shot Tamara a look. I'd known her for a few decades now, and she had a habit of naming every animal she met. This caribou certainly wouldn't be an exception, especially with it being so close to Christmas. I was sure of it.

"Rudolph," she said shyly.

I let out a huff of laughter. Of course.

I took a listen to the caribou's chest and lungs, then moved cautiously toward his head, continuing the check-up.

Tamara refused to make room for me. I shot her a rather dark and slightly exasperated look, that hum of tension cranking up between us again.

"What? He's scared and nervous! And I'm not projecting or anthropomorphizing or whatever."

"I didn't say you were."

"I can see you judging me, Haden Powell."

"I need to check his pupils." I waved my small penlight and

edged closer while still in my crouch, my knee pressing against Tamara's. She should have moved, giving me room, but she didn't.

She was acting weird again.

I pressed harder. "Tamara?"

She wouldn't budge.

"I thought you wanted me to hurry up?"

She sighed. "Fine." She glanced up toward the stall's half wall before shifting out of the way.

I moved in, carefully inspecting the deer's pupils, stroking him gently across the forehead like Tamara had, then down his jaw when he allowed it. I could tell Tamara thought I was giving the wild animal snuggles, but I was actually checking for lumps and abrasions, as well as to see if the animal's jaw was still properly hinged. Because what vet gave a wild animal chin scratches like this? I was acting as though this was the coolest part of my entire week.

Because it actually was. A reindeer just before Christmas Eve? Who would have thought it possible in our neck of the foothills?

Now, though, I truly was scratching the animal's chin. I might not want to dress up my animals, but I did love them. And this guy was a fan of his chin scratches. He was stretching his neck, trusting me, allowing access to a vulnerable area. This wasn't a wild animal by any stretch.

A light feeling of happiness welled up inside, and I chuckled. "I sure hope this isn't one of Santa's reindeer."

The air seemed to grow still, and the caribou's deep dark eyes turned to me. Tamara visibly swallowed as she choked out a weak ha, ha.

I turned back to the caribou, and I froze. I didn't move for a second or two, my hand frozen mid-scratch.

My mind refused to compute the change I saw in my patient.

Still hunkered down in my crouch, I pivoted on the balls of my feet so I could look directly at Tamara for clues as to what was going on because, suddenly, this animal had a red blinking nose.

CHAPTER 8

~ *Tamara* ~

I supposed Haden's sudden shakiness and stunned expression answered my question about whether or not he could see Rudolph's blinking red nose. The eavesdropping herd shifted above me as they peered over the edge of the stall's half wall, eyeing each other, all of us unsure what would happen now that Rudolph had revealed his true identity.

Did Haden see Rudolph and his nose because he believed in his existence, like I did? Or was it because he'd touched him? Or was Rudolph in control of all of it, and had decided Haden should be able to see him?

The magical world was a confusing, layered mess of rules I'd never fully know or understand. I just hoped our actions tonight wouldn't get us into trouble, or mess up the space-time-continuum of Christmas. If there was such a thing.

And...Haden was freaking out. He was frozen, staring at me, the colour draining from his face. Then, slowly, he turned his gaze back to Rudolph, not blinking. He seemed to be speechless.

This was not good. We needed him sane and distracted

from this crazy reality so his brain didn't blow a precious, injured-animal-helping valve.

Sweating, I swallowed my panic and focused on finding a diversion to snap him out of it. Anything!

What did a man like Haden enjoy?

Before I realized what I was doing, I was kissing Mr. Leads Women On. I'd launched myself at him, causing him to lose his balance, and we tumbled backward into the loose straw. He wasn't resisting, but I was aware he had his choice of pretty much any single, straight female in the small town of Eagle Ridge, as well as the surrounding county. And there was absolutely no consent or hint that being mauled by me was what he wanted. None whatsoever.

I drew back long enough to check on my victim.

His eyes met mine with wonder. "You are the weirdest, most interesting and unpredictable woman I have ever met," he whispered.

"Merry Christmas," I breathed, relieved he'd returned to the land of the speaking, but unsure whether what he'd said had been a compliment.

Then, before I could think about things any further, his hand slid into my hair and he guided my mouth back down to his.

Well then. Merry Christmas, indeed.

Very, merry Christmas.

I sighed involuntarily. The man was a great kisser. He'd mastered the right combination of tenderness and commanding pressure, his tongue exploring, but not pushy. There was heat between us, too, and I felt like I could get lost in this moment forever.

A hoof kicked my calf, and I leapt off of Haden, hand over my mouth as I scrambled to my feet, remembering myself. "I'm so sorry!"

In my scattered haste, I nearly tumbled over Rudolph, who was looking at me as if to say, "Don't forget about me over here, all injured and with Christmas riding on my health."

His dark eyes sure could lay a guilt trip on a woman.

"Sorry," I repeated breathlessly, ashamed, and unable to find somewhere safe to look. I was unsure if I was apologizing to Rudolph, his spying reindeer friends, or the man still sprawled in the straw with rosy, kissed lips.

"I'm not," Haden said with a lopsided grin, propping himself on one elbow in the straw.

I made a garbled choking sound, well aware that he was getting the wrong idea. Completely wrong. He led women on, and had probably kissed half the county. To him, kissing me was as meaningful as taking another animal's temperature.

As if to remind me of his popularity, his phone let out a buzz, indicating he had a new voicemail or text or demure photo from a local bombshell with 'accidentally' positioned cleavage behind her supposedly 'ailing' pet. Haden stood, ignoring his phone, and brushed the straw from his jacket and jeans. He glanced at Rudolph, and then at me.

"And here I thought I was going to have a very boring Christmas without you at the Powell family dinners." The corner of his mouth tweaked upward.

I cleared my throat with force, ignoring the heat in my cheeks. This would definitely be awkward from here on out.

I pointed to the injured reindeer at our feet. "So, um, right. Sorry about that. But he's hurt. A little bit in shock maybe?" It was likely best to leave out the fact that he was intoxicated. "Is his leg broken?"

Haden kept darting looks at me, his lips dancing as he fought a smile. He gave a small cough, frowned way too deeply to be genuine, and rested a knuckle across his top lip, allowing his hand to cover his amusement.

This was so embarrassing. He was struggling not to laugh at me for kissing him.

But he'd kissed me back. And he hadn't gone screaming from the barn at any point during the Rudolph reveal, or my mauling.

I wasn't sure where that left us though.

But I think I might be feeling a significant level of gratitude.

"What do we do?" I insisted, more than ready to have his attention off of me.

He was still looking at me with those shuttered eyes that revealed nothing, but saw it all.

"If we could just..." I waved a hand around, gesturing to the area of the stall where we'd kissed "...pretend that never happened?"

Haden remained silent, his brows furrowing. Hands on his hips, he took in Rudolph's nose. He blinked long and hard a few times, as though willing his vision to stop messing with him.

"Haden?" I whispered, afraid he was drifting toward freaking out again.

"Right," he said gruffly. "This is a big problem. Christmas and all." He inhaled a little breath while turning to face me, one finger casually aimed at the caribou's nose, his face paling again. "Can you...? Is that...?"

I nodded, biting my bottom lip.

Hands returning to his hips, Haden stepped back, then forward, as though undecided. Finally, he crouched in front of the deer, staring at Rudolph's nose. "Well."

He was quiet for a long, long time.

"Haden? What do we do?"

He nodded once, slowly. Then he moved down to Rudolph's rear leg. He gently ran his hands up the length of it before giving it a careful, gentle twist. Rudolph didn't react. He placed a palm on the bottom of Rudolph's hoof and pushed upward, causing his knee to bend. Rudolph's eyes rolled back toward the vet, and he straightened his leg to shove Haden's hand away. That earned a tiny hint of a smile from Haden.

"I'm guessing no breakage." He gently patted Rudolph's flank. "He didn't react when I put a little torsion on the bad leg. He would have if it was broken, I should think. It's likely a deep bruise. I'd like to roll him over, and give his other side a good check, too, though."

Rudolph carefully rolled upright with a groan, tucking his front hooves under his wide chest, then his hind legs crookedly under his body so he could shift onto his opposite side with a huff and a snort of effort.

Haden glanced at me, swallowing hard, the colour in his cheeks draining. I shook my head at Rudolph. Real subtle, dude. Show the freaked-out human you understand English.

Then again, it did make things easier. And Santa's reindeer should know English, right? Well, unless they truly did live in Lapland—northern Finland—like some legends suggested. In that case, they'd speak Finnish. But then Santa would be a goat, because Joulupukki was the traditional Finnish Christmas figure.

I shook off my thoughts, noticing that Haden seemed to be focused on his own thoughts as he knelt on the other side of me, his brow furrowed in the most adorable way. His expression was so serious it made my heart hiccup.

As I crept closer, curious as to what he was discovering, I noticed his attention slip, and he gave me a sideways look. Right. Back off. Don't be a bother like I was as a teenager. Let him do the veterinarian stuff alone.

And definitely don't attack him again like he's an object, and not a human being with thoughts, feelings and desires.

I was such an embarrassment. I mean, what had I been

thinking? He didn't do relationships—not that I wanted one with him. The town would flip their lid if we started something. I could only imagine what they'd think if I jumped from one brother to the next. His parents would probably act even more awkward around me, and Kade would go crazy, listing all the reasons Haden was the wrong kind of man for me. It didn't help that Kade was always in competition with his older brother—and always losing.

Why had I kissed Haden?

And why did he find it so stupidly amusing?

Because he wasn't interested, and my actions had always been cute...until they'd become annoying. Little Tamara, crushing on him. Again.

Sigh.

"This side seems okay." Haden rolled from his knees back into a crouch, his gaze drifting to the reindeer's exposed nose. "Normally, I would suggest we wait and see, but since this is a rather time-sensitive injury, I'd like to do an x-ray."

"Is the clinic open?" It had to be way past regular opening hours by now.

He gave me a dry frown. Right. He owned the clinic. It was open whenever he wanted it to be.

Man, his kisses had scrambled my brain a little bit. I wanted to kiss him again. You know, just to see if it unscrambled the scrambled bits.

What was I thinking? I was cracked in the head. Sure, it had been one of the best kisses I've ever had, and with a man I'd fantasized about as a kid. But it hadn't been a kiss-*kiss*. It had been merely a distraction tactic in a high-stakes situation. That was all.

I stood, edging toward the stall's doorway. "Well?" I prompted. "Shall we go?"

Haden chuckled, a warm, friendly sound, his attention

solidly here with me and the woodland caribou. I could see the wheels turning as he worked out the logistics of secretly transporting the animal without raising any questions from our snoopy small town.

His focus was pretty sexy.

Ugh. Cracked brain. This man was not sexy. He broke hearts and led women to believe he was interested when he wasn't. I'd had a crush on him all through elementary and junior high, but had forced myself to get over the unattainable older man when I'd started dating Kade. Unlike the single female population around here. They were still crushing. Hard.

Finally, Haden leaned forward, asking slowly, "Can you walk, Rudolph? Are you in much pain?"

"Dude, he's a deer," I said softly, eyes cutting to our eavesdroppers. I subtly gesturing for them to hide in case Haden could see them now, too. They obeyed, slipping below the stall's divider, disappearing from sight. One less possible thing that might overload this man's precious brain circuits.

"He's a deer who can clearly understand me."

"Okay, fine." I gave a dramatic eye roll. "He understands us."

Rudolph slowly got to his feet, and Haden positioned himself at the ready to help the large animal if need be. The man was strong, but he'd more likely get squashed if he attempted to catch the quarter-tonne animal.

"He can ride in the back seat again," I suggested, "unless you're hauling a trailer?"

Haden shook his head. "I'm not, but I'll go get it."

"We don't have the time."

Honestly, though, I couldn't imagine putting poor Rudolph into one of those livestock carriers. They were cold, hard and bumpy rides. "What's a little more reindeer fur in my back seat?"

"People will see him."

"They won't."

"But we can."

"Yeah, and we're special," I said, not wanting to get into the nitty gritty of magic right now. It was time for action, and I really didn't need Haden's questions or possible panic if I accidentally let it slip that there were ogres and witches out there, too. And maybe dragons.

I glanced at the reindeer, who were doing a poor job of hiding, seeking confirmation that we could ride through town undetected. Well, Rudolph would. I'd look like the crazy person in a convertible with the top down in minus thirty weather.

None of the reindeer contradicted my statement about the town seeing Rudolph.

"I'm glad I didn't call Fish and Wildlife earlier," Haden said, standing at the edge of the stall as Rudolph slowly exited with a hobble.

"Me, too." I addressed our injured friend, "Wait here. I'll drive my car in through the big doors so you don't have to walk as far." It would mean letting out what precious heat the barn had held on to, but the way Rudolph was moving looked painful, and I didn't want him walking more than he had to.

Haden waited inside, ready to open the doors once I had the car in position. As I exited into the biting cold night, I wondered what I was thinking. I was going to voluntarily freeze my face off again by driving with the top down. And the drive to the clinic was even longer than the earlier ride home.

But what else could I do? There was no way I was letting Rudolph ride in a freezing metal trailer.

I unplugged my block heater and started my car, checking in with the GAL PAL texting group. There was a recent one from Josie.

JOSIE

Where are you now? Are you okay?

Aw. Even though she ghosted us half the time, she cared. Another message popped up.

JOSIE

Tam? Are you okay? Please check in.

Okay, now she was starting to sound oddly similar to my mother.

JOSIE

Christmas is an important holiday. Stay away from anything and everything related to it. Please let me know you're okay. And don't touch Rudolph! Just walk away from all of it.

Too late for that.

CHAR

Did you call Haden?

SAMANTHA

I rolled my eyes and sighed. I typed out a quick message.

ME

I'm okay. Rudolph is here, and so is Haden. Going to take Rudolph to the clinic and x-ray his hip and leg, just in case.

JOSIE

Please tell me you're joking. You shouldn't interfere with the magic world.

ME

> But I already did. I hit him with my car. I
> have to help him!

CHAR

> Make sure you kiss Haden as thanks for
> coming to the rescue!

ME

> Already did.

With shaky fingers, I put my phone back in my pocket while it vibrated vigorously with the flurry of incoming replies. No doubt a Josie lecture and Gabby and Char getting excited about the kiss.

Why had I told them about that? Now they were going to hound me about it, and make it more difficult to brush off when nothing came of it. I could already feel the disappointment welling inside me like cold water.

And why should I feel disappointed? It was ridiculous to have any hope at all that Haden would ever be interested in me. He was eight years my senior, and I was sure we wanted different things. I wanted a hobby farm and a family, and I wasn't certain that was on his life's to-do list.

I drove the car into the barn, focusing on the Christmas carols playing on the radio rather than Haden and his kisses. Carols always made me think of decorating the tree with my family. Mom and Dad would get all snuggly, remembering the year they almost broke up before coming to their senses. Oma would come over and make hot chocolate, and we'd play carols for the first time of the season. Together, the four of us would decorate the living room tree. I loved it so much, I'd bought my own tree for this place, but decorating it alone hadn't been the same, no matter how many Christmas songs I'd hummed while doing it.

I got out of the car and pushed the button to let the top down, frustrated by the indecipherable, furtive looks that Haden kept shooting my way.

"What?"

He shook his head, but the twinge of twinkle didn't leave his eyes.

"What?" I insisted.

"Nothing. You're just...different. That's all."

Oh, no. We were *not* going there. That was the whole break up song between me and Kade. How much I'd changed. Like having a surer sense of myself was some sort of betrayal.

Reading my body language, Haden added smoothly, "It's good."

"It's *good*?"

"It's good," he confirmed, not looking up from the message he was typing on his phone.

I leaned into the car, trying to puzzle that one out, and flipped the front seat forward for Rudolph with more force than was needed. A loud bang came from the trunk.

I jolted, having forgotten about the trapped elf. He still hadn't found the trunk's safety release, and I was lucky he hadn't frozen to death.

I moved in front of the trunk, watching Haden with a stiff smile. Could he hear Snarky? He hadn't seemed to have noticed the herd of reindeer behind him. They were doing an incredibly poor job of staying hidden. Their large antlers kept peeking out here and there, and every once in a while, their small cloud of murmurings rose when they thought we wouldn't overhear them. Which maybe Haden couldn't.

Hugo however...

Haden stalked over to the back of my car, hands going to his hips. "Do you have an animal stuck in there?"

I backed against the trunk, patting it loudly with a flat palm to warn Hugo to shush. "What? No. The car's just really old."

He was giving me that 'what on earth are you up to now?' look of his. I hated that look. It made me feel like I was up to something stupid.

And usually I was. Kind of like now.

But in my defence, my actions always made sense to me in the moment. Like pushing the elf into my trunk. Or the time Kade, Haden and I were trying to find a reported injured porcupine as part of Haden's summer job for Fish and Wildlife while he was in vet school. Kade and I had been bickering while walking through the fields. He'd been complaining about my lack of adventure, and I'd set out to prove him wrong when we'd come across an old swing rope at an irrigation lagoon. Feeling brave and adventurous, as well as soaring on the success of my anticipated vindication, I'd leapt up onto the rope, swung far out over the lagoon in my cutoffs and tank top. Then, when the rope broke, I'd belly flopped onto the water's surface so hard it had stolen my breath.

Haden, ever the hero, had pulled me to the pond's edge, shoulders stiff and fists in a bunch, giving me that look—the look he was giving me now. Like he couldn't track my thinking, and maybe he didn't want to.

"It's old?" Haden was coming closer, amusement burning in his eyes. He'd been checking his phone's notifications when I'd brought the car in—you know, being on call for animal emergencies pretty much 24/7—and it was with great satisfaction that he put the phone away, ignoring it over me and this awkward moment where I might be busted for mistreating one of Santa's grumpy elves.

Oh, why did he have to notice me right now? And why was he enjoying this so much? Why couldn't the elf stay invisible and silent to him like the herd was?

"Yeah. Um... You should probably return all of those messages or something, right?"

If Haden met Hugo... Well, nothing could prepare him for that. And I needed him here and helpful, not turning into a babbling bag of testosterone, and thus unable to take charge and save Christmas for me. Because if that happened, then where would the world's children be, come Christmas morning?

Haden narrowed his eyes, and I quickly scrolled through a list of possible excuses for the loud banging and swearing that was coming from the trunk.

I'd tried lying earlier and had failed. Honestly, why would a car, even an old one, make thumping sounds when it was turned off?

"My cat sometimes manages to climb into the trunk—because the car is so old." Oh, I was good. So good. "There's a hole."

"That could be really dangerous for Puss in Boots."

"No, no. It's okay," I said quickly, worried he'd think I didn't care about my cat, while wanting to purr over the fact that he remembered my rescued tomcat's name. "I'd never let him get hurt. He mostly just climbs in there when it rains, and there are blizzards and stuff." Ugh. Now it sounded like I left him out in horrible weather to fend for himself. "But usually he's inside the house. I don't want him to lose an ear to frostbite."

Haden bent over, checking the wheel well for a cat-sized rust hole. I thanked my lucky stars that my car was likely to have such a hole.

He straightened. "How does he get in?"

"Oh, um. It's just when I have the roof down, and I *never* leave it down. He must have zipped in when I was getting Rudolph out. If you go check on him," I tipped my chin toward the hobbling reindeer, "I'll let the cat out of the proverbial bag —er, trunk." I gave a weak, lame laugh at my equally weak and lame joke.

Haden shifted, stepping sideways toward the reindeer, keeping one eye on me. I shot him a stupid smile and moved around to the driver's side to pop the trunk. I was going to have to move fast. Snarky was going to fly out as soon as that latch let go.

The moment Haden turned his back, I pulled the lever and zipped around to the trunk, shoving Snarky Elf back in when he lifted the lid.

"Help! Prancer! *Help* me! Rudolph! She's kidnapping me! Save me! Save Christmas!"

"You stay in there," I hissed at him. "You can't be seen."

"But I'm invisible!"

"Are you really? Because I can both see you *and* hear you, and so can that human." I jerked a thumb in Haden's direction, who was turning around, no doubt hearing the conversation I was having with the 'cat' who'd been thumping about in my trunk.

The elf's mouth snapped shut, and I slammed the trunk closed again before he could say anything else. Then I turned to give Haden a bright smile as he helped Rudolph into the back seat.

CHAPTER 9

~ Haden ~

Tonight was turning into a list of things I never thought possible. I wasn't sure which was top of the list—being kissed by my brother's ex-girlfriend, or meeting one of Santa's reindeer and then smuggling said reindeer through Eagle Ridge's sleepy downtown and into my clinic for an x-ray.

But here I was, as well as refusing to process the logic of what was going on. If I did, I might need to have my mental health examined, and I was way too busy with emergencies to deal with that kind of delay. But Tamara saw it all, too, right? And she was acting stable and fairly calm.

Maybe this was all a dream.

I flipped on the lights in the back of the clinic and pushed Rudolph further inside on an animal gurney so he wouldn't have to walk. As Tamara went to close the alley door behind the three of us, I saw what looked like a herd of reindeer landing lightly in the snow around her car.

I blinked hard, trying to focus further into the dark alley to confirm what my eyes were telling me. Tamara, noting that I was watching her, closed the door most of the way, and leaned her head outside. She was talking to the reindeer.

They were real.

A whole herd. All of Santa's reindeer. The ones who travelled around the world in one night. How did Santa get inside all of those houses? Certainly not down chimneys.

I shook away the endless questions forming in my mind. It was time to be methodical. Be logical.

And none of this was logical.

Plus, I was pretty sure I'd spotted an elf in Tamara's trunk back at her farm.

I looked down at my hands. They were shaking again.

The alley behind my clinic wasn't very private. Many of the buildings had residents who lived above the street-level stores and businesses. And several tenants were smokers who enjoyed their "fresh air" from the rooftops. Their vantage points gave them the drop on a lot of the town gossip. Even in blizzards. What would they say about a herd of reindeer outside my clinic? Tamara had said nobody could see Rudolph. But I could. And so could she. So, what about this herd?

"Are those guys with you?" I asked the red-nosed reindeer sprawled out on the gurney at my side. I angled my head toward the alley.

"Yes," Rudolph muttered.

I blinked hard, giving my mind a moment to focus on what had just happened here in the clinic. Did I imagine Rudolph's response? Or did he speak to me?

"I'm sorry?" I croaked.

"I said yes."

"Oh. Uh. Cool." I nodded, trying to act calm. "Yeah. Yeah, okay. Uh, people can't see them though, right? I mean, other than us? I mean, you can see them obviously. You're a reindeer. You're like them. And you can talk." I clamped down on my flustered thoughts, forcing my mind to be logical, methodical, and to focus on the possible current problem at hand. The herd's possible visibility. "Can other people see them in the alley?"

"Maybe."

"Ah. Okay."

The impact of the night had started to sink in on my drive to the clinic. Now that impact was fully at the front of my mind. Santa and his reindeer were real. And Tamara had injured Rudolph, just hours before he was needed to fly around the world.

And I was the medical professional on the scene.

No pressure.

And what about Rudolph? Was he like a normal caribou? Would I even be able to help him?

Tamara, her toque pulled down low, and her scarf wrapped all the way up her face so only her eyes were exposed, was still hanging out the back door. She must have frozen half to death on the drive over, but knowing Tamara, she wouldn't have it any other way. Because Rudolph needed help, and she'd literally freeze before letting him come to harm.

Well, other than accidentally hitting him with her car.

She let out a squeak like something had surprised her, and I began striding toward her. "Are you okay?"

"Nothing. Yes. Fine. Just fine," she said, over her shoulder, her voice tight and high. She slipped through the door, into the dark alley, saying, "Just need to get something from my car."

Then she slammed the door shut behind her.

CHAPTER 10

~ *Estelle* ~

"What are you doing here?" Tamara growled at me as I appeared before her in the dark, snowy alley behind Haden's veterinarian office.

Her snappish tone received some interesting looks from the reindeer milling about. I nodded to the boys and swept closer to Tamara, my ankle-length faux fur coat dragging through the piling up snow.

The snow wasn't actually landing on me, since I wasn't truly here. Thanks to a splitting spell, I was as snug as a bug in my Calgary office, all warm and toasty. Me being in Eagle Ridge was simply an illusion, as if I'd stepped into a long-distance projector.

"I didn't make a wish," Tamara added. She crossed her arms in her bulky parka. "I'm never making a wish again."

"Well, you should. Then I could help you tonight." Hopefully. I would be circumventing some magical world consequences for the way she was interfering with Christmas, one of our most important holidays. But, as long as we moved now, and quickly, Gram-Gram and I figured a good wish could mend this problem before Christmas was truly ruined.

"I don't need help," Tamara insisted.

"That's not what Char told me."

"I needed you to call Santa. That was all."

The reindeer shifted, all eyes on Tamara. She lifted her arms in their direction. "What? This was before you guys started talking to me! Now I know that you're trying to stay out of trouble." She turned to me. "You don't need to call Santa."

"You boys aren't supposed to be down here, are you?" I asked, turning to them.

"We can leave at any time. There's no rule," Blitzen said. The party animal had ornaments hanging from his antlers, a clear indicator that they'd been up to some serious shenanigans.

"That is correct," Prancer said primly.

It was an implied rule. Gram-Gram and I had looked it up.

"So," I asked innocently, "why are you trying to keep it a secret, then?"

They remained silent, their eyes pleading with me.

I sighed, understanding their need for a bit of secrecy. They were in a sticky situation, and Mrs. C., one of their bosses, so-to-speak, was scary. And I liked the reindeer. When she'd flipped her lid at the summer solstice party after some innocent flirting with Santa, the reindeer had tried to console me. Hugo, the little evil minion elf, had run straight to Mrs. Claus, simpering and trying to calm her. But he'd only made things worse.

Considering that the word on the street was that Mrs. Claus and Santa were still fighting, the reindeer could end up stuffed and mounted above Mrs. Claus's fireplace if word of this disaster got back to the North Pole.

But I could maybe help. If Tamara made a wish.

I reassured the herd with the truth. "I couldn't call Santa through the regional communication system, so nobody knows." I turned to Tamara. "You should know that interfering with Christmas is a serious offence. We need to extract you from this situation."

"I'm not interfering. I'm trying to help Rudolph." She pointed to the unmarked metal door behind her. "He's in there getting an x-ray."

"You've injured Rudolph within twenty-four hours of Christmas Eve, and you're failing to protect the magical world from more human interactions."

"They chose to be seen!"

I glanced at the reindeer for verification, but they all seemed too busy pawing the snow to pay me much heed. I turned back to Tamara. "Please. Make a wish and I'll fix all of this for you."

"I've scrubbed the word 'wish' from my vocabulary."

I'd expected this. Her friend, Char, due to a filing error thanks to her former fairy godmother, who'd been a bit senile, had ended up with incredible debt. But it had all turned out well in the end. Spectacular, really. So, it made little sense that Tamara would give up on us fairy godmothers, and the light we could bring to her life. Or in this case, her salvation from the scariest woman in the white magic world.

Thumping and banging, and a weirdly masculine yet squeaky voice came from inside Tamara's car, which was parked beside me, its top down. I paused. I knew that voice.

I slowly turned from the car to Tamara, a feeling of dread sinking deep into my fairy bones. "Why is Hugo in your trunk?"

"He likes it there." Tamara crossed her arms, clearly trying to look tougher than she felt.

I sighed and rubbed my temples. This was getting worse by the minute. I got the impression that Hugo was Mrs. Claus's favourite. She wouldn't take too kindly toward this sort of treatment. "Make a wish, and I'll do my best to undo all of this."

"This is a magical world fiasco. I shouldn't have to make a costly wish in order to fix it."

"I'm a fairy godmother. I can't fix *your* problems without a wish."

"Isn't this a magical world problem?"

"It started with you."

"Did it though?" She crossed her arms.

"You need extraction."

"Well, I saw what happened with Char. I'm not plumping up your Christmas bonus, or whatever you get for charging people for all their wishes."

"In the end, Char put a lot of good out into the world," I reminded her, struggling to hold on to my patience. "And I can procure a price list for you, if it would make you more comfortable. Or we could ask Char if she'd share her account's credits. I'm sure she'd like to help you."

"Why are you really here?"

"To help."

"You implied I'm in trouble."

"Yes, you could be."

"Am I going to get eaten by Igor?"

It took me a second to realize what she was getting after. "The guy in accounting? No."

"But he's an ogre."

"Yes, but he doesn't eat people, remember?"

She shook her head as though not quite believing me. Seriously, Trish, my rival at Your Fairy Godmother, had made me believe that if my clients didn't pay on time, Igor would eat them. And me. I accidentally let it slip once, and now here we were. This was one big muddled mess of confusion that just wouldn't die, no matter how many times I insisted that Igor was vegan.

"I just want all of this fixed so I can go home, have a hot bath, and go to bed."

"You could wish for that."

"I can't afford it, Estelle. I'm barely making ends meet on my rent, and feeding horses is way more expensive than I realized. Can't you use your magic to help your magical reindeer friend?"

I shook my head. I'd already looked into what I could do from the sidelines—nothing. The only way I could help was if Tamara made a very specific wish. Then I'd be tagged in, and ready to rumble. But her wish had to be solely about herself, and not Rudolph. As in, I wish I'd come home a minute sooner. The impact would be that she'd miss Rudolph on the road and not hit him. Then she wouldn't be wishing about things that involved magical creatures, and I could grant those wishes. It would change their timeline, preventing this unfortunate overlap.

The longer we let this mess run, the more likely bad things would happen. Such as Mrs. C. finding out. She had special powers and was caught between two magical worlds in many senses. She hadn't been born into Santa's world, and her residency was tentative. If she got mad—sorry, madder than she already was—and refused to do her part with Christmas, she could get sent back to her world. Seeing as the woman didn't have a pinch hitter who could jump in for her if she didn't feel like doing her Christmas jobs, the holiday would be screwed.

The non-magical human world would surely notice, and that was a major breach of our inter-worlds contract.

We had to keep Mrs. C. in the dark, and happy. Very, very happy.

The problem was, she was already in a foul mood, fighting her black magic nature and a strong force that could easily take over if given a bit of darkness to grab onto.

Tamara's phone chirped from deep inside her coat. She sighed, bit the end of one of her thick, insulated mittens to hold it between her teeth, then withdrew her hand from within its confines.

"My mom," she grumbled around the mitt. "I forgot to text her that I got home okay after supper."

A blast of snowy air hit her full-force like a punishment and she shivered, tapping on her phone's screen.

"Got home okay," she muttered as she tapped on the screen's keyboard. "Right. I'm alive, so that counts. Not a total lie." A whooshing sound filled the air. "I'm definitely not telling her I went back out into the storm."

"Tamara..."

Her phone chirped as soon as she repocketed it, her hand already burrowing back into the warmth of the fluffy mitt. She groaned. "Wanna help me?"

"Yes!"

"Tell my mom to chill," she snapped.

Now we were talking. Any wish to get the ball rolling was a win. "Simply close your eyes and make a—"

"Estelle. I'm not making a wish."

"You don't understand what you're unravelling here tonight," I stated, trying to walk that fine line between not wanting Tamara to panic, yet somehow make her understand how dire this was. She needed to do something! "You're meddling with magic during one of our most important holidays. Beings from my world might assume you have malicious intent and are a threat. Do you know what they do to threats?"

"No," Tamara said weakly. Under the rosiness from the cold, her skin paled.

"You shouldn't even be able to see the herd."

"I still believe."

"Believing isn't enough to see through the magical shroud at this time of year."

"I think they chose to let me see them. That's what Hugo said."

I turned to the reindeer. They all looked away.

But like Gram-Gram had said, something was still not adding up. Seeing the herd was one thing, severely injuring Rudolph was another. There had to be something wrong with the shroud.

"Rudolph is inside?" I asked.

She nodded.

"With the human? Who can see him?"

"He's a vet. He's helping." Tamara hunched deeper into her mountain of winter layers. Being human looked miserable.

"You look cold," I said kindly, hoping she'd let a wish slip out. We could start small and work our way up to saving her and Christmas, and most of all, avoiding the Magical Court of Rules and its punishments. "Would you like to be warm?"

"I am *not* making any wishes, Estelle. Why do I have to go into fairy godmother debt to clear a problem that has more to do with misbehaving, drunken reindeer than anything of my own doing?"

My mind cleared. "They were drunk when you first saw them?"

"Yes! And Blitzen is even more drunk now. He got into my alcoholic punch."

"You gave him..." I felt woozy. My office flickered in my mind's eye, over the vision of the alley. My splitting spell wavered in my panicked distraction.

"Not on purpose! And I mean, yeah, I was driving the car that hit Rudolph. I admit that's fairly significant. But *still*. They were drunk."

The reindeer being drunk had weakened the wall between

the magical world and Tamara's. That was how she'd done damage to a magical being despite the shroud!

This was important information. And it could lessen the perceived severity of Tamara's actions if she came under judgement. Well, except for her having given Blitzen more booze. That was very bad. As was injuring Rudolph. Even if by accident.

However, the worst part was that because this was a Christmas incident, and it included misbehaviour on the part of magical beings, it all fell into Mrs. C.'s domain. That meant she'd be the one judging Tamara. Yes, it would be a strong conflict of interest on Mrs. Claus's part. One that would *not* work in Tamara's favour. And, to make matters worse, the woman was already mad at Santa as well as resentful of the holiday.

And if she knew Tamara was one of my clients... Who knew what might happen to her.

"You're in a lot of trouble," I blurted, wishing I could spill all the details to Tamara to help her understand. But Gram-Gram had been firm, telling me I could only reveal so much about our world to a human client. "It's too close to Christmas and you're interfering with the magical world. You need to make a wish so I can make all of this not happen."

"It's not my fault!" Tamara pleaded.

"Tamara, you're meddling in something that's well beyond you." My surroundings were starting to blur. My splitting spell that held an image of me here was fading. "Your only hope in avoiding judgement is to correct your actions by making a wish."

The alley around me vanished, sending me back to my office. I could only hope that Tamara understood just how important it was for her to make an immediate wish.

CHAPTER 11

~ *Tamara* ~

Estelle gave me such a headache. This mess with Rudolph was all accidental, and surely everyone in the magical world could see that. I was not going to make a wish, and go into debt over one little oopsie involving a drunken reindeer who wasn't minding where he was bounding.

Then again, the magical world did seem to be a bit ruthless. They'd only given Char three months to pay off her hundred-thousand-dollar debt—a debt that she hadn't even known she was incurring, thanks to an error on their end.

But her experience was just another reason for me to not give in to Estelle. There were too many unknowns.

And I had plans for my money. Namely, rent. I was in over my head with the little farm I'd rented, and my generous offer to feed Dolly. Educational assistants made less than dental office receptionists, and the hours were a lot shorter, too. I also hadn't done the math right when estimating how much it would cost to heat my new house. Natural gas wasn't too badly priced, but all the fees tacked onto the bill made the amount due skyrocket to several times the actual cost of the used gas. As a result, I'd been chopping wood like a madwoman to use in the fireplace.

I let myself back into the clinic and found Haden already x-raying Rudolph. The reindeer seemed much perkier now. Had he been in shock? Or was the tequila wearing off? Maybe that whole time-bending thing they did on Christmas Eve in order to make all of their deliveries also impacted how long they could stay drunk or hurt. For the sake of Christmas, I hoped that was the case. Especially since Estelle's warning had spooked me. I didn't want to get in trouble, but I also didn't want to go into fairy godmother debt. I just wanted Rudolph fixed and home in time for Christmas.

Haden was moving about efficiently, my earlier absence no hinderance to him getting things done. He had shed his coat, and his shoulders filled out his flannel shirt in the most sexy lumberjack sort of way. I found myself hoping I had to kiss him as a distraction again.

Which was silly. We were never going to be a thing.

"I'll bring up the x-ray. Give me a sec." Haden excused himself, heading toward a computer. While one hand navigated a mouse, his other hand had his phone clasped against his ear. I hadn't even heard it ring. Was it one of his many members of the Haden Appreciation Group?

"Yeah, no. Maybe," he hedged quietly. "Can you call her and see if it's a real emergency? I'll send you the number."

For sure a HAG, likely angling for a house call. Well, he was mine tonight, missy. I had a magical Christmas emergency.

Haden ended the call, waving me over to the computer, his focus on his phone's screen where he was tapping and scrolling. Seconds later, his phone was back in his pocket, and we were standing shoulder-to-shoulder, studying x-rays, his attention solidly fixed on me and my animal emergency. Did it make me a petty and small person for loving that my emergency trumped anyone else's?

"Is he okay?" I asked, squinting at the image in front of us.

I was impatient for the results. Because what if I'd given poor Rudolph more than a bruise and a scrape? Then I'd really be ruining Christmas, and would need to go back on my word and make a wish to my fairy godmother.

"Looks like Rudolph doesn't have a broken leg."

"Oh, thank goodness," I said on a gusty exhale.

Haden turned to me with a smirky grin. "Maybe you didn't ruin Christmas after all, Trademark."

I crossed my arms across my 'Oh what fun it is to ride' Christmas sweatshirt, giving him a glare I didn't completely feel since my heart was soaring with the good news. "Ha. Ha."

What a relief. There was no need to make a wish. Rudolph would be okay. He just had to walk it off, or sleep it off, and then he and his pals could get back to the North Pole, and we could all live happily ever after. No fairy godmother debt for me. Yes!

I watched as Haden fussed over Rudolph, seeming so child-like in his happiness, and so unlike the serious older brother I knew him to be. Dare I say it, but he was even more sweet and handsome with that smile than the young man I'd crushed on as a child?

As I took him in with fresh eyes, I realized he was still that truly kind soul I'd seen when he'd dried my tears and tied my shoes on my first day of grade one.

He was a good man, and a natural at helping people and animals. He had a way about him, and had always been here for me, despite our differences. I'd known he'd come help me tonight. He was dependable, whether it was wiping my six-year-old tears, trying to make a scratched truck look less damaged, or even just driving into the city to haul me and my stuff back to Eagle Ridge.

Why was he always here for me? Was it a sense of brotherly

duty that extended to me, the woman everyone assumed would one day join the Powell family?

"So, you can see his nose, eh?" I stated, standing beside him. Rudolph let out a snort of impatience from the gurney when he discovered he'd consumed all of the oats Haden had given him.

Haden shot me a private glance that made me feel wrapped in his arms. It was quick, warm, and accepting, and very familiar.

"It's pretty cool," he murmured.

"Yeah." We watched Rudolph for a beat, his nose glowing bright, then fading like a slow heartbeat. "And you were able to see the...the others?" I asked hesitantly, wincing in case he hadn't, and things got weird.

"The ones in the alley?" He raised his eyebrows, and I nodded.

"They trust you." There was a hint of wonderment in my voice, but it wasn't earned. Of course they trusted Haden. I'd have been surprised if they hadn't.

We shared a smile before quickly looking away, our focus back on something safer than each other. A swell of gratitude washed over me and, unable to resist, I clutched his arm, giving it a quick hug, just barely refraining from throwing myself completely around him.

A flash of uncertainty crossed Haden's face. "Were they in the barn, too?"

I nodded. I could see pieces clicking together, and I hoped he didn't ask about my trunk noises again.

"And they can talk?"

"Um." I glanced at Rudolph, wondering what had happened while I was in the alley that had made Rudolph decide to reveal his English language skills. "Yes."

"And the...elf? Was that an elf?"

I cleared my throat, unable to meet his eye. "Uh, what elf?"

"The one in your *trunk*?"

I sighed long and loud, ready for the older brother lecture that was surely coming. "Yes."

"In your trunk?" he repeated firmly.

"Long story."

"Must be." He gave me a look, one eyebrow raised, clearly holding back a chuckle. "That's the most unTamara-like thing I think I've ever witnessed."

"Hey!"

"Nope. You threw bags of chips at my brother. That was very—"

Unable to help myself, I smacked Haden's arm. "He had it coming. Both of these guys did."

"Remind me not to tick you off." His eyes caught mine, and I saw a flicker of old hurt. I instinctively knew it was over the way we'd gone from being pals to obligated acquaintances with the flip of a coin when I was seventeen. Tentative friendship over.

I looked down, ashamed at the way I'd behaved around him, taking his knowledge for granted, and for how he'd felt as though he couldn't address it with me. "I'm sorry."

His voice was soft, deep. "For what?"

"For being a pest."

"You're not a pest, T.M.."

T.M.? That was a new one. Short for Trademark, no doubt.

"I was annoying. Admit it."

"When?" He pulled an apple from his shirt pocket along with a small, folding utility knife from his jeans. He began slicing the fruit, feeding Rudolph. The reindeer's eyes were big and round, his fuzzy nose wiggling as he sniffed each offered slice before wolfing it down.

"I was always asking you all those questions about horses and stuff. I was so..." I reined in my flash of embarrassed anger.

"You were very kind and patient with me." One of those sweet men that had all the patience in the world for a slightly infatuated, awed young woman. Sweet and gentle, and always respectful. Never making me feel as though I was the pest that I now understood that I'd been.

"Is that why you stopped asking for help? You thought you were a pest?"

"I was. Kade told me."

"He was wrong."

"He said I was annoying you and that you were too polite to tell me."

"I didn't mind. Not at all."

His warm knuckles grazed mine, and it felt intentional.

"Your hands are cold." He gathered my hands, lifting them so he could cup them in his. "We should have switched vehicles. You're frozen."

"Rudolph probably wouldn't have liked it." My jaw chattered, as though suddenly aware of how cold I was. "And are you sure I wasn't a bother? I asked a lot of questions." I stared at Haden, looking for a sign that he was cushioning me from the painful truth. "Kade said..."

"I know my own mind." His eyes met mine over our bundled hands. He blew hot air into the cup of our hands, warming me.

I wanted to focus on what he was doing, what his gesture meant, but all I could think about was why Kade would have told me that if it hadn't been true? One of these brothers was lying. And I didn't think it was Haden, which meant I now had to reconcile my feelings about him. It was a good thing he was the kind of guy who led women on or I'd be feeling some warm and fuzzies over him right now. Especially with my hands wrapped in his, as if I was delicate and his to care for.

There was scuffling outside the back door and reindeer

voices carried to us. It sounded as though Dasher was eager to get going, but Comet, who I'd begun to think of as the herd dad, was telling him to cool his jets.

"They don't seem to do subtle very well," Haden said wryly, his lips curving up in a smile.

"Well, they are all drunk."

He snorted a laugh, delighted. "Really? I'm glad that booze scent isn't coming off of you." He mocked someone drinking from a bottle and then driving crazily.

"Haden! I'd never!"

He laughed, leaning away as I gave his arm another affectionate squeeze, grateful I could share this crazy evening with him.

"I'm glad you're not freaking out," I said. "And I really appreciate you x-raying Rudolph."

"Oh, don't worry," he said easily, "this will all go on your bill."

I must have blanched, because he added, "I'm kidding. You're family. No charge for this one." He gently tapped my arm in what I could only interpret as a buddy-buddy or sibling sort of way. Was it so wrong that I didn't want to be seen as family? That I longed for something different?

And how wrong was that? A man like Haden would never put his brother in an awkward position by dating his ex.

I cleared my throat, trying to act jovial and not gutted by the fact that he seemed to see me as a sister. "Can I extend the family discount to all of my vet bills?"

He smiled, not answering, then reached out to give Rudolph a scratch behind the ears, the apple gone, his pocket knife blade wiped clean on his jeans and tucked back away. "You're in luck, buddy. No broken bones. How are you feeling?"

"Sore," grumbled Rudolph.

Haden jolted, clearly still taken off guard by the fact that his patient not only understood him, but also talked.

"This is going to take some getting used to," Haden said softly. He addressed Rudolph. "I could give you something for the pain. Any known allergies?"

"No."

Haden's cheeks had gone pink, but he nodded.

"Will he be able to fly?" I asked. "With his leg?"

"Not sure." The vet turned back to Rudolph. "You've got some pretty bad bruising. Icing it might help." He eyed Rudolph's hips and legs. "I don't think I have that much on hand, though."

"Well, there's a lot of snow outside," I said dryly.

"Sorry," Haden said, shaking his head. "I'm used to dealing with princess pets."

I cleared my throat and looked the other way, feeling like he could be talking to me. Yeah, I was definitely blocking him from seeing Boot's Christmas post. I had a photo of him in a Santa hat, sitting in a cardboard box I'd shaped as a sleigh.

What could I say? I had a lot of free time on my hands in the evenings.

"We can use snow to bring down the swelling on your back flank," Haden continued. "And I'm also going to bandage the spot where you went through Benjamin's bumper."

Haden shot me a stern look of reprimand as he called my car by name. Yeah, yeah. My driving was notorious. But my heart warmed from the way he referred to my car by his given name. Most people teased me for naming the Sebring.

This man always seemed to understand me on every level. Add in the fact that I hadn't truly annoyed him with my endless animal questions and my once-wounded heart soared. Haden was the best, and if he wasn't careful, he was going to have to add one more member to his fan club tonight.

CHAPTER 12
~ *Tamara* ~

I was driving back to my farm with the roof down to accommodate Rudolph's antlers. Haden was following behind in his truck, having smartly chosen to ride alone rather than freezing alongside me in the convertible. He planned to meet us there to help ice Rudolph's hind end, even though it was something I could do on my own. I wasn't sure if he was simply dazzled by the talking magical beasts, thought I needed the help, or wanted to spend more time with me. I figured it was the former option, but hoped it was the latter.

While Rudolph didn't have a broken leg, it was clear by the way he'd struggled to get back into the car that he was in no shape for flying. I bit my lower lip, wondering how long I could put off making a wish on his behalf. Shouldn't Estelle or some other magical being be here, fixing this situation? Why was it up to me?

I know, I know. I should have been paying more attention or driving slower to avoid an accident. And even though I insisted it was Rudolph's fault, I knew it was more mine than his.

Even though he'd been drunk.

And basically landed in front of me.

In the dark.

In a blizzard.

On a snow-packed road.

Once we were out of town, I raised my voice to be heard over the wind and snow twisting into the cab to bite us. "So, about that Christmas Eve time-bending thing? Does it mean you guys heal faster, too?"

"I don't know," Rudolph replied.

"Can you make a guess?"

"Prancer knows more about how your version of time works."

"He doesn't happen to have a handbook, does he?"

The way I figured it, time must move slower for us than for them. That way the North Pole crew would have more time to do all of their Christmas Eve deliveries in just one night. Therefore, Rudolph would have more time to heal before his flight if he was at the North Pole.

"How do we get you home again? Do you think you can fly?" I assumed he couldn't, but it was worth asking.

"That apple was good," Rudolph said, nosing my shoulder, and referring to the treat Haden had given him back at the clinic.

"I don't have one. We need to return you to the North Pole so you have more time to heal."

"Do you have some oats?"

"No." We'd emptied Haden's tin before hitting the road. Rudolph had scarfed the oats off my palm, tickling my hand with his soft muzzle. I'd probably overfed him, loving the feel of his nose on my skin.

Now, his fuzzy nose pushed forward as he leaned into the front seat, his antlers nearly whacking me as he tried to sneak a bite of the mistletoe bundle I'd tossed onto the passenger seat earlier while trying not to hit him on the road. I snatched it up and hung it on my rearview mirror. Rudolph stretched for it, his pink tongue darting out.

"Stay back there." I grabbed one of his antlers and attempted to angle his head back, away from the front seat, and nearly drove off the road.

"I'm hungry."

"I don't have any reindeer snacks with me."

"Cookies?"

"No cookies."

"They were really good."

"I wouldn't know," I grumbled. After Haden had bandaged Rudolph's leg, he'd offered us a plate of Christmas treats. But before I could accept even one, Rudolph had cleared off the plate with what I swore had been a smile.

The brat.

Haden had laughed, but I'd been a bit miffed. The cookies were a beautiful arrangement of decorated gingerbread men, sugar cookies, and shortbread. All of my favourites. And I hadn't gotten a single one, thanks to the little piggy riding in the back seat.

"How can we get you home if you can't fly? Can Santa come get you with his sleigh?"

He didn't reply.

"Okay, well, just so you know, I'm not making a wish to fix this mess. There are all sorts of magical consequences that come with changing the past that I don't understand. We're in this together, you and me, but I think it would be smarter to tell Santa so he can fly here to help us. The danger of missing Christmas has to be worse than any trouble you could possibly get into for your stag party, right?"

"Do you have any sugar plums?"

"I don't even know what those are. Are they regular plums?"

"Some candy canes?"

"No. And why are you changing the subject?" I glanced in the rearview mirror, hoping to see him despite the darkness surrounding us. For a reindeer, his face was surprisingly expressive, and I prayed I'd spot a helpful tell. But with Haden travelling too far behind us to illuminate my cab with his headlights, I saw nothing but shadows.

"I'm not," Rudolph grumbled.

"Are too."

A muffled voice from the trunk added, "Yes, you are! You big chicken!" Snarky, the elf, started making gleeful clucking sounds.

I'd forgotten about him again. Based on his ability to stay hidden for long periods, I didn't doubt his spying abilities.

"We should let him into the cab," I said, before realizing that he was probably warmer in the trunk since he was at least sheltered from the blowing snow. The windshield protected me a bit, but not enough that I wanted to make driving with the top down a new winter habit.

"No, thanks," Snarky shouted back.

"When we get to the barn, we need to contact someone to come help. Haden's done all he can." I spoke loudly, ensuring my two passengers could hear me over the wind as the car picked up speed on the straight stretch of road.

"You know, I'm feeling a lot better," Rudolph said.

"Those are the pain meds kicking in. We need to give Santa enough time to put his contingency plans in place in case you can't pull his sleigh."

"Think Santa has eight or nine of those contingency plans?" Snarky was laughing, the sound lifting above the wind rushing past the car. "One for each of his naughty reindeer? Oh, I can't wait to see the look on Mrs. Claus's face!"

I was getting a better picture of why the reindeer disliked the elf.

"Cupid can pull," Rudolph said.

"Cupid's drunk. You all are."

"We'll sober up."

Seriously, he was dragging his feet like a naughty kindergartener who was afraid to speak to the principal.

The elf, his delighted cackles partially carried away by the wind, began to sing, "Rudolph's going on the naughty list!"

"I feel better, and nothing is broken," Rudolph said. "We'll get home before anyone has to know we left."

I bit my tongue. It had taken some effort to get Rudolph back in the car again, thanks to his hurt leg, and I was certain we'd added new hoof scratches down poor Benjamin's side panel. In other words, it didn't seem as though Rudolph was flying anywhere in the immediate future.

"She's gonna know you snuck out and played stupid reindeer games!" Snarky hollered. I could hear him surprisingly well, and I realized he'd pushed down the small divider in the middle of the back seat that acted as a pass through into the trunk, as well as an armrest and cup holder for the rear passengers. He wasn't able to lower it all the way because of Rudolph, but he'd opened it enough that he could press his nose and one eye through the opening to see what was going on in the cab.

"What's he talking about?" I asked Rudolph.

"I'm going on the naughty list," he said glumly.

"Santa's bad-kid list? Why? Because you snuck out? Is he a mean boss, worthy of one of those reality TV shows, or something?"

"No. The *naughty* list," he repeated.

I really needed a handbook, because I was starting to get an uneasy feeling in my stomach, not unlike when I ate too much raw cookie dough.

"Right. Well. We're not kids any longer." Sure, I still believed in Santa and the spirit of Christmas, but not some list of bad people that Santa would skip over. I was a grownup, and Santa didn't even bring me gifts any longer.

I blinked. Was that because I was already on his naughty list?

Wait. No. I didn't know *any* adults who still got gifts from Santa.

Maybe we were all on the naughty list for no longer believing in him?

But I still believed. So why would I be on the naughty list?

Oh, right. For throwing bags of chips at Kade when we had our break-up fight in the grocery store. But it had been so satisfying in the moment to take him off balance like that. His surprise at seeing my spine at long last, and my willingness to stand up for myself instead of shying away from conflict and going with the flow. His expression was one I'd never forget.

Except I hadn't been getting Santa gifts even before that fight....

None of this added up.

"You don't want to be on that list." Rudolph was giving me sad reindeer eyes. I kind of wanted to hug him, ruffle his fur, and soothe him.

"I'm sure we can explain everything. It was one big accident, and we're doing our best, right?"

From what I could see, his furry-faced expression grew even more bleak.

He seemed so blue, I momentarily doubted my vow against accepting Estelle's costly fairy godmother help.

"I was drunk, and shouldn't have been on the road."

Rudolph sighed so heavily I was surprised he didn't throw a dramatic collapse in as well.

"Maybe you don't know about cars and roads? You know, being from the North Pole?"

"He knows about roads!" Snarky hollered. "He was acting as dumb as a candy cane! His brain's nickname is shortbread. Get it? As in *short* on brain cells?"

I heard the chomp of a large set of teeth clapping against each other, as if they'd tried to connect with something.

"Missed me," Snarky gloated.

"What *were* you doing on the road?" I asked Rudolph, almost afraid to hear the answer.

"We were playing a game."

"A game?"

"Reindeer games," he said bleakly.

A series of swears rolled through my head. Reindeer games? On the road? At night? Of course, one of them had been hit! I hadn't stood a chance, had I? Those stupid, risk-taking, testosterone-fuelled deer thinking they were invincible!

"Well, I don't care about the naughty list," I said definitively, holding my temper. "We need to save Christmas."

"I won't go on the list," Snarky said primly.

"Because you're her little narc." I heard a muffled thump, like a hoof striking the seat, followed by a squeak.

"Boys!" I snapped. "Fighting won't get us anywhere. We're in this together, remember?"

"I'm going to tell Mrs. Claus," the elf said, a waver in his smug tone.

Rudolph gave a cough, while saying, "Narc."

Rolling my eyes, I slowed Benjamin to a crawl to turn down my winding driveway, Haden following behind.

"And you're going on it, too, lady!" Snarky sounded as if I'd deeply and intentionally insulted him. "You've been interacting with the magical world without proper permission!"

"You guys didn't really give me a choice," I muttered.

"You don't have proper clearance."

"Yeah? Funny, because I didn't see an application form or request booth on the side of the road."

Rudolph let out a guffaw.

"And anyway, my friend Char interacts with your world all the time. Or she did, anyway. So did I. How is this different?"

"That was a business arrangement between you and Estelle," Snarky stated. "And it wasn't an intentional, unauthorized breach of the wall separating the two worlds. Her shroud breach was agreed upon by both parties. It's covered under an inter-world treaty."

He sounded as if he was reading a clause from a book of rules. You'd think he and Prancer would get along, seeing as he'd been quoting similar rules earlier.

"If I don't have proper clearance, how do I see you as well as the reindeer? Just because you chose it? This wasn't a business arrangement or an intentional breach. And I don't think it was agreed-upon by both parties, either."

"We're drunk," Rudolph stated.

"It weakens the walls between them and other worlds," the elf said, starting to sound bored.

Rudolph muttered something to the elf that sounded like, "But she also still believes."

"Does that make it so I can see more?" A bubbly feeling of excitement rose within me, along with the knowledge that I might be special in some way.

"Rules are rules," the elf snapped at Rudolph. "And you broke them! You'll both have to go before the magical courts."

"Well, I'm sure they'll see I was in the wrong place at the wrong time, and am trying to amend the situation."

"She won't listen," Rudolph said.

"Who?" I asked tiredly. "The judge or something?"

"Or something."

I shivered, my imagination running wild. Maybe I didn't want to go there to plead my innocence after all. Then again, the other option seemed to be fairy godmother debt. Unless I got Rudolph up into the air in the next few hours.

"You've injured one of Santa's reindeer," Snarky was saying, his tone prim and bossy, "and detained one of Santa's elves within twenty-four hours of Christmas Eve. That's *very* bad."

"You know there's a glow-in-the-dark pull-tab thing in the trunk, right? You could've let yourself out at any time."

The elf was silent for a long moment, then I heard the tell-tale click and pop of my trunk opening.

"Dude! I'm driving!"

The trunk lid rattled and banged up and down as I made my way through the snow-packed ruts toward the barn. Haden's headlights bounced over us as he followed behind.

"Does Haden still believe in Christmas? He saw the herd outside his clinic."

"Weakened walls. Belief. Touching Rudolph. What does it matter? He's going on the list, too," Snarky informed me in a bored tone. "You've both been interfering with the process of Christmas."

"Haden's innocent. I asked him to help."

"He touched Rudolph. Gave him drugs. He's aiding and abetting in the transportation of the lead reindeer to undisclosed locations within the Christmas bubble of time." He sounded like a lawyer laying out charges, like they were cards in a game of Solitaire.

As I pulled my car up to the big barn doors, I checked the sky for reindeer circling to land or whatever they did. The last thing I needed was to mow down a few more of Santa's drunken finest, and add to my list of growing charges. I grumbled my concerns aloud, becoming aware that I was quickly ending up in a pickle similar to what Char had had with Estelle. The magical world made their own rules and then held unwitting humans to those rules. Even if they didn't know or understand them. And it looked like I was getting caught up in a big mess I had no clue about.

The only option was to get Rudolph healed and back home as soon as possible.

CHAPTER 13

~ *Haden* ~

There was a glow of determination in Tamara's eyes by the time she parked her car and marched Rudolph into the barn along with the rest of the herd. I hoped they understood what they were up against.

Tamara might be a sweetheart, but she also had a way of making things go in the direction she thought best. I'd heard how kind and firm she could be with the kindergarteners in her school, and how she had them following her orders like imprinted ducklings within a day.

Hearing stories about Tamara always filled me with something I couldn't describe. It was part pride and part something else that left me feeling good inside. She deserved to be recognized for all she did for others, and there needed to be more people like Tamara in the world. She was the type of person who inspired others. For example, I probably wouldn't have thought to offer free care to animals in need every day throughout the month of December without her role modelling. And I knew some of her financial constriction this month was due in part for the way she'd filled a few of her student's fridges this holiday season. Stuff like that didn't stay secret in Eagle Creek.

Again, I hoped the reindeer understood who they were dealing with. The woman might give off warm, homey vibes ninety-nine per cent of the time, but that other one per cent? Watch out. You didn't mess with Tamara, because once she decided something or her patience was up, the fuse was lit, and there was no putting it out.

Case in point, her giving my brother what-for in the grocery store during their breakup. When I'd heard the story, I'd felt embarrassed for Tamara, knowing she'd hate the rumours about her. But I'd also felt a lot of admiration and pride that she'd stood up for herself, and finally spoken to Kade in a way he couldn't ignore.

Honestly, I hadn't been able to stop grinning for a week.

She deserved better than my brother and had let him and others know it. She might be kind, and she might sometimes come across as a pushover, but she wasn't.

Not to say my kid brother was a bad guy, but the two of them had never been the right match. He'd helped her open up and be less timid in high school, and she'd helped him cool his jets and get in touch with his calmer side. But Kade needed someone who would push back—constantly. And that wasn't Tamara's style. She was kind and gentle, and needed more space than a man like Kade would ever provide. Not that I believed myself to be the man for her. She needed someone she liked and respected, and somewhere along the line, I'd obviously failed her.

That was a crappy feeling. Failing a woman like Tamara who brought only good to the world.

Right now, despite her take-charge attitude, I'd bet she wanted to go curl up under some blankets with a cup of hot chocolate by her twinkling Christmas tree and lose herself in her next book club story.

I also knew she'd never do that because she was too much like me. She felt responsible to see this through, no matter how weird it was, because the idea of not helping fix Christmas was too huge of a weight.

"All right," she announced, her voice carrying through the barn. She had her hands on her hips and was glowering at the reindeer, who were shifting nervously. I gently closed the door, curious what she'd command us to do.

"How are we getting Rudolph to the North Pole? I need an answer now. One that's helpful and actionable."

There was no reply from the herd. Even Dolly stepped further back in her stall, as though afraid to be in Tamara's line of sight.

These were her boundaries, so firm you could ricochet off them.

"*Now*, boys." She waited a beat. "Either you come up with a plan, or I figure out a way to contact Santa or Mrs. Claus. And might I remind you that I have a fairy godmother?"

A fairy godmother? I found myself taking in the barn, on the lookout for a small woman with wings. I didn't see anyone who fit a fairy godmother description.

"So, it's your choice as to how I proceed," she continued. "Because we're not sitting around any longer."

"Mrs. C. would skin us all," one of the reindeer said.

"Do you think she'd even come?" another asked. "She wants Christmas to fall apart."

"Who? Mrs. Claus?" I asked, sharing a look with Tamara. That didn't seem right.

The reindeer had formed a circle in the middle of the barn, centred around Rudolph, words flowing over each other.

"—handle this the right way—"

"She's still mad about the summer—"

"Santa needs to—"

"She's got to make her—"

"Do we have enough to do this—?"

"No, and we'll have to come back again..."

"What choice do we have?"

"We're going to regret this."

"I already do."

"Okay?" Rudolph asked the group.

"Okay," they replied in unison.

Then, suddenly, they fell quiet.

Tamara and I shared looks, followed by a shrug. I had no idea what they'd been discussing, and it didn't appear that she did, either. I found myself moving to her side.

The remaining seven healthy reindeer, without so much as a look at us, marched toward the barn door. I hustled ahead, opening it for them.

One passed me with shiny Christmas ball ornaments hanging from his antlers and, unable to help myself, I reached out and touched a red one.

The reindeer turned to me. "*Dude*. Hands to yourself."

"Sorry," I said quickly, tucking my offending hand behind my back while the rest of the herd clambered outside. They all nosed into the small pouch Comet had been carrying in a holster like it was some sort of preflight ritual. I realized they were eating. Before I could figure out what was happening, they lifted up into the sky.

The reindeer didn't jump or fly straight upward like I'd expected, though. It was like a hearty, twisting cross breeze had aligned with their flight path. Two of them had even knocked antlers before straightening out again. Was that normal, or were they still tipsy?

The trunk of Tamara's car popped open, and a short man in

a green vest and brown pants jumped into the sky after the reindeer. One of them tried to kick at him, but he swirled around in the air behind it, taking flight as well.

It was the elf. What a night!

I watched them until they were out of sight, which didn't take long given the darkness and falling snow, then closed the door.

I turned from the door, feeling a mutual responsibility for the herd as though Tamara and I had raised them, and were now setting them free, hoping they'd survive. It was an odd sensation, and I shook it off before telling her the deer had set off.

Tamara turned to Rudolph, the tension that had been vibrating through her frame slipping away. "Come on then, let's get you settled and ice that hip." She guided the reindeer back into his earlier stall.

She talked softly to the animal, stroking his forehead. Then she straightened and joined me outside the stall. She went to a dusty old cupboard on one of the outer walls, opening it. She grabbed several big black garbage bags from a box and handed me one. "We can fill these with snow for his hip."

"Are they going to the North Pole?" I asked, referring to the departed deer. I assumed that was where they were going, but I was new enough to this whole talking-reindeer thing that I might have missed something.

Tamara nodded. "I believe they're going to get Santa and his sleigh."

"Well done on bossing them into action."

She snorted, her eyes smiling at me as we removed our mitts to open the big bags, so they'd be ready to fill once we went back into the wind and snow.

"You know you don't have to stay. I mean, there's probably not much else we can do for Rudolph other than ice his hip with the bags of snow." She looked shy, tucking a lock of hair behind an ear.

"And miss out on possibly seeing Santa? Not a chance." I shot her a quick wink, and her cheeks, pink from the cold, turned pinker.

The reindeer didn't seem to be dangerous, but I still felt a protectiveness in case Tamara got herself in too deep tonight with her love for all living creatures, and needed help.

"I just don't want you to feel obligated or responsible, because you think of me as family."

"All the more reason to stick around."

She nodded slowly, chewing on her bottom lip again.

"So, you still believe in Christmas?" Tamara asked cautiously, like she was aware of the strangeness of asking an adult man her question.

"I definitely do now."

We shared a burst of laughter.

"I should have guessed," she said. "Every December you provide complimentary care to several in-need patients each day."

"You inspired me to do that."

"I did?" She looked surprised.

"Yeah, and I wish I could do more." Sometimes that was all the veterinarian care some of the animals got.

"But you believe." There was wonder in her expression, so fresh and bright I wanted to lean in and kiss her again.

"I believe in that elf you had stuffed in your trunk." I raised an eyebrow in her direction.

She gasped, eyes widened. She quickly dropped her gaze to the bag in her hands. "He likes it in there. And, anyway, he let himself out. "

"Who else are you hiding from me?"

"Nobody."

"Really?"

"I swear."

I heard a giggle. I stopped rustling the bag I was opening and listened. I leaned into the stall where Rudolph was giggling to himself. Having never heard an animal do that, I smiled.

"What's so funny?" Tamara asked him. "Are you still drunk?"

"Blitzen sure is."

Tamara and I both automatically looked up toward the sky, even though we couldn't see it or Blitzen through the barn's roof.

"They wouldn't fly if they were too tipsy, would they?" she asked carefully, and Rudolph laughed. She groaned, placing her hands against her cheeks. "What have I encouraged them to do?"

"I guess we wait and see." I crouched and took Rudolph's pulse. "As for this guy, he's probably reacting to the painkillers."

The reindeer's eyes were giant, dark saucers.

"He's high?" she asked, flopping onto an overturned metal feed bucket, using it as a seat. She then moved to kneel in the straw, gently stroking Rudolph's front flank, her voice wobbly. "I'm messing up everything tonight."

"It'll wear off." I took out my stethoscope and listened. "I'm sure he's fine."

"He's not having a reaction or something, is he?"

"No, no. He's okay." I leaned back on my heels, disentangling my hand from Rudolph, who'd decided to lick it. "I've seen animals get a little loopy, but they weren't able to giggle. At least not in a way that I understood."

I caught Tamara's eye, sharing a look. A smile played at the edges of her mouth. Usually, if we were ever in cahoots, it was over ribbing my brother, which had been fun. This, though? It was way better, and I realized just how much I'd missed it. And her. I found my gaze dropping to her lips, aware that our age gap was no longer a wall to keep propped between us, to stop me from admiring her womanliness.

As Rudolph continued to giggle, I couldn't help but smile. "He's pretty cute."

Her eyes crinkled with joy, and she gave me a sweet, teasing smile. "Are you getting soft on him?"

"I want to keep him," I confessed, knowing she'd understand.

"But you can't!" Rudolph giggled again.

The three of us laughed as the spirit of the season wrapped inside me, along with the gratitude that I was the one Tamara had called.

I wasn't sure if she'd forgiven me for the unwanted attention I received around town as a bachelor, though. Everyone assumed I was sending women the message that I wanted them, then dropped them as soon as they expressed interest.

What was I supposed to do? They were kind, and I was kind, and then suddenly I was a big jerk for listening and caring, but not wanting to date them.

Honestly, until tonight, I'd figured that in an emergency, there was a fifty-fifty chance that Tamara would call my back-up veterinarian directly instead of me on my clinic's after-hours line.

Turned out I was fifty percent wrong.

CHAPTER 14

~ *Tamara* ~

Watching Haden tuck the bags of snow around Rudolph, and then cover him with a blanket while talking to him made me wonder what he'd be like as a dad. Obviously he was caring, and with a go-with-the-flow, unflappable attitude. Did I already mention caring? A man who could be vulnerable enough to show he cared, not worrying if somebody called him less of a man for having a tender, nurturing side. It warmed my heart in a way that I couldn't explain.

I forced myself to leave, so I didn't throw myself on the poor man once again.

I stood outside the stall, wondering what I could do next to help Rudolph. I was dying to go back to the house and warm up. But I worried that if I suggested we move locations, Haden might take it as a cue to go home or on to his next emergency. When I'd first called him, I'd wanted him to dart in and out of here as fast as politely possible. Now, however, I was enjoying being around him just like I had all those years ago—before Kade had lied to me.

Still, I needed to remind myself that Haden was here

tonight out of duty and responsibility. He still thought of me as family and, for him, family came first. Even in college, when most guys were out partying, he went on family trips. That was how committed he was. And I was sure it would be a long time before he let me fade from his familial sense of duty.

That was all this was. It wasn't about me as an eligible and charming sweet woman, and I'd be wise to remember that.

Besides, he'd choose a woman who was closer to his age, and not eight years his junior. He'd also smartly choose a woman who didn't cause him to fist his hands whenever she tried to gently and kindly stand up for herself and failed.

The man, despite his shuttered eyes, should never play poker, because his body language made it clear what he thought of me. He was probably fisting his hands to prevent himself from jumping in and fixing me.

Be more assertive. Be louder. Nobody's going to know what you want unless you speak up for what you want. I'd heard countless people dole out that advice, and I bet Haden agreed, but was simply too polite to add to it.

I leaned into Rudolph's stall. "How long do you think they'll take to get to the North Pole and back?" I pushed up my coat sleeve to check my watch. It was almost ten. The herd had been gone about twenty minutes.

"I don't understand time," Rudolph said.

"I know, buddy. Sorry."

Haden shook his head when I looked at him. He stretched his neck from side to side, letting out an exhausted exhale. He'd probably been working since six in the morning, if not earlier. And here I'd roped him into another animal crisis at the end of a long day.

"You sit for a bit," I said, gesturing to the bucket-stool outside the stall. "I've got to put the roof up on my car." Earlier,

I'd been too busy getting Rudolph back into the barn, and the herd off to the North Pole to take care of it.

"I'll help," Haden said, ignoring the offered seat.

"No. Be a good vet, and sit with Rudolph. Make sure he doesn't get cold."

Haden nodded and yawned, moving the bucket into the stall and taking a seat.

I watched him for a second as he pulled out his phone. He had a queue of unanswered text messages. I could see him skimming them, then using some sort of texting shortcut that suddenly produced a long message which he'd then send. I caught the odd word from the message. Symptoms to watch for in the pet, and the clinic's emergency number if things got worse. But, otherwise, it was call in the morning and make an appointment.

I was charmed by his efficiency, and how he instituted boundaries between his private after-hours time, and the plethora of so-called emergencies that plagued him. But I also felt bad for sucking up his night with my own weird animal emergency. The poor man never got a break by the looks of it.

And there didn't seem to be anything more that he could do for Rudolph. "You can head home now if you want," I offered again. I was enjoying his company, but I didn't kid myself that this was the start of something.

"It's fine," he mumbled, continuing to work through his messages.

Still half numb from my earlier drive, I headed back into the cold night where it was snowing like crazy again. A swirl of blinding snow spun and drove downward in a gust, and I worried about the reindeer. The visibility was horrible. And without Rudolph and his 'nose so bright,' I wasn't sure how they'd fare. Could they get lost? Blown completely off course and stuck somewhere foreign, and too exhausted to reach the pole?

The trunk of my car was open, and I peeked inside, not spying the elf. Where had he gone? I checked around the vehicle for footprints. None. Was he okay? Had he beamed his way back to the North Pole? Wherever he was, I supposed I no longer needed to worry about him freezing to death because of me.

I quickly put the roof up, ignoring the drifts of snow on the car's seats. A chill rocketed down the collar of my parka, and I jogged to the two-bedroom farmhouse, located only about thirty feet from the barn, shoulders bunched up to my ears. Inside, I fed my pet gopher Felipe some apple slices when he sat up on his hind legs and chirped at me.

Then I brewed two cups of coffee, figuring it would be a while before Haden and I got a chance to call it a night. Bundling up again in my big boots, parka, scarf, mitts and toque, I opened the door, startled when Boots went tearing past me and out into the freezing night.

"Boots!" I called, but he was already gone. Knowing he could seek refuge in the barn, thanks to the kitty door I'd made, I let him be, even though I worried about him being out in this weather.

Alone, I walked under the row of bare crabapple trees lining the walkway to the barn, heading back with a thermos and two cups. Halfway there, and somewhere above me, I heard a deep male voice shout, "Turn, turn, turn!"

It was followed by a cracking that sounded like a tree branch breaking and I instinctively crouched, eyes to the sky. Through the dampening sound of the falling snow, there was the faint ringing of sleigh bells.

Santa!

The reindeer were back already, and had brought Santa to fix everything!

There was a flicker of white light, some sort of headlight I guessed, and then the shadowy outline of reindeer pulling a sleigh.

I gasped at the brief sight, feeling like a kid as joy filled my heart. Santa was real. *All* of it was real.

More commands, each one sounding more frantic.

Without Rudolph and his nose, Santa must be having trouble landing his sleigh despite the headlight. Almost dropping the thermos, I jogged to my car, flicking on the headlights. They cast a glow across the driveway—a beautiful landing strip. Then I ran to the barn, flipping on the rest of its outdoor lights, including an extra floodlight. Next, I grabbed the huge emergency kit flashlight from my trunk and I aimed it at the sky.

Immediately, I heard a crash. I ditched the thermos and cups in the snow and ran blindly toward the noise, aiming my light. Snow crunched under my feet, and as I stepped off the driveway, my boots sunk into the deep, unpacked snow, pitching me forward. I got back to my feet and slowly waded through the endless white, punching holes in the drifts with my big Sorels, the cold snow tumbling over the tops of the tall boots and freezing my ankles.

The light from the barn had already been swallowed by the falling snow, darkness surrounding me other than the beam from my flashlight. In a storm like this, it would be easy to go too far, get turned around and freeze to death a few dozen feet from safety.

I hesitated, considering turning back. Then I heard muttering and bells ahead, and to the left. I did my best to continue toward them, and just when I was starting to panic again, my light caught something. The sleigh?

I waded through the knee-deep snow, and a few seconds

later, I was running a hand down the side of a majestic wooden red sleigh with gold detailing. A man in red and white was sitting on the plush bench seat, rubbing his forehead. In front of him, his reindeer were pawing at the ground, looking back at me. Everyone was standing, seemingly okay.

"Hey, guys," I called to them, wondering what to do. "You made really good time. You were only gone for about half an hour."

Where was Santa's boisterous 'Ho, ho, ho?'

I came up to the sleigh's door and shone my light on Santa, excitement swelling like I might burst with giddiness. I was about to introduce myself when I realized the sleigh wasn't level. The front end was jacked up and splintered pieces poked jaggedly into the air.

Santa had hit a tree.

No. Not hit. *Slammed.*

~

SANTA WAS NOT ALL RIGHT.

Unable to get the dazed man to reply to my hellos, I tried opening the sleigh's side door, but couldn't find a handle.

"It opens from the inside," Prancer said. He was one of the reindeer closest to the sleigh.

"Thanks."

"Are you okay, Santa?" I repeated. The sleigh was too high. I couldn't reach over the side to find the inside handle with my mittened hands.

Santa muttered something nonsensical.

Comet turned from his spot near the front of the herd. "He might've hit the tree when we stopped. Please check on him."

"I'm trying."

"Hurry up. Climb over the side," Dasher added impatiently

as I tried to figure out how to get my leg high enough to hoist myself over the sleigh's side, which was at collarbone height. I did the odd workout, mostly out of guilt after watching a news story about obesity or preventable illnesses related to physical inactivity, but I knew without trying that I wasn't strong enough to do a full body chin-up lift thing over the side of the sleigh.

"Step on the curly part at the front," Prancer suggested.

I aimed my light toward the front of the sled and, sure enough, the runners curled up into a decorative swirl at the front of the sleigh. As I angled my body into position to launch myself over the front of the sleigh and onto the seat beside Santa, the reindeer began bickering.

"I told you to turn," Dasher said to Blitzen, who I noted no longer had decorated antlers. "Are you still drunk?"

"We all should've turned. Together," Comet said calmly. "We should've slowed down, too."

"I don't do slow," Dasher said simply.

"Only mentally," Dancer said in his Swedish accent, and someone snickered.

"Everyone shut up," Cupid bellowed. "Let the humanoid do her thing. I have a date tonight."

"Her name is Tamara," Prancer said. "Learning people's names is important, Cupid."

"Hey, Cupid," Donner called. Like Blitzen, he'd also ditched the festive decorations from his antlers for the Rudolph rescue flight with Santa. The party was over, and it gave me hope that the herd would be more helpful moving forward. "What's her horse's name again?"

"Luscious," he said with confidence.

"Is not!" several of them chorused.

"Whatever," he muttered.

"It's Dolly," Prancer said smugly.

I swung my light around, still struggling to vault my way into the sleigh. Finally, by some miracle in physics, I managed to hoist myself onto the edge of the cab. I balanced precariously on my stomach for a half second before toppling inside, headfirst, landing on the sleigh's floor. I scrambled in my bulky parka, righting myself, then placed myself on the seat beside the large man in the red and white suit. I took a slow breath to calm myself, excited to be sitting next to the one and only Santa inside his flying sleigh. I wanted to touch him, ask for something fun for Christmas, but the idea that he was real was still so overwhelming. I sat for a moment, simply staring at the man.

His beard was long and thick, a beautiful white, his cheeks indeed rosy. Not a shopping mall wannabe. The real deal.

Was this how Char had felt when she'd first discovered our fairy godmother was real? Excited and slightly lightheaded?

No, she'd been skeptical and freaked out.

Two adjectives that did not describe me meeting Santa.

"Well? How is he?" Comet asked. "Santa? How are you?"

"Mhm," Santa mumbled.

I gently touched Santa's arm to get his attention, shining my light away from his face so I didn't blind him.

"My name is Tamara."

"Tamara Rose Madden. Eagle Ridge, Carl Gerson's farm. You want a boyfriend for Christmas."

I blushed, flicking the flashlight's beam over the snickering herd to my left. Suddenly, they became very studious about watching the falling snow, with the exception of Cupid, who I swore was grinning at me.

Apparently, they actually believed that adult women made wishes to Santa, and that, when they did, they wished for boyfriends. As pathetic as *that* sounded. Honestly, why couldn't they assume the more reasonable explanation—that Santa had bumped his head a little too hard?

I sighed and scooted closer to Santa.

I did want a boyfriend. Living on the farm alone was more isolating than I'd expected. And if my mom was right—and all the good ones had been taken, or were not interested like Haden—then I could use all the help I could get. Including Santa's.

And why was I suddenly thinking about Haden as an eligible man? Sure, there was a fizz of something fun between us, but that wasn't a reason to start thinking of my ex's brother in that way.

"It's nice to meet you," I said to Santa. "It looks like your sleigh hit a tree. Are you hurt?"

"The elves can't make boyfriends in the factory," Santa told me, his expression somber.

Someone was snickering again.

"Do you know what day it is?" Comet asked.

"It's snowing," Santa announced.

A sinking feeling of nothing but pure unadulterated dread took over.

If Santa had a concussion, what would happen to Christmas?

And even worse, would I be blamed? I shivered at the thought of what might await me in the magical realm and focused back on Santa and the snow falling around us.

"It is snowing," I agreed. "Very pretty snow tonight." Mentally I began humming White Christmas. Keeping my tone light, I asked, "What are all of your reindeers' names?"

"Olive."

"Sorry?"

"Olive."

In the silence, a female voice said quietly, "It's an old joke from the song *Rudolph the Red-Nosed Reindeer*."

I nodded. I knew it. I just didn't know what it meant in regard to Santa, and a possible brain injury.

"The line where you sing 'all of the other reindeer'," Donner mansplained to me. "That's Olive. The tenth reindeer."

"Right."

"It's a joke. There is no Olive."

"Thanks for clearing that up."

"No problem."

I peered through the snow, casting my light across the reindeer. There was indeed one more than I'd sent off an hour ago. "Vixen?"

"Yes?" Her voice was sweet and calm.

"Nice to meet you." I wasn't sure what else to say. Other than it was lovely to have another woman around, and that I was sorry for dragging her into this mess.

"Nice to meet you, too," she said, her voice rising with pleasure.

"Olive, huh?" I said to Santa. So he had a sense of humour as well as a possible brain injury. This was going to be so much fun.

"Where's Mrs. Claus?" I asked. I'd half-believed both of them would come to gather up their injured reindeer friend and take him home in their sleigh. The now crashed and damaged sleigh.

Nobody answered, the studying of snowflakes resuming among the deer as though they were researchers working on a thesis.

I sighed. If their fight was bigger than an injured Rudolph, that likely wasn't a good sign.

I addressed Santa. "Can you move?"

"She's upset," he said flatly.

"About Rudolph?"

He leaned awkwardly to one side, muttering to himself about misunderstandings.

"Maybe we can get you out of your sleigh to assess its damage?"

"On Dasher, and Olive and Pickles and Cucumbers!" Santa announced in his booming, jolly voice. He had righted himself, and he wiggled the reins in the air.

"Is that us?" Dancer asked in his Swedish accent.

"Yes!" Dasher cried. The sleigh twisted and creaked beneath me as he pawed at the snow.

"No. Don't move, boys," Comet commanded.

"I think we'd better get you checked out, Santa. My barn is just over there. Let's move inside." I gestured through the storm, realizing I might have trouble finding the barn again through the wildly swirling snow. But it was too cold to stay here. We needed to move.

I got out of the sleigh and began unhooking the reindeer from their harnesses. I told Comet to go get Haden, hoping the animal's instincts would guide him through the dark, and that he wouldn't get lost. Then I began coaxing Santa from the sleigh, hoping Haden would know what to do.

CHAPTER 15

~ *Estelle* ~

T'd been following Tamara's progress tonight, at the ready for when she decided to make a wish. But she'd made no wishes. I'd even been checking the wish catching machine as well as my private, secret wish amplifying app, as if her life depended upon it. Which it likely did.

But no wishes. And things were getting worse. So much worse.

Gram-Gram pulled a chair up to her desk for me to sit in. Trainees were never invited to sit. We never stayed in the big pink office long enough while giving our reports to worry about it. But tonight, the two of us were secretly cramming our brains with archaic rules and regulations after pretty much everyone else had left for the day, reading tomes that didn't even apply to fairy godmothers. We needed a loophole that would allow us to intervene, and her rosewood desk was buried in books. The air smelled like ancient paper and dust.

Gram-Gram had even asked me to use my secret, quick index that I'd made for the book of rules to help me find passages faster. She wasn't supposed to know about it, as I hadn't asked permission to use tech. It made me wonder what else she knew about. But more concerning was that she was looking for ways to circumvent Mrs. Claus's authority, should it come to that tonight.

Because if something didn't fix Tamara's growing problems soon, we were going to have to alert the authorities. And Mrs. Claus. And that was the last thing we wanted to do.

The offices were quiet, and I took a moment to take in the peace. Even the wishing machine in the corner of the bullpen was almost silent. Normally, the head fairy was home by now, along with everyone else. But tonight we were both still here, and I was very aware that this might be my last few hours as a fairy godmother. By not alerting the magical world authorities about the shroud breach, we were breaking protocol. We could get pulled into the Magical Court of Rules and have our titles as fairy godmothers stripped.

But it turned out Gram-Gram had a soft spot for the reindeer, and didn't want them to get in trouble. She'd kind of paled when I told her they were drunk, and that had been the reason Tamara had hit Rudolph with her car.

That wasn't enough reason for us breaking protocol, though. If we tattled about the breach and growing list of problems, we could absolutely blow up Christmas, which was Mrs. Claus's domain. With it being so close to reindeer take-off time, she had the power to make snap judgements if anyone was caught interfering with the holiday. She could even do it without taking them to trial in the magical courts, and we feared tonight's transgressions might tip her angry black magic over the edge of reasonableness. We could send her into a rage that might cause her to destroy the holiday out of spite.

We were taking a risk, but it was a calculated one.

Dread poured through me as my imagination supplied me with plenty of things to worry about. Gram-Gram began pacing in her large office, the big book she'd been reading, ignored.

She was frowning, not looking all that inspired.

She stopped beside my chair. "We need loopholes!"

"We do," I agreed.

"You're good at loopholes."

I smiled proudly. I'd found a few of those last summer. I'd even received a creativity award because of it.

"Now!" She clapped her hands. "We need some *now*."

"Right!" I jumped, brain scrambling for purchase on my slippery thoughts. "But Tamara hasn't made a wish."

"I know."

"She's afraid of the cost."

"We've been over this. She's out of trial offers."

"I know." But there had to be a loophole there. Accounting wouldn't give us a coupon for Tamara to use, unless we told them everything. If we did that, they'd go straight to the shroud's security team and things would get really messy, very quickly. "I suggested she use Char's credits, but she didn't want to. Wait! What if Char made a wish on Tamara's behalf?"

Gram-Gram inhaled through her teeth. "Risky."

"I know. But if I stick to the rules. Like maybe..." I paused, thinking my way into and around loopholes and rules. "What if Char wishes that she'd called Tamara earlier tonight—before the accident—and kept her talking on the phone for too long. That would make Tamara later getting home, and she'd miss hitting Rudolph!"

Gram-Gram stared at me for a full, lengthy beat before grabbing my arm and shuffling me off to the privacy of our late fairy, Paxi's, office. "Splitting spell. Now. Go see Char. I'll watch the door."

~

I cleared my throat, feeling awkward as I stood in Char's hotel room, waiting for her to notice me. She was snuggled up on a couch in front of the TV with James, the patio door open, an ocean breeze rippling the curtain. It was chilly, but nothing like Canada right now.

"Char!" I whisper-shouted, even though I knew James couldn't see or hear me.

Her head turned slowly, and her look suggested she was unimpressed by my arrival.

"Be right back," she told James, planting a quick kiss on his temple while she extracted herself from his arms. He pulled her back for a noisy, passionate kiss that made me look away.

The two were very much in love, and I was pleased for her. I hoped she had children soon. Trish was gaining experience with granting wishes to new moms, and it looked like a lot of fun. It would be a new challenge, too, because of all the rules around impacting the lives of others with a wish, and new moms made a lot of wishes surrounding their baby's behaviours and futures. Plus, babies were super cute with their pudgy little arms and legs, and those uninhibited toothless smiles and giggles, and I'd have an excuse to watch over them.

"What are you doing here? What's wrong?" Char whispered, once she'd locked us in the bathroom. The floor was tiled in orange and blue, and it was very festive and fun. It seemed they liked colours down in Mexico, or at least more than they did in Canada.

"Nothing's wrong," I said mildly. No need to start her off with panic.

Actually, no. I did want her to panic. I needed her to step in for Tamara.

"Then why did you bust in here? Haven't you ever heard of privacy?"

"Oh, but—" I shook my head, realizing we were already

heading off on a tangent, which was typical for most of our conversations. I stated firmly, "Everything's wrong."

Char immediately looked to the door where James was watching TV on its other side.

"He's fine. It's Tamara."

Char crossed her arms. "You were supposed to help her. You were supposed to contact Santa."

"I can't, and Tamara needs to be extracted from a very sticky magical situation."

"Sounds like a job for you."

"And you."

"Me?" Her voice went loud and she immediately hushed herself, whispering frantically, "What do you mean, 'me?' I'm on vacation. I didn't do anything."

"I need you to make a wish on Tamara's behalf."

"What? Why?" She was instantly suspicious. Why did these women find it so difficult to trust their fairy godmother?

"You have credits. Please use them to help extract her."

"I told her she can use them."

"She won't."

"Well, what am I supposed to wish for?" She was shaking her head. "There are so many ways this can backfire. And isn't it wrong for me to interfere with someone else's agency?"

"She—or you—just needs to wish that she was a few minutes earlier or later hitting the road tonight. It will solve everything. A near miss that will be even better than a mile." I grinned at my use of a human expression.

"A miss is as good as a mile," Char corrected.

I was so close.

"So, please agree to make a wish that will create a miss as good as a mile for your friend."

"Ohhhh," Char said, head tipping back. "I know why she won't make a wish."

"But I told her she can use your credits."

Char was smiling softly, and slowly shaking her head. My confidence in my plan faltered. "We can grant her permission."

Char was still shaking her head.

"Don't you want her to be safe? She's meddling with a very important holiday. She'll end up in the Magical Court of Rules."

Char's smile wavered, and I could see her concern growing for her friend. I pressed on. "She needs extraction. We need tonight to have never happened."

"I can't."

"Why not?"

"Because I think she finally kissed Haden."

CHAPTER 16

~ *Haden* ~

Tamara and I, with Santa braced between us, made it through the falling snow to the barn with the reindeer following us. By the time we hit the driveway, the snow had lightened to a few gentle flakes. Santa definitely had a concussion, and likely wouldn't be himself for at least several hours.

As we struggled through the snow, I could feel Tamara silently berating herself for asking the reindeer to go to the North Pole to get help. But there was no way we could have predicted this.

Well, that was a lie. The reindeer were drunk. There was a reason drinking and driving laws were in effect around the world, and it wasn't a stretch to think it should apply to flying animals.

"Mrs. Claus needs to make her flying oats for the reindeer," Santa said. "I don't know if she's making them this year. Do you know if she's made the oats?"

"I don't know," Tamara said, struggling under Santa's weight as one of his shiny black boots slipped in the snow.

Santa. We were carting the real Santa Claus across Tamara's yard. Mind. Blown. Did he wear his red and white suit at all times? Or was it a flight suit? It seemed right that he was in red and white, but also weird since it wasn't quite Christmas. I felt like a kid full of questions and wondered what Tamara was thinking.

A moment later, Santa said, "The reindeer need their flying oats. Will Mrs. Claus be making a batch?"

"Not sure," I answered. "But they were flying earlier. And eating something out of a pouch Comet had."

"Leftovers. We need her oats for Christmas Eve. Has she made them?" Santa asked again.

"We'll ask," I said.

"You know my wife, Mrs. Claus?" he asked warmly, like he was meeting someone he knew would be a friend for life.

"We'll make sure it gets sorted out, Santa," Tamara said.

"Tamara Madden, from Eagle Ridge. I got your letter. For Christmas you want a—"

"Santa! Can I make the oats?" Tamara asked, cutting him off in a fit of inspiration.

"Oh, I'm sorry," he said jovially. "Only Mrs. Claus can make those special oats."

I listened to Santa's repeating loop of conversation as he asked again about if the oats were ready, watching for clues to the depth of his injury. Tamara and I had assumed Santa had an injured reindeer plan. But did the North Pole also have an injured Santa contingency plan?

"What are you doing?"

I came up short at the sound of my brother's voice. His truck was parked near the barn, and Kade was standing in front of us. Apparently Tamara hadn't noticed him either, because she let out a gasp and the two of us nearly pitched Santa forward onto the snowy driveway as we came to a quick, guilty stop.

Could Kade see Santa?

I really didn't want to include him in this. Not just because I was starting to repair things with Tamara—things I suspected Kade was responsible for damaging. But also because my doofus younger brother was likely to try and pull off Santa's beard to prove he was a fake. Kade was gregarious, and the life of pretty much every party—whether invited or not. And he expected the entire world to be charmed by his personality. And sometimes that led to him doing ridiculous things for laughs and a sense of belonging.

And although he was social and outgoing, he lacked Tamara's natural kindhearted acceptance, which was what we needed right now. The woman had returned to Eagle Ridge with a confidence that made her dazzle.

What had Tamara ever seen in Kade? Yeah, he was fun. He brought everyone out of their shells and was a generous guy to boot. But he and Tamara were so different from each other, and it was easy to see the strain he put on her sometimes. She deserved a man who accepted and loved her personality, and Kade wasn't that guy.

Kade eyed us, his gaze landing either on Tamara or me, and never in between us. I wondered what he saw, if not Santa. Tamara and I with our arms out, as if we were supporting an invisible person or giving each other a long-distance pat on each other's shoulder?

"Hey," he said easily to me, "what are you doing here?"

"Helping with an animal emergency."

"Yeah, well." He hesitated a second. "Mom's looking for you."

"Thanks." That was a weird comment from him. I'd been

checking my phone plenty, and there'd been no text from Mom. If I didn't know better, my little bro didn't like me being here.

Was he like this with any guy who entered Tamara's orbit? Was he afraid she'd find someone who made her happy, and glow in the way she truly deserved, and he'd have to sit and watch, all lonely and down in his cups?

Or was his issue specifically with me being around Tamara?

"What's up, Kade?" Tamara asked. I wanted to believe I heard a slight impatience in her voice.

"Oh, right! Christmas gift." He jogged back to his truck while we helped Santa get a few feet closer to the barn door.

Kade returned, handing Tamara a small, red-and-white bag jammed with tissue paper.

"I'm sorry," she said to Kade, straining under Santa as he leaned her way, mumbling something about presents and Christmas, "I didn't realize we were doing gifts."

"Yeah, no worries." Kade shrugged easily. He was still studying us, but there was no pause or lingering look at the man in the red and white suit, nor the herd of reindeer who'd gathered behind us.

"Well, um, thanks," Tamara said.

Santa called out jovially, "Onward, Pickles!"

Kade didn't even blink, and Tamara let out a gusty exhale, as if she'd been holding her breath.

"What's up? You seem stressed," Kade asked Tamara. He moved to her side, lifting his chin in my direction in a joking manner. "This guy bothering you?"

"What? No, I'm fine," she chirped back. "He's fine."

My phone let out a series of beeps from my pocket, and I sighed involuntarily. It was not the ringtone for our mom, but was, more likely, another well-intentioned, overly attentive pet owner. It felt conceited, but I was tempted to find a woman who'd pretend to be my girlfriend, so the never-ending texts and calls from the women of Eagle Ridge would ease up.

Maybe I could convince Tamara to be my fake girlfriend. It would be worth it not only for the cessation of unnecessary calls and texts, but also to see my brother's head explode. Because I knew it would. Especially since I'd finally realized it had been his insecurity that had tossed the bomb into my friendship with Tamara. I had a feeling he'd been the one orchestrating the growing space between us. I sincerely hoped he hadn't, because it didn't say a lot about my brother or his trust in the two closest people in his life. And yet... I was pretty sure he had.

Plus, faking something with Tamara would give me plenty of excuses to figure out why kissing her felt so right. Spending time with her tonight reminded me of how much I enjoyed hanging out with her. I'd missed her. Now that she was no longer joining the family for holidays and dinners, they were bland and boring. There was nobody willing to keep Kade in check, and the conversations tended to centre around him as a result. Which was fine—he was always interesting and amusing —but I missed Tamara.

"Does your phone ever shut up?" Kade asked with a hint of bitterness as my phone chirped a second time. He was the life of the party, but felt I got more of the type of attention he craved. Honestly, I think he'd believed that when he broke up with Tamara, he'd be up to his eyeballs in women. He only needed to spend a day in my shoes before he'd realize the attention wasn't quite what it was cracked up to be.

"No. It does not."

"What if it's your mom?" Tamara asked, the edge of her mouth fighting a grin.

"She has her own text sound."

"Why are we standing out in the cold?" Kade asked, making

a point of rubbing his hands together and hunching down into his coat. He stamped his feet in the snow, then turned to Tamara. "You got some hot chocolate? The kind with mini marshmallows?"

"No, I don't think so."

We needed Kade out of here. We couldn't very well start attending to an invisible jolly Saint Nick with him peering over our shoulder.

"Bummer. I sure could go for some. How about you? You look cold," he asked Tamara. He shoved his hands deeper into his jacket pockets, clearly opting for no gloves in hopes of looking cool despite the biting, dangerous temperatures.

"I've got to get to work here," I told Kade. "Tell Mom I'm fine, and that I'll call her when I'm done."

As one, Tamara and I wordlessly started propelling Santa toward the barn again. There was a gash on Santa's forehead, and I hoped to give him a better once-over than I'd been able to perform in the sleigh, to ensure it was superficial. Hopefully, things weren't worse than Santa's obvious concussion, and possibly his cholesterol. The man had some serious weight behind him. Weight that had worked against him when the sleigh had made contact with the tree. To say Santa had rung his bell during the crash was an understatement.

Kade didn't take the hint and began following us to the door.

"What's wrong with Dolly? Boy, Carl's going to be ticked if anything happens to her on your watch, right?"

"Her landlord trusts her with his horse," I said, my tone more biting than I intended.

"I was making conversation. Loosen up, man."

"The horse is fine," Tamara said kindly.

"You work too much," Kade told me as we entered the barn. "Take some time off. Hey! I know. Let's go to Louise and shred it up on New Year's Eve. Then hit the town, meet some ski bunnies."

Lake Louise, the ski hill and small mountain town, would be a nice place to bring in the New Year, but I wasn't interested in hooking up with strangers. I was more of a 'family and friends' kind of guy. My inner circle was small, but filled with ride-or-dies. I could count on every person in my friend group.

My brother, on the other hand, baffled me. He knew just about everyone in the county and had about a thousand Facebook friends and acquaintances. But did he have a core group of friends that would be there if he needed them? Somehow, I doubted it.

"Come on, don't make a face. It'll be fun. My treat. Well, the hotel and a beer or two. Lift ticket prices have gotten out of control. Although the hotel might set me back more than a lift ticket." He followed us into the barn, negotiating with himself over what he'd cover for me if I went with him. He gave a little hop over the wooden threshold, closing the door behind him, and before the reindeer could enter. A huff of frustration came from outside.

"Did you get a new horse? Why are we in here, and not the house?" Kade asked.

"We're, uh, looking for the cat," Tamara replied.

We sat Santa on a bale where he muttered to himself. Again, I wondered what Kade saw us doing.

"Your cat, Shrek?" My brother had begun eyeing me, as if he was picking up on a Tamara-and-I-had-secrets vibe, his shoulders squared and chest puffed out almost as though he expected a fight. The two of us had ganged up on him enough before our falling out that he was instantly suspicious whenever Tamara and I seemed to be on the same page. It likely didn't help that we'd made it a habit to poke at him. Maybe that was the real reason he didn't want us hanging around each other.

"The cat's name is Puss in Boots," I said, tone low, near a growl. I couldn't help it. The guy couldn't even be bothered to learn her cat's name. He clearly didn't deserve Tamara.

"Yeah. From *Shrek*. Close enough. So, what's the emergency?"

"I'll have him better in a jiff," I said, using my older brother authority. "You can head home."

"I'll wait."

"Why?"

"'Cause. I'm bored, Golden Boy," Kade stated, making himself at home on a bale beside Santa. I bit back a smile, thinking that he'd crap himself if the man next to him suddenly became visible.

"I'm not the golden boy." Our parents were proud of me, but they fawned over Kade. He could do no wrong. It was to the point where I wondered if they regretted spoiling him so much, seeing as his precociousness was less cute now that he was an adult, and he'd driven away the woman they adored like a daughter. "And don't you think it's weird Mom would send out her *second* son, if she was concerned about her first one being out in this weather?"

"She didn't *send* me. She was just asking where you were." Kade bunched his bare hands into fists. "And I'm not second. Not like that."

"Sorry? Like how?" I asked innocently.

He glowered at me while Tamara and I shared a quick, darted look. I saw the hint of a tiny smile playing at her lips. Oh, those lips. I wanted to kiss her again and wasn't sure why. She'd always been more like a kid sister to me. But that one kiss had turned the tables.

"You know, I should call Mom," I said lightly, patting my coat as if searching for my phone. "Tell her we're both okay."

"No, no," Kade said quickly, standing. "It's fine. I'll call her later."

"I'm sure she's worried." I had my phone out, and caught sight of Tamara's dancing lips, silently egging me on, just like old times.

"Both of her sons out in this storm? Oh, my," Tamara said with mock seriousness. "She *will* be worried."

She was struggling not to laugh. Was what we were doing unfair? Definitely.

But fun? Also, definitely. And so satisfying as well.

We hadn't picked on Kade in ages, and I missed it. It might make me a cruel older brother to admit that, as well as how much I enjoyed having her on my side, but I was okay with it.

"I said it's fine," Kade said. "What's wrong with the cat?"

Tamara grew serious, clearly eager to get Kade out of here. Lying wasn't her thing, but how else were we going to make Kade leave? Tell him the truth?

Let's see how that would go... Hey, so Tamara hit Rudolph with her car. Santa has a concussion. Oh, and we kissed.

Pretty sure that wouldn't expedite his exit.

Knowing Kade, he'd find a way to be able to see these Christmas characters. Then he'd try to ride a reindeer, or post a photo of the crashed sleigh on social media. Assuming it could be photographed.

"So," I announced, "this is where I do my veterinarian thing. You're off the hook, little bro. You can go home before the storm gets worse." I placed a hand on Kade's shoulder and started steering him toward the barn door. I paused, as though coming up with a new idea. "Unless you want to help make a cat barf? I could use someone to hold him. You have gloves, right?"

He shrugged me off. "What's up with the two of you?"

"Nothing. I'm working."

Tamara swiftly stood in front of Santa, who was muttering about oats again. "Yeah. Nothing."

She was a horrible liar. Her face was flushed, and she couldn't meet Kade's gaze. I feared we were one small slip-up away from awakening his stubborn streak. He was already close—he obviously suspected something was going on. But if this went much further, it would take him forever to back down.

A weekend, several years ago, Tamara came to a wedding with the family, and Kade had become convinced that the two of us had hidden his tie. Of course, that had been an asinine assumption, seeing as we'd both been avoiding each other at that point.

Kade, of course, had forgotten it at home, but that hadn't stopped him from accusing us, turning the hotel rooms upside down as well as rummaging through everyone's bags. It had made the weekend a weary one, even though it had been fun having someone sane to share weary smirks with—Tamara—as Kade lost his mind. I may have also kept him wound up by egging him on a teensy bit. It had just been too easy. And it had seemed to make Tamara smile and forget the stress of meeting every extended family member we had. That alone had made it well worth the lecture I'd received from my mom later on.

"You're acting weird," Kade told us.

"You're acting weird," Tamara retorted quickly.

"Am not. I worry about you, T."

"I'm fine."

"You're out here alone so often. It's not good for a person."

"I like it," she said firmly.

"Yeah, no, of course." Kade nodded, as if he understood Tamara. He was good at pretending to listen, then convincing her to do whatever he wanted instead. Or at least he used to be. I had a feeling Tamara had outgrown his little tricks. "You're just alone. A lot."

"Kade, let her be," I said, knowing I didn't need to stand up for Tamara, but feeling the need nevertheless.

"Why'd you come here after hours?" Kade asked me, his tone accusing. "You're not the only vet around here."

"She's family," I said firmly, and a bit too loud.

"Yeah," she said softly, her voice filled with disappointment. "Family."

I nodded, unsure why her expression seemed so hurt. Maybe she'd hoped to rid herself of all the Powells when she and Kade broke up.

I turned back to my brother, and focused on the point I was trying to make. "She *should* call me if she needs help. Any time."

"She's not family, and you're not her personal hero."

"Family," Santa said sadly. "It's important. Has Mrs. Claus made her oats?"

My phone chirped, then seconds later, rang. I popped out my phone, checked the caller ID, then the text that had preceded it, and finally silenced the whole thing.

"All the single ladies?" Kade chirped.

"Only Haden Powell can fill their lonely pre-Christmas emptiness," Tamara added flatly. Great. Now she was ganging up on me? Where was her loyalty?

"If only he could make up his mind which one to choose," Kade said, but Tamara didn't smile.

"I'm keeping my options open," I snapped back, fingers flexing hard on my phone. I forced my hands to relax and silently cursed how the female attention I received brought out my brother's insecurities. The irony was that he wanted to play the field, and I was the one who wanted to settle down and move on with life.

"According to the latest census info from Stats Canada," Tamara said, her chin tipped upward, "I'd say there's about five hundred options within a short radius. And I'm sure you've already sampled at least half of them. You've got to be close to finding the woman of your dreams."

I rolled my eyes at the dig. Clearly she didn't know me as well as I thought if she believed I was the kind of man who would run through women like that.

Still, I respected the fact that Tamara was willing to bust my chops about it. It might mean she'd allow me to clear up any misconceptions she carried.

"I'm going to change my phone number," I told the both of them. "Remind me not to give it to either of you."

A plastic cooler fell over with a dull clunk. Blitzen had taken advantage of our distraction and his invisibility to nose the empty container, licking up tiny puddles that remained inside it.

Kade glanced toward the cooler but didn't react to the reindeer. "You making yukaflux? Sweet! Party at Tamara's! When? New Year's Eve?"

"Uh. Guess not. I seem to have spilled the batch."

"Bummer. Hey, where's your cat?" Kade's eyes narrowed.

"Not sure. He ran outside on me earlier. But he has a cat door to let him in here as well as into the house."

Tamara crouched down and called Puss in Boots, crossing her fingers behind her back, clearly hoping her healthy cat didn't come running.

Santa chimed in, calling, "Kitty! Puss, puss, puss!" and I saw Tamara cross her fingers so hard, I worried she might dislocate a knuckle.

Mew!

Well, apparently her crossed fingers had been a worthless waste of time—or maybe Santa's magic overrode what little she could summon. Either way, her ebony-coloured cat ran in, clearly a healthy beast.

Santa scooped the cat into the air.

Surely Kade saw the flying feline, right?

"Cat seems fine," Kade said, and I choked on a laugh. What did he see? Clearly, some sort of illusion that didn't include Santa making cute chirpy sounds while Boots purred in his arms several feet above the barn floor.

"What are you two really doing in here?" Kade asked, eyes narrowed at my not-quite-controlled mirth.

"Fine! It's a Christmas surprise," Tamara blurted out. "Haden's helping me, and you're ruining it."

"It's for me?" The hope in his voice was ridiculous. "What is it?" He glanced around, spying the bag he'd given Tamara sitting next to Santa. "You haven't opened your gift yet."

I stepped in front of him. "Not everything is about you."

"I didn't say it was. Chill out, you big psycho." He leaned around me. "Open your gift."

"I'll open it on Christmas morning."

"Open it now. While I'm here."

"You know I like to wait."

"Magic of the holiday," Kade said impatiently. "Come on, I want to see your face. You're going to love it." He yanked the tissue paper out of the gift bag, and unfolded a navy-blue T-shirt, holding it up for us to see. It said 'I love horses.' But there was a heart instead of the word 'love.'

"That's nice. Thank you." I could see the way the gift had hit the right note, softening Tamara. Why hadn't I thought to get her a present? I used to, when she was still dating Kade.

"Yeah? You like it?" Kade asked.

"Very thoughtful," I murmured. My brother, for all his faults, really wasn't a bad guy.

"It was. I like it. Thank you. But, um, not to be rude, but can you please go so we can work on my cat?" Tamara asked tentatively.

"Maybe I can help?"

"No," we both cried in unison.

"You two are always in cahoots," Kade complained, clearly put off by our sharp reply.

I glanced at Tamara. It felt like his accusation was about more than just us ganging up on him. Could he sense that we'd kissed tonight, or that I was seeing his ex-girlfriend in a new romantic light?

And why had she apologized for kissing me? Especially after I'd pulled her in for a second one. A really nice kiss, if I were to judge it. How could I have made myself more clear that a kiss was *not* something she needed to apologize for? Not with me.

I couldn't get her out of my head, and kept finding my attention straying to her lips. Sadly, I got the sense she wanted that one kiss to be a one and done. She was smart, kind, and I was the last man she'd ever choose.

It annoyed me. I needed to convince her to give me a shot.

"You two are so alike," Kade complained. "Always quietly sitting around and bonding. Or leaving me out and picking on me."

"Bonding?" Tamara's unimpressed look set me back. I knew she wasn't a fan, but wow. I had my work cut out.

"You're always sharing these funny looks, like you're in some special club."

Tamara sighed heavily. "We don't give each other funny looks."

"We do, actually," I said, rolling my neck, releasing the tension that was building. I shot her a look that immediately made her expression relax and lift.

"Oh. Those." She tried to hide a small, shy smile, but giggled instead.

Yeah. Those. Those little looks that made me feel as though she understood what was going through my head. Someone who shared the humour of the situation, or the annoyance. The little looks that brought my stress levels down from a ten to nonexistent.

Kade was right. Tamara and I were alike, and often in cahoots. Or, at least, we used to be. And I hoped that tonight would bring us back into cahoots more regularly. But if I wanted to get that ball rolling, I needed Kade out of here and Tamara back in my arms for another kiss.

CHAPTER 17
~ *Tamara* ~

"You want me to leave." Kade's expression was so down, I felt myself cave. It wasn't his fault he no longer believed in Christmas, and didn't belong in this barn tonight. And it wasn't his fault I'd gone to the city to see more, do more, be more, and had supposedly changed on him. Still, I was entitled to my own life, and the way I was living it made me happier than when we'd been together—even though I hadn't yet managed to completely create the life I wanted.

Hello? Horse of my own? Where were you? Same with the farm that I could own for more than a month at a time, or the husband and kids and... I needed to stop thinking about all the goals I'd failed to reach.

But come to think of it, it actually *was* Kade's fault I'd changed. He'd broken up with me the first time because he'd wanted to have more, see more, too. Jannifer Eric's boobs, to be specific.

I'd gone off to the city and gotten a better sense of myself, what *I* wanted, and a snippet of the confidence I needed in order to get it. Or at least a watered-down version of it. Live it, be it, have it all.

I think the real issue, though, was that I was an introvert and Kade was an extrovert. We both felt like the other person was from a different planet.

"The two of you have a secret thing going," he said, referring to me and Haden. "You always have."

I tried not to look at Haden as heat rushed to my cheeks, remembering our earlier kiss and how it had felt to have Haden's hands tangled up in my hair while we'd been lost in the moment.

I'd profusely apologized for kissing him, even though it was an unexpected experience I knew I'd think about often. Had I called it a mistake? I hoped not.

"What are you talking about?" I asked, my voice catching on the guilt that was rising up my throat.

"You like him."

"Haden? Of course. He's a nice guy."

"You know he leads women on." He pointed to Haden, whose gentle hands had formed into tight fists. "Listen to his phone. It's always blowing up."

"I'm a veterinarian!" Haden growled.

"That many emergencies? Do you think we're dumb?"

"I don't invite it."

"You're always listening to everyone like they matter. That's an invitation!"

"It's called kindness," Haden said, his tone feeling like a roar even though he didn't raise his voice.

"Guys," I said nervously, afraid the brothers were going to come to blows over me. Me, someone who wasn't even family, despite what Haden said.

Kade turned back to me. "Don't fall for his act. You know what he's like."

"Kade," I said, struggling to stay calm. I had a fleeting, quickly discarded thought of what it might cost to wish Kade away right now. "I get that you're trying to look out for me, but can you please just go so we can work on my cat?"

Kade lowered his voice. "He's not right for you."

"Kade..." My entire being flamed in embarrassment. Were my secret feelings for Haden—that old crush that I'd extinguished eons ago, and was rearing up again—showing? Otherwise, why was Kade having this conversation with me? Here? Now? In front of his brother? It was beyond mortifying.

"You need someone who gets you out of your shell. He'll let you turn into a hermit."

"Kade... Stop!" I could feel Haden moving closer, his body as tense as a mountain lion's, stalking its prey.

"You need to get off this farm, and get out more. A life with animals isn't the end-all, be-all. This isn't good for you."

"Kade...."

"There's a big bash on Boxing Day with some really cool people I met through an online social club. Come with me. Meet someone nice." He darted a look at his brother. He'd noticed Haden, his tight fists, the displeasure rolling off him in waves, and he backed up half a step. "Someone who will want only you."

"I don't like big parties, Kade."

"You don't want to hang out with me?"

"No, yeah. Maybe? I don't know." He always got me so turned around. "It's not about that." I didn't mind hanging out, and I still wanted to be friends with Kade, but a room filled with strangers was grossly unappealing.

"So, let's go. It's going to be epic."

"You know I don't like big, loud parties, filled with people I don't know. Especially—"

"You need to get over your social anxiety."

I raised my voice. "—especially because you tend to forget about me, and then I'm stuck—"

"I only forgot you once."

"—in the corner talking to someone I don't even like."

"You need to make more friends."

"When I go places with you, I go there to be with you."

"Oh." His demeanour turned perky. "So, you wanna go out?"

The man was giving me a headache. Why couldn't he just listen to me in the way Haden did? "Kade..."

"We could go for supper. No, let's do drinks first at the Monkey Top. And there's this hopping new restaurant—"

"Kade, we broke up. I'm not—"

"I know. It's not a date-date."

"Back off, Kade." Haden was growling, using a voice I'd never heard before. It sent Dolly further back into her stall, and even Santa had quirked his head, watching us.

"I don't think going out is a good idea," I said gently.

"We're still friends, Tamara. We'll always be friends."

"Yes, but we're also two very different people, and we want different things. And we have different ideas of fun."

"But we had fun when were together. We went out and did stuff."

"I know."

"It was good for you. We had fun."

"We did." That was truthful. It had been fun. But I'd also needed time at home to recharge after most of our outings. There was only so much of Kade and his energy that I could handle before I desperately craved some downtime. In high school, I'd known I needed to get out more, and he'd made it easy. But why I'd ever believed he was someone I could be with long-term, I wasn't sure. Maybe because I didn't understand my introverted needs back then. And I hadn't trusted myself enough to try to understand what I wanted and needed.

"So, what's up? You don't like me now?" He looked so hurt, my spirit fell.

"Please, Kade, I'm tired." And feeling too warm in all of my outdoor gear. I tossed my mitts on the bale beside Santa. "Can we talk about this some other time so Haden and I can help Boots and go to bed?"

"Together?" Kade was staring at Haden like someone had gutted him, and it took me a minute to pick up on his train of thought.

"What? No. Not like that. I just want to call it a night. Alone." I turned to Haden in exasperation, looking for backup on this ridiculousness. He was always so good about not interrupting when Kade gave me the runaround, but I was tired and out of patience. "Did you drop him on his head as a baby?"

"Only once."

"That's not funny," Kade said, when a burble of laughter escaped my throat. "The two of you are always..."

"Always what?" Haden had lost his sense of humour, his hands still in tight fists—like they seemed to be whenever I tried to gently let Kade down with kindness and, hopefully, some sensitivity.

Kade had a way of railroading me into doing something extroverted without me even noticing, because I was so busy trying not to hurt his feelings. For someone so outgoing, he could be sensitive.

As for Haden, it always seemed like he was holding back from punching something, or someone. Or was he bunching his hands to prevent himself from shaking some sense into me. I knew what he was thinking. I was too soft. Too patient. Not bold and direct enough. I was too small-town. Too quiet. Too...*me*. I needed to speak up for myself, have a spine, not be a pushover.

But any time I stood up, firmly and bluntly, I laid awake at night worrying about the other person's feelings. I never wanted to be mean, and boundaries were so tricky to maintain, especially with someone like Kade.

"You don't want me here," Kade stated, and I sighed without thinking.

"Why can't I want what I want? Why can't the things I want be more important than anything else for once?"

He blinked at me for a long moment. "What do you want?"

"For you to drop this so I can take care of my cat."

"I'll go home if you promise to go to the Boxing Day bash with me."

"Kade!" I exploded, suddenly out of patience. "You never listen to me, or take into account what I want or I need. I don't like big parties!" My hands were shaking and my voice trembled. "And right now, I just want you to leave so I can take care of Boots."

"Fine. Why didn't you just say so?"

"I'll help you find the door." Haden stepped into his younger brother's space, making him back up, moving him closer and closer to the barn door with every step. Now that I'd spoken my piece, he no longer had that prowling vibe to him, but rather was more protector, shoulders squared as he escorted Kade out.

"Dude, I know where the door is. What are you? Her bodyguard?"

"I have a cat to heal." Haden gestured toward my cat as though illustrating evidence. He spotted Boots being held up by Santa, who was touching noses with him, and quickly turned back to Kade, angling himself between the cat and his brother.

Boots was purring loudly and rubbing his chin and cheek against Santa's beard. I frantically snatched my cat back in case Kade saw something. He'd been around the reindeer for a while now, and with that thin veil between the worlds, or whatever it was, what if he grazed a reindeer, and suddenly saw what Haden and I did?

"I have a cat to heal," Kade mimicked, making his voice high, and very unlike Haden's timber tone.

"Yup." Haden's chest was practically touching Kade's. He reached around him and opened the door, letting in a blast of winter air along with a flurry of snowflakes.

"You're up to something, and Tamara..."

"Tamara what?" Haden nudged Kade's chest with his own, causing his brother to stumble over the barn door's threshold. Wide-eyed reindeer squeezed through the doorway whenever there was a chance to get by.

Kade was trying to form words, but Haden cut him off. "I have work to do. So, if you'll excuse us."

"I'm telling Mom you're acting like a—"

Haden closed the barn door on him with a curt, "Fine. Drive safe."

I SAGGED in relief as I heard Kade's truck start, then the crunch of snow as he drove away, into the storm and away from the magic in my barn. Haden reopened the door once the truck sounds had faded, letting the few remaining reindeer that were still outside come in with us.

Boots squirmed in my arms, trying to get back to Santa, and I set him back on the straw bale so he could do just that.

Haden was giving me the side eye, his shoulders still puffed up, his hands clenching and unclenching.

"I know! I know," I said wearily, feeling the weight of his gaze. "I'm a pushover. So shoot me."

Haden's eyes were dark, brows low. The intensity of his gaze was like a pin, poking into me, and reminding me that I often failed at standing up for myself, or at making my voice heard without causing a big stir.

"Do you still love him?"

"What? No."

"But you did?"

"Of course. We were together for years." And it hadn't been all bad. We were simply at the crazy-making stage of being in a former relationship.

Haden stepped closer, cupping my chin with his large, warm hand. His eyes looked so serious, I felt shaky.

"Love shouldn't hurt like that."

"Like what?"

"Love shouldn't hurt like that," he repeated quietly, releasing me and stepping back. I had to take a step forward to regain my balance.

"Oh," I said softly. I felt like I'd been kissed. The way that left you breathless, wondering if the world always felt this warm, always this beautiful.

My mind eventually found its way back to my worries, like there was a well-trod groove to them from every happy thought I ever had.

"He's..." I swallowed, unable to say his brother's name after the way Haden had bared himself without even showing me anything. "He's going to think we're up to something."

Haden's voice was low, steady, and clear. "Is that a bad thing?"

I crossed my arms, feeling pinned by his heavy gaze. "You know what I mean."

"You're too good to him, and for him."

I bit my lip, a little wobbly inside. I felt bad for the easy way I'd fallen into old habits, building Kade up, putting him first. I'd once thought that was how relationships worked.

I hugged my arms around my gut, feeling like a failure for

not figuring things out between us sooner and for trying to placate Kade tonight. I wanted Haden to think good things about me. I wanted him to see me as more than just that much younger, too eager to please, naive girl I'd once been.

Haden was still standing too close, watching me as though he could read me.

"What?" I asked, an edge to my tone. Quite frankly, I hated what The Book of Tamara might be telling him right now.

He moved further into my personal space, and I forced myself to hold my ground. Everything this man did, he did with reason.

Gently and slowly, as if he was afraid to spook me, he brushed a strand of hair off my cheek.

"I think you're amazing." His right hand, warm and thick, found mine. He gave my hand a squeeze. "I don't know how you do it."

"Do what?"

"Hold on to your patience. You're so kind, and strong, and generous with everyone. I literally have to clench my fists so that I don't throttle him when he treats you that way."

My lips parted, the words stuck in my throat. He made fists because he wanted to protect me? Stand up for me? Not because he thought I was frustratingly incapable of fighting my own battles?

His head tipped toward mine, our lips slowly lining up for what would I knew would be a spectacular kiss.

"TM, why didn't I meet you first?"

I melted into his chest, completely overcome by the sincerity and depth of emotion behind his words. Our lips were drifting closer, and my heart swelled at the idea that Haden had a regret in life, and that it was about missing a chance with me.

The barn door slammed against the wall, and Haden and I jumped. A low, gruff voice carried across the room, "Santa! I have a report to file on these humans and their mistreatment of magical beings, including myself! I told Mrs. Claus and I'm going to tell you, too!"

Our would-be kiss was forgotten as the most annoying member of the North Pole entourage reappeared after a blissful absence.

Haden had sheltered me with his body when the door slammed, ready to protect me. Now we stood side by side gawking at Hugo. "Is that the elf?" he asked.

"I've been saving the best for last," I said, my tone expressing just how peeved I was by the unwelcome guest's interruption. "Meet Snarky."

"That's not my real name!" the elf snapped as he marched past me, coated in a layer of snow, and clearly near freezing.

"Snarky, meet Haden."

"My name is Hugo!"

Using my best educational assistant voice, I said, "If you're going to join us, you have to be nice."

"I told Mrs. Claus you locked me up," Snarky told me, brushing the snow from his pants.

"You could have gotten out at any time! And why are you half snowman?"

"I was hiding."

"Where?"

"Under the sleigh that just crashed because of you!" He glared at me, waltzing across the barn as though he owned the place.

"*Under* the sleigh?"

"I don't fly like the reindeer. I had to make sure the coast was clear before coming out."

"Santa wouldn't let you into the sleigh?"

"Santa!" He began marching toward the man in red and white, ignoring me.

"Oh, boy," Haden whispered. His torso was pressing against my arm and back as he stood close. It was feeling mighty warm in here. "Now I can see why you locked him in the trunk."

"Yeah. He's a treat."

Haden's hand was rubbing my arm in a soothing, intimate way, and I wished Hugo had stayed out in the storm for at least another five minutes.

Why didn't I meet you first?

That line was going to be circling in my brain for the rest of the night.

"Santa! Your irresponsible reindeer snuck out. And they got *drunk!*"

Snarky pulled himself up to his full height in front of Santa, knuckles planted on his hips.

"On, Cucumber!" Santa declared. He cuddled my cat closer. "This is my *new* number one elf. Meet Sir Fluffball."

Snarky blinked at Santa, momentarily thrown, his face falling. He cleared his throat. "Sir, we have a number seven issue. As well as an eleven, an eighteen and a twenty-one. Also, a category E problem that could quickly become an F. Not to mention—"

"That's enough business for now. Go help Mrs. Claus make oats for the reindeer," Santa said, patting the elf on the head. "It's almost Christmas Eve. It's time to forgive and be happy. So good to have you back." He began humming *Feliz Navidad* as he cuddled Boots closer, getting another chin rub from the cat.

"Forgive?" Haden whispered to me.

"Long story," I muttered to Haden. "Still getting to the bottom of it."

Haden shed his winter coat, and I noted that it had grown oddly warm in the barn despite there being no heating system. Had I accidentally made a wish to Estelle in the alley to be warm? Or was this simply something about Santa and his presence?

I shrugged out of my own coat, noting that a fully decorated, ten-foot-tall Christmas tree was now in my barn. Where had that come from? I was tempted to run a hand through its branches to see if it was real or just an illusion.

Was the wall between worlds weakening even further? I spun slowly, on the lookout for any other changes.

"Has that always been there?" Haden whispered, gesturing toward the new tree. I shook my head.

Snarky, red-faced, his fists clenched at his side, glared up at me. "What did you have Estelle do to him? I heard you two talking outside *his* clinic!" He jabbed a finger in Haden's direction.

"What? Nothing! I haven't made a single wish!" Even though I'd skimmed a recent text from Char suggesting that I do just that, and to use her credits when I did. It seemed Estelle had visited her, too. But Char was on my side. She told me to do what felt right to me. And avoiding a tangle with more magical creatures—AKA my fairy godmother—seemed like a wise move.

Although maybe less so now, since my big plan to get Santa to fix everything was clearly a dud.

"We hit a tree," Donner explained, coming over, his hooves making a slow beat on the barn floor. "A couple of trees, actually." His gaze swung to Blitzen.

"The last one did it, though," Dasher said cheerfully. "Smashed into it, right good." He made a prolonged smashing and crashing sound effect that would have delighted a small child.

"The sleigh's damaged," I added.

Snarky's face turned white. "No. It's just parked funny. I saw it."

"Did you look at the front panel or runners?"

"Why?"

"They're broken."

"No. No, no, *no!*"

"Possibly. It's quite bad," I added, fascinated by his meltdown.

He sat cross-legged on the straw-strewn dirt floor, head in his hands, his little striped hat slipping to one side.

"He's taking it better than I thought he would," Prancer said, looking down at the elf.

"Christmas is *ruined*," the elf moaned.

"Well, you chose your side, so this really isn't your problem." Donner addressed the rest of the reindeer. "I vote the narc out of here."

"We can't, though, can we?" Cupid said sadly.

"Why does he even care about Christmas? He chose his side," Donner said, giving a huff as he moved to the other side of the barn, far from the elf.

"I still care!" the elf wailed. "All I do is care!"

"You just went and told Mrs. Claus everything," Donner said. "How is that supposed to help us or Christmas?"

"She can fix this."

"Will she though?" I asked. "Or will she put us all on the naughty list?"

"Naughty list?" Haden whispered to me.

"It's real," I mumbled to him under my breath. "And it's not about toys."

"Chilling."

"So, is Mrs. Claus coming?" I asked the elf. "Christmas is her holiday, too, right?"

"She does lots of stuff behind the scenes to make the holiday work," Prancer said.

"I really like Christmas." I gave a little pause, trying to signal to these goofballs just how important this holiday was to many of us on the non-magical earth.

"I do, too," Haden added.

"Baking cookies with my Oma and wearing the same sweatshirt is a tradition I look forward to every year."

Nobody said anything, and I continued, even though I was laying it on pretty thick. But I spoke from my heart, hoping to spur them into some form of action involving teamwork and a solution. "And seeing people donate to the less fortunate, to ensure they have a good Christmas always makes me smile. It renews my faith in humanity, and I always feel so proud of my community. Christmas is a holiday that brings out the best in people during one of the coldest and darkest months of the year."

We were all watching Hugo.

"Well?" I prompted. "Will her most magical being come and help us?"

His voice was small with shame as he said, "She said this doesn't concern her."

A few of the reindeer gasped. My heart dropped, and I momentarily doubted my plan to try and fix all of this without Estelle's magical fairy godmother assistance.

But if I made a self-serving wish at this point, it wasn't going to help the ongoing problems at the North Pole. Christmas might be doomed no matter which option I chose—wish, or no wish.

I chewed on my lip, unsure which plan of action was the best.

"Has she forgiven me?" Santa piped up, his tone hopeful as he looked over at me.

"Doesn't sound like it," I told him.

"Oh." His shoulders drooped.

I crouched in front of him. "Can you share some of your

Christmas contingency plans so we can start prepping...in case we need them?"

"Top secret," he replied cheerfully. He tapped the side of his nose and gave me a wink. He was so jolly and loveable, I felt bad for the third degree I was going to have to give him.

"Yes, I'm sure they are. But it's time to make them less top-secret."

"No can do, Tamara Madden of Eagle Ridge."

"Santa, Christmas is in danger. You have a concussion. Your sleigh is broken. Rudolph got hit by a car and is injured. Blitzen is drunk. And Snarky..." I looked at the elf, who was now sobbing and throwing himself around on the floor. "Well, he's having a breakdown. We need to activate contingency plans."

Preferably soon, so I could wriggle my way back into Haden's arms and see what he had in mind for me.

"Mrs. Claus takes care of Hugo now." His tone held a hint of sadness.

"What do you mean?"

"He's her *Numero uno*. He chose his side."

"Oh? Okay. Well, can the two of you kiss and make up?" The reindeer inhaled as one, taking a step back as though choreographed. "Christmas is on the line, and I get the feeling we could use your wife's help."

"She needs to make the oats," Santa said bleakly. His blue eyes looked damp.

"Right," I said softly. I glanced at Haden, but he just shrugged. "So, she needs to mix up those oats. Can't I make them?"

"Top secret!" Santa made a tsk-tsk sound, his bright eyes sparkling merrily, his earlier moroseness gone. "Have you met Sir Fluffball? He has such an exquisite name."

"Um. Yes. Fine. It's lovely."

He leaned closer to me, and I echoed his move. "Do you

find it odd that I know people and their names, but I don't know their pets?"

"Well..."

"Poor Sir Fluffball can't ask me for Christmas gifts." He rubbed his cheek against the cat's back. "A real oversight, I'd say."

"I agree." I cringed at the idea of any of my cat's wishes coming true. I pretty much let him have run of the house, but had chased him out of my cereal bowl the other day. I mean, I wasn't finished yet! And I was fairly certain I'd read somewhere that cats were actually lactose intolerant. He'd sulked for hours, even though I'd been looking out for him.

Naturally, I dreaded to think what might appear on his Christmas wish list.

"Hugo?" Santa commanded.

Snarky elf stood immediately, snapping to attention, face impassive, as though nothing had ever been wrong. "Yes, sir?"

"Look into that."

"What, sir?" His eyes shifted from side to side, as if he had done something he shouldn't have, and was waiting to be caught out.

"Why can't animals make Christmas wishes?" Santa turned the cat so he was looking at Boots, face-to-face. "It seems very unfair to me. Don't you think so, Sir Fluffball?"

Puss in Boots gave a small meow of agreement, his purr filling the room.

"I'll add it to the list, Santa, sir." The elf pulled a spiral note-book from a pocket in his pants and began scratching the item onto an existing and lengthy list.

I met Haden's eyes, and he shot me a look I knew. It wasn't a secret glance, like the kind Kade despised. It was simply the shared knowledge that Christmas was definitely in trouble.

I turned back to Santa. "What do I need to do to make the oats?"

"Are you a witch, Tamara Madden of Eagle Ridge?"

"No."

"Oh, that's too bad."

"Why?"

"Because that's how Mrs. Claus makes them. She's a witch."

CHAPTER 18
~ *Haden* ~

Tonight was getting weirder and weirder. Mrs. Claus was a witch? That sweet old woman with the curly white hair?

"Haden," Tamara whispered, waving me over to a quiet part of the barn. She was leading one of the reindeer by his collar, and her look meant business.

"What's up?" I asked, instinctively running my gaze down the length of the reindeer for injuries. Crashing the sleigh had to have been hard on them, too.

To be truthful, I was hoping to find another private moment with Tamara. I'd only started to express how I felt about her before that danged elf came banging his way back into the barn.

"You okay?" I read the reindeer's medallion. "Prancer?"

"Just fine," he replied primly.

"Give us the straight goods," she demanded, releasing his collar.

"What straight goods?"

"About Mrs. Claus, her witchcraftery, the oats, the fight, Hugo, the naughty list. All of it."

"This is confidential magical world business."

"Prancer, don't give me that crap."

"I'm not a narc," he said loudly, the rest of the herd nodding in agreement.

"Come on, boys. You know Christmas is screwed."

My jaw slackened at Tamara's no-bull attitude. Prancer pawed the barn floor and twitched his head, sending his rack from side to side.

"This is no time for rules," she insisted.

"You're going to have to lock me in your trunk," he said, lifting his head in defiance. "Rudolph will confirm that we are not to reveal these integral and vital pieces of information to a non-magical human."

He was still nattering on, lecturing Tamara even though she was already stalking toward Rudolph's stall.

"Santa, I need a minute with Rudolph," she said loudly. I strode after her, wanting to be a steamroller to any obstacles in her way. That was my job, my role. Give her the space to shine, so she could be the kindness the world so desperately needed. Or in this case, so she could grill the reindeer about the inner workings of the magical world.

"Of course, Tamara Madden. Oh, hello, Haden Powell. Did you enjoy your dirt bike? Oh, but you were just a boy then. You're a man now."

"I am, yes." I smiled at the warm memories the machine brought up. "I loved that bike. Thank you, Santa."

I helped the man up off the bale we'd set in the stall earlier, and he winked at me, then smiled at Tamara as though he was keeping some juicy secret from us. I settled him outside Rudolph's stall on the stack of bales close to Dolly, and I rejoined Tamara, curious about what she was up to.

Like a practiced interrogator, she already had Rudolph spilling magical world secrets.

"She's a black magic witch," he was telling her.

Prancer stood in the stall's entrance. "Don't tell her anything! It's against protocol!"

"She needs to know what she's dealing with," Rudolph stated.

"Maybe you could keep Santa company," I suggested to Prancer, trying to gently steer the rule-follower away from the stall so Tamara could get all the info she needed from the herd's leader.

"Naughty list, Rudolph!" Prancer called out as I managed to edge him back. "I won't protect you."

"I'm in charge," Rudolph snapped.

Prancer finally turned from the stall. "It's your funeral, *boss*."

"Remind me why you're not friends with Hugo?" I mumbled to Prancer as he trotted away, giving a defiant little kick as he went.

"Santa's magic is white," Rudolph continued to Tamara. "Good, pure. They fell in love, and now she lives in our world. But they aren't allowed to have children."

"Why not?" Tamara asked.

"Interworld species propagation is forbidden, unless permitted under special circumstances."

I nodded. That made sense to my scientific mind. You didn't really want inter-species propagation here on the non-magical earth, either. Things tended to go funky when different species mixed and matched.

"Okay. And?" Tamara prompted.

"Santa really wanted kids. So, they created Christmas. In a way, all of the earth's children became theirs, and they could spoil them once a year."

"That's really sweet." Tamara was beaming, clearly liking this warm and fuzzy workaround the no-kids thing. "And she makes you and the rest of the herd fly, too?"

"She makes enchanted oats for us each year. And she wraps additional spells around us to keep us secure and protected when we travel."

"Did she remove that spell? Is that why we can see you?" I asked.

"No, it's because they were drunk," Tamara said. "It weakens the wall between the worlds."

"It also weakens the effect of her spell," Rudolph said. "Plus, she only wraps us in that protection spell once a year, and last year's spell is wearing off."

"She sounds integral," Tamara said, catching my eye. I could read her worry, and I wanted to ease it and make things better for her.

She absently stroked the side of Rudolph's neck, and the animal's earlier agitation waned.

"Christmas is a strain on her," Rudolph confided, "and I worry..."

"Worry about what?" Tamara asked when he didn't continue.

"She won't want to come back to us. With the herd sticking with Santa, I think she felt excluded and alone."

"Yeah, Hugo isn't much of a prize, eh?" she asked, knowing the elf had chosen her side in the fight. Tamara's joke fell flat, and her brown eyes flicked to mine, then to Rudolph. "I'm sure she still loves you all very much."

"That might not be enough."

"Why not?"

"Being in our world means that she's constantly fighting against her black magic nature."

"But she loves Santa, too, right?"

"TM," I warned, knowing love didn't solve everything, especially if Mrs. Claus was battling major forces within herself.

"She does," Rudolph said, looking at me as though I was out of line for warning off Tamara. "Because of him, she does the work, stays civil, and acts like she has natural white magic. But Christmas reminds her that she can't give Santa what he truly wants, and that she will never fit in or be accepted."

"Oh, that's awful," Tamara murmured, and I moved to her side so I could place an arm around her in comfort.

"On summer solstice she can go before the council of white magic to request the hex be lifted—" Rudolph shivered, and I instinctively checked his ice packs to make sure he wasn't getting too cold.

"What hex?" Tamara asked.

"The one that keeps her from having kids. Last summer, she was denied again."

"But they're so old. Surely it's too late?"

"It's become about being accepted by the white magic community," Rudolph explained. "She's always upset and angry after she gets denied. And then she saw Santa with a fairy. She hates fairies. She tries so hard to live up to her public image, and fairies are naturally cheery and good. She resents them and the ease in which they flit about the white magic world. So when Santa and that young fairy godmother with red hair almost kissed—"

Tamara gasped. "Wait! *Estelle*?" She pointed to her chest. "*My* fairy godmother? Oh, no." Tamara's gaze dropped to the floor, her fingers resting on her bottom lip.

Rudolph nodded. "Mrs. Claus lost her mind."

"What? What does this mean?" I asked. I understood that a woman in love, one who'd had her trust and heart broken, was a powerful force to reckon with. And this one had super powers called black magic. She wasn't simply going to throw harmless bags of potato chips at someone in the grocery store. But the question was, what *was* she going to do?

"She hates my fairy godmother—she was the source of their fight. And now I'm ruining Christmas. Mrs. Claus is the judge at the magical court of rules, and I'm on her naughty list because of tonight. If she learns I'm associated with Estelle... Or I make a wish to Estelle to get out of this mess... What happens to me?" Tamara sucked in a swift breath and gave me the most plaintive look I'd ever seen.

I gave her elbow a gentle squeeze. "You okay?"

"Mrs. Claus loves doing the white magic world's dirty work with her naughty list. She holds us and others accountable, and she's ruthless. It's the one way she's permitted to release her dark magic nature into our white magic world."

Tamara had gone pale.

"And how does Hugo tie in?" I asked.

"He tried to play peacemaker, and now she says she won't make our flying oats."

That meant the herd couldn't fly on Christmas Eve—even if Rudolph was feeling better.

The state of Christmas was looking grimmer by the minute.

CHAPTER 19

~ *Tamara* ~

A deep feeling of dread hit me as Haden and I left Rudolph's stall to sort out our new knowledge and what it meant.

Santa and Boots were cuddling. The reindeer were talking in a huddle, and Hugo was sitting outside the circle.

Christmas felt doomed. How was I supposed to convince a hurt and angry witch to do her part for Christmas, especially when I was aligned with her rival? That was even assuming we could fix the Rudolph and Santa issue...

Haden, as though reading my mind like he so frequently did, pulled me in for a hug, resting his cheek on the top of my head. I didn't know what his comforting embrace meant. Was it a prelude to finally having that interrupted kiss? Or did he see me as little Tamara, in need of consoling?

He'd said he wished he'd met me first. As in, before his brother did. Was it a deal breaker that I'd once dated Kade?

Or was he simply under the influence of magic, and none of his feelings were particularly real? Magic was all around us tonight, and it could no doubt impact the way we felt.

I felt him stifle a yawn, and I pulled my head back, looking up at him.

"Hey, adorable," he said softly, his gaze lingering on my lips. If I were a mind reader like he was, I'd say he was wondering how to get a second kiss. And I wondered how I could subtly make that happen.

"I can only imagine how many emergencies you've dealt with today," I said. "You must be tired."

"Not too tired for this."

I could see and feel the solidity and power behind his words. He was here until the end, willing to help me.

He still had his arms around me, and I fidgeted with the button on his flannel shirt before realizing I had accidentally undone it. I smoothed my hands flat over his pecs, delighted by how firm they were.

If I cared about him, I should convince him to leave before he got so tangled up in this that something bad happened to him. But if I wanted to find love—which I sorely did—I should keep him around so we could explore how deep our seemingly mutual—and our possibly long-hidden—feelings might go.

I sighed, my sense of ethics and responsibility kicking in. "I should warn you that we're likely in really big trouble with the magical world."

"Okay."

"And it's scary, and I don't know what will happen, but I think we broke some big rules."

"We're trying to help."

"I know, but Hugo said our help could be construed in a bad way."

"I see."

He didn't seem to be listening, even though his focus was on my mouth again.

"We could end up in their court, facing Mrs. Claus."

His body stiffened ever so slightly, a sign that, as always, he had been listening and I hadn't recognized it.

I swallowed hard. "What I'm getting at is... I think you should leave."

"Do you want me to go?"

"I want you to be safe."

His arms tightened around me again. "And I want you to be safe. That means there is no way I'm leaving, unless you specifically order me to."

I wanted to roll up onto my toes and kiss him. Instead, I said, "You're welcome to stay, but bad things could happen to you."

I shuddered, my imagination automatically filling in all sorts of blanks for me. Blanks which were now filled with hungry ogres. I know, I know. Igor was vegan, but I just couldn't get that beast out of my imagination. It had locked onto him, and would not let go.

Haden brushed a strand of hair off my cheek. "If bad things are going to happen, then let's face them together."

My heart wanted to believe that he meant as more than friends. But all that came to mind was his earlier comment to Kade that he was here because I was family. It was the same reason he wasn't charging me for his services.

Yes, tonight had been peppered with kisses and sweet words that I wanted to believe. That, however, was lovely and new.

If I looked at the history of the man, it was obvious that he was a natural-born fixer. And there was a very high possibility that he was here tonight not to woo me, but because of some sense of familial obligation.

"Right," I said firmly, reminding myself to keep my hopeful heart in check. "Family." At his questioning glance, I realized I'd said *family* like it was a dirty word.

CHAPTER 20

~ *Haden* ~

Family. That word didn't feel right coming out of Tamara's mouth, or even in this context. Not when I had my arms around her, craving desperately to kiss her. Her lips were in a pouty frown, and I could sense their gravitational pull. I let out a shuddery breath and focused hard on her words and on what her expression was telling me.

It wasn't good. I'd hurt her somewhere along the line tonight. She doubted me and my sincerity.

I kept catching hints of her recently reapplied lip gloss. Coconut. I wondered if kissing her would make my lips taste like coconut, too.

I needed to concentrate on her feelings, not her lips and the desire dragging my mind places it shouldn't go. I couldn't let this moment pass us by before I fixed it. We'd spent years avoiding each other, and I wasn't going to let that happen again.

"Family," I whispered, willing my brain to focus on the problem, to bring it into clarity so I could understand it, remedy it.

She was chewing on her bottom lip, and for an instant, I could read her again. She wanted me here. And not just for my medical skills. But there was something else I couldn't quite reach.

She was hurt, but what had wounded her?

"I'm not family." Tamara blinked hard, cheeks flushed. Her delicate, slender hands had been resting on my pecs, and she dropped them, stepping away from me. She crossed her arms over her chest, looking as if she didn't want me touching her.

"Not officially, no," I said carefully, holding myself in check. It was like a cold, giant rock had formed between us, the lightness gone, and in its place a giant, spiky boundary of wrong words. Did she no longer want to be a part of the Powell inner circle? Was that why she'd been avoiding me around town for so long? She wanted out?

"But you're family to me," I said. She was part of my life. She could call me any time, and I'd come running. And my parents would, too.

"Please don't."

"Don't what?"

"I know you're not charging me because you feel like you can't. But you can. Okay? I'm not family."

"Do you want out?" My voice felt small, my tone level and emotionless, even though her answer had the power to devastate me.

"It's not that." She tipped her head to the side, her expression pained. "If you think of me like a sister, just charge me your usual fee tonight."

She had such a sorrowful look I wanted to scoop her into my arms and kiss away every doubt she had about what she meant to me, and where she placed in my life. She was brave, kind, and generous. She offered lifelines to people I'd have cut out of my life. She gave people a second chance to rise to the occasion, and to her expectations of them. And if they failed, she still continued to be kind. She received the best of everyone, but sometimes their best just wasn't enough.

I wanted to be my best. I wanted to be enough for her.

But I didn't know how to get from here, to where I wanted to be. I'd resisted any romantic feelings or attraction toward her for so long that I no longer knew how to clear the invisible hurdles I'd put up to block myself.

"I'm not charging you. And it's not just because I don't have a line in my accounting software for magical flying reindeer," I said gruffly.

"So, you *do* think of me as a sister?" she asked.

"I would never..."

I screwed my eyes tight, realizing this was the watershed moment for us. The moment when I could make her understand.

I opened my eyes and stepped close, our bodies tight together. She lifted her chin defiantly.

"I would never...*ever*..."

My voice was almost a growl.

I scooped my hands into her hair, loosening her ponytail as I lined up our mouths, prepared to release the storm of pent-up longing battling inside me.

"...kiss a sister."

CHAPTER 21

~ *Tamara* ~

Haden knew exactly how to kiss me. His hands were in my hair. His lips were angled just so. His tongue was dipping and diving, meeting mine. It felt so good to be in his arms, to be cherished and held. He was the perfect height, so easy to kiss, and I wanted every future kiss in my life to be this magical.

Feeling bold, I ran my hands over Haden's waist and up the curve of his back. He was muscular and fit, the planes of his torso perfect under my palms. His fingers tightened in my hair, sending a delicious shiver down my spine, and I inadvertently moaned into his mouth, immediately feeling self-conscious for showing my pleasure.

I angled my lips, tipping my head so he wouldn't try to kiss me again. I needed to get a grip on myself. I needed to focus on all the reasons Haden and I shouldn't be doing this. I needed to work on the broken logic in my brain that had to be swept up and set straight again.

Because none of this made sense.

He wanted me.

He most definitely did not think of me as a sister.

His lips had moved to my neck, and I shuddered with pleasure, sagging against him as he left a trail of magic down my nerve endings. Was it actually possible that this man had secretly wanted me for so long, too? That we'd both been burying our attraction and denying it, and that Kade had seen what we'd refused to recognize?

Had he been trying to keep us apart? To keep me from this bliss?

And what was *this* exactly? Temporary bliss influenced by the magic around us, or something more?

Before I could settle even one shard of shattered logic into place in my aching brain, my thoughts scattered. My hands, without much guidance from my brain, had slid under Haden's soft flannel shirt and cotton tee, hitting the hard, smooth skin of his lower back as we clutched each other, as if we needed to hold on so we wouldn't fall. Then his lips were on mine again, and I never wanted to stop. I didn't want to think or worry or be responsible for anything in this world. All I wanted was to be in his arms, and feel every bit of him pressed against me, the way he was in this moment.

When we finally broke apart, dazed and slightly breathless, it took a minute for thoughts, and then reality, to weave their way into my brain.

Haden was a hottie.

A hottie who'd just kissed me senseless.

I'd liked it.

My crush on Haden had returned with a breathtaking force.

Haden was my ex's older brother.

It was Christmas. I'd hit Rudolph.

Santa Claus had a concussion.

And all of that was happening here in my barn, where we'd been making out, oblivious to it all.

A soft sigh of realization escaped as my mind put new pieces together. If I wished that I'd never hit Rudolph in order to fix this Christmas fiasco the way Estelle wanted me to, I'd never kiss Haden. I'd lose this.

Haden was studying me with an unreadable look.

I shifted, pulling myself from his arms, afraid that I'd misread him and mauled him once again. Afraid that he didn't want this with the same urgent desperation that I did.

He led women on, didn't he? That would explain these amazing kisses. He was well-practiced, and this was just a fun and distracting game for him.

"You need your head checked, TM." With a tug at my waist, Haden had me back in his arms for a quick kiss.

"What? Why?" I tried to step back, but he pulled me close once again. He trailed a knuckle softly down my cheek, his expression warm, open, and filled with what I could only hope was affection.

"I can't believe you would ever think I'd see someone as amazing as you as a mere *sister*." He said the word with the same amount of disdain I felt for it.

His lips, plump from our kisses, covered my mouth again, and we were lost in a new lust-hazed, delicious pink cloud of wondrous feelings.

When we pulled apart, we were both smiling. We rested our foreheads against each other's, delighting at our mutual attraction.

Playboys who led on women didn't act like this. They were simply cool, because kissing someone was blasé. *This* was something more. I could sense how our kisses had shifted something for Haden, too. He was feeling something, something he wouldn't have felt with the fan group flavour of the week.

He glanced around, as though tuning into the silence that surrounded us. There were no hoof sounds scuffling through the straw strewn across the barn floor. No bickering. No hiccuping. Not even the sound of Boots purring.

"Where are the reindeer?" I asked, a feeling of uncertainty tipping me between hope that they'd solved every problem while we'd been kissing, and a fear that everything had slid into absolute chaos.

"They went to get Mrs. Claus," Snarky said. He wore an expression of delight as he hopped down from one of the bales beside Santa. The old man in red was dozing, Boots curled up in his lap.

"I thought she wanted nothing to do with Christmas?"

The elf shrugged. "They're dumber than a box of candy canes."

"Well, hopefully they can convince her to come."

While the idea of meeting a black witch was terrifying, the idea of Santa's wife coming and taking charge was reassuring. Yes, it was possible she could extend some of her Christmas anger my way, but I was hopeful she wouldn't. In my dreams she simply wafted in, set things straight, and Christmas was saved.

"How will they get her here? The sleigh's broken," Haden pointed out.

Snarky explained that there was another sleigh that had been retired. It was rickety, and too small to handle the demands of the world's current population, but had been kept for posterity's sake more than as a reliable back-up. The reindeer planned to use it to carry Mrs. Claus as well as a couple of Santa's handyman elves who would fix the main sleigh, which was currently wedged against the giant poplar.

"That's great," I said, still steadfastly trying to avoid thinking about the fact that they'd be bringing a potentially very unhappy witch onto my property sometime in the next hour or two.

I spied a reindeer dozing in the corner of the barn. "Wait. Blitzen is still here."

"He was grounded from flying by Rudolph until he sobers up. Plus, they didn't have enough flying oats to get him home."

"Oh. That's not good." Could Blitzen be stuck here forever along with Santa? What if Mrs. Claus refused to make more oats? Everyone would be stranded where they were.

Haden, as though sensing my rising panic, took my hand and tugged me toward our coats. "Let's go check on the sleigh."

His warm fingers entwined with mine were a fine distraction, and I felt my worries ease up a notch.

In this moment, with Haden choosing me, I didn't even care what the town might think about me moving on to a different Powell brother.

My spirit rose at the idea of having a man like Haden to call mine, and at the idea of finally living the dream with the sweet man I'd crushed on for so many years.

There was no more squelching my truest feelings for this smart, handsome, and kind man.

As we exited the barn, Haden said, "Maybe we can bring the sleigh inside, so when the elves arrive, they can work on it in the light and warmth."

"That's a good idea."

Snarky tagged along with us to the crash site, Haden taking the lead with the giant floodlight from his veterinarian truck.

What if the elf was stuck here forever? That was a distasteful thought.

"So, you rode underneath the sleigh?" I asked Hugo, wondering how he'd managed such a feat. It must have been a cold and wild ride.

"What's it to you?" Hugo snipped.

"Just making conversation. Also," I continued, "why didn't you go back with the reindeer to get Mrs. Claus?"

"Do you need special oats to fly, too?" Haden asked him.

"I'm an *elf*. We don't fly."

"But I saw you fly away with the reindeer when they went to get Santa."

"You did?" I asked, surprised by this new info. Maybe I wouldn't be stuck with Sir Nasty Pants after all.

"I wasn't *flying*. I was surfing in the wake from the reindeer."

So he was a hitchhiker, huh?

When we arrived at the sleigh, Haden ran the beam of his light over its damage. The front right runner was badly broken, and the cab, or whatever you called it, had a jagged hole near where Santa had sat.

"Might only be cosmetic," Haden said, testing the strength of the pieces surrounding the hole.

"Are you an engineering or construction elf, by any chance?" I asked Snarky.

"No." He stood in the snow, shoulders sagging, expression glum.

"Do you have magic that could help us?"

"I'm not allowed."

"But you have magic that could help us?" I edged closer, tuning out Haden's verbal monologue about what was wrong with the sleigh, and the possible fixes.

"I don't think Santa can fall out of that hole, if that matters," I called over to him, then crouched beside Hugo.

"Probably won't help the sleigh's aerodynamics," Haden muttered back.

"Hugo, what kind of magic do you have, and how can it help us?"

"It's not magic. It's knowledge. And I can't use it here."

"Why not?"

"Rules and regulations."

"Don't you think an emergency situation such as this would lead to an exception?"

Hugo refused to say anything further, his arms tightly crossed over his chest.

I sighed and went back to the sleigh. Haden stood at its front corner, and bracing himself, pushed up on it. The whole thing twisted, creaking and moaning. He swore under his breath. "I think the hole's weakened it, structurally."

I felt my shoulders drop like the elf's. "What should we do?"

"Let's get it into the barn for a better look."

"This is really bad, isn't it?" the elf howled, flopping into the snow, fists to his eyes as he bawled unabashedly. "Everything is going wrong. Mrs. Claus will hate me, everyone hates me, and Christmas is *doomed*."

"Yeah," I muttered, feeling as though I had to be strong since he'd called dibs on falling apart. That had been my plan. Because everything did feel rather doomed at the moment.

I sucked in a breath and bent over to pat his shoulder. "We'll figure it out, Hugo."

I nodded, reaffirming to myself that I was with Mr. Fix-Everything—Haden—and that the herd had gone to get the one woman who could magic us out of this mess. It was all going to work out. I wouldn't even have to make a costly wish to my fairy godmother. There was no need for me to sit down and howl in the snow alongside Hugo.

Look at that. Bright side.

"Let's get Blitzen hooked up to this thing and see if he can pull it to the barn," Haden suggested. He let out an ear-piercing whistle, which I guessed was intended as a call for the drunk reindeer, Blitzen.

"Have I ever mentioned how much I appreciate your take-charge personality?" I asked Haden.

"I don't think you have." His voice dropped low, confiding like he was sharing something private. I realized he was flirting, and I caught a hint of his smile in the shadowy light from his lantern.

"Definite oversight on my part," I whispered, crunching a bit closer to him in the cold snow.

He chuckled, holding my arm through the thick layers of my coat.

"Think he'll come?" I asked, referring to Blitzen. The wind wasn't blowing at the moment, but he was in the barn. How good was a reindeer's hearing? Make that a drunk reindeer.

"If not, I'll go get him. Let's sort the reins."

We began untangling the muddle of leather reins and harnesses from when I'd unhitched the herd after the crash. I hadn't focused on keeping them organized, desperate to free the reindeer, and now the leather straps were frozen into messy clumps.

The elf, startled by Haden's whistle, had stopped crying and was hiccupping from his spot in the snow, watching us work.

Progress.

I moved around the fully grown poplar tree, tucking a handful of reins into the sleigh's cab. "Man, this thing is really wedged against the tree." With Haden's floodlight, I could see more than I had earlier with my own light. The sleigh must have come to a very abrupt halt when it hit this tree. Poor Santa. No wonder his brain was so scrambled.

"Hello," Blitzen said merrily, appearing rather stately out of the darkness. I always forgot how much beefier and shorter reindeer were than I expected until I was standing close to them. "Was that whistle meant for me?"

"Well done," I whispered to Haden, very impressed.

"Can you help us take the sleigh into the barn?" Haden asked, a flurry of flakes landing in his dark hair. His nose was bright red from the cold, and I tucked my chin deeper into my scarf.

"You know who could?" Blitzen said. "Dasher." He looked over his shoulder as though ready to goad on his competitive herd mate into doing his work for him. Then, as if realizing he'd been left behind by his pals, he sighed and moved closer. "Where do you want me?"

Haden and I worked on hooking the sleigh up to Blitzen, who wouldn't stop moving. At least he could stand up straight now, giving me confidence that we wouldn't run into more trouble as he pulled the sleigh over the snow for us. The only issue was that the storm was picking up again, and our visibility was rapidly being eaten away. I hoped he had a good sense of direction.

As soon as Haden and I cleared ourselves from the sleigh, Blitzen began pulling.

"Hold up," Haden called. "You're hung up on the tree." The wood sleigh was creaking and protesting, screaming as it was pulled against the thick trunk.

"I can do it. I am as strong as anyone!" Blitzen boasted.

"I know," I said soothingly. "You totally are."

"Just give us a second, okay?" Haden said. He directed me to stand beside him by the poplar up near the front of the sleigh.

"Push here," he told me, breaking a branch off the tree so I had room at his side. I lined myself up in the freshly made space so we were shoulder to shoulder. I ignored the way my body hummed, reminding it to chill out. The man really didn't need me focusing on our recently released lust for each other. He needed me to get this sleigh unstuck while admiring how strong and capable he was. Well, admiration was a bonus.

Together, we put our entire weight into pushing the sleigh's front corner away from the tree, tipping it upward so Blitzen could slide it past the trunk.

Blitzen, all fired up, and still pulling with all of his might, surged forward as the sleigh tipped up and away, the resistance against the tree disappearing.

Haden and I, unprepared for the sleigh's sudden movement, lost our balance and tumbled against its side as it crashed back against the trunk. Haden wrapped his arms around me, trying to keep us from going under the moving runners blazing through the snow at our feet.

"Stop!" Haden shouted, but Blitzen was on fire. He continued to thrust forward, the sleigh scraping against the tree, no doubt adding a long, deep gouge into the gorgeous red and gold side as he pulled it free.

Haden and I tumbled against the side of the sleigh like clothes in a dryer as it zipped by, barely staying on our feet. Then the sleigh was in the sky, with Blitzen calling out something I couldn't hear, Santa's sleigh bashing like a pinball against trees and branches.

No longer having anything supporting us upright, Haden and I tumbled into the snow, with me landing with a glorious thump on top of him.

~

HADEN SAT up much too quickly for my liking, practically tossing me into the surrounding fluffy snow as if I was an annoying weight—and not his future girlfriend, if he played his cards right.

I'd been prepared to enjoy being on top of him with the snow tumbling around us, the feeling of his chest rising and falling, and dreaming of what it would be like if my cold lips rested against his in a kiss again.

But no. He was squinting into the dark sky, hands cupped around his mouth, calling Blitzen. I stood, pulling the cold snow out from between the cuffs of my jacket and big mitts. The mittens were thick, full of insulation, my fingers cuddling like buddies and yet still half-frozen thanks to the late December cold.

"Where is that reindeer going?" Haden grumbled. He ran forward a few steps as though he believed he could catch the reindeer and pull him back to earth.

I winced as the night filled with the distant sounds of breaking branches. I supposed that a runaway reindeer who was crashing Santa's sleigh was a tad more important than cuddling with me in the snow.

But only because we were so close to Christmas.

"We forgot to tell him not to fly, didn't we?" Haden said, as I brought myself up beside him, both of us staring into the darkness.

The sleigh's harness system wasn't properly balanced to have only one reindeer pull it through the air. No doubt the sleigh was tipping precariously to the side, impossible to steer and dragging Blitzen downward and to the side. There was also the issue that he hadn't eaten any flying oats before taking off, so he was likely running on magic fumes from his earlier flights.

Haden shone his spotlight into the sky, but the beam went nowhere. The falling snow ate up the light before it could go further than several feet.

The sound of breaking branches continued as Blitzen, and the sleigh failed to clear the obstacles. What had we done? Blitzen was going to get hurt, the sleigh completely trashed, and my yard was going to look like a tornado had gone through it.

The plan had been for Blitzen to pull the sleigh into the barn. On the ground. Through the snow. Not the air.

"Maybe he thinks he needs to take it to the North Pole?" I suggested as Haden asked, "Did he forget where the barn is?"

There was a harsh sound of wood crashing into wood.

"I think he found it," I said, horrified by the screeching. I began jogging through the deep snow as best as I could in the direction of the noise.

Through the silence, I heard a chirpy little reindeer voice say, "You have arrived at your destination!" It was followed by a guffaw.

He was still totally loaded, wasn't he?

Haden yanked my arm back mid-run. I stumbled, flailing in an attempt to regain my balance. I fell against Haden's chest, and was promptly engulfed in his strong arms. When he placed me back on my feet, he seemed to hesitate before releasing me.

"Don't go running off into the blizzard," he growled. "Follow the trail." He pointed his light toward our feet. Even though it was snowing madly, you could still make out the impression of a tamped down valley of snow due to our earlier trek from the barn.

"Right. Thanks," I said, breathless with shame. I knew better than to run blindly into the dark in weather such as this. Within a few hurried steps I'd already veered into the cocoon of falling snow that surrounded us, completely missing the trail.

Haden shone the light to the left as he gathered me in like a lost duckling, and I spotted the elf huddled in the snow. I bent down, reaching for his hand. "Come on. Sounds as though we have another problem to fix."

BLITZEN WAS STUCK on the roof.

As we craned our necks to stare up at the faint outline of the reindeer, I could feel a headache coming on.

I was trying to deal with the growing heap of problems in a methodical and cool-headed manner like Haden, but this newest mess took the whole freaking cake. I wanted to scream. I wanted to go into my house and slam the door, take off all my winter gear, curl up under a thick warm blanket with a bottle of wine and pretend tonight had never happened.

That was what I wanted. And I wanted it right now.

Well, except I wanted Haden to come with me.

"I can't deal with this," I muttered to Haden, trying to blink back the wetness of futility forming in my eyes. It had to be near midnight and I was spent.

"I've got it," he said, giving my shoulder a squeeze, and I leaned into him momentarily, relieved. "You and the elf go check on Rudolph and Santa."

"I have a *name*," Snarky said.

"Sorry, Snarky," I muttered.

"It's Hugo!"

The elf and I entered the barn where Rudolph was keeping an eye on the concussed Santa while Haden dutifully began tackling the issue of figuring out how to get a broken sleigh and drunk reindeer off the barn roof.

"Was that Mrs. Claus?" Rudolph asked when we reached his stall. "Did they land on the roof?"

"Mrs. Claus?" Santa perked up from his spot on the bale near Dolly. "She came?"

Rudolph shushed him and with a mumble, Santa dipped his head back down, as though deciding to nap.

"Um..." I glanced at the elf to see if he wanted to break the news to his reindeer friend—or foe, or whatever their relationship happened to be.

"Your drunken colleague landed the broken sleigh on the roof," Snarky announced. "Apparently, he doesn't understand instructions. Surprise, surprise."

"Haden is dealing with it," I said with a calmness that surprised me. I gave snoring Santa a pointed look. "Have you been waking him up?"

Rudolph had been under strict instructions to wake Santa every half an hour. I realized now that my directions had been myopic. Not only did the reindeer lack a watch, but he also probably couldn't tell time. Further, his sense of time seemed to differ from mine here in the regular world. And then there was also the fact that, due to the painkillers, Rudolph kept dozing off as well.

"Santa?" I gave his thick shoulder a gentle shake. "Santa? Can you wake up? Do you know where you are?"

"Well! Hello there, Tamara Madden from Eagle Ridge," he said warmly. "What would you like for Christmas this year?" He tipped his head to the side, giving me a gentle, playful look. "And you know I can't deliver a boyfriend. Not a real, live one at least!"

He gave me a meaningful wink, and I shuddered. Beside me, the elf snickered.

"I'm working on it here on my own. So, you can scratch that off your list!" I said cheerfully. "No magic or wishes required!"

My mind immediately flitted to Char last summer. She was a wishing machine, and had thought her new boyfriend was under a love spell, thanks to Estelle and a poorly made wish. It hadn't been easy for her, believing that he only loved her due to magic. That kind of extra emotional turmoil, while falling in love and sorting out all of those fun insecurities about whether a guy likes you or not, wasn't something I felt the need to repeat. And knowing that Santa had nothing to do with Haden's desire to kiss me tonight was reassuring.

"Santa, do you know where you are?" I asked, refocusing my efforts on the problems at hand.

Maybe this year was the last time I'd need to ask for love. My mom was going to be delighted I'd found someone...although she might be perturbed that I was hopping my way across the branches of the Powell family tree.

"I am here with you, Tamara Madden. And look, there's Rudolph. Hello, old friend."

"Hello, Santa," Rudolph replied cheerfully.

"*Santa*, bring me a *boyfriend*," Snarky said in a high-pitched voice, just loud enough that I could hear him, but quiet enough that Santa and Rudolph would probably miss it.

I whirled, giving the elf my best glare. Oh, how I longed to punt that big-eared annoyance right out of my barn and straight into the New Year.

Satisfied by how Hugo had rocked on his heels in surprise after my split-second glowering, I turned back to Santa. *That's right, you little punk.* I could be scary. It might be a façade, as everyone pretty much knew I was a small-town softie.

Except my kindergarteners. Okay, okay, they were onto me, too. They respected my authority because they were five, and I helped them open tough packages and containers at snack time.

There was another thump on the roof.

"Is Mrs. Claus here?" Santa asked, perking up again. Then, like a memory hit him, his expression quieted and he let out a sad little "Oh."

I was already getting too warm in the barn, thanks to Santa's magic, and I pulled off my coat.

"Santa, do you have some magic that could help Rudolph?"

"What a festive sweatshirt," Santa said, and I looked down at the 'Oh, what fun it is to ride' horse graphic on my front. "I do enjoy your spirit. Always have."

"Really?" I couldn't help but beam at him. "Thanks. My Oma and I do a new sweater every year."

"She has a good sense of humour," he said, his eyes twinkling. My smile dropped.

"How do you know?"

He winked and tapped the side of his nose with his index finger. What did that mean? He was spying on my Oma?

He began cheerily humming *Jingle Bells*.

I resisted the urge to drag another bale over for me to sit on and sing carols with Santa Claus while forgetting about our little time crunch. Instead, with a reluctant sigh, I asked, "Santa, Rudolph hurt his leg, and he needs to pull your sleigh in a few hours. Are you able to heal him?"

My eyes drifted to the barn roof, where all the banging and scuffling was coming from. I didn't want to know what was going on up there, or what kind of danger Haden might be putting himself in, as it basically sounded like hooves were pulling a sack of lumber across the shingles. Sadly, I didn't think that assessment was too far off, with the once pristine sleigh being the lumber. If Santa could heal Rudolph, maybe he could deal with the sleigh after that.

"Oh, are you hurt, Rudolph?" Santa said tenderly, his kind blue eyes turning to his reindeer friend.

Rudolph nodded sadly. "This woman hit me with her car."

Oh, heck no.

"Santa, would you like to hear the full story?" I said firmly, giving Rudolph a stern look. He blinked at me with giant, gooey reindeer eyes filled with pain and innocence. Dang, he was good.

"Look! There's Tamara Madden," Santa said. He gave me a cheery wink. "You know I can't deliver you a boyfriend for Christmas."

"Okay. That's fine." Feeling snippy, I added, "I'll talk to Estelle about it instead."

"Estelle!" Momentarily, the fog in Santa's eyes faded and a

look of alarm flashed before he saw Snarky. Then he leaned forward, eager and intense. "Hugo? You're here? Is Mrs. Claus okay? Has she sent me a message? Is she making the oats?"

"I'm sure she'll make the oats," I said impatiently. "I just need you to heal your lead reindeer as well as your muddled-up, bruised brain. That's why you're here! To fix things. And as a cherry on top, could you also sober up Blitzen, and get your broken sleigh off the roof of my barn? And then fix it, so it'll fly? Can you do that? Please? Because that's what I actually, truly and very deeply, want for Christmas this year."

Beside me, Snarky sat in the straw and began whimpering and rocking. Santa, however, simply blinked at me a few times.

I braced for the irritating broken record of him being surprised to see me, Tamara Madden of Eagle Ridge. His jovial sweetness was so innocent, I couldn't stay upset, but it was still incredibly irritating.

"Rudolph is hurt?" he asked seriously, no hint of the jovial, blundering man I'd been dealing with for the past hour or so. It was like a moment of clarity, allowing me to finally see the man who ran the North Pole.

"Yes," I said firmly, afraid he was going to revert back to fun-loving, loopy Santa any second. "What can we do to help him heal quickly?"

Santa's gaze slowly shifted to the elf who was still hugging himself in the straw. His voice was firm and commanding. "Hugo?"

"Yes, sir!" The elf jumped to his feet, practically vibrating with eagerness.

"A potion to heal Rudolph."

"On it, sir!"

Santa patted the elf's back. "I've missed you, Hugo," he said soberly.

"I've missed you, too," the elf said, his voice trembling.

"Come in for a hug, will you?" Santa put out his arms, folding the little elf into his embrace. And in that moment, I didn't see Snarky the meanie narc, but rather a hurt, lost elf who saw Santa like a father. One he'd been estranged from for months, not unlike a small child of divorce.

Blinking back tears, and aware that the banging, dragging and clopping of hooves up above had ceased, I gave the men a minute, and went outside to see how Haden was faring.

~

OUT IN THE YARD, Haden was looking up at the roof, left hand on his hip, right hand shining the beam of his giant flashlight upward. I followed the beam, but saw nothing beyond the darkness and falling snowflakes.

"How's it going?" I asked.

He grunted.

"That good, eh?" I stood beside Haden in the freezing cold, shivering and stamping my feet to try and ward off the freezing air nipping at me.

He put an arm around me, pulling me against his side. "You should go back inside where it's warm."

"I wanted to tell you that it sounds like Hugo can make something that'll help Rudolph."

"He can make a healing drink if he has the right ingredients," a voice behind me said. I jumped and whirled to find Blitzen blinking at me.

"You're down here again!" I searched the area for the sleigh. When I didn't see it, I looked up again.

"In the spring, I'm going to have to re-shingle in a few places for you," Haden said, finally turning away from the barn.

"Where's the sleigh?"

"Over there," Blitzen said. Now that I knew where to look,

I could see its faint outline. It wasn't a pile of kindling. At least not completely. But, even from a distance, it was clear something was quite wrong with it.

"I was thinking you and I could bring it the rest of the way inside," Haden said carefully. "Blitzen has worked so hard."

"Yes, of course." I nodded, one eye on Haden. I turned to Blitzen. "Why didn't anyone say something about Hugo's healing mumbo-jumbo?"

"You didn't ask."

I threw my hands in the air. "How am I supposed to know about the magical world?"

"There are a lot of restrictions," Blitzen said in a bored tone. "Hugo is like Prancer. Rule-follower and boring."

"Well, Santa told him to make one, so we should be good in that regard." I was feeling a bit steamed that Hugo hadn't offered to heal Rudolph. I was certain it would have helped him rebuild his relationship with the herd. And it would have prevented a lot of other issues as well. Such as Santa's concussion and his broken sleigh.

"Do you have any magic that'll fix the sleigh?"

"Do I look like an elf?" Blitzen said in a tone that suggested I was crazy for even asking.

I huffed in frustration. "Can Hugo fix it? Or Santa? He had a moment of clarity a minute ago."

"Nope. Have more of that cooler juice?"

I rolled my eyes and headed back inside the barn with Haden.

On Santa's request, Snarky made us a list of the things he needed, his pencil whizzing across the page of his notebook. It appeared as though any rift between Hugo and Santa had been mended, and I took that as a hopeful sign that the rest of the North Pole problems would soon be resolved.

Moments later, the elf tore the list from the book and handed it to Haden.

Reading the paper around his very broad shoulder, I noticed that it was basically just a bunch of herbs and vitamins.

"And this will fix him up?" I asked, daring myself to place a possessive hand on Haden's hip and lean into his personal space to read the list a second time. His posture softened, welcoming the contact, and a warm fuzziness flowed through me. "Your magic potion?"

"It's not magic," Hugo snapped. It seemed as though his warm mood was reserved for North Pole citizens only.

Although, I guess I did lock him in the trunk for an hour or two...

"It'll help him heal faster?" I confirmed, trying again for a firm answer on what was what with this weird list of ingredients.

"It's anti-inflammatory." Snarky gave a shrug while tipping from side to side, as though mentally weighing out the other technical aspects of the drink he planned to make. I hoped there were no chances of it backfiring.

"And you're sure it's safe?" Haden confirmed, as if reading my mind.

"Yes!" Despite his certain tone, Hugo scratched his forehead with the end of his pencil, taking back the list to read it again. "It won't do any harm, even if it's off by a few ingredients."

"Um?" I gave Haden a panicked look.

He shrugged. "It's just a lot of botanicals."

Wait. *Botanicals.*

No.

"You know, vitamins and such," Haden added. "How is this a potion?"

"How did your x-ray help heal him?" Hugo replied.

"Good point." Haden turned to me. "Shall we?"

I was already shaking my head back and forth.

No.

Eagle Ridge was a small town. There was only one place where you could buy the 'botanicals' on this list.

And all the shops were closed.

That meant we had to call in favours. Big favours. From people I never wanted to speak to again.

No, no, and no.

Haden turned to me as I backed away, almost tripping on a square bale. "What's wrong? Where are you going?"

"Nope. Not me. We should wait for Mrs. Claus."

"TM, we need this."

"Nope." He couldn't sway me with that sweet nickname. I wasn't budging. "I am not going." I laid the tip of my index finger on the end of my cold nose, the childhood sign for 'not it'. He could call me all the cute names he could think of, but I was not changing my mind. Not for anything. Not even if he kissed me and asked me out to dinner.

Well, actually for that, I'd cave like a house of cards in a windstorm.

"What are you doing?" Haden asked, his lips quirked as I kept my finger on my nose.

Hugo, watching me with big eyes, slowly repeated my action. Then he turned to Haden to see what would happen next.

"Last person to put their finger on their nose is it," I explained. "That's Haden. So he has to do it."

Snarky snickered. Maybe I liked him after all.

"Do what?" Haden asked, his brow adorably scrunched in confusion.

"There's only one person in town that sells this stuff, and it's after midnight. That means we have to call in a favour."

Well, come to think of it, I didn't have Jannifer's number,

even if I'd wanted to have a chat with the woman Kade had originally left me for. And since I doubted Haden had her number, since she was a pet-free weirdo, I amended my earlier statement. "Probably two favours."

I knew someone who had Jannifer's number, and that someone was related to Haden. A someone I'd already kicked off my property once tonight.

Kade. The last person I wanted to talk to just hours after doing some steamy kissing with his older brother.

I was pretty sure that all added up to me getting a free pass when it came to this situation.

The elf was looking between Haden and me as though following a tennis ball at a Wimbledon match. "What? What?" he squeaked impatiently.

Haden's face lit up with what I could only describe as a slightly evil smile. "You're upset because we need Jannifer Eric."

Yeah, maybe I didn't like Haden so much after all.

CHAPTER 22

~ *Haden* ~

"I'd rather break in," Tamara told me as we waited outside Jannifer's herbal shop in downtown Eagle Ridge. We were in my idling truck, the heat blasting. She'd offered to drive, but the thrill of riding to town in the snowdrift she called her convertible wasn't my thing. Plus, she had a bit of a reputation for bumping into things. To be fair, after hearing about all the reindeer on the road story, I wasn't sure I would have fared any better than she had. In fact, since I tended to consider the speed limit a gentle suggestion, it likely would have been way worse.

When we got back to her farm later, I needed to remember to get all the snow out of the cab of her car in case a chinook melted it into her seats. Being this close to the Rockies, warm air came over the mountain ranges from the Pacific Ocean, and we got "snow eater" weather, as the Blackfoot called it. The temperature could go from minus twenty Celsius to twenty above in less than twenty-four hours. That much melted snow in such a short time would certainly wreak havoc on her heated seats' electrical system.

I also wanted to snag the mistletoe she kept hanging from her rearview mirror and put it to good use.

"We're not breaking in," I replied absently, swiping to delete all the useless notifications on my phone's lock screen, one after another. Fake emergencies. Invites to Christmas dinner. Stupid questions that could be answered by a tiny bit of common sense or a quick online search. Questions that had no real answer that were used to hook me into a lengthy conversation.

I didn't get a thrill out of ghosting my clients or sending them canned responses, but there were only so many hours in a day, and if you nibbled on the line of questions, soon you were fighting off an avalanche. It was something I hadn't learned nearly early enough in my career.

"I guess she'd know it was us if we broke down her door." Tamara turned up the radio where Celine Dion was singing *Happy Xmas (War is Over)* and pulled out her own phone, making me feel like I was being rude for checking my own.

"Sorry," I said. "Just scanning for any emergencies." There seemed to be more than usual tonight.

"You get a lot of messages," she noted, interrupting her own humming along to the song. On her side of the truck, the streetlight was decorated with holly and coloured Christmas lights, giving her a rainbow-like glow. It reminded me of the decorations the reindeer had been sporting earlier in the evening.

"Guess so."

She scrolled through her messages and smiled.

"What?" Did she have someone sending her sweet nothings? Sending her memes that tickled her funny bone? I didn't like the thought of that.

"My friends—my old roommates..." she said.

"Right. I met them when I helped you move."

"They never change. They're the best."

I shifted, looking at her, putting my phone away. It was past midnight, an ungodly time to be replying to business messages. "How so?"

She shrugged. "Samantha is freaking out about her boyfriend getting more serious than she is. Gabby has a major crush on her live-in friend and brings him up every chance she gets. Josie is AWOL, like a healthy human being taking a tech break. And Char's in the midst of an adventure."

Tamara put her phone back in her parka pocket, chewing lightly on her bottom lip, and trying to hide a smile, as if the gals had all been dishing juicy gossip. I couldn't help but wonder if some of it had been about me.

Tamara was staring at Jannifer's store, a slight scowl forming. "Do you think this will even work? How are vitamins supposed to fix Rudolph's sore hip?"

"I have no clue."

"And seriously," Tamara said with a disgusted shake of her head, pointing to the large store window. "That display does not say Christmas to me."

I followed her gaze to the front of Jannifer's Botanicals, amused by her annoyed attitude. "I like the garland."

Tamara snorted.

"Christmas lights woven around big containers of protein powder doesn't get you in the holiday mood?" I teased.

She gave a huff. Disgruntled Tamara was entirely the cutest of all the Tamaras I'd gotten to know over the years. It was like seeing an upset kitten. You wanted to take it seriously, but...it was cute. Really cute.

Angry Tamara was different though. She was fierce and absolutely nothing to laugh at. When she was angry, it made me angry, too. Partly because something had managed to bother her that much—which wasn't an easy feat—and partly because she deserved... I don't know. Everything good.

It brought out the steamroller, fist-making side of my

personality where I just wanted to right her world's wrongs for her.

I probably should have agreed to come here alone so she wouldn't have to face Jannifer—the woman who'd caused her first break-up with Kade.

Seriously, what was wrong with my brother? If you loved a woman, you never let her go for anything in the world. You cherished her, you protected her, you fixed the small pieces in her life so she could be unburdened and shine in the way the universe had intended her to.

Kade had clearly never truly loved Tamara in that deep, everlasting way that she so rightly deserved. So, maybe it was actually a stroke of luck for Tamara that Jannifer had caught Kade's wandering eye.

"This town never changes," Tamara mused, taking in our surroundings and pulling me from my thoughts.

I glanced up the street, trying to see what she did. Eagle Ridge was still going hard on its mid-century, small-town prairie vibe. It had been so fully embraced that even some of the new buildings had false fronts extending above the squat buildings.

"False fronts never go out of style," I stated.

"They make me think of a short woman wearing high heels."

I burst out laughing. I'd never see these buildings the same, and would surely smile every time I drove down the street.

Tamara scooted forward in her seat, craning her neck to see the roofs lining Main Street. "Is Lady MacBeth out having a smoke?"

I scanned the street and found the insurance agency, a few doors down from where Lady MacBeth lived in the apartment above the shop. During the day, if you were driving a pickup and were at the right angle, you could see the top of Lady

MacBeth's faded rooftop smoking couch lined up along the edge so she could watch the street below.

Rumour was she used to butcher geese to sell at the farmer's market. Someone had seen her walking around town with their blood on her hands, hence the nickname. Truthfully, I'd heard it was actually paint from helping make sets for a community comedy night, but the nickname had stuck, and I wasn't sure that anyone under the age of thirty knew her real name.

Tamara shivered. "Think she's watching us?"

I put the heat on max and continued to peer upward, on the lookout for the small red glow of her cigarette.

"Too cold tonight." I often saw her when I was running off to middle-of-the-night emergencies, since my clinic was within her range of view.

"Think she's coming?"

"Jannifer?" I asked. "Or Lady MacBeth?"

"Jannifer."

If she didn't, I'd go bang on her door until she did. Even though Tamara had won the finger-on-the-nose thing, Kade wouldn't pick up my call, so I'd left the next attempt to Tamara. It had taken a lot of cajoling and promises to get my brother to agree to call Jannifer. It had made me want to grab her phone and threaten Kade with bodily harm if he didn't help Tamara.

This woman was bringing out my protective side tonight, just like the time she'd foolishly swung out over the lagoon on a crappy, tattered old rope, belly-flopping the wind right out of her lungs. As soon as I heard the loud gunshot smack of her body hitting the water, I'd known it wasn't good. Kade had doubled over laughing at her spectacular entry, believing Tamara was hamming it up. I was already front crawling my way to Tamara before she'd even surfaced, praying she was still conscious.

She'd scared me that day, and that wasn't something I often

felt. Not even when I was cornered by an ornery bull. If it had been Kade in her shoes, tumbling toward the water, I'd have laughed on the shore until I lost my breath. But Tamara.... There was a tightness in my chest just thinking about all the ways things could have gone so very wrong that day.

As for Kade, he better darn well show up. The man owed her for humiliating her in the grocery store last summer. For bringing her home, and then breaking up with her. And before that, for breaking up with her in the first place for someone he clearly hadn't loved.

According to my calculations, Kade owed Tamara for pretty much the rest of his life.

I flexed my fingers on the steering wheel, trying to encourage my growing rage to ease off, while Tamara sagged deeper into her seat.

"I just want this done and over with so I can go to bed," she mumbled sleepily.

I reached across the space between us and laid my hand over hers. "Your hands are cold."

"From October to March. How are yours so warm?"

"Probably helps that I wasn't driving around in a convertible tonight."

"Yeah." Her eyes danced, and a weak smile wavered. It was clear she was loving tonight's adventures, despite the stress of it all. And who could blame her? It was pretty cool meeting these Christmas characters. Maybe tomorrow, we could meet up and take the time to let it all sink in.

I gestured to the store when she yawned again. "Do you want me to take over so you can get some sleep?"

"This isn't your mess."

"I'm used to late-night animal emergencies."

And while there wasn't anything more I could do for Rudolph, I was unfamiliar with healing a concussed Santa, and wasn't sure if my handyman skills would extend to fixing a flying sleigh, I'd try, for Tamara's sake.

Snowflakes gently floated down, melting on the truck's warm hood.

"Think she'll show?" Tamara asked, shifting so she was facing me better, her hand rolling under mine so we could clasp palm-to-palm.

"She'll show."

"What makes you so certain?"

"You need her help, and my brother will be there."

"I don't know. The vibes I've been getting off her since I returned home haven't exactly been friendly."

"She'll love that you need her."

"For a middle-of-the-night 'herbal emergency?' It's stupid."

"She likes Kade."

"And she thinks I'm a barrier to getting him back? Great. That puts her in the unstable, mean girl category." She shot me a wicked smile. "Think I could push Kade into her waiting arms?"

I really liked hearing that there were no hopeful 'what ifs' rolling around in her mind about another chance with Kade. In fact, I probably liked it too much.

Tamara sat forward, looking down the street for Jannifer's approaching vehicle. No sign. "We should break in."

Instinctively, I glanced upward, checking out the spot above the insurance agency for a glowing cigarette tip.

The streets were deserted, and it likely wouldn't be long until the town cut the power to the lit-up decorations lining the street to save a bit of money.

Tamara yawned again, her eyes watering.

"Quit yawning," I muttered through a huge yawn of my own. "You wouldn't even know how to break in."

"We could break the glass and just..." She let go of my hand

and flung her arms out like she was trying to hug a big oak tree. "Grab everything."

"You'd chicken out. You don't even speed."

"A speeding ticket doesn't seem worth it, in terms of cost-benefit analysis. You gain a few extra seconds in your day, and risk paying several hundred dollars for it? Plus, getting pulled over would eat up all those extra minutes you'd gained, anyway."

A knock on the truck's passenger side window made her jump, and I wondered how I'd missed Kade's truck rolling up. I put down the window, wishing he was on my side so Tamara wouldn't have to deal with the bitter wind whipping into the cab.

"Hop in," I told him, hitting the power locks button to release the doors.

"I'm fine," he said.

"Tamara's not. Hop in." I put her window up again.

Kade, grumbling under his breath, crawled into the back seat. He grabbed the sides of our front seats and scooted himself forward so he was practically between us. "So, the surprise is for me, right?"

"What fresh, new insanity are you talking about?" Tamara snapped, not even turning to look at him.

Yeah, she definitely didn't want a second chance, unless it was to bury him up to his chin in the sand, sprinkle his hair with bird seed and let the magpies and crows go at him.

I think I'd want to help her, if it ever came to that. Because seriously? How did I end up with such a self-centred brother? Did he really believe this late-night shopping trip was related to the fake Christmas surprise in Tamara's barn? And that it was all for him? It made me feel guilty that our parents passed along all the brains in the family to me before he showed up.

"I mean, you know I think vitamins are the bomb." He

gestured to Jannifer's store. "And here we are, even though you believe they're an overpriced farce."

"I don't think they're a farce. I just think—"

"And tonight you need vitamins for an *emergency*." He sat back, pleased with the belief he'd figured us out. "So, it must be a surprise for me."

Tamara scrubbed her forehead, as if her knitted toque was itchy.

I glanced at Kade in the rearview mirror. Would he be able to tell that Tamara and I had kissed tonight? I felt a slow smile, curious how he'd react when he found out. It almost made me want to tell him. Almost.

I valued Tamara too much to subject her to his possible temper tantrum, though, because that kiss...

I wanted more. A lot more.

It had been like touching a live wire of bright white energy.

I'd felt something. Something I hadn't felt in a very long time.

CHAPTER 23

~ *Tamara* ~

I didn't know what Haden was thinking—as usual—but he was sporting a slightly evil grin. He shot me an in-cahoots look so tender and filled with affection that, even though I didn't know what he had in mind; I knew I was game. This man was quickly becoming my ride-or-die, and I couldn't help but wonder what something deep, meaningful and long-term between us might look like. Because although we'd only kissed a couple of times tonight, I felt incredibly close to him, as if this was a step we'd always been meant to take.

Haden was quiet, but protective. Understanding, but also willing to prod me along when I got worried and started to seize up. And most of all, he wouldn't let me deal with a crisis alone.

A true ride-or-die. And, to boot, his kisses were heavenly, and his woodsy scent was something I wanted to bottle and sneak sniffs of until the end of time.

I caught myself leaning in, angling for a kiss, flinching when Kade spoke. How had I forgotten he was in the back seat? Then again, I realized that when Haden was around, he had a subtle way of eclipsing everyone, my focus narrowing in on him like some sort of homing beacon programmed deep inside my

222

DNA. No wonder Kade got so loud and demanding around him. And no wonder he'd tried to push us apart with a few strategic lies. Haden was the man I was meant to be with.

"Sure is cold." Kade rubbed his bare hands together.

"Get some gloves," Haden said mildly, a sting of irritation in his tone.

"Dude," Kade said, arms out. "Seriously? It's the season for being nice, and all that crap."

"It's called a blizzard. Dress for it."

"Thanks, *Mom*."

Jannifer pulled up before the brothers could escalate their bickering to fratricide. Eager to escape, I braced myself before opening my door to the full arctic blast called the great outdoors. Some Canadians loved to go out in the cold, and found it invigorating and bracing, but personally, give me a thick blanket, a cup of coffee, and a book or horse magazine any day of the year.

"Ready to pay way too much for a bunch of ground up plants in capsule form so we can save Christmas?" I muttered, dropping my feet onto the snow-covered street. A wintery blast hit me and, despite my layers, I shivered. The temptation to give into Estelle's urging, and make a wish to be warm was like a tauntingly sweet devil on my shoulder.

Haden came around to my side of the truck, letting his shoulder brush mine. "Next year, let's take a page out of Char's book and go to Mexico for Christmas."

Unable to help myself, I smiled, filled with hope that something like that might actually happen. I knew it was just a passing comment, but the idea that Haden could be thinking about there being an 'us' in twelve months—a strong, travel together on couples' trips, kind of strong... Well, it did funny things to my heart and mind.

"I'm in," I replied with a grin.

Haden and I hung back while Kade chatted up Jannifer, where she was standing by her store's front door, jingling her keys like she was searching for the right one. She was watching us all, no doubt trying to figure out what was really going on.

She wasn't wearing any makeup, and her calf-length parka revealed the cuffs of her pyjama pants. Wordlessly, she unlocked the store, made her way through the dark room like an expert, flicking on lights, then turning off the store's alarm.

Seriously? Was she afraid of break-ins? Who'd bust their way in for a bunch of supplements? Broke bodybuilders? Besides, nobody used cash anymore, so it wasn't as if money was left on the premises each night. Honestly, it was probably a difficult time in history to be a regular thief. Especially with Lady MacBeth smoking on the rooftop a few buildings down.

Kade stopped just inside the door and looked around as the lights came on, catching my eye and then performing a fake cringing jump away from me when he realized he was beside a rack of organic vegetable chips. With wide eyes, he took a giant step away from them, staring at me in manufactured fear. Haden glared at him, inserting himself between us.

"How are you feeling, Tamara?" Kade asked in a tremulous voice, peeking around his brother's wide shoulders. "Not mad for any reason, are you?"

"Want me to kill him for you? I promise to dig the hole deep enough nobody ever finds him," Haden muttered.

I shook my head, feeling steamed. Seriously. You throw a couple of bags of chips at a guy, and he never lets it go. Okay, so I sorta whipped them at him while yelling insults at the top of my lungs. Not my finest moment.

"Too bad we didn't break up in the canned good aisle," I muttered to Kade.

Haden choked on a laugh.

Kade, cheeks pink, crossed his arms and glowered at us. "I don't like it when the two of you hang out."

"Too bad," Haden growled. "We've decided we're besties."

"Best friends for life," I chirped, shaking off a mitt so I could lift a crooked pinkie finger in the air, hooking it on Haden's like some sort of secret handshake.

"You guys are really annoying when you're together," Kade complained, but I could see the corner of his mouth quirk upward, the start of an unwanted smile.

"We try," Haden said lightly.

I went to drop Haden's finger, knowing we were pushing on Kade again. But Haden gently twisted his grip, catching my hand in his so he could pull me to him. I felt my eyes widen, and my mouth fall open. Was he going to drop me into a backward dip and kiss me right here in front of everyone? But instead, he lifted his arm, spinning me in a tight circle, then out, before back into his arms. I felt like a dancer on stage, graceful despite my clunky winter boots.

With a small smile, even more special than an in-cahoots one, he said tenderly, "'Curiosity keeps leading us down new paths'."

"Liking the Walt Disney quote," Jannifer said.

"Lame-o nerd," Kade grumbled. "Tamara doesn't like showoffs, you know."

Haden still had his gaze locked on mine. He gave my hand a squeeze before releasing it while saying, "Curiosity is *never* a bother."

I held in a sigh. Haden thought I was special, and was telling me I'd never been a bother, unlike his brother's claim. This, right here, was the most romantic thing I'd ever experienced.

The room was silent for a moment, nobody quite knowing what to say. Haden had made a declaration. To me, it was one of love and affection, but what the others saw, I wasn't sure. All I knew was that Kade would likely get down-right upset if he figured out that his brother and I had romantic feelings toward each other. It wasn't his business, and he'd learn about us soon enough. But right now, I wanted to savour being with Haden and the tender bloom of affection between us without a dark cloud marching in and putting a damper on it all.

I hurried over to Jannifer, clearing my throat.

"Thanks for doing this, Jann." She gave me a severe look, and I quickly added "—ifer. Jannifer." I cleared my throat. "I—we—really appreciate it."

She grunted frostily, her eyes darting to the brothers who were waiting near the door. They both had their arms crossed, and were glowering at each other.

"What do you need?" Jannifer asked. I held up the list from Hugo. She gave me a strange look, then grabbed a small basket. "When did you take up alternative medicine?"

"Um. Just...I. Um."

Still casting me a suspicious look, she began walking down her aisles, flipping bottles of pills into a growing collection as she went. It didn't even seem as though she was paying any attention to what she was doing. Either she knew her store like the back of her hand, or I was learning the truth about herbal supplements—it didn't matter what the label said, as long as you believed it was going to help you, it would.

"Uh. It's actually for a friend."

Her gaze was cold. "You don't believe in alternative medicine?"

"I—it's for a friend," I repeated.

"They're not well?" She was eyeing the list with a practiced eye, and I felt a stirring of doubt. Her eyes met mine. They were cold, hard, and totally unimpressed with me.

"They're not well," I repeated slowly. Maybe we weren't

being as clandestine as I'd assumed. Maybe she could look at the listed ingredients and figure out exactly what we were up to.

But there was no way she could guess that it was for a reindeer.

Right?

"Are you part of this?" she asked casually, as she passed Kade on her way to the shelf along the far wall. Her tone was much friendlier with him, and about nine hundred degrees warmer.

"It's a surprise," he said, dropping his arms and grinning.

"A surprise?" She was drinking him in, her body leaning toward his.

He leaned an elbow on a nearby shelf. "For Christmas."

"Really? That's interesting. What kind of surprise?" She'd completely forgotten her task of filling the basket and had sidled up beside Kade. She was pretty when she wasn't scowling. She had great hair—the kind that always had that slightly voluminous tousled look—and what I think you'd call Cupid's bow lips. I bet she could do a sexy pout without appearing farcical.

"I'm not sure." Kade shifted, looking my way.

Oh, boy. We did not want anyone asking for details about this.

"Is that everything?" I asked Jannifer, peering into her basket.

She shot me a dirty scowl.

Honestly, we didn't have time for her to flirt around the bush—or in this case, an oblivious Kade. We had a major holiday to save.

"Kade, weren't you asking me earlier if I knew what Jannifer was doing for Christmas Eve?"

He shot me a scrunched-face look of confusion, and I didn't dare glance at Haden. I was close enough I could smell his wonderful earthy cologne, that hint of pine and manhood that was so him, and feared one look and he would distract me from my mission. I could practically see him shaking his head at me for meddling where I shouldn't.

Some wingman he was.

But we had a timeline to adhere to. Jannifer liked Kade, Kade was single. Two birds. One stone. We had to get to it and get out of here.

"Are you free tomorrow?" I asked Jannifer.

"Why? Do you want to throw a bag of chips at me?" She tipped her head to the side. "Because, if so, I'm busy."

I gulped air, trying to find words that wouldn't express my sudden rage. Beside me, Kade let out a burst of laughter. He didn't even try to squelch it, out of politeness.

"I think you two should meet up for coffee," I said between gritted teeth. I turned to Kade. "Does that work for you?" He was struggling to breathe through his laughter. "Great. Pick her up at, say, three?"

Nowhere in town would be open for them to go have coffee on Christmas Eve. Everything would be closed for days. But that really wasn't my problem.

Jannifer was staring at me.

"What? It's the least he can do after dragging you out of bed." I tried to take the basket from Jannifer, but she tugged it tight to her body. However, she was now eyeing me in a way that suggested that maybe she wouldn't be slicing my tires anytime soon.

What a win.

"I'll throw in a bottle of Vitamin C, because this time of year, with all of these family gatherings, there are so many germs. Keeps your immunity up." She went to the shelf, and knocked a couple more plastic bottles into the basket, then re-consulted the list before moving to the cash register. She fired it up and put all of the bottles on the counter in a tidy row.

"Um. Thanks." I smoothed the tape over one of the posters tacked to the front of her checkout counter.

"You're different, you know." She was peering at me like I might be a doppelgänger, and not the real Tamara Madden she'd grown up with.

I inhaled deeply, summoning patience. If one more person told me I'd changed...

"In a good way. You're more you."

"I agree," Haden said, his fresh outdoorsy scent enveloping me as he joined us at the counter. He had a soft smile, one that made me feel squishy inside, and I wasn't sure where to look, how to act. He liked the way I'd changed? It felt like my face was turning red, and my arms were suddenly too long for my body.

It was going to take me a few days to get used to the way we were revealing our true feelings to each other. I had years of habits to undo, such as making sure I didn't look at him too long, or didn't allow myself to notice just how amazing his shoulders were or how kissable his lips were. Or acknowledging how sweet and kind and patient he was, and how lucky his animal patients were. Or indulging in those fantasies where we somehow ended up in the woods together, and I was injured and he had to use his veterinarian medical skills to take care of me...

Oh, wow. Who was I kidding? I'd been crushing on this man for eons, and had used a very heavy dose of denial to make myself believe otherwise.

"You hanging out with your Oma tomorrow?" Kade asked me, leaning against the counter and knocking over a stand of pamphlets.

Ugh. Seriously, I'd just set him up with Jannifer. How many bags of chips did a woman have to throw at this guy before he understood she was done? Chat up Jannifer! Not me.

Haden angled himself between Kade and me, waving his

credit card in Jannifer's direction. "Sorry, still have lots to do tonight."

"Yes, lots," I agreed. "Is that everything?" I asked Jannifer, hoping to speed up our exit before the truth came out about what we were up to. I could just imagine. These two would have us shipped off for a full psychiatric workup.

But what were we going to do when there was no Christmas surprise for Kade? Maybe we could tell him it all went wrong, and we'd had to throw it out?

"Everything on the list?" I confirmed when Jannifer continued to ignore me, running her handheld scanner over the barcodes on each bottle.

"All of it?" I repeated.

She shot me a dark look, not appearing nearly as pretty as she had earlier.

"Great, okay," I chirped. "Thanks."

Dang, but she was well-stocked for reindeer emergencies. I had to admire that.

"Need a bag?" she asked coolly. "They're fifteen cents each."

I opened my mouth to argue. I could see our grand tally stretching into the hundreds of dollars, and she couldn't even throw in a cheap paper bag that had probably cost her a fraction of a cent?

Where had my friendly, I'm throwing-in-Vitamin-C Jannifer gone? Because if she forgot, and charged me for those extra vitamins as well as a bag, this woman and I were going to have words.

Haden, his wallet already open, smoothly crowded me out of the way, no doubt noting the way Jannifer and I were digging in, as we had so many times over the years when I'd been dating Kade. We'd never come to blows, but we'd come close. And drinks had maybe 'accidentally' been spilled on each other a time or two. Or three. Okay, four. But it was mostly her doing the spilling, and me having to go out and buy new shirts.

"However many bags you think we need, Jannifer," he said evenly.

"I should pay." I patted my parka pockets, horrified to realize I hadn't even thought to grab my wallet before jumping into Haden's truck.

"I got it."

"But it's—"

Jannifer snatched Haden's credit card and shoved it into her machine instead of letting him do it himself. "So your emergency is a surprise, or is your surprise an emergency?" She caught my uncomfortable expression and smirked. "Run someone over with your car?"

Kade coughed, holding up a hand to barely cover his smile.

"Yeah," I said lightly, giving Kade a glare, daring him to pick on me and my driving. "Something like that. And I'm still in the mood to hit something else."

HALF AN HOUR LATER, with Haden still chuckling over my parting remark to his brother, we had the bottles of vitamins, herbs, botanicals, and supplements (or whatever they all were) safely in Snarky's tiny hands. While the elf worked, Haden and I sat at my kitchen table near the window overlooking the darkened backyard, eating my Christmas baking and sipping freshly brewed coffee. I'd tried to locate the abandoned thermos and cups from earlier, when I'd dropped them in the snow during the sleigh crash, but couldn't find them.

It was a bit past one in the morning, and there still weren't any signs of Mrs. Claus and the reindeer, which I found concerning.

Santa, however, was at least becoming a bit more coherent, and conversations with him were leading to fewer repeating loops. A part of me was holding out hope that everything would somehow resolve itself before dawn, and without needing Mrs. Claus and the rest of the reindeer crew to intervene.

I winced as Hugo, standing on a chair to make himself tall enough for my kitchen counter, tore apart more capsules, sending powder flying everywhere. To say he was a neat and tidy chemist would be a lie. I was going to have quite the mess to clean up later. But if it got Rudolph back on his feet, it would be well worth it.

"Oh, I wasn't thinking," I said to Haden, shutting my eyes at my error. "You switch to tea in the afternoons. I should make you a cup of tea instead."

I went to stand, but he said, "Actually, I think this is a job for coffee." He took a sip of his brew as though proving my lack of thoughtfulness was just fine. "I've always wondered if you like tea. You make this funny face whenever you drink it."

"I don't really care for it."

"But you drink it?"

"To be polite."

"Hm."

Yeah, another instance where I was that polite pushover again, eager to please and trying to preserve other people's feelings at the expense of my own desires. Drinking something I thought was gross. Why did I do that? And why was it such a hard habit to break?

Then again, I'd made what I wanted tonight—coffee—and not what Haden preferred. So maybe I was breaking habits? Or maybe, I was simply too tired to properly access my memory banks.

"Tell me the truth," Haden asked with a slightly wicked grin. "What do you really and truly think of tea?"

I huffed a laugh over the rim of my cup.

"Come on. Don't be chicken. Lay it all out there."

Feeling strangely nervous, I blurted out, "It's like licking someone's garden."

He laughed, light, warm, and free.

"This is where you tell me I just haven't tried the right kind of tea," I said helpfully.

"Never." He reached out, tapping my hand, then resting his over mine. Warm and wonderful. "Just be you, TM."

"Okay," I said softly, feeling more than a little tickled at the way he always wanted the unvarnished truth from me. It was liberating, and scary as heck.

Hugo exclaimed, "Thundering *reindeer* hoof beats! Where's that—*there* it is."

Haden and I shared amused looks over the rims of our coffee cups.

"I was thinking..." Haden said carefully and slowly, like he was broaching a topic that was sensitive, yet possibly exciting.

My heart lifted. Was he going to talk about us, tell me what he wanted from a relationship? Would it be the same thing I wanted?

"I have an idea if we can't get Rudolph back on his feet," Haden said in a low tone, so Hugo wouldn't be able to overhear.

"Oh. Right." I nodded seriously, feeling sheepish that Haden was creating contingency plans while I was daydreaming about him as my boyfriend, worrying over the elf's mess, and fantasizing about slipping off my bra and curling up under a thick blanket. Such bliss. I could almost feel the relief just thinking about it.

Maybe I was more tired than I'd thought.

"I've an idea about how we might help the remaining reindeer do tomorrow night's job without their leader." He checked his watch and feebly corrected himself with a gentle clearing of his throat. "Tonight's job. I could beg my cousin Justin to open up his hardware store, and we could buy out his night vision goggles. Fit them to the reindeer, and voila. They can see."

"Tech is always the answer," I said with another yawn, quite in love with his idea. I blinked away my fatigue, taking another sip of coffee, forcing myself to focus on Haden and his plan. It could work.

A large bang made me jump, and I sloshed coffee onto the tabletop. Lacking a pestle and mortar, Hugo slammed my hammer down on a pill to crush it. Judging from the sound of the banging, I was going to lose my damage deposit when the landlord saw the countertops.

I glanced over as Hugo raised the hammer again. "At least use a cutting board under the pills, please."

"I've got this," Haden said, swiftly getting to his feet and moving into the kitchen to stand beside the elf.

With commanding gentleness, Haden helped guide the elf into working in a way that didn't destroy my kitchen.

Haden came back to the table, and I slid the plate of gingerbread men his way.

"Thanks." He grabbed one, biting off its head.

"How's it look for getting my damage deposit back when I eventually buy my own farm?"

He tipped his head to the side in thought. "Not great, but there's still a chance if you strategically place some fruit bowls during move out—no, that won't work. All is lost. Sorry."

I giggled, despite my annoyance at the likelihood of losing my deposit. Especially if Carl saw the barn's battered shingles, thanks to Blitzen and the sleigh.

Although, maybe Haden would come and fix my shingles on a nice, warm spring day. He would wear his toolbelt and jeans slung low on his hips, his white T-shirt stretching over his pecs and biceps. I'd bring him lemonade, and we'd kiss under the crabapple trees as petals from its fragrant flowers drifted down around us...

I cleared my throat and blinked away the images of him working on the barn, realizing I'd been gazing at his chest, almost drooling.

I pulled at my horse-themed Christmas sweatshirt, my earlier chill suddenly long gone.

Haden, looking at my shirt, asked, "You still want to own your own farm?"

I nodded, nibbling on the feet of my gingerbread man cookie. "A hobby farm, so just a couple of acres. Some horses, goats, chickens. Kind of like what I've got here. But I want to own it, so I don't have to worry about my landlord potentially not wanting to renew my lease."

"That's what I imagined I'd be doing when I bought my acreage. Creating a small hobby farm."

"Really?" There was no way he had the same little dream. The idea that we wanted the same things made my stomach feel undeniably fizzy.

"Yeah," he said, leaning back in his chair, arms stretched overhead as he yawned. "But my work's too unreliable to have the number of animals I want."

"You can't afford it?" I asked, surprised. I'd assumed he was raking in the money based on his fees. If I could afford to start my own little hobby farm, then surely he could.

Then again, I drove an old beater of a car, and maybe he'd put all his money into his fancy veterinarian truck with its mobile medical unit thingy. As well as being a sexy landowner.

And then there was also his veterinarian practice, which he'd bought off a retiring veterinarian. Haden had a lot of debt, for sure.

Not to forget all those years of university.

In some ways, Haden had inspired me. I'd never wanted to go to college, but I also hadn't known what I wanted with my life other than a few inklings. Seeing him out there, away from home, bettering himself, but still having ties to his community had intrigued me. Then when Char had moved to the city, and gotten excited about it, I'd caved. Seeing Haden and Char thrive had given me the courage to try attaining my own dream for myself.

Because who was I? What did I want?

I felt like I knew the answers now, but back then, I hadn't yet learned to listen to myself. Or, for that fact, ask myself the right questions.

It turned out that living in the city had been a bit like dating Kade twice. Worth trying, so I'd know if it was something I truly wanted...but in the end, it wasn't for me.

With Kade, I'd known what I wanted—love—and the second time around had confirmed that he couldn't give me what I needed. But I'd had to try. With a stitch of nostalgia for home, and a belief that we'd both matured enough to make a relationship work, I'd come home to give us that second chance.

When I'd moved to Calgary, I knew something was missing in my life, but I hadn't figured out what. Living with the GAL PALs away from home, I'd learned how to listen to myself. I'd discovered that I truly did belong in the country. I was okay being introverted. I wanted a horse of my own, and I craved love and a steadfast sense of belonging in a relationship. I'm not sure I would have figured that out if I hadn't moved to the city. It likely would have just remained fuzzy little moments of unfocused wanting.

"Getting chores done in a timely manner is also difficult with my schedule," Haden clarified. "Animals deserve better." He looked around the room. "Speaking of animals, where is this fabled gopher I often see on social media?"

"Probably sleeping under my bed." I was glad I'd taken in Felipe when I'd moved home. And he seemed to love it here. Strangely enough, the critter and my cat got along fine, their positions in the food chain seemingly irrelevant. "Want me to go get him?"

"Nah." Haden gave me a slow, warm smile. "Another time."

I liked the idea of him being a regular guest at my place.

"Where's the turmeric?" Hugo squeaked. A moment later, orange powder surrounded him in a cloud, making him sneeze. It was a cute, small and innocent sound, so unlike the attitude the elf was so skilled at dishing out.

Haden and I shared a silent giggle, necks tucked into our collarbones so we wouldn't get noticed by the grumpy elf.

"For some reason," I said to Haden, once we'd recovered, "I thought you didn't want animals. Not that I ever really thought about it. I guess I just assumed that because you take care of them all day long, when you get home, you want to do something else."

"I'd love to have a hobby farm," he said, acting almost embarrassed. But I could see the hint of a smile, the sparkle in his eyes as he said wistfully, "Collecting my own eggs. Maybe even making my own goat cheese."

"Then, I suppose in order to satisfy that dream, you'll just have to take me in along with my animals—just the cat and gopher so far, sadly. Dolly has to stay here. But we could make that hobby farm, and you'd have someone to take care of everything when you couldn't."

Man, that dream felt vivid, full of colour, hope and happiness.

Realizing I'd basically leapt from us kissing a few times to suggesting I move in with him, I dipped my head, blushing.

"My door is always open," he said calmly. So calmly, it made me look at him twice. It almost felt as though he was serious about that semi-invitation.

"I can't move in with you," I protested, feeling slightly panicky at the idea that he might actually be serious. That Haden and I might move way too fast on something very deep, intimate and real.

"Why not?"

He seemed so serious. Weren't there steps between where we were and moving in together?

I started babbling. "Your family won't survive the whiplash. Plus, about eight million single women in the county would make voodoo dolls of me, and I'd be dead within a week."

He chuckled. "You're obsessed."

"Am not."

He grabbed my hand, smiling warmly. "Are you jealous?"

"Of the HAGs?" I scoffed. "No."

"HAGs?"

"Haden Appreciation Group. Women with fake animal emergencies, vying for your undivided attention."

"HAGs," he repeated, this time with amusement, his thumb tracing very distracting circles over the back of my hand. "How long have you been secretly crushing on me, TM?"

"I'm not. I haven't." I sucked in a breath. Haden was my safe space. I could tell him anything. And if I couldn't, it was best to know now. Not later. Not after my heart was deeply invested.

I sighed and rolled my eyes at him. "Do you really want to know?"

He'd edged his chair closer to mine, his five o'clock shadow giving his look a slightly rugged and dangerous edge.

"Since the first day of grade one."

"What?" He looked confused.

"When I fell and scraped my knee."

He turned his head, eyes still on me. "I think I vaguely remember that."

"I fell and started to cry. You came and dried my tears, retied my shoe, and found a teacher to bandage me up."

"I did that?"

"Yes."

His smile spread like liquid warmth. "And you started crushing on me then?"

"I never really stopped. Well..." I waved a hand through the air. "Maybe for a bit."

His eyes shuttered, and he leaned away ever so slightly. "Kade."

"He made me think you found me—"

"A pest. You weren't."

"I know that now."

We were silent for a moment. It wasn't quite awkward, but there was a tentative vulnerability in the air we were both afraid to disrupt.

"Know what he told me?" Haden asked.

"What?"

"He said I was an annoying mansplainer."

I laughed, surprised. "Furthest thing from it. You taught me a lot."

Haden moved his chair again, pressing his knee into my thigh. He stroked the side of my cheek and I leaned into him. "You were a very curious young woman. Still are." Those shadows that kept me from understanding him had dissipated, and for the first time, I felt like I could read Haden. Really read him.

"How long have you liked me?" I whispered, my heart thundering in my ears as I waited for his reply.

"I don't know. I think for quite a while. It wasn't appropriate to have those sorts of feelings when you were younger, and then when you were dating my brother." He was looking at me, his gaze prolonged, and not shy like mine. "I found you interesting and fun. I liked hanging out with you. And then somewhere, that turned into an attraction that I definitely denied. It's been a while." He grew quiet, his attention dropping to our intertwined hands. "The first time I realized I was attracted to you was the day we were shoeing my dad's Clydesdale."

"That's when Kade said all that stuff."

"He must have seen how I felt."

"And me." Shyly, I ducked my head and cleared my throat from the shame I felt for feeling things for Haden while dating his brother. "I was crushing pretty hard that day, too." It had felt wrong, but it had also felt more like an unattainable fantasy than a viable crush. Sort of like the kind of feelings you might have for a celebrity you'll never actually meet. But those feelings had made it easy for Kade to separate me and Haden.

"I don't think I ever moved on," Haden admitted.

My head popped up, my curiosity taking over. "Sorry? What?"

He shook his head, mind elsewhere.

"What? No. Tell me."

"I think maybe you're the reason I don't really date."

His eyes met mine and I could see the truth of his words in the bottomless depths of his blue eyes, right down to his soul.

"*Me?*"

"Nobody's ever been as fun, sweet or curious. They all fall terribly short, and I can see it after just one date."

Oh, my word. It was me. I was the reason he seemed like a womanizer, moving from woman to woman without ever settling into a relationship.

Haden's lips grazed my cheek, his words a whisper. "Some people are hard to get over."

CHAPTER 24

~ *Estelle* ~

Gram-Gram was pacing her office.

"Is Tamara actively trying to ruin the holiday?" she complained.

"She's trying to help," I said meekly. The head fairy had not been pleased when I told her about my earlier failed visit to Char. She was even less pleased now that I was unmistakably in a make-a-wish standoff with two of my clients and losing.

"Permission to explain her situation more fully to her, please. Tamara doesn't know about magical world extraction, and how much she needs it."

"Permission *not* granted."

"Ma'am, with all due respect—"

"Don't start."

"—the severity of this situation—"

"Rules, Estelle," she said coldly.

"But this is unprecedented, and there are severe conse-quences for both worlds if we continue to allow this to unravel."

The head fairy had lowered her elbows to her desk and had propped her temples between her fingertips. She was rubbing slow circles like she had a headache. "There are consequences to everything we do. Christmas isn't our domain, and with our clients refusing to make wishes, it means our hands are quite tied."

We were quiet for a moment, and I took a second to mentally check in on Tamara, to tune into her frequency. I sucked in a slow breath, gathering a quick picture of the current state of affairs. A lot had happened over the past several hours.

"Santa's hurt."

"What!" Gram-Gram crept closer, as though I was a crystal ball she could look into. "When did that happen? Haven't you been checking in on her?"

"Yes! I mean, not all the time. I'm trying to respect her privacy. Maybe it happened when I was in Mexico. It looks like the reindeer went and got him so he could come help Rudy, and they crashed." I added in a small voice, "Still drunk."

The room felt frozen for a moment. Then the head fairy's voice turned to ice as she spat out, "*They did what?*"

"I know. Please, can't we just—"

"Where is Mrs. Claus?" Gram-Gram was near frantic. "Can you see her?"

"No." I'd only be able to see her if she was with one of my clients. It was a stopgap to prevent fairies from spying on other beings with our fairy vision.

"She's not there." My voice trembled, and I sucked in a steadying breath. "But it seems as though they've summoned her, ma'am."

And that was the first time I ever heard the head fairy curse.

She began shoving me toward the door, across the pink bullpen where the trainee cubicles were laid out in a grid. Then over to Paxi's office again, her hands insistent bites at my back as she urged me forward with a "Go, go, go!"

CHAPTER 25

~ *Tamara* ~

Hugo fed Rudolph the bowl of goopy, brown disgustingness that had set Haden back around three hundred dollars, and made Jannifer that much richer. For the sake of Christmas, I hoped the elf's home-made concoction worked. I also hoped that Blitzen didn't spill it, as he'd convinced himself Rudolph was getting a 'wobbly pop,' which was what he called my cooler of yukaflux. He kept trying to stick his head in Rudolph's bowl, their antlers knocking each other about, the liquid sloshing precariously close to the rim.

"Boys!" I scolded, giving Rudolph the opportunity to successfully lick up the last bit of the elf's potion.

I froze, swearing I'd heard sleigh bells.

"Is that Mrs. Claus?" I asked.

I heard the bells again. Unable to contain my excitement, even though I knew she was supposedly some sort of angry black witch, I grabbed Haden's hand.

"Mrs. Claus is here! She's here!" I dragged him toward the barn doors, not pausing to grab our coats first.

Outside, a woman in a svelte red outfit, with white fur

trim, was standing, feet wide apart, arms crossed as she glowered at the smashed sleigh parked beside the barn. Snow swirled around her under the yard light. Her white hair was done in stylish short spikes, emphasizing her striking, high cheekbones.

"I hear my husband has run into trouble," she said in a low, cold tone as I came to a halt just outside the barn doors. Haden bumped into me from behind, his right arm circling my middle as he clutched me against him to prevent us from tumbling to the ground.

Mrs. Claus, in all of her very tall glory, marched toward us. There didn't seem to be a speck of her that resembled the image I was expecting to see. She was slim, younger than Santa, and scary. She pointed a gloved finger in my face like it was a magic wand.

"You? You're the one who started all of this?"

I nodded mutely, my eyes crossing as I focused on her fingertip, worried it might start glowing with pent-up black magic.

She pointed to Haden, who was still behind me, arms slung around my middle. "And you can both see and hear everything that's going on?"

I felt him nod, his warm exhale creating a cloud in the frigid night air.

Mrs. Claus's lips pursed and her eyes narrowed. "We'll deal with that later."

I swallowed hard and shared a look with Haden.

Behind Mrs. Claus, the reindeer were hitched to a rather plain, red sleigh. They pawed the ground and looked at their hooves, avoiding eye contact. Obviously, they had no plans to do anything other than stay clear of Mrs. Claus's radar.

"Santa's in the barn," I whispered, unable to find my voice. I shivered in the freezing late-night temps and Haden tightened his hold. My Christmas sweatshirt was cozy, but no match for the weather.

Haden shuffled us away from the doorway.

"We'll get out of your way," he said diplomatically. "As I'm sure the reindeer have brought you up to speed on the...issues we're facing."

"They most certainly have." She gave me a glare, as if I'd intentionally mowed down Rudolph, then flouted all of the rules of her queendom.

I shared a quick look with Haden as Mrs. Claus continued to stare us down.

Maybe I should have made a wish to Estelle and suffered the possible financial woes as a result, because this woman was terrifying. For the first time tonight, I felt the full gravity of what the reindeer and elf had tried to warn me about.

This could be the kind of trouble that was impossible to escape, even with a hefty dose of logic, and a sound argument couched with good intentions.

Haden, who'd released me, was in a bow like he was greeting royalty. He gestured to the open door beside us. "Your...highness?"

"Oh, enough grovelling." Mrs. Claus pushed past us with an unimpressed huff, muttering something that sounded a lot like "men" as she entered the barn. But I noticed the flicker of pleasure in a tiny smile as she passed Haden.

Soon, the woman's loud, scolding voice echoed through the structure. She barely paused for breath while scrambling ensued. I'd laugh if she wasn't so terrifying.

Why did the world believe Santa's wife was a sweet, rotund, cookie-bearing woman? I suppose nobody got the warm and fuzzies from a tough woman whose personality leaned closer to Snarky's. Too bad I couldn't exactly lock her in my trunk when I grew tired of her.

And seriously? Her and Santa? Talk about opposites attract. She was the grumpy to his sunshine. And the black magic to his white. No wonder they were having relationship issues.

Haden and I, hunched as deep into our shirts as we could go to battle off the cold wind, approached the reindeer hitched to the old sleigh.

"What took so long?" I asked them.

The reindeer huffed, but didn't reply. Had they been forbidden from talking to me?

"It's a lot smaller," Haden said, running a hand over the sleigh, "but at least, it's not smashed, and still flies. Looks pretty good."

A small face peeked up over the sleigh's side and I startled. It was a trembling female elf in a green and red stripped hat.

"Is she gone?" she asked in a tiny voice.

"Mrs. Claus is in the barn," I said gently. "I'm Tamara. This is Haden."

The elf's eyes grew very large, and she shrunk down again, disappearing back into the sleigh.

I exchanged a glance with Haden and asked the reindeer, "Should we unhook you?"

They shook their heads furiously.

"So, then, what can we do to help?"

Nobody replied.

"She seems pretty upset," I offered, gesturing to the barn.

"Very," one of the reindeer muttered.

"I thought she was going to shoot us."

"There's still time," Donner mumbled.

"I wouldn't look good above the fireplace," Cupid replied.

"Never seen her like this before."

"Not even when Dasher ran the training sleigh through her garden."

"But at least she came." My remark was met with silence,

and my hope that all would be neatly wrapped up and taken care of wobbled and waned.

Haden, who was breathing into his cupped hands to keep them warm, shoulders hunched up near his ears against the cold, said, "Not to be a chicken or to shirk responsibility, but I think maybe we'd better make ourselves scarce. I have a feeling things are going to get scary."

CHAPTER 26

~ Haden ~

"I'm not leaving." Tamara gave me a big, brown-eyed look, pleading with me.

"I'm not leaving, either, but I think we need to lie low."

"But I—"

I shushed her with a kiss before she could argue, wrapping her in my arms to keep her warm against the pervasive cold.

"The animals are spooked," I said. "Trust their instincts."

"I am, but we also need to help. *I* need to help."

"Well, whatever we do, we need to do it while staying out of the way. That woman looks ready to zap someone."

Tamara shivered in my arms, but this time I knew it wasn't from the cold.

Mrs. Claus stormed back out of the barn, Hugo scurrying to keep up with her swift strides.

Tamara shuddered again, and I opened the long-sleeved flannel shirt I wore over a tee, wrapping it closed around Tamara and myself.

Mrs. Claus pointed to the trembling female elf who was peering over the side of the newly arrived sleigh.

"You," Mrs. Claus announced to the little elf, "one job, and one job only. Fix this." She waved a hand in a circle as though opening a portal around the broken sleigh beside us, except nothing happened. Or at least nothing I could see. Beside me, Tamara was watching, eyes wide, her breath coming out in clouds.

The small elf climbed down out of the old sleigh, a toolbelt strapped around her tiny waist, and crossed over to the broken sleigh. She stared at it with clear apprehension.

Mrs. Claus pointed a black-gloved hand at the sleigh that had brought her here. "Hugo, be a boss and burn Number One."

Burn it?

I snatched Tamara's hand and pulled her to my side as she moved to intervene. This was not our business.

"Lie low," I whispered.

"Ma'am?" Hugo squeaked, eyes widening as he took in the old sleigh, which had been kept for posterity and sentimental reasons. He stepped forward with obvious hesitation, as though his ears may have deceived him.

"Sparkles needs motivation," Mrs. Claus said coolly.

The female elf turned from her thumping and banging on the broken sleigh, eyes round with terror. Fixing Number Two seemed to be entirely up to her, and I wondered if she was actually able to do it, given the time constraints and severity of the damage.

I'd expected a cluster of elves, working at high speed, creating fixes with magic, not one terrified small being with a toolbelt.

Sparkles dropped out of sight inside the broken sleigh, and the loud sound of random banging filled the night air.

"*Now*, Hugo," Mrs. Claus said sharply.

Tamara moved again, and I hugged her from behind, shushing her quietly.

"This is so bad," she moaned.

"You're going to get yourself zapped," I whispered.

Mrs. Claus heard me, her lips quirking, a pleased glimmer to her dark eyes. She tipped her head to the side, addressing Tamara, the pleased look becoming frosty. "Are you doubting my elf's ability?"

"Uh, no. I just think that—ooph!" I gave her midsection a tight squeeze, temporarily knocking the air out of her, for what I hoped was her own good.

A blast of fierce wind hit us, showering us with flakes that swirled off the barn roof.

The witch's eyes warmed into a fiery red, and she glowered off to our left, her body expanding as though about to shoot fireballs or something equally terrifying.

"Why are you here?" Mrs. Claus growled. Beside us, a woman with violently dyed red hair and black leather pants smirked, trying to cover up her obvious fear.

"I believe Tamara would like to make a wish." She swirled a pointed finger upward as though it was a magic wand.

Tamara nodded. Hugo, having forgotten his task, was watching with his mouth ajar.

"Who's that?" I whispered to Tamara. The tall, slim woman's unnaturally bright hair was startling against the subtle blues, pale greys and white surrounding us.

"Estelle. Fairy godmother."

"*What*? Where are her wings?" She didn't look anything like the fairy godmothers I'd heard about. Then again, Mrs. Claus didn't look the way I'd expected, either. Santa's appearance and demeanour, however, very much met my expectations.

"Trying to circumvent me?" Mrs. Claus asked Estelle. Her

voice was low, her stance wide, her body poised, as if she was about to duel with the fairy.

"They're trying to be helpful," Estelle said.

Mrs. Claus sashayed toward us, reminding me of a tiger coming to toy with its wounded prey. I could practically feel her well of confidence draining Tamara's.

"And you're one of *hers*?" she asked Tamara.

She nodded, mutely.

"She's not here to meddle," Estelle said.

"And how do you know she's not?" the witch asked. Her eyes were still red, and I didn't think I'd ever be able to reconcile the image of the sweet, doting grandmotherly type with Mrs. Claus ever again. Not even if I visited Santa's Village in Bracebridge, Ontario and saw an actress embodying the image we all believed in.

Tamara was leaning into me, and I backed us up a half step at a time, trying to create distance between us and the witch without her noticing.

"Christmas is a very important holiday," Mrs. Claus said, eyes narrowed at Tamara.

"We recognize that. Tamara asked me to x-ray Rudolph. Nothing is broken, but he—"

"*Darling*," Mrs. Claus said in a clipped tone, "you know *nothing*. Absolutely nothing. And you are interfering where you are not only unwelcome, but also with something so much larger and grander, and immensely more important than your tiny little human lives."

"You can't touch them," Estelle said, stepping forward.

Tamara was talking under her breath, seemingly arguing with herself. I couldn't make out the words, but I sensed panic and a great internal debate.

"They have to be tried in the courts before you can touch them," Estelle warned Mrs. Claus.

"I am the judge, and Christmas is my domain." Her voice was getting louder, more powerful, as if she was summoning energy from the universe. "We don't have to be in court for me to make my ruling, as they are clearly interfering with *my* domain."

I began edging Tamara backward again, toward the barn door. My plan was to grab our coats, my truck keys, and then sneak out the small door at the back. We'd circle around when it was safe again, and escape.

Mrs. Claus, without turning to look at the sleighs parked behind her, snapped her fingers. "Hugo! Sleigh. Now."

Hugo did a hop, then with his legs a blur, zipped to the old sleigh. He flicked a lighter under the rails, and sparks and the odd flicker of flame appeared in the darkness.

In a panic, Tamara and I moved as one unit, heading straight to the reindeer, our concern over hiding out from the witch forgotten. I hadn't needed to worry though, as the two women began screeching at each other.

Tamara and I scrambled to unhook the massive harness system holding the reindeer to the old sleigh. The herd watched us while Hugo studiously obeyed his orders and tried to light their sleigh on fire.

As soon as the reindeer were free of the sleigh, I grabbed Tamara's freezing hand, ready to make a beeline for the safety of the barn. But before we could move, the fighting women turned to face us. Mrs. Claus's eyes were a burning red, and as she lifted an arm, Tamara froze, her breathing stilled, eyes squeezed shut.

CHAPTER 27

~ *Tamara* ~

"TM? Are you okay? Where are we?" Haden was still holding my hand. He pulled me into his arms and patted me as if he was checking for injuries.

I let out a breath, realizing where we were, and that we were safe.

"We're in Justin's hardware store," I said.

"What? No, we're not. Wait. How did we get here?"

I'd never been in this back room before, and the faint glow of the few security lights left on in the store filtered into the storage area where we stood. Still, I recognized it.

I looked down. We were wearing our winter coats like we'd bundled ourselves up and driven here. There was even snow under our boots. But we hadn't driven here. And we hadn't gone into the barn to retrieve our winter gear.

We were here because I'd made a wish.

I closed my eyes, realizing I'd panicked and done the one thing I'd promised I wouldn't do during this whole fiasco. But when Mrs. Claus turned toward us with her terrifyingly empty, burning eyes, and with rage coming off her in waves, I'd feared for Haden and wished us away.

Thank goodness Estelle had instantly granted my wish. There was probably a smouldering crater outside my barn where we'd been standing moments ago, thanks to the angry Mrs. Claus.

The reindeer had been right to fear her, and to choose Santa's side. Mrs. Claus made me want to wet my pants.

Haden, assured I was okay, released me, taking in our surroundings.

"How did we get here?" he repeated. He reached out, tentatively touching a wall with chipped paint and layers of scrub marks. When it didn't give way, he turned to me for an answer.

Inhaling slowly, and very aware that my sensible new boyfriend—Could I call him that already? I think I could— might really lose his mind over this one. I could, too, if I paused to think about it. So, it was probably best not to.

"I made a wish. Estelle sent us here."

"You wished to come to the hardware store?"

I nodded, wondering if Mrs. Claus would be able to follow us. "I wanted to get somewhere safe. I was thinking about ways to help while lying low, and I thought about your plan to get night vision goggles. I thought about coming here."

Hearing the quiver in my voice, Haden tucked me into his arms. He pressed a kiss into the crown of my head. "Good thinking."

He released me, moving to the back door and opening it wide. "My truck's out there." His voice was mystified. "How did I... Did I drive it?"

"I have no idea." My legs were getting a bit shaky. The more I thought about the details and what we'd possibly just avoided back at the barn, the more worried I became. "I'm sorry I got you wrapped into this whole mess, and then wished you here without permission."

He turned to me with an expression of disbelief. "Are you

kidding? That was really quick thinking. Any time I'm about to get zapped by a black witch, feel free to send me somewhere else!"

Then he swore under his breath and jogged past me to a box on the wall containing the store's security system. He punched in a code, then another as the light began blinking faster. It went out with his second attempt, and he sagged in relief.

"Security system," he said.

"How do you know the code?"

"Justin uses our grad date for everything."

"Secure."

Haden came back over to me, rubbing my arms. "Are you okay?"

I nodded, not daring to speak.

He cupped my cheek, tipping my head up, then gazed at me for a beat. "You sure?"

I nodded again, biting my lower lip. The adrenaline was waning, making me shaky.

He pulled me into an embrace and I let out a shuddery breath, relieved we were both safe. Whatever that wish had cost me, it had been worth every penny.

Realizing how close Haden had come to harm because of me, I reconsidered Estelle's plea to make a wish and erase my accident with Rudolph.

Haden released me, taking my hand and pulling me through the dimly lit back room. He had a small smile on his face, his eyes unshuttered, letting me see every thought he had tonight, from love and excitement to fear.

I couldn't wish this away. I just couldn't. I knew it was selfish, but we had to find another way to fix this Christmas fiasco so we wouldn't lose this.

"How about we get the night vision goggles," he suggested, "and then sneak back to the barn in a bit? If it's safe, of course."

"Okay."

So far there was no sign of Mrs. Claus, and I was fairly certain she'd immediately follow us, if given the option. I relaxed, letting Haden lead me through the backroom maze of shelves, doorways and random boxes. The organization system seemed to be the exclusive kind—where it only made sense to the person depositing the boxes willy-nilly. Seeing as I'd never been in here before, I was a bit dazzled that I'd managed to magick us here at all. Maybe wishing wasn't always so bad after all.

Haden placed a hand on my lower back, guiding me toward the hunting section.

"Oh, wait." He stopped, his hand dropping. "Gotta grab the key to open the case. Back in a flash." Haden turned and disappeared into the dark hallways behind us and I shivered, feeling exposed and alone without him.

I sent a quick text to Char.

ME

> Made a wish. Please, please tell me I can still use your credits.

It was around two in the morning, and well before Char would rise and shine down in Mexico, so I was surprised when she texted back.

CHAR

> Thank goodness! I was getting worried. Are you okay? How's Haden? Rudolph?

I texted back with shaking hands.

ME

> Mrs. Claus is scary. We're hiding from her. She and Estelle got in a massive fight.

CHAR

How's Haden?

I rolled my eyes. My life was in possible danger, and she wanted to know about the man I was crushing on?

ME

Fine.

CHAR

Come on. How's he really? You've been in love with him since forever.

In love?

My reaction was to deny it, even though it struck a chord of truth within me. I had loved him for a long time, hadn't I? I just hadn't quite recognized it, or allowed myself to see it for what it truly was. Or how deep and real it was, and that it might be the kind of love I was looking for.

ME

He's fine.

CHAR

No dishing, no credits.

ME

You're mean.

CHAR

You're holding back!

ME

Fine. He's good, and tonight with him has been good.

CHAR

Good? That's all?

I smiled.

> **ME**
>
> Really good. Really, really good.

CHAR

You kissed?

> **ME**
>
> Yes.

I bit my bottom lip, allowing my worries to surface so my best friend could help me through them.

> **ME**
>
> Kade is going to freak.

CHAR

His problem. Not yours. Can't wait to hear all about H. Call me in the morning.

> **ME**
>
> I know it's not his business...but...

CHAR

No buts!

An unwelcome thought popped to mind, and I shot another text to Char, my heart beating wildly.

> **ME**
>
> You didn't wish for anything on my behalf, did you?

I closed my eyes, barely daring to breathe as I awaited her reply.

CHAR

What do you mean? Tonight? No.

ME

Ever?

CHAR

No, not that I'm aware.

Wait. Do you think Haden is under a spell?

ME

Is he?

She would know better than I did.

CHAR

Not because of me. I promise!

ME

You sure?

CHAR

YES! Not knowing if your boyfriend loves you because of magic is the WORST. I worried about it too, and would never wish that upon you. And definitely not with Haden.

I exhaled and nodded to myself. I knew that as much as Char wanted me to have love and happiness, she'd never mess with my life and put me through that same emotional wringer she'd gone through.

ME

Thanks. Had to ask. Sorry.

CHAR

No worries. I'm going to bed, now that I know you're okay. But call if you need anything!

> And make as many wishes as you want. My
> credits are your credits. Stay safe tonight.
> Save Christmas. Stay out of trouble. Save
> yourselves. And get more kisses! He likes
> you—no magic!

Could I believe that? I sure wanted to.

CHAR

ME

> Thanks. You're the best. Get some sleep.

Haden returned, jogging as he held up the key. "Got it!"

I caught the smile that was for me. Only me. Nobody else. This was real. I could feel it. He was himself, and so was I. Everything we were feeling was heartstoppingly real. No spells required.

"Why does Justin carry night vision goggles?" I asked as we entered the hunting section. "It chills me that armed people are out in the dark, trying to shoot things. What if they mistake me for a buck?"

"I'm pretty sure you look different than a buck."

"I don't know, night vision goggles just feel so over the top. Who's giving animals an advantage? What if some doofus sees a green blob, and gets trigger-happy? Then the next thing we know, someone like me is pushing up daisies."

I turned to the case filled with compasses and fancy gadgets, feeling jittery after our close call with Mrs. Claus, and the fact that we were now surrounded by weaponry. Someone like Josie was equipped for this, but not me. She and her friends were always doing Live Action Role Playing skits where they had mock battles. Me? Again, I liked a cosy blanket, a cup of coffee and a good book or horse magazine so I could dream about becoming a barrel racer from the safety of my living room. Not LARPing followed up by real life action.

"You'd avenge me if I got hit?" I asked Haden. "Right?"

"Of course," Haden replied seriously, placing one hand over the spot where his heart resided under layers of winter coat. "You'd do the same for me, too, right?"

"Darn right! Especially now that I know the codes to get in here. I'll be able to arm myself properly for a thorough avenging mission." I gave him a gleeful, slightly manic smile, and pretended to check out the gun rack behind us. Honestly, I had no idea what I was looking at. They all looked very heavy...and dangerous.

"You know you can't come in here without permission, right?"

"Relax. Don't get your panties in a twist. Could you imagine me hunting someone down?"

"Yes."

I giggled and placed a hand against my chest, sobering myself. "Me? Innocent, little old me?"

"You kept one of Santa's elves locked in the trunk today for how many hours? Not to mention you mowed down Rudolph, and threatened to do the same to my brother."

I opened my mouth to defend myself, but he continued on, imitating my earlier excuse. "My cat sneaks into my trunk."

"Hey! I had to hide Snarky from you!" I gave him a playful shove and, to my delight, he caught my hand. I wasn't sure how to encourage him to keep touching me, so I stepped into his space like I was truly captured, and he wrapped his arms around my waist like I belonged in his embrace.

"And, for the record," I said, "it's your fault he was in there so long. He was hiding from you."

"So, let me get this straight. You'd rather freeze an elf than trust me?"

"There is no one in town that I'd trust more with this problem than you."

His lips curved into a smile, his eyes dancing. "You know I'm just messing with you."

I snorted in disgust and pushed him away. "You're the worst."

Much to my disappointment, he let me go. "Really? I'm the worst?" He gave me puppy eyes. "Because I thought there was no one else you'd trust the way you trust me?"

Grumbling to myself, I scanned the various displays. "Are you sure Justin has night vision goggles? And what do we do when he comes to work tomorrow, and we've cleaned him out?"

Oh, and how were we going to get these goggles back to the reindeer without getting ourselves killed in the process?

"I'll leave him a note," Haden said, "or shoot him a text in the morning."

I fiddled with a toy bow and arrow with suction cups for tips in a nearby wire bin. An idea came to me as I causally suggested, "You should probably leave him a note now so you don't forget. You know how snippy he gets if you forget."

"One time. It was one time."

"Mm."

With a sigh, Haden turned. "Be right back."

In high school, he'd let himself into the store one night to get a tow rope to haul a friend out of a muddy ditch. He'd left a note for his uncle, Justin's dad, who'd owned the shop at the time. The note had gotten lost, and Justin had been blamed. By the time Haden remembered to follow up with his uncle on how much he owed him, Justin had already served several days of extra chores. It was a bit of a sore spot with Justin, although I think he enjoyed holding it over his cousin's head.

Still. We didn't want to give him a second thing to hold over Haden.

Carefully, I opened the bow and arrow package, knowing I shouldn't. But having recently and, very narrowly, escaped death made messing with unpurchased products feel tame in comparison. And I *had* to do something with all this amped up fight-or-flight energy I had coursing through me.

I crouched behind a display case with the bow drawn back, arrow poised to get Haden when he returned. I shifted, the backs of my knees starting to feel weird, as if I was cutting off the circulation to my lower legs. Crab-crawling to a different spot, I stretched out, rolling onto a hip and elbow to peer around a shelf corner to watch for Haden.

This was boring. How did hunters sit in their blinds for hours?

I rolled onto my back and sighed. Using the bow, I poked at the items on the shelf beside me.

"Well, look what we have here," I muttered. Night vision goggles. Toy ones, so probably not the high-end ones from the locked case that Haden was hoping to put on the reindeer, but still, they might be better than nothing if Haden couldn't get at the others.

Convincing myself that I was merely testing out the product we planned to purchase, I opened the package, slipping a pair out of the box and over my head. I gasped as my vision changed. This was just as cool as in the movies.

Armed again with my bow and arrow, I got to my feet and crept forward, standing behind a rack of insulated camouflage jackets.

"Done," Haden called out from somewhere deep inside the store. "And I scheduled a text to go out to him at six, too." He still hadn't turned on the harsh overhead lights, and I waited for a green blob—Haden—to appear in my vision.

And there he was. Barely able to hold in the giggle, I pulled back the bow's string and struck.

The toy wasn't very robust, and the suction cup feebly grazed Haden's shoulder before falling to the floor.

"What the...?"

"Got you!" I called triumphantly, my fears and worries that had followed me all night dissolving.

"Where are you?"

I stepped out from behind the rack.

"Are you wearing night vision goggles?"

"Toy ones. I thought we should test them."

He stooped, picking up the arrow. "And this?"

"Also testing," I said seriously. "We don't want Little Johnny getting a crappy gift this Christmas."

"And who is Little Johnny?" he asked, amusement tingeing his voice as he set the arrow on top of the display case he was unlocking.

I leaned over the case filled with tech. "Think we should test these ones, too? After all, Christmas is on the line. If the holiday fails tonight, it might disappear forever."

I shivered at the thought. Christmas with my Oma meant everything to me. Was it possible Christmas could disappear if we didn't fix things? Could the implications be that massive?

I cleared my throat, trying to keep things light despite the sudden heavy foreboding weighing me down. "So, we'd better be careful about our selection."

There were several different brands inside, and Haden stacked a couple of sets on the glass counter. "I don't want to abuse my privileges."

"Of course not," I said as I watched him open a box, adjusting the strap before putting on the night vision goggles. His jaw softened as he let out a soft gasp.

I couldn't help but smile at his sense of wonder.

"Cool, right?"

He cautiously moved his head from left to right, taking in the room. "We should turn off the security lights."

"On it." I hurried toward the back of the store, looking for the few lights that stayed on twenty-four-seven. "Where are the switches?"

"I got 'em," he called from my left, and we were immediately plunged into darkness. Ambient light from the streetlights outside filtered in, giving the goggles enough light to work with. Crisper forms than before emerged, letting me see the room.

"Nerf guns?" I dared.

"Definitely."

"Good, 'cause that bow and arrow definitely sucked. Little Johnny would've been very disappointed."

"Then, for the sake of Christmas, we'd better test something else."

"Speaking of Christmas, we should also give Mrs. Claus ample time to cool down before we head back," I added.

"I like the way you think."

We ditched our winter coats, and Haden pulled on my hand. "Nerf guns are over here."

Giggling, I followed him to the toy section, loving that I could see everything. Within minutes, we were armed and ready for battle, hiding behind shelves on opposite sides of the store.

"Ready?" he called.

I was already moving. I crouched low, my thighs burning, heart pounding.

I heard the release of his Nerf gun's spring and the plastic *chunk* sound as a foam bullet fired. It hit my calf, just above my winter boot, stinging with the impact.

How did he move so fast? He was a blur of green. I caught sight and began firing, hoping for a hit.

He opened fire in return. Foam darts nailed me, and I rolled to the floor, splaying onto my back like I'd been taken down.

Haden knelt beside me. "Tamara! Are you okay?"

I kept my eyes closed before realizing he couldn't see them through the goggles.

"TM?" he whispered.

Oh, swoon. He was shortening my Trademark nickname again. I felt like I was falling, my heart singing, my spirit lighter than it had ever been in my life.

"I think I need CPR," I whispered weakly, pushing up my goggles. I cracked an eye to quickly peer at him before shutting it again. I couldn't see his eyes through his goggles, or really anything, after using mine.

He let out an amused huff, then swept me into his arms, and said in a dramatic voice as he brushed the hair from my face, "Don't go towards the light!" He rocked me in his arms like I was truly dying, and his act warmed my heart. Honestly, I'd never had as much fun as I was having right now, faking my own death. "Stay with me."

"Give me something to live for," I whispered just as dramatically.

"It's too soon," he crooned.

I opened one eye and said feebly, "Haden? Is that you?"

He pulled off his own goggles, his lips lowering to mine.

And then we were kissing.

I could feel the press of his mouth against mine, his arms holding me against his broad chest. His warm hand slipped under the hem of my green Christmas sweatshirt with the faux cross-stitch of a horse, and then my T-shirt, gliding across my lower back and sending delicious shivers through my torso. I fought the temptation to suck in my belly so that I felt like someone else under his touch. Someone slimmer and fitter.

Someone worthy of making it to the top of the pyramid-like food chain of women who'd been scrambling for his affections.

As his hand roamed across what I knew to be obvious love handles, a low growl of satisfaction rumbled through him, and his kiss grew more urgent. I shoved my insecurities aside, determined to enjoy this sacred moment. He smelled like snow and fresh straw, and in the darkness, I could release my fears and believe that he wanted me as much as I wanted him, and that come morning, we would be the couple I'd never allowed myself to dream we could be.

CHAPTER 28

~ *Haden* ~

Tamara's fingers slid into the hair at the nape of my neck, pulling me close for another kiss and sending electric fireballs down my spine.

Her lips drifted from mine.

"You okay?" I asked, hoping she wasn't going to tell me I was pushing too fast. Now that the door had opened between us, I wanted all of her. Now.

"Am I really the reason you've never dated anyone for longer than four months?"

"Four months?" Had she been keeping track of my past relationships?

"Yeah."

I paused, considering my conversational options. I didn't want to talk about exes right now. I wanted to keep kissing Tamara. But I got the impression that if I didn't talk about my exes, there would be no more kissing.

With a sigh, I ran a hand through my hair. "What's the point of staying with someone when you know you'll never fall in love with them, because you've got feelings for someone else?"

She sighed in my arms, and it was the happiest sigh I'd ever heard. It made me wonder if we would have dated in high school if we'd been the same age. If it hadn't been necessary for me to put up mental blocks and walls to keep things appropriate between us for so many long years.

Before Tamara could ask anything more about my long-buried, not-fully-understood feelings about her, I grazed her lips with mine. I'd never get tired of her and her coconut lip balm. The tender touch of her mouth. The way her lashes fluttered down before mine did when we kissed, the way she lost herself in being touched by me.

The light kiss turned into something more, a need that made our kisses suddenly turn frantic and deep.

I suddenly jolted back, freezing as I processed what was going on around us. Something had clanged. Was it a door? Had Mrs. Claus found us?

Could Tamara magic us away again with another wish? The seamless way we'd travelled here made me wonder if someone else's wishes had ever impacted my life before. Maybe the renewed friendship between Tamara and myself tonight was nothing more than a product of someone's wish.

I'd be okay with that, as long as the wish didn't wear off. Right now, her sweet lips were millimetres from mine, and I felt their pull, my libido wrestling for control. This felt real. So very real.

I heard the whisper of fabric, maybe the squeak of a rubber sole, and the instinctual part of my brain tightened its grip on my focus.

Something wasn't right.

Tamara was still gathered in my arms, and I pulled her into a full upright position, releasing her.

"Did you hear that?" I whispered as I heard another undefinable noise. I slipped my night vision goggles down over my eyes again. The store was cold without Tamara pressed against me, my jaw pleasantly tired from kissing.

"I didn't hear anything," she whispered back. She was feeling around in the dark for her own goggles, which had gone skittering across the floor at some point. I passed them to her.

"Is it Mrs. Claus?" she asked me.

"I don't know."

Flickering security lights strobed, streaking the store's ceiling. Had we accidentally tripped the alarm? I was sure I'd turned it off.

Adrenaline thundered through my veins as I heard a boot land on the hard floor somewhere to the right. I slid Tamara behind me, trying to gauge where the intruder was, and whether I should announce our presence or not. If it was Mrs. Claus, we wanted to stay completely off her radar.

I picked up my Nerf gun, prepared to throw it once I had a target.

"Police!" a deep male voice shouted, and Tamara jolted, hitting her head on the boxes on the shelf behind us. Large sounding feet, in some pretty serious boots, stomped across the floor in our direction.

Was it really the police, or was Justin playing a prank on us? He could have installed cameras without me knowing, and thought he'd come scare the crap out of us. But the red and blue lights rotating on the ceiling...yeah, it could be the police.

Tamara and I scrambled to our feet, listening. She backed against a wire rack and it swayed, dropping whistles and keychains around us. She squeaked, and the footsteps came closer.

"Police! Stay where you are!"

"We're unarmed," I shouted, realizing just how far south this situation could go if we weren't careful.

"Drop your gun!" Tamara said to me, and I let the plastic toy clatter to the floor.

"He's armed!" the police yelled, and Tamara screamed.

"We're not armed!" I hollered back. "It's a toy. A Nerf!"

The overhead lights flashed on, blinding me as the night vision goggles bloomed out in a sea of greenish white. Footsteps. Scuffling. Hands spinning me, pushing me to the floor. I didn't resist, letting out a grunt as my stomach made contact with the cold, gritty floor. There was a clink of handcuffs, and I was bound.

"Hands in the air," a female hollered.

"Tamara!" I shouted, imagining the worst.

"Hey, Stacy. Um, sorry?" Tamara said sheepishly. I turned my head, the goggles twisting off my face, and saw Tamara, hands raised, looking embarrassed.

Stacy, a member of the local police who also acted as the school resource officer, had her taser trained on Tamara, feet planted far apart.

"Is it just you and Haden?"

"Yes."

Stacy relaxed, looking around the store, her weapon still raised. She studied me, and I smiled apologetically. She took in Tamara from head to toe.

"Stand down," Stacy said to the officer behind her, placing her taser back in its holster on her belt.

"We got a call about the alarm. That you?" Stacy asked.

"Does Lady MacBeth *ever* sleep?" Tamara grumbled.

"We didn't break in," I said, wondering how we were supposed to explain our situation. It was true, though. We technically hadn't performed a break and enter.

"Right," Stacy said, clearly unconvinced. "It's the middle of the night, and all of the security lights are off. Justin called us about an unexpected, de-armed alarm."

Of course he did. He got notices for that, but no cameras to see it was just me?

"We were Christmas shopping," Tamara said lamely.

"Christmas shopping?" Stacy's tone made it clear she knew it was a lie. She kept eyeing Tamara like she didn't quite know what to believe. I understood the feeling. She'd thrown me for a few loops tonight, too.

Everyone said she'd changed, but I didn't think so. It was more that she was finally showing people who she truly was—fun, adventurous, bold, and yet also still that loving, quiet, unassuming woman. And now they could actually see her, since she wasn't being overshadowed by my brother and his large personality.

"Stuff for a Christmas stag party," I said from my spot. My cheek was getting cold from the floor, but at least they hadn't cuffed Tamara. "I have the security code. I didn't want to wake Justin." Truth, truth, and more truth.

The officers were staring at us. Then Stacy eyed Tamara again, her eyes drifting to the discarded bright orange plastic gun. "Nerf gun war?"

Tamara nodded.

"Ever go paintballing?"

"Yeah. Char likes to go."

"We need someone for our team."

"I like to play," I said from my spot on the floor.

Stacy held out a hand to shush me.

"We need a female." She was still watching Tamara. "I didn't ask you before because you're so sweet with the kids at school. I didn't think you'd want to shoot people with paint."

She glanced at me for a second before returning her attention to Tamara, like she was sizing her up anew.

"But if you can actually hit someone with bags of chips, and like to sneak into stores in the middle of the night to have toy gun wars, you might be the kind of woman we need on our team."

"I'm really not very good," Tamara said. "Char always nails me, and Haden got me more than I got him tonight." She gave Stacy a hopeful look. "Can we go home?"

"Hm. Shopping, was it?" Stacy asked. She looked between the two of us, and I swear she could tell we'd spent most of our time in here goofing around and making out. And basically having the best night I've ever had with a woman. No exceptions.

"Yes," I confirmed.

"One moment." Stacy took a few steps away, speaking into the radio clipped to her lapel. She waited to hear a garbled reply, then said to me, "We're going to need confirmation from Justin that it's okay for you to be in here."

Great. What kind of mood was my cousin in tonight? Hopefully not the kind where he'd find it funny to send us to the clinker.

"But we didn't break in!" Tamara protested. "Haden knows the security code. Please?"

"I'm sure half the town knows it. We need to ensure you have proper permission, and it doesn't sound as though you do." Stacy said to her partner, "You can uncuff him."

"You sure?" asked the recruit.

"I know where he lives."

"You know where everyone lives," the man muttered under his breath as he released me. Man, it felt good to be able to stand up, use my arms, and get my cheek off the grimy floor. I moved to Tamara's side, wanting to hug her, even though she was clearly okay.

"I sure wish Justin would answer his phone, and let us go," I said pointedly to Tamara as Stacy waited to hear something through her walkie talkie. "Don't you wish that?"

Tamara rolled her eyes at me and shook her head. What? What was the point of a fairy godmother if you didn't use her liberally?

275

CHAPTER 29

~ *Tamara* ~

Once Justin confirmed that it was okay for us to be in his store as long as I baked him one of my chocolate cakes, Stacy and the new officer let us go. But not before watching Haden send payment to Justin. Once again, Haden refused to let me pay.

It was charming, but a bit old-fashioned. Since it was my fiasco, I thought it was unfair that he was the one paying for everything. A small part of me wondered if, deep down, he still saw me as tiny Tamara, in need of rescue.

His remarks about my wishing our way out of our scrape with the police had made me a little grumpy, too. We both knew Justin wasn't going to send us to jail. And while Haden didn't understand the complications and cost that came with having a fairy godmother, I was too tired to take it all in stride. Especially since a part of me worried that I was falling too fast, too hard, and by daybreak, I'd somehow be without him in my life. Like this magical night with him was just that—magic.

And magic was dangerous. If I wished this messy night away, what else would I be wishing away? Haden and our kisses? Because if I hadn't hit Rudolph, there would be no

Haden in my barn, and then no kissing. We'd still be avoiding each other like before tonight.

And even if I wished tonight's mess away, with a plan to woo Haden tomorrow, since I now understood he had feelings for me, would I even remember come morning? Neither of us knew how we got to the hardware store, and yet Haden's truck had been waiting for us outside. Was that a bit of magic that had placed the vehicle there, or had we driven here without memory of it, thanks to the magical weaving of time to make my wish happen?

Too many questions, too many risks.

Haden drove us away from the store, and down the alley, the truck bouncing and jiggling in the dark gulley between buildings as we went from one snowy pothole to the next.

From above, a blip of red—a glowing cigarette—burned above the insurance agency. Lady MacBeth. Would *she* remember tonight? How long would it take for the juicy story of Haden and me being busted by the police to circulate?

On the bright side, it might distract people from trying to solve whose stag party we'd been shopping for. In a small town like Eagle Ridge, everyone knew everyone. And the topic of marriage? Well, that would get everyone talking.

Haden's truck pushed through the deep snow on the unplowed country roads. As we drew closer to my farm—as well as the fight I'd wished us away from—a feeling of dread settled in the pit of my gut.

"Maybe we shouldn't go back," I said. When I'd made my wish, what else had been set in motion? What consequences might we face if we returned? And how would Mrs. Claus feel about us slipping from her grasp?

Haden took his foot off the gas pedal, and I felt the truck slow as it got bogged down in the fresh snow.

"You want me to pull a U-ey at the correction line?"

I bit my bottom lip, debating if I wanted him to turn us around at the upcoming T-intersection. A feeling of responsibility crept into my brain, refusing to release its prisoner.

"No. It doesn't feel right to bail on the reindeer or Santa. Or that poor fixer elf."

"I guess if things go south, you can always wish us out of there again," Haden said hesitantly. I could hear the trace of thrill in his voice, like when he'd first met Rudolph. He was loving all this magic stuff. Maybe a little too much.

Again, my brain prodded me with the thought that the magic of tonight might be playing a role in his sudden romantic interest in me. What if he found the everyday, sit-at-home-and-read-a-book version of Tamara boring like his brother had?

"Wishes are a last resort," I said sternly. "There are always consequences." I nodded firmly, my decision made. "We'll go check things out, but keep your keys at the ready in case we have to get out fast."

"Okay."

Haden turned down my driveway, and the wind let up as the trees lining the gravel trail protected us. The storm was dying.

As we moved toward the barn, I caught sight of a faint red glow. Something was burning. The original sleigh? It looked like it had burned down to embers, occasionally letting out a burst of flame, as if fighting against its untimely murder.

"I guess we have some North Pole relationships to save on top of a holiday," I muttered, the small fire bringing my attention back to our present task—to save Christmas.

"Is this what it's like having kids?" Haden asked.

"I think there are significantly fewer crises."

"Thank goodness. Having a family isn't something I'm ready to give up on yet."

"You want a family?" I asked.

"Of course." He said it nonchalantly as he parked near a drift that hadn't been there yesterday morning, and we hopped out with our stash of goggles.

Haden wanted a hobby farm *and* kids? And he wasn't freaking out over this magical business, and didn't like big loud parties, either. Was it possible he was truly perfect?

"Where's the broken sleigh?" I asked, stopping in front of the barn.

"Do you think they fixed everything and left?" Haden asked.

"That would be nice."

"Hey." Haden caught my hand, his expression dark and serious. "Whatever we meet in there, be careful, okay?"

"You, too."

He pulled me closer, giving me a very lovely, deep kiss that made my whole body sing and sigh. Kissing Haden, I felt so light I could fly. If there was a way to bottle this feeling, there wouldn't be a problem with the added weight, or a lack of aerodynamics, with a poorly repaired sleigh. I'd just sprinkle some of this over it, and the reindeer would be off.

Haden released me, then opened the barn door, nearly dropping his stack of goggles at the sight of utter chaos that greeted us. Santa was shouting at Mrs. Claus, and she was wagging her finger at him like she planned to divorce the man if he didn't come around to her way of thinking. The reindeer were cowering in a cluster near the back corner of the barn, kicking and braying. The broken sleigh had been brought inside and was resting close to us, not looking any better than it had an hour ago. Hugo was standing between the married couple, his neck swivelling from side to side as he tracked each participant in the argument. He looked close to crying.

We hesitated on the threshold. There was no sign of Estelle.

"Um, we have night vision goggles for the reindeer," I said quietly.

Nobody noticed us.

I ventured over the threshold, but Haden grabbed the elbow of my coat, holding me back from going further. "Maybe we should let them be."

I'd stopped just inside the doorway, and Sparkles, the timid fixer elf, appeared beside us, arms raised to take the boxes.

I shifted half of my load of goggles into her arms, holding on to the rest.

"How is fixing the sleigh going?" I whispered.

"Not good. And Santa is mad that Mrs. C. burned our backup plan."

"How's he doing?"

"Getting better."

"And Rudolph?"

"Getting better."

"Where's Estelle?"

Sparkles shook her head.

I gasped. "Dead?"

"Banished."

"What does that mean?"

"Mrs. C. made her leave. But she can come back any time you make a wish. And Estelle can banish Mrs. Claus if she goes after a client while she's granting wishes." Her voice went so small, I could barely hear her when she added, "But that would cause a really big banishment fight."

"Oh, boy."

I'd once wondered what it might be like to have two men fight over me, as it had sounded a bit thrilling to be wanted that badly. This kind of battle though? With Mrs. Claus wanting to punish me, and Estelle wanting to save me? It was spine-chilling.

Still, I wasn't conceited enough to think they were merely fighting over me. I knew there were a lot of periphery issues in play—ones I didn't want to think about right now.

I turned back to Haden, unsure of what we should do. Run and hide? Try to help with the sleigh? Wade into the argument and play peacekeeper?

"Let's see if we can get these goggles to fit the reindeer," Haden said, as though reading my mind. He drew me behind the broken sleigh, crouching down so we'd be out of sight of the fighting couple. Then we began unboxing the goggles, trying to sort out how we'd fit them on the reindeer, while Sparkles went back to her impossible repair job on the sleigh.

We caught snippets of the argument going on near the stalls. "I was only nineteen." And "You're always like this."

It didn't sound as if they were arguing about tonight's mess, and it made me feel helpless. Bringing Mrs. Claus had only made things worse.

Their fighting also reminded me of my parents, before they split temporarily, and of Kade, during our final days as a couple. Only we'd been screaming things such as "You've changed" and "You haven't."

Either way, in my experience, fights like this had a good chance of being deal-breakers. And that didn't say much for the state of Christmas.

HADEN and I had fallen asleep against the sleigh, unable to successfully lure one of the reindeer past the fighting couple, and over to us for a night-vision goggle fitting.

Now, something was wiggling my foot, disturbing my sleep. I grunted, pulling my foot closer as I snuggled further into Haden's wonderful embrace and wide chest. He was prefect for snuggling, and as comforting as my Oma's rice pudding Christmas dessert.

"Tamara!" hissed a voice.

"More sleep," I muttered. The rhythmic thud of Haden's heart under my ear made me feel as though everything was, and always would be, okay.

Someone hauled on my foot and I shifted upright, grumpy and dazed. Estelle was crouched beside us behind the sleigh, her short red hair tucked behind her ears.

"Shh. Sorry," I whispered to Haden, settling him again with a pat on his chest. I extracted myself from his arms with difficulty, because he kept drawing me back in. There was nowhere else I'd rather be, but apparently I had to talk to my fairy godmother about the stupid magical world and its growing issues.

"What?" I asked, crawling over to the other end of the sleigh. The barn was quiet, still warm. When I poked my head up over the sleigh's side, I could see the Christmas tree winking, but was unable to spy anyone other than a few reindeer resting in the straw.

I took a better look at Estelle. "What happened to your hair?" It was singed, her face red like a Canadian who'd gone out on the first sunny day of June without sunscreen, and gotten smacked about by the unfamiliar ball of fire in the sky called the sun. "And your skin?"

"Banishment."

I felt my jaw drop, and I think even my shadow took a gulp of horror and surprise at the physical impact of what had happened to her when she'd been shuttled back to her own world against her will.

"We need to get you out of here," Estelle whispered. She handed me a slip of paper. "This is the wish you need to make for everything to return to normal."

My hands shook as I read the simple, carefully worded wish.

"Both the head fairy and I looked at it from every angle, and wrote this out. It'll undo tonight, and should get you out of any trouble with Mrs. Claus."

"And Christmas?"

"This wish would take you out of this timeline."

"But will that save Christmas?"

Estelle paused. "We can't read the future, Tamara."

I glanced back at Haden, folding the piece of paper with the handwritten wish. "Will I remember tonight?" I looked up at my fairy godmother. "Will he?"

Estelle placed a hand over the one holding the wish, not meeting my gaze. "This is for the best. Char says you can use her credits. There will be no cost to you. No unforeseen consequences."

"We'll lose tonight though, won't we?"

"It's my job to protect you, and it's very important we extract you from this timeline immediately."

"But what about Christmas? What happens to it? What if the reindeer still get drunk and are out partying on the roads, and the walls remain weak, and someone *else* hits Rudolph? Only it's worse because they're speeding? What if they don't stop and help him? What if Santa and Mrs. Claus stay angry at each other, and she doesn't make the magical flying oats? What if Christmas is ruined either way?" I looked down at our hands, slowly removing mine from under hers and standing, my mind made up. "This is too important, Estelle. I have to try to fix Christmas."

CHAPTER 30

~ *Estelle* ~

I was crying softly, worried for Tamara. She seemed to think she could save Christmas. Why were humans so ignorant and stubborn? Yes, Haden would forget tonight if she made that wish, but this was her life! She needed to stop worrying about everything, and everyone else.

Gram-Gram patted my shoulder as my tears dropped onto her office's pink carpet, making the rose pattern bloom and change with every drop. It was beautiful and almost made crying worth it in order to see it animate.

"Look up," she commanded, dabbing my burned skin with a lotion that smelled like spring rain. It soothed my scorched face, which was thanks to Mrs. Claus unceremoniously banishing me from the barnyard after I granted Tamara's safe passage wish, sending her and Haden to the hardware store.

"The first time always hurts the most," Gram-Gram said. "A bit of your pride gets burned, too, doesn't it?"

"You've been banished before?"

Gram-Gram chuckled. "The best fairy godmothers wind up on the wrong side of other magical beasts from time to time." She smiled. "I like to think it's in our DNA, but it's probably because of the way we steadfastly adhere to our guiding rules whenever our client is involved in something."

Keep the client safe, happy, making wishes, and improve their lives. Yeah, those rules had definitely landed me on the wrong side of Mrs. Claus tonight.

Gram-Gram was still fussing over me, and I leaned away. "I'm fine. Really." I ran a hand through my hair, horrified to find the bits around my face had been singed, too, and were now a brittle disaster.

"Oh, sweetie," Gram-Gram clucked. "It'll grow back."

"I didn't even fix Tamara's mess. She's not safe." My palm was littered with fragile black strands of what had once been my beautiful hair. I patted the rest of my head, ensuring Mrs. Claus hadn't done more damage than to just the fringe around my face.

"You got Tamara and Haden away from Mrs. Claus's rage," the head fairy said. "That's keeping your client safe, which improved her life. You granted her wish, which made her happy. You're four for four on the guiding rules, and that granted wish will give Mrs. Claus time to cool down."

"It's not enough. Tamara needs to reverse time."

"Reversing time means she has to give up love. She's waited for years for this man to show her affection. It's unfair to expect that wish from her."

I sighed. What did I truly know about love? The one time I'd thought a guy was into me, it turned out he was Santa Claus, and married to a much-feared and powerful black witch. Now she was terrorizing my client as well as ruining my signature hair style and enviable complexion.

"You gave Tamara the wish to use, if it comes to the point where she needs it," Gram-Gram said soothingly. "We've done all we can for the moment. We'll stand by and watch the wishing machine so we can take immediate action if she calls upon us. Tamara's fate is in her own hands. Not ours."

"Letting humans have agency in their own lives is stupid!" I exploded, my emotions getting the best of me.

What was I going to do if Mrs. Claus got to Tamara? What if the witch used her anger with me against my client? I'd lose Tamara, and I'd fail at all the promises I'd made when accepting her file. I'd fail at keeping her safe and happy, and I certainly wouldn't have improved her life.

"Did you know I wear green and red on Christmas Eve?" Gram-Gram said coyly, clearly trying to cheer me up.

"You don't."

She laughed at my tone. "You're right. I don't. I much prefer pink. But you can wear green and red. And I heard you have a new pair of green stilettos to wear."

She was trying to distract me. I shifted, facing her more fully. "We have to do something, Gram-Gram. Something more."

She put an arm around me. "Destiny and fate will do what they can, and so will we. Tamara has a good sense of self-preservation. She's saved herself once tonight with your help, and you've given her the tools to do it again. Let her choose her own path. Even if it's a dangerous one."

CHAPTER 31

~ *Haden* ~

"Wake up!"

I woke to the sound of Tamara's voice, and saw her marching out from behind the sleigh and its protection. I blinked away the sleep, scrambling to catch her, but she was already well beyond my reach and was hollering her command across the barn.

The building was quiet and still warm. There was no fighting, no sleigh reconstruction sounds, and the mysterious Christmas tree was blinking in the corner.

The reindeer, who'd been curled up sleeping on the floor, lifted their antlered heads as Tamara marched toward them. Mrs. Claus appeared out of a stall. She was smirking.

I caught up with Tamara, already not liking whatever was about to happen.

"Well, there you are." Mrs. Claus's tone was commanding, smooth, and in control. It sent shivers down my spine, and I instinctively took Tamara's hand.

"We need to take care of Christmas," Tamara said with authority. "It's everyone's holiday and—"

Mrs. Claus snapped her fingers. The air around Tamara and

me turned cold, then warm again, then cold, as dancing shadows filled the periphery of my vision. I wrapped my arms around my girlfriend, trying to shield her from whatever magic had us in its binds.

The world around us faded away.

CHAPTER 32

~ *Tamara* ~

For a moment, I thought I'd lost consciousness, even though I could still feel Haden's hand tightly clasping my own. Everything had gone black, the temperature flashing between pleasantly warm, and the harsh cold of a western Canadian winter.

Then it remained icy, the world almost too bright for me to open my eyes. Squinting, I took in our new surroundings. We weren't in the barn. Nor were we in the four-in-the-morning darkness of my yard. We appeared to be on top of a long, sheared off mountain slope, the wind picking at our shirts, the sun already high in the sky.

"Are we on Rundle?" I asked, referring to the angled mountain that served as an iconic backdrop for the small town of Banff, Alberta. I'm not sure why I thought we might be there, other than the sheared off slab of rock that went on forever, and the snowy drop offs that surrounded us. Wind was wisping off the edges of the mountain, creating clouds along the cliffs.

I'd hiked up here one summer with a guy from Calgary, completely exhausting myself. It had been our first and last date. In fact, at the time, it had made me miss Kade and his love of parties because I could opt out whenever I wanted, simply by sitting in a quiet corner and reading a book on my phone.

"Maybe. How long did we sleep? It's already day." Haden, his hand still clasped in mine, shifted, moving his body like a wall, ready to shield me from whatever we were to face. Or maybe he was just trying to protect me from the biting wind. Either way, I curled into him, accepting his warmth.

Here on the mountain, we seemed to be in a makeshift courtroom. To my right, sitting in a snowdrift, was a judge's stand, and in it, stood Mrs. Claus. She was wearing a black robe over her red and white outfit, seemingly unbothered by the strong, cold wind. To the left were two empty desks covered with a light dusting of snow. And standing on either side of Haden and me were shadowy figures I couldn't quite focus on. Whenever I tried looking directly at them, they shifted, always seeming to remain just within the edge of my periphery.

Black magic.

There were no lawyers or a jury. It was the two of us humans, shivering in front of Mrs. Claus, the judge.

"Tamara Madden and Haden Powell," Mrs. Claus said severely, and I swore there was a hint of joy in her voice. "You have been summoned to the Magical Court of Rules. You have been placed on the naughty list for tampering with the magical world, interacting with its inhabitants without proper permission, as well as interfering with the holiday known as Christmas. On these accounts, you are hereby sentenced—"

"Stop!" I hollered, startling Haden, my teeth chattering. "We didn't do any of that with intention. We have been trying to help. Hitting Rudolph was an accident because of a weak shroud beyond my control, and I've been—"

"You have also been brought here on the charges of brutality and kidnapping. The severity of these charges increases, due to the proximity to Christmas. The serious endangerment of Mr. Claus will also not be ignored, nor will your summoning of creatures from the North Pole with the intent of preventing and delaying Christmas."

"You have it all wrong!"

"You are welcome to present your evidence at this time."

"Evidence?" Haden asked me, his face turning white.

"There is no evidence, and she knows it," I complained under my breath. The tips of my ears were starting to lose feeling, and my nose felt ready to fall off. Even if we survived this unfair trial, we'd go home with frostbite.

"We would like to speak to a lawyer," Haden declared, wrapping me further in his warm embrace as I shuddered against the brutal, biting cold.

A lawyer? How we were going to find someone who understood what was going on and help us?

Make a wish.

I felt my spirit deflate. What other choice did we have? We didn't understand what was going on, and we didn't know how to get out of this mess. We needed someone on the inside. We needed a fairy godmother. *My* fairy godmother.

The only issue was that Mrs. Claus liked to brutally banish Estelle whenever she showed her face. But what had Sparkles, the fixer elf, told me about banishments? If I made a wish, Mrs. Claus couldn't banish Estelle if she was helping me? But Estelle could banish Mrs. Claus....

And start a war.

"Fine. I have assigned you the goat," Mrs. Claus stated, turning her head to one of the previously empty tables where an overweight grey and white goat appeared.

"Joulupukki? The Christmas goat?" I gasped.

Haden clutched me tighter, and I could tell that he knew the creature from Finnish folklore.

The goat was casually chewing its cud, looking bored and

more like a barnyard animal than a lawyer about to extract us from this sticky mess. My excitement waned. He made me think of the Three Billy Goats Gruff from a storybook I'd read as a kid.

Didn't one of the goats headbutt the troll at the end of the story?

Maybe the goat would make a good lawyer.

~

HAVING the goat as our lawyer was not good. I wasn't sure how the legal system worked in the magical world, but if it was anything like ours, we were in a hot mess. The goat seemed infinitely more interested in gnawing on the table than helping us.

"Ask her what evidence she has of our intent," I shout-whispered to the goat across the space that separated us. He stared at me, mindlessly chewing. "Well? Ask her!"

"Her mind is already made up. Make peace with it," he suggested.

"But this is unfair!"

"*Life* is unfair," Mrs. Claus growled at me, her eyes flaring red.

I straightened my spine. "And it's doubly unfair that you're keeping Haden here. I *asked* him to help me. He would have had nothing to do with this situation, otherwise. He's innocent, and I take all the blame."

"Tamara! What are you doing?" he whispered hoarsely, gripping my arm and pulling me back as I tried to step forward, my voice trembling.

"Trust me," I said, shaking him off. I couldn't stop, or I'd chicken out, the way I had been doing all night. It was time to end this, even if it wasn't in the way I'd hoped. Even if it meant giving up my own happily ever after.

"You need to let him go," I said firmly. "He's innocent."

"I *chose* to help her. I'm a veterinarian."

"He only came to help because I begged him to," I said, the bitter wind almost stealing the words from my mouth.

"I had a choice," Haden protested.

"I left him several panicked voicemails."

"I could have ignored them."

"I brought him into this, knowing I shouldn't let him see Rudolph or the others. I knew what I was doing when I breached your rules."

"Yes, that is a problem," Mrs. Claus said mildly. She was staring at Haden as though mulling over the pros and cons of keeping him as a slave, or possibly feeding him to some beast such as a dragon.

I tried to keep my spine straight, to prove I was strong enough to take the punishment for both of us. That I was the one worthy of her rage. The wind howled, numbing my ears, my chin, my hands. My cheeks ached from the buffeting blasts of stinging snow crystals and, unable to help it, I hunched into myself, teeth chattering.

Haden gathered me into his arms, hugging me tight, his flannel shirt against my cheek as he wrapped himself around me like a shelter. I leaned into him, feeling his reassuring solid weight press back.

"I'm so sorry I got you into all of this," I whispered with a shudder. Haden didn't deserve this. He was a good man in every way, and I'd never forgive myself if he lost out on a single thing because of what I'd pulled him into tonight.

"Nah," Haden said casually, "this has been fun."

I let out a laugh. It hurt.

"Please, let him go," I begged Mrs. Claus, my jaw trembling with the cold. "Punish me instead."

"Tamara, stop," Haden said.

"You don't understand," I told him, giving him a look I hoped he could read. I was not backing down. I was not going to let him lose his beautiful life, or have it tampered with because of me.

Even if it meant losing him. Even if it meant losing the love, I felt I was meant to have.

"Please," I begged. I wasn't even sure who I was talking to any longer. Haden? Mrs. Claus? God? Estelle? Myself?

I'd held off losing him as long as I could, but now we were at our magical crossroads, and it was time to say goodbye.

"TM, no," he said softly, as though able to read my resolve.

"I'll miss you," I said into his chest, savouring the warmth coming off his body. I hugged him hard, a cold fist of dread seizing my gut as I stepped away. In my periphery, I could see Mrs. Claus raising her glowing finger, decision made.

I held in a choked sob as I released him, tears in my eyes, momentarily freezing my lashes together whenever I blinked. "Please don't forget me. Don't forget tonight."

I vowed to myself that if I was still alive tomorrow, I'd find a way for us to stumble back toward the love we'd shared, no matter what.

"TM..." He reached for my hand, and I could see into those depthless eyes. I could see the love, and I held it in my heart, knowing I may not see it again.

I lifted the tips of my frozen index and middle fingers to my lips, hoping he knew I felt the same.

"Haden Powell." Mrs. Claus said his name with the gravity of a legal summons, which, I suppose, in this world it was.

Cold dread swirled through me like an unexpected, powerful storm.

Mrs. Claus snapped her glowing red fingers. "Out!"

Haden vanished. I stumbled forward, screaming despite myself, terrified by the empty space where he'd been standing only seconds ago.

"Where did you send him?"

"I returned him to your world. And as for you..." Her finger was glowing again, matching the ruby colour blazing in her eyes.

My gaze cut to my so-called lawyer. He was currently curled up in a ball, napping in the snow, a belly full of desk.

I felt panic welling up, choking my throat, clouding my mind with fear. I'd saved Haden, but now I had to face Mrs. Claus on my own. I needed to speak up for myself, but was scared I'd do it wrong. That I'd make things worse.

I gave myself a shake. If Haden were here, he'd tell me the truth about myself and I'd believe him. Tamara Madden was no longer the sweet, quiet pushover who waited for others to determine her fate. That woman had changed. She now spoke up for herself, and for what she wanted. She was kind, generous, and strong. But most of all, she was a woman who understood Mrs. Claus's heartbreak, and might be able to reach her beneath the tremendous burden of hurt.

"Mrs. Claus..." My voice came out clear and loud. "If I might speak before you make your final ruling? I know, from speaking to the reindeer and Hugo, that your powers are well-admired. But I've also heard that you haven't had it easy."

Her expression was stern, jaw unyielding like her gorgeous cheekbones. I blundered on, my words stumbling over each other in my haste, scared she'd dole out her punishment before I could make an argument.

"I understand how important you are to the holiday of Christmas, which is why I asked the crew to bring *you* to my barn. I had a feeling you were the one working tirelessly behind the scenes, making the holiday work, from creating the magical oats for the reindeer so they can fly, to other things they didn't disclose to me." Okay, so I was fibbing a tiny bit, but I *had* asked them to bring her into the loop early on, and had since realized just how vital she was to the holiday.

"I can tell that you, like so many of us women here on the non-magical earth, are not recognized. Santa gets all the credit, doesn't he? It looks easy because of all the work you put in behind the scenes supporting him. And I know this holiday can't happen without you, and your very special powers."

I bowed my head. "I tried saving Christmas tonight, and I failed." I lifted my head again. "I failed because we needed you."

"Christmas doesn't matter." Her finger was still glowing, but it was no longer pointed at me.

"Yes, it does! And it's so much more than just Santa leaving gifts for children. The spirit of the holiday starts when we're children who believe in Santa. We may stop, but the spirit of your holiday, and the hope it brings us, stays with us. As adults, we use that spirit to make the world a better place. Christmas is a time of generosity and caring for one another." I thought of my parents, and how their short breakup paralleled the Claus's own fight. "It's a time for second chances.

"If you stop what you're doing, Mrs. Claus, the holiday will die. Generations will lose the holiday spirit, and the hope that comes with it. We will lose that belief in miracles and magic.

"We humans need that, Mrs. Claus. More now than ever. Please don't abandon us. What you do matters. If you don't help your husband tonight—today—your holiday will be missed, and by extension, so will you."

"Mrs. Claus is just a façade," she growled. "I'm a black witch. Filled with evil." She waited for me to flinch but, to my credit, I didn't. "Mrs. Claus is a fake. A ruse. A charade. She isn't real."

"I think evil is a choice—something you've chosen to leave

behind, because you *are* Mrs. Claus. *You* are the embodiment of the image we humans have created. That image grew from our feelings toward you, and all that you do for the holiday and for Santa."

The intensity of the burning scarlet in her eyes wavered.

"We see and feel the way you care," I continued. "We see and feel your love, and your acceptance and benevolence. We see a sweet, kind woman who accepts and loves us like we're her own. Please continue to be her for us. Please save Christmas."

She had lowered her finger; the glowing extinguished. She looked tired, deflated. I soldiered on, my voice wobbling. "My biggest fear is that this holiday will cease to exist today. I could have wished my way out of this mess several times tonight, but I didn't because Christmas was in danger."

"Be honest." Her tone was chilly. "You didn't want to lose that man you tried to protect."

"Yes. That's true. And a bit selfish of me. But beyond that, I couldn't wish for us out of this night because it meant I'd be giving up on Christmas. The idea that I might be able to help save it... I couldn't have lived with myself if I'd wished my way out of it. Especially if we lost Christmas."

"What does Christmas matter to an adult? It's for kids. Christmas is just an excuse for you humans to overspend, over-consume, and act greedy."

"Some of us do that," I admitted. "But personally, I love seeing the generosity your holiday instills in others. It warms my heart to see people helping others in need." I took a deep breath. "You probably won't believe how important the traditions I have with my Oma are to me. I know I won't have her forever, and our time together at Christmas is irreplaceable. We started creating holiday rituals when my parents separated when I was thirteen. They got back together, but it was a scary time for me, and the traditions Oma and I created that year saved Christmas for me.

"Each year, those rituals remind me of that special time with my Oma. Celebrating your holiday brought my grandmother and me closer and gave me something I will always cherish. So, for the sake of Christmas, and all of the people who love your holiday, I want to help. I want to do whatever I can to make sure the children of the world—your children—wake up in the morning with a sense of wonderment, excitement, and joy. I want them to have this because of you."

"You're human." Her tone had lost its fierceness, and I could hear a tremor of defeated, long-standing, unresolved hurt. "And you have meddled. You have kidnapped and detained my elf, Hugo. You have injured my husband." The tremor intensified. "You have held his herd here on earth. Convinced them to perform reckless acts in a storm. You have given Rudolph human drugs for his pain. Pain that you caused with your carelessness. You have interacted with and harmed magical beings."

Her sentences were coming faster and faster. I sensed she was battling something, but I wasn't sure if she'd win or not. "You have breached the shroud. You have, without a doubt, interfered with a major magical holiday, and put it at great risk with your continued actions. You, Tamara Madden, are someone who needs to be made an example of."

I cringed, shivering with my eyes screwed shut, waiting for the zap that would end me.

Her decision was made. There was no saving Christmas.

I peeked through my lashes, determined to make one last attempt to change her mind.

"Please, Mrs. Claus. Santa still loves you."

"Irrelevant!" She clamped her hands over her ears.

"He wants to get back together. He misses you."

She shut her eyes, her body bending forward as though under a great weight.

"You're all he talks about. He would even live in the black magic world with you. He loves you so much. He'd give up *all* of this for you."

She straightened, her arms at her side, head held high. "Stop!" Her voice trembled, loud and fierce, as though a storm was ripping her apart from the inside. Her finger was glowing red, casting a scarlet glow into the cloud of snow swirling around her like a devil-possessed tornado. The finger was aimed at me.

I had one more option. Someone who could protect me.

Even though calling upon her meant losing tonight and losing Haden.

I unfurled the folded handwritten wish from my pocket. I read it to myself, then closed my eyes, hoping I wasn't too late.

CHAPTER 33

~ *Tamara* ~

The snow was falling gently around me and it was cold, nipping at my nostrils with every inhale. The sun was starting to paint the horizon with pale pink streaks.

I must have been gone for hours. I moved my feet, noting I was leaving tracks, the snow making that squeak-crunch sound it did when it was minus thirty. I could see my breath. I patted myself down. I appeared to be alive.

My wish had worked.

I spun in a small circle, on the lookout for Haden.

There were no burned sleigh remains on the driveway, meaning it had either been cleaned up or covered with fresh fallen snow.

I sprinted to the barn, yanking open the door. Familiar smells enveloped me. Dolly snickered a hello, and I murmured to her as I walked further inside, seeing my warm breath come out in clouds.

It was cold. Silent.

I stopped, taking in the building. There was no damaged sleigh. No night vision goggle boxes littering the barn floor. No reindeer. No Santa. No elves. No Christmas tree. I jogged to

Rudolph's stall, swinging my way through its entrance. No reindeer. No melted ice packs.

Shaking, I took a few steps, my boots shifting the straw and dirt at my feet. It was like they'd never been here. My yukaflux cooler stood upright, lid closed. I opened it. It was full.

Everything was back to normal.

I flew to the barn door and looked outside. There were no ruts in the fresh snow from us coming and going last night. I stumbled back inside and fell to my knees in the straw, sniffing away my tears.

I was wearing my winter coat again, and I found my phone, typing out a text to Haden.

ME

Did you get home okay?

I scrunched my eyes closed, my cold fingers cramping as they gripped my phone, waiting for a reply. He *had* to reply. He kept his phone on him, 24/7, because he was always on call.

Gripping my phone, I stared at the screen, willing a reply from Haden.

"Please, please, please," I whispered. Please let him remember us.

Bubbles appeared on my screen to show he was typing, and I held my breath, anticipatory tears welling in my eyes.

"Come on, come on."

Haden's message popped up.

HADEN

Yeah. Some storm, huh? Merry Christmas
Eve. 🎄

I frowned at the message, trying to decipher what it meant. The longer I stared at it, the more the letters blurred into nonsense, and the more my chest tightened with an inkling that felt more and more true by the moment. One I didn't want to accept.

I got up and made it as far as a square bale of straw before collapsing onto it in a defeated, heartbroken heap. A chickadee landed near my feet, then another, ready for their morning treat of sunflower seeds. I filled my palm from the nearby container of seeds and held it out for the chickadees. They landed lightly with their chilly, claw-like feet, taking turns, one after another, like a well-coordinated airport. Grab a seed and fly off. Grab a seed and fly off.

Haden had forgotten last night. We were back to avoiding each other. Back to the layers of misunderstandings that had added up over the years.

My phone vibrated with another message, and I peered at it.

HADEN

I hope my mom didn't pester you while I was out working in last night's storm. If she did—sorry.

I let out a strangled squeak and dropped my phone, pressing the heels of my hands against my eye sockets. I focused on my jagged breathing, trying to settle it.

No, no, no.

He was gone. My wish had undone everything.

I sniffed, then again, aware tears were streaking down my cheeks.

The door opened to the barn, and I stood so fast, I got woozy. "Haden?"

Someone was approaching, the dawn light at their back. "He won't recall anything from the magical world, or anything related to it."

Estelle. Her look of soft sympathy crushed me even further.

"He'll remember *nothing*?"

She nodded, her hair still singed from last night's banishment.

"But we fell in love last night..." I was sure we had. Shouldn't that overcome everything else?

"I'm sorry, Tamara. You know that rewinding the night to let things play out without you hitting Rudolph was the only way to safely extract you. He was a bystander, and all bystanders lose their memories when we do time mending. It's a very minor consequence."

"No." I stood, shaking my head. I couldn't imagine the cruelty of me remembering the fun we'd had, and Haden being oblivious to it all. "I still remember."

"Would you like your memories erased as well? I have the ability to wipe them, but the head fairy thought you would want them as a memento."

"*No*! You don't understand. He has to remember, too. He *has* to!"

Estelle sniffed, avoiding meeting my eyes. "Santa and his entourage are all okay, and have been returned to the North Pole. Christmas will proceed as usual, thanks to your wish, and whatever you said to Mrs. Claus. She is proceeding with Christmas, and you have been removed from the naughty list. Very well done."

I waved off her compliment. Mrs. Claus had only needed someone to make her see her own self-worth, and how much she was loved.

"I want to make a wish."

"A wish?"

"Just one. Help me get Haden's memories back from last night, so he remembers falling in love with me."

"I can't."

"We can skip over the magical interaction stuff. Just let him remember that he loves me, and remember that I also love him.

Something—anything along those lines. He doesn't have to remember being here, or Rudolph, or any of that stuff. Please."

"I can't. I'm sorry." Estelle gave me a sad frown. "This is where we part ways."

"What do you mean? Why? I'll pay for the wish. Whatever it costs. I'll find a way." The idea of losing Haden was horrible. What if I couldn't get him to love me without the magic of last night? What if I wasn't enough on my own? "I need your help. Please, Estelle."

"You've been banished," she said softly.

"Banished? No, I haven't. Look at me. I'm not singed or sunburned." I held out my arms to show her. I likely looked a mess, but I hadn't been scorched like she'd been.

"You've been forbidden from having any interactions with the magical world, including making wishes."

"But..."

"You got off easy. I'm sorry." Estelle turned and walked back out of the barn.

A sob rushed up my throat, escaping before I could catch it.

CHAPTER 34

~ *Tamara* ~

"What are you still doing in bed!" My mom had to be standing right over top of me, given how loud her voice was. I scrunched my eyes tighter and pulled a pillow over my head. "We have to be at Oma's in fifteen minutes."

She tugged at my pillow, and I groaned, rolling out of reach.

Oma's Christmas Eve brunch. I used to look forward to it, especially the rice and pineapple dessert she'd make for me with the half-melted mini marshmallows in it. She only whipped it up once a year, and she always did a double batch, just for me. She'd made it every year since I was thirteen, and only once had she tried making something else—a chocolate log. To me, nothing said Christmas like her rice dessert, and I'd been so disappointed in the log that she'd gone straight into the kitchen to rush out a batch of the rice dessert.

It had made me feel guilty, spoiled, but also so very cherished and special.

Oma would always be my favourite person in the world.

But today, even the thought of her holiday dessert couldn't rouse me from my heartache.

I'd saved Christmas, Haden, and myself, but I'd lost something precious. I'd lost Haden and his love, and I needed some time to come to terms with it. I needed a good wallow before picking myself up by my bootstraps and faking a smile until it finally felt real again.

"You're not even dressed!" my mom chirped. The drawers of my dresser screeched open. "Where's your Oma sweater?"

I sighed and flipped onto my back, bringing the pillow with me. I felt hungover. Was this a side effect of being pulled into the magical world, and then spit back out again?

"Tamara," my mom said in exasperation. I peeked out from under the pillow. The room streamed with sunshine, and she was done up in her usual Christmas outfit, dressed in red and green from head to foot.

I pulled the pillow tighter over my eyes. Everything about Christmas reminded me of last night. The laughs. The kisses. The fun we'd had. I didn't want to get up. I didn't want to face the holiday. Not this year.

"Get a move on. Where's your Oma sweater?"

"Wearing it," I mumbled. Oma and I wore our matching ugly Christmas sweaters or sweatshirts for every meal and gathering during December to ensure we got our money's worth. In our family, that meant I'd worn my Oh-What-Fun-it-is-to-Ride sweatshirt last night, and would wear it again for today's brunch, and tomorrow's supper.

My mom had tried to get in on the tradition, but unfortunately for her, that was during her separation from Dad, which meant I'd been a hissing, scratching and biting thirteen-year-old who'd snarled at her like a feral stray who wanted to be left alone.

Needless to say, the sweater thing stayed between me and Oma.

"Go ahead without me," I mumbled from my mini haven of sorrow and lost love. "I'll catch up."

"We are *not* going separately. Your father is delivering last minute Christmas hampers, so he's arriving on his own. I don't want us all straggling in one at a time, as if we don't like each other."

I sighed, knowing I wasn't winning this one, but was willing to give it one last-ditch attempt.

"I don't like Christmas anymore. I'm staying home."

A cool hand immediately slid between the pillow and my forehead. There was a pause, then my mom said in a motherly tone filled with affection and impatience. "No fever. Time to wake up, because you're dreaming. You love Christmas." She gave me a gentle pinch.

"Ow!" I protested, even though it hadn't hurt. I lifted my head out from under the weight of my pillow. Was that all last night had been? Dreams? From the flying reindeer to Haden's kisses, all just fiction thanks to a lonely, overactive imagination that had gone into overdrive while I'd been asleep?

"A dream?" I asked.

The bedding was whipped off me. A throaty noise of disapproval came from her direction. "Did you sleep in your clothes?"

"Mm-hmph. I told you that already." I covered my eyes with an arm, wincing at the light. The lull between last night's storm, and tonight's oncoming one meant the sun was uninhibited, and sending its rays ricocheting off the bright white snow outside, into my room to attack my retinas. "Close the curtains."

"You need to get dressed." My mom sighed, and the sound of my dresser drawers opening and closing took up their banging again. "How many Christmas sweaters do you have?" she asked in wonder.

"Lots." Well over a decade's worth.

I rubbed my fingertips together, marvelling at their tender sensitivity. A nip of frostbite. Last night hadn't been a dream.

I rolled onto my stomach, head back under my pillow. I could hear Mom sorting through my drawers, and I was fairly confident she was picking out fresh undergarments for me, like she had when I was two. I should never have given her a key to my place.

Cringing at the thought of her pawing through my delicates, I hauled myself out of bed. "I'm up."

She handed me a stack of folded clothing. "Go shower."

I flung the bra she'd stacked on my sweater and jeans into the corner. "That one's itchy." I grabbed a fresh one. It was no longer white, more of a sad grey, with its elastic all stretched out, but beautifully comfy.

"You smell like the barn." There was an unfamiliar hint of approval in her tone, and I wondered briefly if Estelle had messed up last night while setting my life back to normal.

MY MOM's car plowed through a snowdrift at the end of my driveway, with me in the passenger seat. I'd tried to drive, getting as far as sitting in Benjamin, who was free of snow and reindeer hair, as well as hoof holes and paint scratches. But he wouldn't start. He hadn't been plugged in. I'd snatched the bundle of mistletoe from my mirror on my way out, clutching it like a magical lifeline back to kisses with Haden.

I sagged into my mom's car, and hung the green sprig from her rearview mirror, staring at it like it held the answer to last night, and how to carry on now that I was the only one who remembered it all.

Mom's tire tracks were still in my driveway from her

earlier arrival, as was the rectangular levelling of snow where her car's undercarriage had dragged through the drifts. But there were no tracks from Haden's truck. Had he really not been here, or had the wind filled in the tire ruts while I'd slept?

The idea that he hadn't seen Rudolph, or laughed with me over Blitzen, or kissed me after playing Nerf gun tag in the hardware store made me glum. I leaned my arm on the door and rested my head against it.

"I was thinking about you, and your lack of a male companion," my mom started.

I groaned. "Please, no."

"I was *thinking*," she repeated firmly, "how Kade was never quite right for you. The two of you just never quite clicked in the way I'd like to see. He didn't get to know you properly. Not in the way a partner should."

I blinked once, twice. Had she really just said that?

I lifted my head to look at her. This was not a normal conversation with my mom. Something had definitely been set back incorrectly when Estelle had time-hopped me out of my sticky magical problem last night.

"Say that again?" I requested.

"You need a man who'll stick up for you, and help you reach your own goals."

My mind immediately thought of Haden, and all the ways he'd stood by me last night. Everything from unsuccessfully refusing to let me shield him from Mrs. Claus in court, to paying for all of our supplies and x-raying Rudolph.

"I do?" I asked.

"Yes. Someone who understands you, and who'll have your back. Maybe someone like..." She laughed, her hands coming off the steering wheel for one precious second of terror as the car slipped a few inches to the right, caught in the fresh snow, before correcting itself back into the packed-down snowy tracks. "Silly idea."

I sat up. Who did she have in mind for me? I could tell by her tone it wasn't Teddy, the borderline alcoholic bachelor she was certain would turn himself around if he just dated the right woman. Or if it was someone I might already have in mind. "Tell me who."

"Oh, it's silly." Her cheeks flushed. "But I was thinking how you and Haden always get along with your little smirks that drive everyone crazy and—"

"We smirk?" That sounded annoying.

"Oh, I can't describe your connection. I think you're a bit of an introvert, Tamara. And he's a bit more your speed. And while I know he's a lot older than you, he does like horses."

I laughed, the feeling like rusted barbed wire vibrating in my chest. "Well, he is a vet."

"You know what I mean."

"Do you think he likes me? You know, like that?" I asked, feeling pretty much as though I'd reverted back to being an insecure teenager again, but unable to help myself. Kade seemed to have been able to see the attraction between Haden and me, or at least, suspected it. If my mom recognized it, too, it gave me some hope that even if Haden had forgotten last night, we might be able to start something anew.

"And can you slow down?" I needed more time to explore this conversation, and we were nearly at Oma's.

"It's fine. The roads aren't that bad. Not like last night. I heard five people hit the ditch, and Teddy claimed he saw reindeer!" My mom laughed and shook her head. "What I'm trying to say is that you're a strong woman, Tamara. You need to make the decisions that are right for you. But I do understand how awkward things might be, given that you dated his younger brother."

"Do you think it's possible, though? That he might think of me in that way? Do you think his family would be on board?"

"Well, I don't think Kade is quite ready to give up on you yet. He misses the way you love him. He doesn't have that same depth in his relationships with others." She laughed. "So, you might need to wish for some outside help on that one."

I leaned against the door, feeling unsettled by her word choice. "Sadly, my fairy godmother's cut me off."

My mom laughed again before growing more serious as she pulled into her mother's driveway. "Well, I hope that you find love, and that everything works out well for you. That's my Christmas wish for you."

CHRISTMAS EVE BRUNCH was the same as it was every year. Oma had made pancakes, sausages, eggs, and a mother's helper casserole, which went in the oven and had eggs and bread. It was a recipe she promised she'd pass down to me when the time was right. I assumed that meant when I had a family of my own. Although, my mom was still waiting for her turn at the hostess reins, so maybe it was a promise as empty as my heart.

"Plug in the tree, dear," Oma commanded. "I'll check on the casserole." She took in my lacklustre enthusiasm and added, "I made your special dessert." She patted my cheek.

"Thanks, Oma."

I did as she asked, and plugged in the tree in her living room, lighting up its giant multi-coloured bulbs that had been popular sometime in the seventies or eighties.

My phone buzzed with a text, and my heart leapt. Haden? Was he starting to remember last night?

No, it was Char. I was way behind on the GAL PAL chat, having not checked in since sometime in the night. Honestly, I'd been too afraid to check the chat this morning, worried that Estelle had erased their memories, too, and that I'd be all alone with the truth about Christmas and how close it had come to disaster.

Estelle had said Christmas was a go, but was Mr. and Mrs. Claus's relationship fixed, too? What if Christmas was still on the line, but for other reasons?

Char was texting me directly.

CHAR

Are the skies clear?

ME

Yeah. Blizzard's over. Another on the way, though.

CHAR

Did our mutual friend help you out?

Too late, I realized she was talking about Estelle and my Christmas problem, and not the weather. I had a whole lot of explaining to do to get her caught up, so I dialled her number.

"Yo!" She sounded happy and sleepy.

"How's Mexico?"

"Fabulous." There was a lift in her voice, and I could tell she was in love. "Tell me about Haden and last night."

"You remember last night?" I confirmed. "Everything? Rudolph and all that?"

"I wasn't that drunk!" she protested. "It was two drinks over three hours, Tam-Tam."

"Just checking!"

I climbed the old wooden steps to the house's second floor, where the bedrooms were located. The steps creaked as I went, the dry winter air making them extra vocal.

"Haden and I kissed last night."

"Right, and…? How are things this morning? Did he stay over?"

I heaved a sigh. "No…"

"Oh, no. What happened?"

"Things were going well. And then we…" I checked the hallway and whispered, "We got summoned."

"Summoned? By who? To where?"

"The magical courts."

"It's real?"

"Very."

"Dang. Then what?"

"I'm pretty sure I used up all of your last credits last night."

"That's fine."

"Brunch in five!" hollered my mom. "Tamara? Where are you?"

"Up here!" I called before saying into the phone, "Mrs. Claus was going to—"

"Mrs. Claus?"

I realized just how out of the loop my friend was with everything that had happened last night while she'd been sleeping.

I quickly gave her an overview of the entire night, starting with hitting Rudolph, which she knew about, to Hugo, Santa, and my feelings for Haden, which I'd felt were being returned. Then on to being in court, and waking up this morning with everybody else's memories erased.

"No," Char breathed. "Tam, this is awful. I'm so sorry." The sorrow in her voice brought tears to my eyes.

I lowered my voice. "And things feel different."

"Different how?"

"My mom said Kade wasn't the man for me."

Char gasped. "What? No way!"

"Yeah." Man, I missed my bestie. It felt good talking to someone who knew my life, my history and all the nuances, so when one thing fell out of alignment, she immediately understood the deeper impact. "She actually suggested that Haden would be a good match for me."

"What? *No*! For real?"

"I swear I've pinched myself so many times that my arm is bruised." I could feel the dinner bell clock countdown happening downstairs. I needed a solution to my Haden issue. "What do I do?"

"There's no way we can recreate last night for Haden," Char said in a tone that was thoughtful. "But maybe there's a way we can jog his memory, or start over or something. Did you ask Estelle about wishing his memories back?"

"I've been banned."

"Oh, right. Sorry. You mentioned that. That's super unfair. You basically saved Christmas."

"Clearly, Mrs. Claus doesn't see it that way."

"Time to eat!" my mother hollered up the stairs.

That was only two minutes, not five!

"Just a minute!"

"Who are you talking to?" she called.

"Char."

"Tell her I hope she's having a good Christmas, even though it won't be a white one down there in Mexico. And be sure to tell her to be careful about the cartels. And—"

"Okay! Thanks, Mom!" I lowered my voice to relay the Merry Christmas bit to Char, "She also says—"

"I heard her. Tell her Merry Christmas, and that I'm too heavy for the cartels to kidnap."

I snorted and called down to Mom. "She says ditto, and thanks!"

My mom muttered something about me being a horrible messenger, then added firmly, "Time to eat. *Now,* Tamara."

"Sorry, I gotta go," I told Char. "Text me if you figure out a loophole to get Haden's memories back."

"I'll ask Josie. She might know a way."

"Tamara Rose!" my mom hollered.

"I'm coming!"

"Go eat your brunch before your mom turns into an ogre."

We giggled and ended the call, my heart filled with gratitude that at least Char still remembered last night, and was willing to try to help me find a way to make Haden remember, too.

I hustled downstairs to find Mom and Dad bickering over where everyone was going to sit, even though it was just the four of us. In the end, we all sat in the living room, as always, because Oma made up a plate and went straight to her favourite armchair. Some things were irrefutable, immovable traditions that could never be changed. Thankfully.

We were just finishing the meal when the doorbell rang. I snapped to my feet, a feeling in my gut telling me that someone was here to see me.

"I'll get it!"

I flung open the front door, sending Oma's pine bough wreath flying from its hook. It rolled off the front step, and into the fresh snowdrifts lining the sidewalk.

"Merry Christmas Eve," Haden said, stooping to collect the wreath for me. Moving a gift bag in his left hand, he hung the wreath on its brass hook behind me as clouds of warm air escaped the house.

"Haden," I said, my voice embarrassingly breathless. "Merry—hi. What are you doing here?"

Was he here to kiss me? Sweep me into his arms, and tell me he remembered everything?

He looked tired, and like he'd been up all night with me. He hadn't shaved yet, and his black toque was pulled down over his forehead, making his guarded eyes look even more closed than usual. In such a short time, I'd become accustomed to being able to see deep into his soul, the way I had last night. Seeing those familiar shuttered eyes made me miss him all the more.

I felt my heart drop its hope like a heavy burden, landing in my gut. Would I ever be able to see into his soul again? Would I be allowed past the barriers and gates that kept most people at bay?

He was one step lower than I was. Oma's front step was only really big enough for one unless you wanted to stand toe-to-toe with your visitor. Which I kind of did—but in a friendly way.

Haden shifted uneasily, his eyes searching mine. He looked a little lost, and I wondered what Mrs. Claus had done to him when she'd sent him back to our world. I hoped she hadn't scrambled that impressive brain of his.

"So Rudolph comes tonight, huh? I mean, Santa," he said, his tone slightly gruff and uncertain. He scratched his brow and winced, as though cringing at himself.

It felt like there was a whisper of a memory begging to be recalled. Why else would he mention Rudolph and Santa? Sensing that it was a place to start, I scrambled to figure out where I could place my crowbar in order to open him up.

"Close the door!" my dad bellowed. "Heat ain't free!"

I was starting to shiver in the cold anyway, so I stepped back into the house, waving Haden inside. "Come in," I said, rubbing my arms.

His smile was shy. "I like your Christmas sweater. Same as your Oma's?"

I nodded and gestured to the gift bag he was holding. "What have you got there?"

"Oh, yeah. I saw this." He looked at the bag doubtfully, but didn't offer it to me.

"Yeah?"

"I was helping Justin at the store this morning. Last-minute shoppers. And..." He stopped talking, fiddling with the bag's handles. His cheeks had turned an endearing pink, and he looked like he wanted to run.

"That's nice of you to help him. I thought maybe you'd be busy with emergencies."

"Yeah, no. It's been strangely quiet today." He pulled his phone from his back pocket, waving it at me as if I'd get the reference he was making—that the single ladies of Eagle Ridge were too busy with family commitments to make up any animal emergencies for the town's most-eligible bachelor. He frowned at his phone and put it back in his pocket.

"The HAGs are busy, eh?"

"Guess so." The corner of his mouth quirked up in the most adorable, sheepish way.

Wait! He remembered what I called his fan group? Or was he just playing along, like he was following my form of crazy?

My breath caught in anticipation as he leaned back on his heels, his chest expanding as though bolstering himself. "So, yeah." He handed me the bag. "For you. I think my brother has something for you, too, but he's out having coffee with Jannifer."

"He is? Wow. That's great." What other little extras had Estelle slipped into last night's wish?

"It's nothing much." Haden pointed at the bag. "But it made me think of you for some reason." I could tell he wanted to explain the gift away, but, to his credit, he owned it.

"Oh. Uh, thanks."

He opened the door, pausing to look at me for a long moment before stepping outside again.

"Merry Christmas," I said, giving him a hopeful smile.

He'd leaned in like he was going to kiss me, then caught

himself and wrapped me in a brief and wonderful smelling hug. "Merry Christmas, TM."

TM. My breath froze in my chest as he headed back out into the cold. As the door clicked shut, I exhaled and peeked in the bag. Inside was a Nerf gun.

~

WITH A GROWING sense of urgency and panic, I opened the GAL PALs chat, which was blowing up. Char had filled in the girls while I'd brunched with my family, and now I hunched over my phone at the sink, pretending to wash the dishes before dessert to get myself caught up, as well as to share the latest Haden development.

Had Mrs. Claus's memory scrubbing not worked? Or was her spell still finding all the nooks and crannies to wipe clean?

And why had Char sent my problem out to all five of us? Samantha and Gabby were never going to believe, and Josie ghosted us most of the time, like she was a boomer who only bothered to check her phone once a day.

ME

Haden almost kissed me. Right now. At Oma's. Then he caught himself.

CHAR

You should have grabbed him and kissed him.

JOSIE

What? How? His memory was erased.

I was surprised to see her in the chat, and sad that she didn't seem to have found any loopholes that would help Haden get his memory back. If anyone knew the answer, it would be her.

Instead, she'd lectured me about how very, very lucky I'd been to get out of court the way I had.

Yeah, thanks. Loving the support.

GABBY

He remembers? OMG that's so romantic.

ME

I thought you didn't believe in this magic stuff?

GABBY

I believe in love!

CHAR

You should have kissed him and made him remember.

GABBY

Like in the fairy tales! I love fairy tales.

ME

Did someone make a wish for me? One where he'd get his memories back?

I crossed my fingers, hoping someone had.

CHAR

No.

GABBY

Of course not.

SAMANTHA

Seriously. Get ur heads checked. Fairy godmothers ARE NOT REAL.

GABBY

What about Cupid? Is he real?

CHAR

He's a Roman god. So, different kettle of
fish. Eros is the Greek version, FYI.

SAMANTHA

CHAR

I'm proud to be a nerd. Have you seen my
new job, and all the cool travel I get to do?

GABBY

Well, if Cupid is real, and on the loose like
your fairy godmother, send him my way.
Preferably on Valentine's Day weekend. 

JOSIE

It doesn't work like that, Gabs.

GABBY

So? I need a boyfriend. I don't care who
Cupid shoots so he falls in love with me.

JOSIE

Tamara, don't forget—you've been banned.
Wishes can't be granted on your behalf, or
for your benefit.

That was actually a bit of a relief. Other than nobody being
able to release Haden's memories.

ME

Haden gave me a Nerf gun.

SAMANTHA

Lame. Weirdo.

ME

We played with Nerf guns in the hardware
store last night and made out.

SAMANTHA

What? I missed everything! You big rebel.
Way to go.

ME

Today he brought one for me. He dropped it
off, but didn't know why. What does that
mean?????

GABBY

CHAR

We need to find out.

GABBY

Maybe kissing him undoes the spell that
was put on him. You should kiss him, just in
case.

ME

So now you believe in spells?

GABBY

I believe in romance. And this is so
romantic.

SAMANTHA

Gabs, come on. They're all cracked in the
head.

GABBY

But it's so romantic! It's like a movie.

ME

Maybe some memories were missed when
they cleared him?

JOSIE

Magic is complicated.

CHAR

What should Tam-Tam do?

JOSIE

Thinking.

Could Haden be in love?

GABBY

Of course he is!

JOSIE

Because, if so, you can't unmagic deep feelings like that. Love finds a way.

CHAR

Nice Jurassic Park reference.

JOSIE

It wasn't one. The movie quote was "LIFE finds a way."

CHAR

Josie was our resident magic expert, thanks to all of the paranormal romance she read. Even though she was super analytical, if she believed in the power of love to overcome magic, then that was good enough for me.

GABBY

I think he's in love. Definitely. Kiss him. I bet all his memories come back. But hurry. Because what if there's some magical window that's open right now, and it closes if you wait too long?

The gals all chimed in, very clearly on board with the idea of me kissing Haden to see what happened.

I mean, yeah. I wanted to believe in the power of love. It was a happily ever after of the finest order. Movies and fairy tales had been made on that premise. Everyone felt good about the theme of love conquering all.

But was it all simply wishful thinking? If I kissed Haden, would it ruin what little we had left?

On the flip side, what if there really was a magical window, and it was closing on us?

I finished the dishes for Oma, my mind swirling.

Yes. No.

Real. Not real.

I felt like it might be love.

But could we have fallen in love in just one night?

Unless we'd spent years slowly falling in love, and last night, it had all just slipped into place, finally becoming a real, tangible thing that even magic couldn't erase.

I LEFT brunch as soon as possible, wolfing down Oma's special Christmas dessert, and then begged the car off Mom. She could ride home with Dad, whereas I claimed I'd forgotten to check on Dolly, and needed to hurry back to make sure her water hadn't frozen.

Instead, I crossed town, passing memory after memory. Jannifer's shop, the hardware store, and finally Haden's clinic. I had so many memories I couldn't share with the one person who'd been there with me. Haden would pass these buildings, never knowing what had existed inside them for just one night.

I parked my parents' car behind Haden's clinic, beside his truck, and wondered if showing up unannounced was the wrong move. If I'd been thinking, I could have created an excuse to track him down...like giving him a Christmas gift. And then kissing his face off.

What if kissing him didn't work?

What if he looked at me with those blank, shuttered eyes again?

I felt frantic. Desperate. Hopeful. Scared.

"Why can't this be easy?" I hollered, my head tipped back.

I immediately felt embarrassed. What if Lady MacBeth was watching me and had heard me scream through the car windows?

Sighing, I gripped the steering wheel. At least I knew where to find Haden. Imagine my frustration if I didn't even know where to look? Since it was Christmas Eve, I knew his parents' house was usually stuffed with extended family. And every year he arrived late, sliding into his spot at the table beside me just before grace. I wasn't sure how he timed it so precisely each year, or why when he loved spending time with his family.

I got out of the car, terrified by what I was about to attempt, and the knowledge that I could truly ruin what little there was left between us.

CHAPTER 35

~ *Haden* ~

Someone was knocking on the clinic's back door, and I grumbled over the interruption. Every Christmas Eve, my clinic was my sanctuary. I'd hide out until supper, then slip into my spot just before grace to avoid Tamara and her cocoa-butter scent. But mostly to avoid seeing my brother fawn all over her. Every Christmas, I was on edge thinking that this could be the year he'd pin her down with a ring.

Even though she wasn't coming this year, and even though a proposal wouldn't be happening, I was still avoiding the house out of habit.

It didn't help that I couldn't get Tamara out of my thoughts today. Every time I got close to thinking about something else, my groggy mind would pull up snippets of daydreams that felt like reality.

I opened the metal back door, realizing I should be grateful for the distraction and my increasing insanity. I mean, I'd bought her a Nerf gun today? Why? All I could say was that I'd been compelled by some unexplainable inner compunction. Why a Nerf gun? Were we twelve? No wonder she'd spent the past few years avoiding me. Not only did I mansplain veterinarian facts to her as if she was a curious little kid, and not a grown woman capable of researching things on her own, but I acted like a fool.

A blast of icy December air hit me as I peered out at my visitor. I took an involuntary step back. Tamara. Cheeks flushed, bottom lip clamped between her teeth, brown eyes round and worried.

I immediately stepped forward, wanting to take her into my arms.

"That's not safe, you know." She came inside, gliding past me.

"What isn't?" I felt a stab of panic, and fisted my hands so I wouldn't grab her, wrap her in my arms and protect her from whatever danger she thought might be lurking in my perfectly safe back alley.

She ignored my question, patting my chest with a gloved hand as she passed. "I like the Christmas colours." I watched her touch my red and green flannel shirt, and felt as though I was having an out-of-body experience. We didn't usually touch. In fact, we very carefully avoided each other. She looked cautious, but also like...

I couldn't put my finger on it, which was odd. Usually I could read her.

"Well, not everyone dresses like their Oma," I quipped, thinking about her adorable sweater tradition with her grandmother.

Tamara snorted, trying to hold back a laugh.

"Something wrong with Boots?"

"My animals are okay."

A pressing need to touch her was rendering me mute. Finally, I asked, "What's dangerous?"

"You shouldn't open the door without knowing who's out here." Her tone turned playful. "It could be a black witch, or a lawyerly goat set on eating you out of house and clinic."

Something wasn't adding up. She was watching me incredibly carefully, her words echoing through my mind like a joke where I'd once known the punchline, but now couldn't retrieve it.

I nodded, holding eye contact with her for longer than we usually did. She didn't look away, didn't pretend she didn't see me watching, or quickly start talking about something random.

"I have a camera that overlooks the alley."

"Did you check it before opening the door?"

"Never."

"And you always open it?"

I shrugged. Only deliveries came to the back. "Pretty much."

She was running a hand over a metal gurney—the one for large animals that had been left out in the middle of the room for some reason. "Ever had Rudolph come by in need of an x-ray?"

I slowly shook my head. Her question felt like a secret password, meant to unlock something. But I couldn't find the box it would open.

I felt a warmth gazing at her. I didn't bother looking away, and took her in. Why did it feel as though that old curtain that had always hung between us, making everything with her feel forbidden, had been lifted?

"What do you need? Are you okay?" I was growing concerned by her unorthodox visit. We were out of pattern in nearly every way.

"It's fine. You're busy." She was heading for the door she'd just come through. Her voice wobbled, becoming quiet. "I don't... I don't want anything. Thanks."

I caught her arm, knowing she'd come here for something.

Something pivotal. "What you want right now is more important than anything else."

Tamara's face went pale, and she slowly turned to me, looking as if she'd seen a ghost. I dropped my hand. "What I want?" she asked, her voice hoarse.

"Yes."

"It's important?"

Her words felt like an echo. "What you want right now is more important than anything else," I repeated, something stirring inside me. Another password, another key, another mystery.

"Even more than what you want?" she asked.

"Yes."

"You heard me say that to your brother." There was a wonderment in her voice, and I nodded, her statement ringing true, even though I couldn't remember when we might have said such things.

"You heard me?" she repeated. "And you remember?"

"Tamara, when you're talking, I'm always listening." It was the truth. The tender, honest truth.

Before I could follow my instinct to draw her close and cup her jaw, she suddenly spun on the heel of her clunky winter boots, racing back outside.

I followed, unsure if I should apologize.

She placed a knee on the driver's seat, reaching into her mom's car.

"What happened to Benjamin?" I called, referring to her Sebring.

"I hit a reindeer with it last night." She climbed back out of the car, returning with a sprig of mistletoe that I swear had been hanging from her rearview mirror at some point. Now it was in her mom's car. Everything felt slightly out of place today.

"Wait. Did you say reindeer?" I asked, as she hurried to the clinic. "This isn't their usual range. Did you report it? They're a species at risk."

"Rangifer tarandus," she confirmed, delighting my nerdy veterinarian heart. "Woodland caribou. He's okay." She lifted the mistletoe above her head. "Also, I feel bad that I didn't get you a Christmas gift, too, so I thought I'd say thanks..." Her voice faltered.

My eyes slowly moved to the sprig of green above us. I repeated her words over and over in my brain. Thoughts that felt like memories came tumbling through my mind. Reindeer. Kisses in the hay.

Tamara. Tamara in my arms. Tamara laughing. Tamara kissing me.

Her cheeks started to flush, and I could tell she was about to leave, embarrassed.

Instinctively, I grabbed her around the waist and drew her tight to my chest, kissing her long and slow, the feeling both familiar and new. But also, so very right.

MY LIPS WERE BRUISED, my heart happy, and my brain confused by a flood of impossible memories. I pressed Tamara against the clinic door and kissed her again.

Memories were everywhere in this room.

X-raying Rudolph. Trying to offer Tamara my leftover Christmas baking from a client, and Rudolph eating them all. The herd out in the alley. I chuckled, a memory of Tamara driving Rudolph around in her convertible in last night's blizzard.

She was amazing.

And we'd kissed.

I'd felt things.

I pulled her back for another kiss, confirming to myself that she was real, and so was this.

I'd secretly thought about this moment for a long time.

"Haden?"

"Shh. Kiss me again," I growled, pulling her tight to me. I needed about a million more of these moments with her.

Finally, breathing hard, we pulled apart. My nerve endings were singing. How had we gotten here, her and I? How had we gone from avoiding each other, to kissing like we were made for each other?

And what were all these crazy images in my head?

"I had the wildest dreams last night," I said, leaning my forehead against hers, hoping she'd help me sort out the impossible insanity I was facing. We'd lost the mistletoe, and I planned to find it later and keep it so I could reinvent this moment over and over.

My hands had wound their way through the hair framing her face, and I was holding her like a lover would. I wanted to kiss her again. I wanted to be her everything. I didn't want to go home. I didn't want to leave this moment in time, even though I didn't understand it.

"What was the dream?" she asked.

"It was about you. We had to...to save Christmas." My thoughts were cloudy, memories not yet settled. It all felt too make-believe to be real. And yet...it felt real. Like a true memory.

"And?" she asked impatiently.

I tentatively grazed her jawline with my thumb, still unsure how we'd become so comfortable in each other's arms. I'd missed something big.

Tamara leaned in, inhaling me.

"Rudolph could talk," I said.

She nodded. "Yes. He can."

"He can," I repeated.

"Because he's real."

"He's real?" I felt like a parrot echoing her, trusting her.

I savoured Tamara's warmth, the feeling of her in my arms. This was real. Not a memory. But it was also a memory, too.

"In Justin's store this morning, I kept having weird flashes." It was unsettling. They weren't memories, but more of a shifting sense of déjà vu. "You and I had broken in. No, not broken in. But we were in there and we shouldn't have been."

"And we made out?" The corner of her mouth lifted, her eyes glittering with devilish sparkles.

"Yeah." I gripped her elbows, pulling her against me as my lips instinctively found hers. It was like my body remembered last night, and wanted to recreate the moments, make the memories more vivid and strong. The kiss was long and slow, her tongue meeting mine, our bodies humming as if they were singing the same song, one composed just for us.

The gauzy mist that had been holding me all day was releasing its hold, almost like a waning spell.

My memory flashed open, revealing one of those secrets it had been keeping. I blurted, "Mrs. Claus is a witch."

"What else do you remember?" Tamara asked, her words quiet and soft, similar to the way I spoke to an injured animal.

Had I been hurt? Was that why my brain felt so fuzzy today?

"What happened last night?" I asked.

"A lot."

"Did we save Christmas?"

"I hope so."

A flood of memories rushed through my mind, little vignettes of Tamara being her sweet self. Helping the animals, trying to right a mounting pile of accidental wrongs.

And locking a cranky elf in the trunk of her car.

I tipped my head back and laughed. This woman. Oh, this woman.

"Tamara," I asked her softly, "why didn't I meet you first?"

Her expression softened, her gaze tracing a line across my brow, down my cheek, over my lips and back to my eyes where they locked in place. "You did meet me first. We just weren't ready for this yet."

She stepped tight against my body, pressing into me. Her hands slid up my chest with a practised and surprising confidence, as if she knew exactly what was in my heart and welcomed it.

"And how about now? Are you ready now?" I whispered.

She kissed me like this was real, not a dream, and like it could never be taken away.

CHAPTER 36

~ *Tamara* ~

When we broke apart, Haden's hands were still bracing my face, and his lips were curved into a rare half smile. Then it faded and his eyes fogged with confusion.

"Why am I having trouble remembering?" he asked.

"Because..." I sucked in a deep breath, unsure of what he could remember, and worried that telling him the full truth would be a breach of my banishment from the magical world. Revealing everything could also set him back, rather than bring the rest of his memories forward.

I decided to risk it all, like a Vegas gambler riding on a high. Go big or go home.

"Because of Mrs. Claus."

He looked to the side, focusing on something in the distance. Paperwork that needed to be done? An uncapped bottle of antiseptic? Or was he recalling everything?

And did it matter if he remembered everything? He remembered me, and us.

His gaze cut back to me. His voice was low when he continued, as if he feared I might be the one to label *him* as crazy, "So, *all* of that was real?"

I nodded.

"And you remember everything from last night?" he asked.

"I think so."

"We kissed."

"Several times," I confirmed.

I liked that he circled back to that again. I also wanted him to announce that we'd fallen in love, too. But maybe it was a bit early for those sorts of proclamations.

His thumb brushed my cheek. There was a lightness in his eyes now, as though he'd finally received something he'd been wishing for. "We like each other."

"Yes."

"A lot." I could see into his soul, and I wanted to dance and sing. I was the luckiest woman in the world. I pulled Haden into a tighter hug, listening to his heart, then lifting my face for another kiss.

His voice dropped, filled with mischief. "Are we a couple?"

I tempered myself. I wanted to pick up where we'd left off at high speed, but I also didn't want to scare him away.

Was this how spouses felt when their true love got amnesia, and didn't remember who they were and what they meant to each other?

"Would you like to be?" I asked.

His head angled, focusing on my mouth before lifting it to meet my eyes. I had to look away. His focus was so intense, so unreadable. "What would you like, TM?"

TM.

He'd called me that last night.

Haden could have any woman he chose. Would he choose me again in the light of day, now that we didn't have magic swirling around us, making everything more exciting? Did he want the quiet version of me, who loved curling up with a book or movie or saddling up a horse for a long ride through the bush?

"What would you like?" I whispered, my voice wobbling. I wanted to lock eyes and let him see how much I wanted this. But I was scared to show him how much it meant to me, and how frightened I was of losing him.

I wanted us to be a choice—his choice. No chance of magic.

His thumb traced the big knuckle of my pointer finger, slow and gentle.

"What would *you* like?" he repeated back to me.

I know he was asking about us, but it also felt like an invitation to finally speak all of my dreams to someone who'd listen. No judgement, no gentle corrections. He'd just listen to what was in my heart. Something I'd only recently learned to listen to.

I tried to take a half step back and break his grip, but he held me tight, flexing those strong arms that could hold a frightened goat.

"What do you want, Trademark?"

My fear felt like lava forcing its way up through my throat, ready to spew forth. I felt mocked by life, by fate, and the magical realm.

I wanted easy. For the first time in my life, I wanted a man to love me the way I was. I wanted him to fit into my life like he belonged there, as if he was an integral, important, vital, and happy part. I was so exhausted by trying so hard, and pretending, and putting so much into a relationship just to make it fly.

His arms gave me a light squeeze, locking me into his embrace, and I loved it while simultaneously fearing it.

"I want a life here in Eagle Ridge," I confessed. "A full one. I want my own farm with animals. I want love. I want a man who is easy to be with, and always has my back."

My whole body felt weak and shaky, like it had been forced to be strong on its own for far too long.

"Someone who says nice things to me, and makes me feel like I can do anything if he's there with me," I added.

My voice was thick and wet from held-in tears. A small voice inside my head told me to shut up, that I was humiliating myself with my raw vulnerability. But if Haden and I were going to start something, I wanted to start it off right, and in the direction that would allow me to be my fullest self.

"I want someone who cares about me and what I want," I continued. "Who believes it's okay if I want something different, or if I change my mind. Someone who believes that nothing about me needs to be changed or kept small or made bigger. I need someone who won't give me a weird look when I dream up something to try out an idea. Or when I stretch and aim for something really ridiculous."

"And what do you want right now?" Haden's tone was curious and kind.

"Everything! Nothing! I don't know." I gave a slight maniacal laugh, the feeling of being in such a vulnerable limbo testing every fibre of my newly acquired self-assurance. "I want to start barrel racing, even though I've never done it, and I feel too old to start, and it's scary."

"Okay." He gave a short nod, like it was all taken care of. Done.

"Okay what?"

"Go do it."

"Go do it?"

It was like the air had been sucked out of me. This conversation was supposed to be about us, not him telling me to pick up a frivolous new hobby.

"Right. I'll just walk over to my money tree and..." I swung an arm through the air.

"You have a decent horse—old and retired, but experienced. You won't be able to compete with her, but she'll teach you. Slowly. And you have the space to train so you can test the idea."

"But I want it right now. The practice barrels, the training, the truck and horse trailer." I swallowed a hard sob. This was why I didn't dream big. It was all so hopeless. Too much to accomplish. My stomach caved, letting me slouch. "And how did this become about barrel racing and not us?"

The skin around his eyes crinkled. "Because—" he took my hands again, and I let him, "I want a happy woman." He snuggled my body against his. I risked letting my cheek rest against his firm chest. His flannel shirt was cozy and soft, his heart thrumming a steady beat of calm. "I want someone who's following her dreams, and able to speak up for what she wants."

He lowered his head, resting his cheek against my crown. "In case you haven't noticed, that woman is you."

I shifted so I could look up at him.

"It is?"

"I might listen to every word you say, TM, but you also have to say things so I can hear you."

I nodded. That made sense. I hadn't always done that with Kade, and I realized it was silly that I'd assumed he'd know what was in my heart and mind, as well as my dreams.

Haden did a good job listening to me, as well as reading my thoughts and feelings. But it wasn't his responsibility to always be the one figuring me out. I needed to make a point of sharing things that were important to me, too.

Haden stroked my cheek again, and I leaned into his palm like a cat. He let out a long sigh. "I wish you'd wanted me first. Before him."

Kade.

"It wouldn't have worked," I said softly, worried that today my shared past with his brother might be a deal-breaker. "I was too young for you."

"I know." His sea cave eyes were flooded with light, and I could see the long-buried sorrow, longing, and years of denial.

But most of all, one thing. He was in love with me.

With me!

I pressed my hands on either side of Haden's cheeks, staring into his beautiful eyes and gave him a gentle, loving kiss.

The idea that he'd wanted me all these years while I'd been figuring myself out, sent something swirling inside me.

I tried to drop my hands, but Haden clasped them, holding them against his five o'clock shadow before cupping them in front of his mouth, giving each palm a kiss.

"Is it weird that I dated your brother?" I whispered, almost afraid to ask.

"Yes."

I sighed. He was always so honest with me. Couldn't he have at least tried to kid me about this one thing?

"Hey." He tipped my chin upward, so I'd look at him.

"I hate that it's weird," I mumbled, unable to meet his gaze.

"Does it matter?"

I nodded. What Haden thought of me had always mattered, and always would.

"Because it doesn't matter to me," he said.

"Are you sure?"

"TM, you've always deserved better than a half love, and I hope I can love you as fully as you deserve."

A half love? That was such a perfect way of describing my relationship with Kade. He had half-loved me, and he'd half-loved our life together. And I'd half-loved him right back. The other half of our relationship had been filled with us not quite sure who we were, stuffing it full of wishes and blind stabbing around in the dark, wondering if this was what love was supposed to feel like.

"What if you and I get together and I change?" I asked.

"I hope you do. Every day."

"What?"

"That's what I like best about you. You're curious about life. Everyone changes a bit if they're still curious and growing."

"But you'll still be here?"

"I'll be here no matter what today's dream might happen to be."

"Really?"

"That's what love means to me."

"You love me?" I asked shyly.

"Yes."

It was such a rare idea, that love could stick to you no matter how much you changed.

The certainty of his conviction was novel to me, and it felt so deep-seated. It gave me the self-assurance of a woman who'd been married to the love of her life for twenty-five years. Such weighted trust, pinned and immovable.

"How can we know that we won't grow away from each other?"

He pulled me close, giving me a gentle kiss. "Because in all the years I've known you, I've only grown fonder."

"Even though we avoided each other for years?"

"Even then."

"You sure?"

"You're impossible to miss."

"You saw me?" I confirmed, my thoughts on love still sorting into place. I knew now that you couldn't fully love a person you didn't truly see. Just like with Kade and me.

But Haden saw me, and he always had, even when I'd

believed I was hiding. All those shared, secret looks that drove our families mad had been Haden seeing me, and me seeing him right back.

Only now, I could finally also see myself.

CHAPTER 37

~ *Tamara* ~

It was Christmas Eve—or maybe it was already Christmas Day—and Haden and I were curled up on the couch at my place. We'd been sitting, talking, and kissing long into the night. At some point we'd fallen asleep by the Christmas tree and fireplace, wrapped in each other's arms. I woke up, hearing something beyond the dying crackle of the fire. I leaned forward, peering toward the window to see what it was.

I squeaked and fell back as a red nose lit up the dark night. I was on my feet in a second, sending Boots scrambling in a flurry of claws, trying to gain purchase on the hardwood floor. The blanket that had been over me and Haden dropped to the floor, nearly covering my gopher Felipe, who'd fallen in love with Haden, and had been sleeping near our feet.

"What is it?" Haden asked, his voice groggy, his tone indicating he was already on high alert. Felipe did a high-pitched warning call before scampering for safety behind my TV stand.

Haden was already standing, one arm swooping around my waist, as if he planned to swing me out of danger's way should anything come at me.

How I adored this man.

341

"Rudolph," he whispered in awe.

I sprung from Haden's embrace and jogged in the direction of the front door, eager to see my reindeer friend. Behind me, I heard the window open despite the storm buffeting against the house. The second storm had arrived while Haden and I had crashed out on my couch after a very thorough make-out session in his clinic. We'd only been apart for family dinners, making our quick excuses to vamoose.

Next year, we planned to split our time between our families, but this year, we hadn't quite been ready yet to reveal our new relationship. We had a how-we-got-together story to set straight first.

"Hey, pal," Haden crooned, and I slid back to Haden's side in my stocking feet.

Rudolph was at the window, sticking his blinking nose inside. Behind him, his pals all said their hellos, their bells jingling.

"Rudolph!"

The herd was hooked up to a sleigh, but in the dark I couldn't tell which one it was. I was guessing it was Number Two, the newer, bigger one, seeing as the backup sleigh had been burned in my yard. Although, had it? I wasn't sure what was permanent about yesterday.

"How are you? How is everyone? Are you okay?" I tried to peer around Rudolph, but I was more concerned about him than his friends.

Wait. Hadn't I been banned from seeing and interacting with the magical world? Theoretically, the wall between worlds should be super strong again. Had Mrs. Claus not performed all of her Christmas duties? Or were the boys breaking rules again?

"I'm fine," Rudolph said.

"How's Santa? Is the sleigh fixed? Is Mrs. C. mad at everyone? And me, too? Everyone was gone by the time Estelle got me out of court."

"Hugo lost the bet," Donner said. "He thought you'd be a total goner. Not many people make it off the naughty list."

"Well, I did get banished, and they erased Haden's memories. Sort of."

The reindeers' eyes all turned to him.

"I remember most of it now," he said, rubbing his forehead while tightening an arm around my waist. "Although it feels a bit dreamlike."

"We don't have much time," Rudolph said. "But we wanted to say thank you for your help last night. Both of you."

"You're welcome. And I'm sorry about hitting you with the car."

"It never happened."

"Oh, right." I rubbed my forehead, trying to wrap my head around what had truly happened versus what was simply a memory. "But you remember last night?"

"We all do. Mrs. Claus let us retain our memories, even though Estelle backtracked time for you."

"Really? Why did she do that?"

"She wanted us to remember our lesson about sneaking out," Prancer said.

"It wasn't sneaking out!" Blitzen complained. "There's no rule!"

"And for us to remember that she saved us all," Prancer said primly.

"She does a lot for you and the holiday, you know," I said. "You should try thanking her sometimes." The poor woman was surrounding by a sea of testosterone up at the North Pole. No wonder she'd been tempted by her dark side.

"She forgave Santa," Vixen said in her sweet voice. "I don't know what you did, but she's like her old self again. And they're both very happy. They solved all of the Christmas problems together, and plan to take a small trip to the black magic world next spring."

"I'm glad they seem to be doing okay again."

Beside me, Haden gave me an affectionate squeeze.

"So Christmas is truly all right?" Haden confirmed.

"It is."

"Mrs. Claus was angry that you wished yourself away before receiving judgement," Vixen said.

"She would have incinerated me!"

"Maybe, but once she calmed down, she set to work on fixing Christmas."

"Is she still feuding with Estelle?"

"I don't think they'll ever be friends."

"Fair enough. I'm glad everyone's okay, and that you stopped to say hi. I hope you won't get in trouble for this—because of my banishment."

"Mrs. Claus opened a small portal for us," Rudolph said.

"She did?"

"She says thanks."

"Thanks?" That was an ending to our little dispute that I hadn't predicted.

"And she said to stay out of our world because you're still banished," Prancer added. "You forgot to tell her that bit."

"Whatever," Rudolph muttered.

Santa let out a ho, ho, ho! Then he called out the reindeers' names as well as a command. Their image began to shimmer and shake.

"Look under your tree," Rudolph said quickly.

I swivelled, but saw nothing under my heavily decorated tree.

"The *other* one," Rudolph called as they all disappeared.

Haden and I looked at each other. He was a bit pale.

He let out a gust of breath. "All of it was real. All of it." He sat on the couch. "Wow." He pushed a hand through his hair, making it stand on end.

I sat beside him, still trying to puzzle out Mrs. Claus's seeming change of heart toward me. To say I was relieved was an understatement.

"Are you okay?" I asked Haden.

He was smiling, his grin growing wider and wider. He pulled me into his arms with a laugh. "I'm doing amazing!"

I laughed with him, happy to be able to share the spirit of the season, and our magical secret adventure with him again.

He kissed me long and slow, my body softening against his. I could do this all day.

Haden broke the kiss, his eyes narrowed in confusion. "What other tree?" There was still the odd thing that didn't quite click into place for him from the other night, but, as for this clue, I wasn't sure what it meant, either.

"The Christmas tree in the barn?" I mused. "Except it disappeared with Santa."

Haden inhaled sharply, eyes bright. I could see a memory lodge itself more fully, fitting into the story I'd told him to flesh out the fleeting, fuzzy memories he'd retained.

He pulled me to my feet. "I think I know which tree."

And even though the clock said it was two in the morning, and we were in the midst of a second winter storm, I followed.

"WHAT ON EARTH?" I was standing under the big poplar Santa's sleigh had hit, in the glow of Haden's giant flashlight, surveying my 'Santa gift' with amazement. "How did they know? How did they get these here so quickly?"

Haden reached out and gave the closest racing barrel a nudge, seeming to not quite trust his eyes. I knew the feeling.

The barrels I needed to race my horse around were real. And they had been left by Santa.

"I have so many questions," I whispered.

"Tell me about it."

"I also hope the reindeer aren't still drunk. Because what if they stole these from a neighbour as some ongoing stag party game?"

Haden laughed. He'd been doing that a lot over the past couple of nights, shedding that serious older brother skin he'd so often worn.

"I don't think they were drunk," he said. "Besides, would Santa allow such blatant thievery?"

"Probably not."

Snow was falling, collecting along Haden's dark toque. I leaned over, going up on tiptoe to give his cold lips a warm kiss. I could get used to this, to him. He pulled me close with a happy groan, deepening the kiss.

"We're wearing far too many winter layers," he complained. "I can barely enjoy your soft curves." He began pulling me back toward the house, but a soft crackle caused us to look up.

"Haden? Look!" The snow that had been falling only moments ago had cleared. We had a straight view to the dark, star-studded sky where the aurora borealis was ablaze, streaks of green and pink dancing across the heavens. As the auroras moved, they dipped so low, it felt like I could reach up and touch them.

"Beautiful," Haden murmured. His arms slid around my waist, and I leaned back against him. Silently, we watched nature's show, our breathing synced as the lights danced and shimmered, grew brighter and closer, then retreated, fading, before appearing again.

"Where did the storm go?" I asked.

Haden pointed to the night sky. Off to the right, in the direction of town, was the silhouette of a sleigh being pulled by nine jaunty reindeer.

I swore I heard a faint ho, ho, ho!

As soon as Santa dipped over the horizon, on to the next house or town, the northern lights faded, and like a stage curtain being drawn, the snow started up again.

"Tamara?" Haden asked, letting me slip from his arms.

I turned to him. "Yeah?"

"How come I can remember stuff if Mrs. Claus tried to erase my memories?"

I wrapped my arms around him, hugging him with pure joy in my heart. "Because some things are so real, they can't ever be erased."

CHAPTER 38

Epilogue

~ TAMARA ~

New Year's Eve

We broke up.

My thumbs hovered over my phone's keyboard, debating several responses to Samantha's text. She and Malachi had broken up and gotten back together two times since Christmas. Was the third time a charm? The poor man had tried to propose on Christmas Day, instigating the first break-up.

In our group chat, Char had declared it too soon for that kind of commitment, but Gabby had been over the moon about the idea. She'd been crushed when Samantha had decided the proposal was break-up worthy.

ME

Come hang out with us tonight.

Samantha and Malachi, upon getting back together the first time, had booked last minute tickets for a New Year's Eve party in Calgary for tonight. I assumed that was no longer a go. And while I was disappointed for Samantha, I was happy the full GAL PAL gang would once again be spending the evening together.

SAMANTHA

Send me a pin.

Yes! She was coming!

I opened a maps app on my phone, pinned my location, then sent it to Samantha to use while navigating to my farm.

ME

It's not that hard to find.

SAMANTHA

Yes, it is. All the roads look the same.

Be there in a bit.

A few hours later, Char and her boyfriend James, looking tanned and relaxed, and very much in love after their Mexican vacation, were in my kitchen cuddling Felipe and eating chocolate cake. Not long after, Josie and Gabby arrived, serving themselves a slice of cake and a cup of yukaflux. It had magically replenished itself, and I was a little hesitant to serve it, even though, due to the unwinding of time, was unlikely to have Blitzen slobber in it.

Haden texted to say he was on his way. I'd half expected a fake emergency from a HAG to make him late, but his business seemed to have settled down to a reasonable, less fake-emergency-laden pace since we got together on Christmas Eve. I wasn't sure if this was due to a touch of magic, or if the women of Eagle Ridge could sense when a man's heart was off the market.

I went to get the door when Samantha arrived, a tremor of excitement zipping through me at the idea of the seven of us being together for New Year's Eve. I had planned some games and movies, as well as set out drinks and snacks. I marvelled at my mood as my little house filled up with people. A few years ago, I would have cringed at the idea of hosting a party, and might have turned into an actual recluse if it weren't for my years with Kade. But spending time with him had taught me that sometimes, being around a big group of friends was indeed the best thing—as long as they were the right people. I was so blessed to have such amazing friends.

"Sorry to hear about you and Malachi. Um, again," I said, taking Samantha's coat. She'd marched straight into the kitchen, plunking down in front of the chocolate cake I'd made. In fact, all of my friends, knowing I'd made cake, had pretty much beelined it into the kitchen like little kids.

Char was already on her second slice by the time the rest of the gang got seated with a generous portion.

Samantha closed her eyes as she took the first bite. "Mmm. I missed living with you."

"This is amazing," James agreed.

"Can I take a slice for Lamonte if there's any left?" Gabby asked, and I nodded, making a note to slide a piece into a container for her before someone else ate it.

I couldn't help but think about her recent change of heart in regard to magic, and her desire to have Cupid find her a boyfriend. She claimed she was no longer crushing on Lamonte, but she still mentioned him 24/7. While Estelle couldn't interfere in interpersonal relationships on a deep level, maybe Cupid could. I was certain that would initiate a whole new bucket of issues, though, ones Gabby might not be ready to deal with, even in the name of love.

Josie, elbows on the table and looking tired, simply rolled her eyes at Gabby's cake-saving request, and kept eating. Her new business as an inventory specialist had been going nuts by the sounds of it, throwing more work at her than she could handle. I was glad she'd been able to make it tonight.

"So, who's moving out?" Char asked Samantha, as she shovelled another bite into her mouth. "You or him?"

I caught her dropping a tiny speck of cake crumbs for Felipe. It was hard to read the gopher's emotions, but I think it was safe to say the two had missed each other. He'd spent most of the afternoon so far either in the crook of her arm, or sitting on her foot while she ate her cake.

"He will," Samantha said.

"Why'd you break up? What did he do again?" James asked. He was a stacked guy who used to work security, but now had a desk job in Calgary near where Char was working.

"Nothing," Samantha said, crossing her arms.

"*Everything*," Gabby said, giving James a warning glance. "He proposed."

"What a jerk," James said with a light scoff, sharing a darted look with Char.

Josie snorted in amusement. "Right?"

Gabby frowned and rolled her eyes. "Some people just aren't romantic enough, like our big, tough old Samantha." She fake-punched her friend in the arm and received a scowl.

"Malachi wasn't the right guy?" I asked, trying to get to the root of Samantha's weird relationship fears. Maybe she was like me, and still discovering herself and what she wanted. If so, I could see how the idea of pinning herself to someone else could be scary.

"Yeah, he's not Caleb," Gabby said with a smirk.

Samantha hadn't exactly hidden her crush on our old neighbour, an Irish hottie. From what I'd seen, he was the only guy who'd ever made her blush. In other words, it was true love. On her side, anyway. We weren't entirely sure Caleb knew she existed. And anyway, we'd all moved out, so we were unsure if he still lived downstairs from where we'd once been, or if he was lost to Samantha forever.

"Malachi had annoying habits," Samantha said, her nose crinkled. "I couldn't imagine marrying him. At least not without murder happening somewhere down our timeline."

She stabbed her fork into her slice of cake, breaking off a large chunk, which she then shoved into her mouth.

"Can you afford the rent on your own?" Gabby asked, her brow pinched with worry.

Samantha shrugged while I nodded, having wondered the same thing. I shook my head, remembering that Samantha wasn't quite like the rest of us. She got an allowance, or rather a trust fund payout, each month, which kept her in a lifestyle none of us at this table were accustomed to. She acted financially normal around us, and I often forgot she was a small-time heiress. But she was. My guess was that no apartment was beyond her financial reach within the city of Calgary.

"There's someone who works at Lamonte's garage who's looking for a roommate if you need someone," Gabby said helpfully.

"Thanks, but I'll make it work on my own. I think I'm done living with anyone for a bit."

"But none of this makes sense. Malachi was Irish!" Gabby exclaimed.

"He tried to steal her Lucky Charms," Char joked in a fake Irish accent.

Samantha let out a long sigh. "He was adorable, but not the right leprechaun for me."

"Leprechaun?" I giggled at the idea of our stylish, trendy friend with a little gnome-like man. A lack of sleep, thanks to long make-out sessions with Haden over the past week, was making me a bit loopy.

"I wouldn't turn one down," Samantha said slyly.

She was met with a chorus of 'Ew's.

"So, everything's still fine around here since Christmas Eve?" Char asked me quietly as the other three started gossiping about something else.

I nodded. "Thanks again for letting me use your credits."

So far, there'd been no bill from Estelle for the wishes I'd made on Christmas Eve. I had thought that, even if banished, I might have to pay for her magical services if Char's credits didn't cover it all.

"Of course. And how are things with your families?" She lifted her eyebrows meaningfully. "Is Mrs. Powell still hugging you every time she sees you and saying 'welcome back'?"

I laughed. She was. And probably secretly knitting baby booties. I hadn't expected her to be so delighted. Honestly, she had the best reaction out of everyone.

In my family, my mom was excited, my dad indifferent, and my Oma said she was happy that I was happy. And that was about it. Done deal. Carry on with life.

The Powell side, however, had reacted a bit differently. When we'd told Haden's family, his mom had squealed in excitement, Mr. Powell had looked alarmed at his wife's response, and Kade had stalked out of the room. Both Haden and I had tried to go after him, but Mrs. Powell, with a determined look, had pushed us both aside and gone to speak with her youngest, herself.

"And Kade?"

I scrunched my nose. "He's still getting used to the idea."

The next time we'd seen Kade, a few nights later, he'd been quiet, barely daring to look at us through his hurt. But he'd mumbled that he was happy for us. Honestly, it could have been worse. With time, I figured he'd warm up to the idea, especially since I'd heard he and Jannifer had gone on a second coffee date.

"Knock, knock!" Haden's warm, deep voice filled the room as he shut the front door.

Char winked at me as I leapt from my spot. "Speak of the devil."

I jogged to the entry, where he caught me, holding me in his arms. The cold from his coat seeped through my sweater as he gave me a long hello kiss.

Bliss.

"What did I miss?" Haden asked, still holding me close. I adored the way his eyes were always unguarded around me now. I could look at him and see inside, warmed by the knowledge that I was the one he loved, had waited for, and then finally been able to choose. It was a wonderful feeling.

"Just me." I gave him another long, slow kiss over his huff of amusement at my bold statement. Yes, that was right. I was going to be *that* kind of girlfriend—mushy and cheesy—so he'd better get used to it.

He released me, unzipping his coat. He was in my favourite flannel shirt. The soft red and green one he'd been wearing on the night we'd fallen in love. He'd learned I liked it, and I adored the fact that he was going to wear it to bring in the new year.

"So," he whispered, "yesterday I got this dreamlike feeling that I'm supposed to fix your barn roof?" He raised his brows. "Am I?"

"Oh..." I waved off his concerns. "The magical world fixed it when they tried to erase everything else. But thanks." I shook my head with a smile. "Is it weird that I kind of miss Blitzen and his antics?"

Haden's eyes lit up and his head fell back in laughter. "That drunk little rangifer tarandus."

"Latin, huh?" I slipped my arms around his neck. "You sexy science nerd."

"I try," he said, snugging me closer.

"Well, it's working. It's sexy. Very sexy."

He'd drawn me close, his nose nuzzling mine, his lips angling to line us up.

"Are your friends in there?" He gestured toward the kitchen with his chin, his lips centimetres from mine.

I kissed him as they erupted in laughter, making their presence known.

Haden's arms tightened another notch, and his kisses roamed down my neck. I angled my head to the side with a sigh.

"Give me the rundown on them again?" he whispered between kisses.

"You're procrastinating."

His smile was crooked, lifting higher on the right, and filled with mischief as he leaned back to look at me. "You in a rush to go in there and behave?"

"Never." I tightened my hold on him. "You know Char, of course. By the way, her boyfriend James wants you to teach him how to wrestle a steer to the ground."

"What?"

"Just kidding! Samantha's secretly rich, and wants to date a leprechaun."

He narrowed his eyes for a second before shaking his head at me. "Okay, now you're just being a brat and testing me." He released me from his arms, toeing off his winter boots, his right hand still on my hip, as if he didn't want to let me go.

"Are leprechauns even real?" he asked.

I shrugged. I hadn't really thought about it.

"What about Cupid? Dragons? Hobbits?"

I giggled, holding his arm. "I don't know." I was actually a bit relieved that I'd been banished. It meant I'd never have to come face to face with anything magical ever again. "But seriously, Samantha loves everything Irish. Josie is a mystery I will never solve, and Gabby's in love with her roommate, who is also her best friend. Watch. She'll bring Lamonte up a ton. It should be a drinking game."

He pulled me back into his arms. "Did you used to slip my name into conversations?"

I shook my head slowly. "Never." I tangled my fingers in his thick locks as I kissed him long and slow, unable to stop myself.

He broke the kiss, resting his forehead against mine. "Never?"

"I was too scared to mention you. You were the man-who-must-not-be-named."

"Why's that?" His hand had slipped up the back of my sweater, like he couldn't resist feeling my skin.

I focused on his chin, the tiny bit of five o'clock shadow he'd missed under his lower lip when he'd shaved, probably at some ungodly hour while running out to an animal emergency. I knew he kept an electric razor in his truck so he could take care of shaving while out and about. I loved that about him.

"I was afraid if I mentioned you, people would realize how infatuated I was. And I was afraid that if I looked at you, you'd know how I felt. I thought I was just upset with you for not telling me I was a bother, but really, I now understand it was more about trying not to show or admit how badly I was crushing on you."

"Infatuated, huh?"

He loved hearing about my secret crush. Insatiable brat.

He lightly kissed my hands again with a reverence that sent a shiver of delight through my nervous system. He lifted his eyes. "Promise you'll never hide how you feel from me again?"

"Of course I won't."

"Promise?"

"Hey, you hid your feelings, too!"

"You were dating my brother." A cloud of darkness shuttled across his eyes.

"And you were so much older, unattainable, and wouldn't let me see *any* of your inner thoughts," I teased.

He tapped the side of his nose, mimicking Santa from the other night. "Top secret, Tamara Madden from Eagle Ridge."

I giggled, and he pulled me into an embrace. His voice was low and confiding as he said, "You were the only reason I ever went on those family vacations when I was in college."

Unable to hide my reaction at his ludicrous claim, I blurted out, "I was not."

"My mom's guilt trips aren't that strong. And you made them fun." His look was tender. "I never knew when you were going to put Kade in his place or wind him up with some poking. I've always loved being in cahoots with you."

I twisted my hand into a fist, pressing it under Haden's, then opening it so I could interlock our fingers. "I like being in cahoots, too."

Haden rested his forehead against mine. He sighed. "Why didn't I meet you first? We could have saved so much time."

"I wasn't ready for you. I didn't understand love yet. I didn't know what I wanted or deserved."

He folded my hand into his, kissing it. "I would have shown you."

I laughed, my imagination running wild with the idea of having dated him when I was younger. "I'd never have believed that a man as handsome and self-assured as you would ever choose me. You have your pick of the town."

"I do?"

"Every woman wants their own Haden Powell."

"But the only woman Haden Powell wants is you."

"Yeah?"

"I choose you."

"I choose you, too." I smiled into the next kiss, my heart expanding. The past week had been amazing, and I couldn't wait to see what the future held for us.

CHAPTER 39

Epilogue #2

~ ESTELLE ~

February

Perfect Trish danced past me on her way back from the head fairy's office in her pretty little pink ballerina flats with the delicate carnation-shaped ribbons. So far, she'd earned more from her client wishes than I had this quarter, and she was up for more awards, too.

For the first time as a trainee fairy godmother, I was up for none.

To make matters worse for me, I hadn't been able to talk about what had gone down on Christmas Eve. None of it. And every single one of Tamara's big wishes had been paid for by Char's remaining account credits.

Because Gram-Gram and I ignored several protocols when Tamara breached the shroud between our worlds, we'd had to keep everything related to that night hush-hush. Even the way Mrs. Claus had banished me back to the magical world. And that had been hard to hide, since I'd sported the evidence of that banishing with my scorched hair and skin. But I wasn't allowed to talk about it. And sadly, Gram-Gram hadn't been able to heal my hair or skin, thanks to archaic rules about using magic on ourselves or on each other. If I'd been ill, yes. A medic fairy could have helped me. But not ease the mark of a banishment.

In the end, Tamara had saved Christmas, and won the love of her life. Mrs. Claus was happily back at the North Pole with Santa. The reindeer were all fine, other than a bit of scolding from Mrs. C.. In fact, I'd heard everyone at the North Pole was pretty much kissing her butt these days.

In other words, everyone was enjoying their happily ever after.

Except me. And I was suffering my way through a sizeable work slump.

A slump to end all slumps.

Nobody was making wishes, at least not the big ones that required a bit of creativity on my part, or were award earners.

I sighed and leaned against my stupid bubblegum pink desk.

At least my hair had mostly grown out around my face from my banishment, so I was no longer wearing my shame for all to speculate over.

"The head fairy wants to see you, Scorch," Trish whispered snidely, leaning close and startling me.

My new nickname, however, would never fade like my banishment marks.

I shoved my office chair back, hoping I'd hit the other trainee 'accidentally,' but she moved fast in her delicate flats.

"Maybe you're being summoned to the Magical Court of Rules to talk about that *banishment.*"

I smirked, knowing it annoyed the fairy lights out of her that I'd clearly been a part of something—something potentially risky and exciting—and she had no clue what it was.

Because the truth of it was that trainees never got banished by another magical being. And only a few high-powered ones could do such a thing.

I loved that not knowing was turning Trish inside out.

I smirked. "Been there, done that," I said breezily, lying about being in court. Tamara had been there, but that was in a confidential file nobody but the higher-ups would ever see.

Trish paled. And delighted with shutting her up for once, I added sweetly, "Please excuse me. The head fairy is waiting."

I crossed the bullpen of pink fairy cubicles and entered the large office with the tall gold door.

"You wanted to see me?" I asked, taking my usual spot in front of the head fairy's rosewood desk. The carpet was plain, no longer animated like it had been on the night when I'd sat in here and cried over Tamara's possible fate, and my powerlessness to change it.

I supposed it was good we'd let her exercise her own agency, as she'd come up with a result I couldn't have predicted.

"Yes," Gram-Gram said, her lavender eyes sweeping over me. "Think you can handle another client being added to your roster? We had someone activate."

I inhaled, swiftly straightening my spine. "Did Trish get a new client, too?"

"That's none of your business," Gram-Gram scolded. "Can you handle another client on your roster? She hasn't made a wish yet, but she now believes. So, it's likely just a matter of time." She caught my excitement and tempered me by saying, "It could be hours, it could be years. It could be never."

I nodded eagerly.

The head fairy handed me a pristine pink folder. So new, so flat. So unlike Char's file, which had spilled and burst with all of her old wishes and notes from her former fairy, Paxi.

I'd never had a newbie client before, and it was exciting to be her first contact with the magical world.

This quarter ended soon—the day after Valentine's Day. I could set the tone with this client, and make the next quarter my best one yet, in terms of granted wishes and client happiness!

"Who is it?" I turned the file to read the name along the folder's tab.

"I believe she's a friend of Char and Tamara's."

With a growing smile, I read the last name Morales. The most romantic woman in their GAP PAL group: Gabby.

And she was all mine.

~

THANK YOU FOR READING RUN, RUN, RUDOLPH. I hope you enjoyed Tamara and Haden's Christmas story.

Ready for Gabby's story? She's up next. And she's on a road trip with her crush Lamonte and Cupid! What could go wrong with that combo, right?

Enjoy THE PROBLEM WITH CUPID next.

Glossary of Canadian Stuff

Here in Canada we are quirky. We measure distances in time, kilometres, and miles. Oh, and yards. Sometimes metres, too. And feet. And volume? Well, we have litres, millilitres, gallons, cups, pints, and on and on. It's like we have our own little secret language up here and we've spent our long, cold winters dreaming up silly ways to confuse outsiders. And ourselves.

So, in case you haven't heard some of these terms, bud, I've set you up with a little glossary of words that are as Canadian as Canuck.

Good luck, eh? And sorry for the confusion.

ALSO NOTE: This book uses Canadian spelling which is basically British spelling. *(Except when we veer off like a startled rabbit and use a different form of spelling. What can I say? Our little melting pot includes spelling.)*

Ready? Let's hit it. Here's your glossary:

Toque: (rhymes with duke) a warm knitted hat to keep your noggin warm so you don't freeze your ears off.

Noggin: Your head.

Mitts/Mittens: Not just for little kiddos. These typically keep your hands warmer than gloves, and have plenty of insulation which will hopefully keep your digits from freezing. Your fingers basically hang out in an insulated room together, and your thumb has its own 'sleeve' like in gloves.

Parka: A thick winter coat for the coldest weather. Typically reaches down to mid-thigh or lower, and has a hood which is often trimmed with fake fur.

Sorels: A formerly Canadian winter boot company (now owned by Columbia). These boots were originally made specifically for the frosty Canadian winters so you could ice fish or stand around as a liftie all day without freezing your toes off. I have a pair that are over 30 years old, and they're still warm.

Liftie: A person who 'throws chairs' at the ski hill. Or, in plain speak, a person who stands out in the cold, and runs the lifts that carry skiers up the mountain.

Celsius: Temperature unit measurement. Quick reference: -25 Celsius is -13 Fahrenheit. 0 degrees is the freezing point in Celsius.

Block heater/Oil pan heater: Canadians often plug in their gas-powered vehicles when it gets to about -20 Celsius or lower. Why? This little heater prevents the engine oil from getting so viscous that the engine can't turn over (start).

North Pole: Where Santa lives in Canada's north. Sorry, Finns. We believe he's Canadian. Then again, what does Joulupukki need the North Pole for? He's a goat.

Joulupukki: (My mom pronounced it yo-loo-pookey) A Finnish Christmas figure who happens to be a goat.

Yukaflux: Chopped up fruit tossed into a bucket of alcohol such as rum or vodka.

Fish and Wildlife: A department under the Alberta government that deals with the regulations and legislation regarding fish and wildlife species, and their management within the province. This includes a staff of enforcement officers and biologists who deal with fish and wildlife questions, issues and incidents.

Alberta: A province in Canada that has two NHL teams, because we're just that Canadian. (I'm not speaking for the minority separatists here, who think we'd rock it solo. They have maybe forgotten that we live on indigenous lands, and there are treaties protecting their land and those associated rights.) Alberta's landscape ranges from the prairies to the beautiful rocky mountains.

NHL: National Hockey League, which is actually international since it includes teams from both Canada and the states. Alberta is home to the Edmonton Oilers and the Calgary Flames.

The States: The United States of America.

Chinook: (pronounced shin-ook) A term attributed to the Chinook people. A warm wind that blows over the rocky mountains from the Pacific Ocean. Referred to as a "snow eater" by the Blackfoot people. The region around Calgary can go from -20C to +20C in a 24-hour period during a winter Chinook.

Eagle Ridge: Fictional town.

SRO/School Resource Officer: A member of the RCMP or local police service that works in schools. The idea is to prevent crime, act as a liaison, offer guidance, and promote safety, as well as foster community relationships.

RCMP: Royal Canadian Mounted Police. Canada's national police service which was formed in 1873.

Oma: German for grandma.

Eh?: (rhymes with hey) A truly Canadian expression we tack onto the end of sentences. Although, these days it sounds like more of a 'hey' than an 'eh?'

Eh is a signal we are done talking, and the other person may now speak without interrupting us. It can also be a casual way to confirm agreement, or to check if the other person is still following what we're saying.

Yeah, no.: Yeah, I hear you and my answer is no (just softened a bit so as not to hurt anyone's feelings).

Yeah, no. Of course.: Of course.

Yeah, no. Maybe: Maybe.

No, yeah: No, of course. You're right. I agree.

Twenty-sixer: A bottle of liquor that is roughly 26 ounces, and even though Canada now uses millilitres, we still call the 750mL bottle a "twenty-sixer" or a "2-6" or a "two-sixer" even though we no longer measure in ounces. Not to be confused with a two-four, which is a pack of 24 beer.

Millimetres (mm) and Millilitres (mL): Units of measurement.

25.4 mm = 1 inch.

4000 mL is roughly 1 U.S. gallon.

Appies: Appetizers

Boxing Day: The day after Christmas. December 26th. This is a big day for store sales in Canada where you may find great deals on everything from clothing to electronics.

U-ey: U-turn. When you turn your car 180 degrees to head in the opposite direction in which you've just come. You may also hear it referred to as: "pull a U-ey" or "whip a sh*tty."

Correction line: In Alberta, the prairies have roads which, for the most part, are set out in a grid pattern. (Some of the remaining main routes that were used a hundred to a hundred-and-fifty years ago, which linked the various forts between the bigger towns of Calgary and Edmonton, for example, still remain. These old cattle trails meander a bit, and you can see it in parts of the 2A, and the C&E Trail (Calgary and Edmonton Trail).)

Anyway, since the earth is round, laying down a grid doesn't totally world. It gets warped and wonky after a certain distance, hence the need to correct that grid to return it to its lovely square dimensions. That leads us to correction lines.

In Alberta, the back country roads are set out with a road every two miles going north-south, and one every mile going east-west. To fix the round-earth-induced warped wonkiness, the north-south road are off-set to the west by a bit every few miles (leading to a T-intersection), and creating a "correction line."

Riding/Ridden shotgun: When you ride where the shotgun goes—in the passenger seat.

Sorry?: Sorry, I didn't catch that.

Sorry: An apology.

Sorry: Also, sometimes not an apology, and just something Canadians say such as, "Sorry, just gotta scoot past you." Or, more popular, "Sorry," when we bump into something inanimate. That is an apology, though. Just not a particularly necessary one.

Stats Canada: Statistics Canada. A marvellous group of sociologists collecting census data, and more, on the Canadian population. (AKA someone I would be if I desired city life. Lucky for you, I chose the unstable career of an artist. Yay.)

Christmas hamper: When for the less fortunate, it's usually a box of foodstuffs, along with other items such as gifts for children and teenagers. Essentially ensuring that they, too, get a nice Christmas meal and some gifts.

To boot: Example: *He was a generous guy to boot.* No, you're not going to take the boots to him/kick him. This simply means 'he was also a generous guy.'

Find a full, up-to-date book list of Jean Oram's books at www. jeanoram.com/books

Or shop direct from the author and save at:
Shop.JeanOram.com

Fairy Godmothers and Other Fiascos

Fairy Godmothers Aren't Cheap

Run, Run Rudolph

The Problem with Cupid

(With two more novels planned!)

Hockey Sweethearts

The Cupcake Cottage

Peach Blossom Hollow

Chocolate Cherry Cabin

Peppermint Lodge

The Huckleberry Bookshop

Sugar Cookie Country House

The Gingerbread Cafe

A Tiny House Christmas

The Cowboys of Sweetheart Creek, Texas

The Cowboy's Stolen Heart (Levi)

The Cowboy's Secret Wish (Myles)

The Cowboy's Second Chance (Ryan)

The Cowboy's Sweet Elopement (Brant)

The Cowboy's Surprise Return (Cole)

The Summer Sisters

Falling for the Movie Star

Falling for the Boss

Falling for the Single Dad

Falling for the Bodyguard

Falling for the Firefighter

Veils and Vows

The Promise (Bonus prequel: Devon & Olivia)

The Surprise Wedding (Devon & Olivia)

A Pinch of Commitment (Ethan & Lily)

The Wedding Plan (Luke & Emma)

Accidentally Married (Burke & Jill)

The Marriage Pledge (Moe & Amy)

Mail Order Soulmate (Zach & Catherine)

Blueberry Springs

Whiskey and Gumdrops (Mandy & Frankie)

Rum and Raindrops (Jen & Rob)

Eggnog and Candy Canes (Katie & Nash)

Sweet Treats (3 short stories—Mandy, Amber, & Nicola)

Vodka and Chocolate Drops (Amber & Scott)

Tequila and Candy Drops (Nicola & Todd)

Champagne and Lemon Drops (Beth & Oz)

Indigo Bay

Sweet Matchmaker (Ginger and Logan)

Sweet Holiday Surprise (Cash & Alexa)

Sweet Forgiveness (Ashton & Zoe)

Sweet Troublemaker (Nick & Polly)

Sweet Joymaker (Maria & Clint)

For the Kids

1,001 Boredom Busting Play Ideas

Acknowledgements

Thank you to my readers for patiently waiting for this series, for reading my books and leaving me little love notes about my books around the internet. Whenever I come across one it always makes my day.

Thank you to Brenda Chin for naming this book, suggesting Vixen be a gal and Cupid a guy, and for letting me know when my sense of humour hit the mark so I didn't delete those bits. Also, thank you for getting me and encouraging me to be 'full Jean.' I appreciate it.

Thank you to the many readers who embraced the first book in this series (Fairy Godmothers Arne't Cheap), even though it was different than my first thirty-nine books (which lacked fairy godmothers and other magical beings). I appreciate the way you found the humour in my newly released quirkiness, and embraced the Canadian vibes and spellings sprinkled throughout this new series. Every chuckle, and every side joke you cracked about that book was like an encouraging whisper that said, "Keep going. Keep going." So, here's book 2! I hope you actually wanted it and weren't just being polite!

A special thank you to my long-time beta readers, Margaret and Donna for speeding through this one, and offering such amazing feedback—as always.

Thank you to my error finding team. You make proofreading fun! Ha! Bet you didn't know that was possible, eh?

About the Author

Jean Oram is a *New York Times* and *USA Today* bestselling romance author. Inspiration for her small town series came from her own upbringing on the Canadian prairies. Although, so far, none of her characters have grown up in an old schoolhouse or worked on a bee farm. Jean still lives on the prairie with her husband, two kids, and big shaggy dog where she can be found out playing in the snow or hiking.

Shop Jean's store: *Shop.JeanOram.com*

Jean's Newsletter: www.jeanoram.com/signup

Become an Official Fan: www.facebook.com/groups/jeanoramfans

Website & blog: www.jeanoram.com
YouTube: www.youtube.com/@authorjeanoram
Instagram: www.instagram.com/author_jeanoram
Facebook: www.facebook.com/JeanOramAuthor